DANCE OF THE GODS

CIRCLE TRILOGY #2

DANCE OF THE GODS

NORA ROBERTS

THORNDIKE
WINDSOR
PARAGON

This Large Print edition is published by Thorndike Press, Waterville, Maine USA and by BBC Audiobooks Ltd, Bath England

Thorndike Press is an imprint of Thomson Gale, a part of The Thomson Corporation Thorndike is a trademark used herein under license.

Thorndike Press® Large Print Core.
The text of this Large Print edition is unabridged.
Other aspects of the book may vary from the original edition.
Set in 16 pt. Plantin.

LIBRARY OF CONGRESS CATALOGING-IN-PUBLICATION DATA

Roberts, Nora.
    Dance of the gods / by Nora Roberts. — Large print ed.
    p. cm. — (The circle trilogy ; no. 2)
    ISBN 0-7862-8678-4 (hardcover : alk. paper)
    1. Vampires—Fiction. I. Title.
PS3568.O243D38 2006
813'.54—dc22

2006023542

BRITISH LIBRARY CATALOGUING-IN-PUBLICATION DATA AVAILABLE

Published in 2006 in arrangement with The Berkley Publishing Group, a division of Penguin Group (USA) Inc.
Published in the U.K. in 2007 by arrangement with Judy Piatkus (Publishers) Ltd.

U.S. Hardcover ISBN 13: 978 0 7862 8678 2
U.K. Hardcover: 978 1 405 61622 5 (Windsor Large Print)
U.K. Softcover: 978 1 405 61623 2 (Paragon Large Print)

Printed in the United States of America on permanent paper.
10 9 8 7 6 5 4 3 2 1

To Logan.
You are the future.

What we learn to do, we learn by doing.
— ARISTOTLE

We few, we happy few, we band of brothers.
— SHAKESPEARE

PROLOGUE

When the sun dipped low in the sky, dripping the last of its fire, the children huddled together to hear the next part of the tale. For the old man, their eager faces and wide eyes brought the light into the room. The story he'd begun on a rainy afternoon would continue now, as twilight settled over the land.

The fire crackled in the grate, the only sound as he sipped his wine, as he searched his mind for the right words.

"You know now a beginning, of Hoyt the Sorcerer and the witch from beyond his time. You know how the vampire came to be, and how the scholar and the shifter of shapes from the world of Geall came through the Dance of the Gods, into the land of Ireland. You know how a friend and brother was lost, and how the warrior came to join them."

"They gathered together," one of the

wide-eyed children said, "to fight, to save all the worlds."

"This is truth, and this happened. These six, this circle of courage and hope were charged by the gods, through the messenger Morrigan, to fight the army of vampires led by their ambitious queen, Lilith."

"They defeated the vampires in battle," one of the young ones said, and the old man knew he saw himself as one of the brave, lifting sword and stake to destroy evil.

"This, too, is truth, and this happened. On the night the sorcerer and the witch were handfasted, the night they pledged the love they'd found in this terrible time, the circle of six beat back the demons. Their valor could not be questioned. But this was only one battle, in the first month of the three they'd been given to save worlds."

"How many worlds are there?"

"They can't be counted," he told them. "Any more than the stars in the sky can be counted. And all of these worlds were threatened. For if these six were defeated, those worlds would be changed, just as a man can be changed into demon."

"But what happened next?"

He smiled now with the firelight casting shadows on a face scored by the years. "Well now, I'll tell you. Dawn came after the night of the battle, as dawn will. A soft and misty dawn this was, a quiet after the storm. The rain had washed away the blood, human and demon, but the ground was scorched where fire swords had flamed. And still the mourning doves cooed, and the stream sang. In that morning light, leaves and blossoms, wet from rain, glimmered.

"It was for this," he told them, "these simple and ordinary things they fought. For man needs the comfort of the simple as much as he needs glory."

He sipped his wine, then set it aside. "So they had gathered to preserve these things. And so, now gathered, did they begin their journey."

CHAPTER 1

Clare
The first day of September

Through the house, still as a grave, Larkin limped. The air was sweet, fragrant with the flowers gathered lavishly for the handfasting rite of the night before.

The blood had been mopped up; the weapons cleaned. They'd toasted Hoyt and Glenna with the frothy wine, had eaten cake. But behind the smiles, the horror of the night's battle lurked. A poor guest.

Today, he supposed, was for rest and more preparation. It was a struggle for him not to be impatient with the training, with the planning. At least last night they'd fought, he thought as he pressed a hand to his thigh that ached from an arrow strike. A score of demons had fallen, and there was glory in that.

In the kitchen, he opened the refrigerator and took out a bottle of Coke. He'd developed a taste for it, and had come to prefer it over his morning tea.

He turned the bottle in his hand, marveling at the cleverness of the vessel — so smooth, so clear and hard. But what was inside it — this was something he'd miss when they returned to Geall.

He could admit he hadn't believed his cousin, Moira, when she'd spoken of gods and demons, of a war for worlds. He'd only gone with her that day, that sad day of her mother's burial, to look after her. She wasn't only blood, but friend, and would be queen of Geall.

But every word she'd spoken to him, only steps away from her mother's grave, had been pure truth. They'd gone to the Dance, they'd stood in the heart of that circle. And everything had changed.

Not just the where and when they were, he mused as he opened the bottle and took that first bracing sip. But everything. One moment, they'd stood under the afternoon sun in Geall, then there'd been light and wind, and a roar of sound.

Then it had been night, and it had been Ireland — a place Larkin had always believed a fairy tale.

He hadn't believed in fairy tales, or monsters, and despite his own gift had looked askance at magic.

But magic there was, he admitted now. Just as there was an Ireland, and there were monsters. Those demons had attacked them — springing out of the dark of the woods, their eyes red, their fangs sharp. The form of a man, he thought, but not a man.

Vampyre.

They existed to feed off man. And now they banded together under their queen to destroy all.

He was here to stop them, at all and any costs. He was here at the charge of the gods to save the worlds of man.

He scratched idly at his healing thigh and decided he could hardly be expected to save mankind on an empty stomach.

He cut a slab of cake to go with his morning Coke and licked icing from his finger. So far, through wile and guile he'd avoided Glenna's cooking lessons. He liked to eat, that was true enough, but the actual making of food was a different matter.

He was a tall, lanky man with a thick waving mane of tawny hair. His eyes, nearly the same color, were long like his cousin's, and nearly as keen. He had a long and mobile mouth that was quick to smile, quick hands and an easy nature.

Those who knew him would have said he was generous with his time and his coin, and a good man to have at your back at the pub, or in a brawl.

He'd been blessed with strong, even features, a strong back, a willing hand. And the power to change his shape into any living thing.

He took a healthy bite of cake where he stood, but there was too much quiet in the house to suit him. He wanted, needed, activity, sound, motion. Since he couldn't sleep, he decided he'd take Cian's stallion out for a morning run.

Cian could hardly do it himself, being a vampire.

He stepped out of the back door of the big stone house. There was a chill in the air, but he had the sweater and jeans Glenna had purchased in the village. He wore his own boots — and the silver cross Glenna and Hoyt had forged with magic.

He saw where the earth was scorched, where it was trampled. He saw his own hoofprints left in the sodden earth when he'd galloped through the battle in the form of a horse.

And he saw the woman who'd ridden him,

slashing destruction with a flaming sword.

She moved through the mists, slow and graceful, in what he would have taken for a dance if he hadn't known the movements, the complete control in them, were another preparation for battle.

Long arms and long legs swept through the air so smoothly they barely disturbed the mists. He could see her muscles tremble when she held a pose, endlessly held it, for her arms were bared in a snug white garment no woman of Geall would have worn outside the bedchamber.

She lifted a leg behind her into the air, bent at the knee, reaching an arm back to grasp her bare foot. The shirt rose up her torso to reveal more flesh.

It would be a sorry man, Larkin decided, who didn't enjoy the view.

Her hair was short, raven black, and her eyes were bluer than the lakes of Fonn. She wouldn't have been deemed a beauty in his world, as she lacked the roundness, the plump sweet curves, but he found the strength of her form appealing, the angles of her face, the sharp arch of brows interesting and unique.

She brought her leg down, swept it out to the side, then dropped into a long crouch with her arms parallel to the ground.

"You always eat that much sugar in the morning?"

Her voice jolted him. He'd been still and silent, and thought her unaware of him. He should've known better. He took a bite of the cake he'd forgotten he held. "It's good."

"Bet." Blair lowered her arms, straightened. "Earlier rising for you than usual, isn't it?"

"I couldn't sleep."

"Know what you mean. Damn good fight."

"Good?" He looked over the burned ground and thought of the screams, the blood, the death. "It wasn't a night at the pub."

"Entertaining though." She looked as he did, but with a hard light in her eyes. "We kicked some vampire ass, and what could be a better way to spend the evening?"

"I can think of a few."

"Hell of a rush, though." She rolled any lingering tension from her shoulders as she glanced at the house. "And it didn't suck to go from a handfasting to a fight and back again — as winners. Especially when you consider the alternative."

"There's that, I suppose."

"I hope Glenna and Hoyt are getting a little honeymoon time in, because for the most part, it was a pretty crappy reception."

With the long, almost liquid gait he'd come to admire, she walked over to the table they used during daylight training to hold weapons and supplies. She picked up the bottle of water she'd left there and drank deep.

"You have a mark of royalty."

"Say what?"

He moved closer, touched a fingertip lightly to her shoulder blade. There was the mark of a cross like the one around his neck, but in bold and bloody red.

"It's just a tattoo."

"In Geall only the ruler would bear a mark on the body. When the new king or queen becomes, when they lift the sword from the stone, the mark appears. Here." He tapped a hand on his right biceps. "Not the symbol of the cross, but the claddaugh, put there, it's said, by the finger of the gods."

"Cool. Excellent," she explained when he frowned at her.

"I myself have never seen this."

She cocked her head. "And seeing's believing?"

He shrugged. "My aunt, Moira's mother, had such a mark. But she rose to queen before I was born, so I didn't see the mark become."

19

"I never heard that part of the legend." Because it was there, she swooped a fingertip through the icing of his cake, sucked it off. "I guess everything doesn't trickle down."

"How did you come by yours?"

Funny guy, Blair thought. Curious nature. Gorgeous eyes. Danger, Will Robinson, she thought. That sort of combo just begged for complications. She just wasn't built for complications — and had learned it the hard way. "I paid for it. A lot of people have tattoos. It's like a personal statement, you could say. Glenna's got one." She took another drink, watching him as she reached around to tap herself on the small of the back. "Here. A pentagram. I saw it when we were helping her get dressed for the handfasting."

"So they're for women."

"Not only. Why, you want one?"

"I think not." He rubbed absently at his thigh.

Blair remembered yanking the arrow out of him herself, and that he'd barely uttered a sound. The guy had balls to go with the gorgeous eyes and curious nature. He was no slouch in a fight, and no whiner after the battle. "Leg giving you trouble?"

"A little stiff, a little sore. Glenna's a good healer. Yours?"

She bent her leg back, heel to butt, gave it a testing pull. "It's okay. I heal fast — part of the family package. Not as fast as a vamp," she added. "But demon hunters heal faster than your average human."

She picked up the jacket she'd tossed on the table, put it on against the morning cool. "I want coffee."

"I don't like it. I like the Coke." Then he smiled, easy, charming. "Will you be making yourself the breakfast?"

"In a little while. I've got some things I want to do first."

"Maybe you wouldn't mind making enough for two."

"Maybe." Clever guy, too, she thought. You had to respect his finagling. "You got something going now?"

It took him a moment, but he tried to spend a little time each day with the miraculous machine called the television. He was proud to think he was learning new idioms. "I'm after taking the horse for a ride, then feeding and grooming him."

"Plenty of light today, but you shouldn't head into the woods unarmed."

"I'll be riding the fields. Ah, Glenna, she asked if I'd not ride alone in the forest. I don't like to worry her. Were you wanting a ride yourself?"

21

"I think I had enough of one last night, thanks to you." Amused, she gave him a light punch in the chest. "You've got some speed in you, cowboy."

"Well, you've a light and steady seat." He looked back out at the trampled ground. "You're right. It was a good fight."

"Damn right. But the next one won't be so easy."

His eyebrows winged up. "And that one was easy?"

"Compared to what's coming, bet your ass."

"Well then, the gods help us all. And if you've a mind to cook eggs and bacon with it, that'd be fine. Might as well eat our fill while we still have stomachs."

Cheery thought, Blair decided as she went inside. The hell of it was, he'd meant it that way. She'd never known anyone so offhand about life and death. Not resigned — she'd been raised to be resigned to it — just a kind of confidence that he'd live as he chose to live, until he stopped living.

She admired the viewpoint.

She'd been raised to know the monster under the bed was real, and was just waiting until you relaxed before it ripped your throat out.

She'd been trained to put that moment off

as long as she could stand and fight, to slash and to burn, and take out as many as humanly possible. Because under the strength, the wit and the endless training was the knowledge that some day, some way, she wouldn't be fast enough, smart enough, lucky enough.

And the monster would win.

Still there'd always been a balance to it — demon and hunter, with each the other's prey. Now the stakes had been raised, sky-fricking-high, she thought as she made coffee. Now it wasn't just the duty and tradition that had been passed down through her blood for damn near a millennium.

Now it was a fight to save humankind.

She was here, with this strange little band — two of which, vampire and sorcerer, turned out to be her ancestors — to fight the mother of all battles.

Two months, she thought, until Halloween. Till Samhain, and the final showdown the goddess had prophesied. They'd have to be ready, she decided as she poured the first cup. Because the alternative just wasn't an option.

She carried her coffee upstairs, into her room.

As quarters went, it had it all over her apartment in Chicago where she'd based herself over the last year and a half. The bed boasted a tall headboard with carved dragons on either side. A woman could feel like a spellbound princess in that bed — if she was of a fanciful state of mind.

Despite the fact the place was owned by a vampire, there was a wide mirror, framed in thick mahogany. The wardrobe would have held three times the amount of clothes she'd brought with her, so she used it for secondary weapons, and tucked her traveling wardrobe in the chest of drawers.

The walls were painted a dusky plum, and the art on them woodland scenes of twilight or predawn, so that the room seemed to be in perpetual shadow if the curtains were drawn. But that was all right. She had lived a great deal of her life in the shadows.

But she opened the curtains now so morning spilled in and then sat at the gorgeous little desk to check her e-mail on her laptop.

She couldn't prevent the little flicker of hope, or stop it from dying out as she saw there was still no return message from her father.

Nothing new, she reminded herself and tipped back in the chair. He was traveling, somewhere in South America to the best of her knowledge. And she only knew that much because her brother had told her.

It had been six months since she'd had any contact with him, and there was nothing new about that, either. His duty to her had been, in his opinion, fulfilled years ago. And maybe he was right. He'd taught her, he'd trained her, though she'd never been good enough to merit his approval.

She simply didn't have the right equipment. She wasn't his son. The disappointment he'd felt when it had been his daughter instead of his son who'd inherited the gift was something he'd never bothered to hide.

Softening blows of any sort just wasn't Sean Murphy's style. He'd pretty much dusted her off his hands on her eighteenth birthday.

Now she'd embarrassed herself by sending him a second message when he'd never answered the first. She'd sent that first e-mail before she'd left for Ireland, to tell him something was up, something was twitching, and she wanted his advice.

So much for that, she thought now, and so much for trying again, after her arrival, to tell him what was twitching was major.

He had his own life, his own course, and had never pretended otherwise. It was her own problem, her own lack, that she still coveted his approval. She'd given up on earning his love a long time ago.

She turned off the computer, pulled on a sweatshirt and shoes. She decided to go up to the training room and work off frustration, work up an appetite lifting weights.

The house, she'd been told, had been the one Hoyt and his brother, Cian, had been born in. In the dawn of the twelfth century. It had been modernized, of course, and some additions had been made, but she could see from the original structure the Mac Cionaoiths had been a family of considerable means.

Of course Cian had had nearly a millennium to make his own fortune, to acquire the house again. Though from the bits and pieces she'd picked up, he didn't live in it.

She didn't make a habit out of conversing with vampires — just killing them. But she was making an exception with Cian. For reasons that weren't entirely clear to her, he was fighting with them, even bankrolling their little war party to some extent.

Added to that, she'd seen the way he'd fought the night before, with a ruthless ferocity. His allegiance could be the element that tipped the scales in their favor.

She wound her way up the stone stairs toward what had once been the great hall, then a ballroom in later years. And was now their training room.

She stopped short when she saw Larkin's cousin Moira doing chest extensions with five-pound free weights.

The Geallian wore her brown hair back in a thick braid that reached her waist. Sweat dribbled down her temples, and more darkened the back of the white T-shirt she wore. Her eyes, fog gray, were staring straight ahead, focused, Blair assumed, on whatever got her through the reps.

She was, by Blair's gauge, about five-three, maybe a hundred and ten pounds, after you'd dragged her out of a lake. But she was game. Having game held a lot of weight on Blair's scale. What Blair had initially judged as mousiness was, in actuality, a watchfulness. The woman soaked up everything.

"Thought you were still in bed," Blair said as she stepped inside.

Moira lowered the weights, then used her forearm to swipe her brow. "I've been up for a bit. You're wanting to use the room?"

"Yeah. Plenty of room in here for both of us." Blair walked over, selected ten-pound weights. "Not hunkered down with the books this morning."

"I . . ." On a sigh, Moira stretched out her arms as she'd been taught. She might have wished her arms were as sleek and carved with muscle as Blair's, but no one would call

27

them soft any longer. "I've been starting the day here, before I use the library. Usually before anyone's up and about."

"Okay." Curious, Blair studied Moira as she worked her triceps. "And you're keeping this a secret because?"

"Not a secret. Not exactly a secret." Moira picked up a bottle of water, twisted off the cap. Twisted it back on. "I'm the weakest of us. I don't need you or Cian to tell me that — though one or the other of you make a point to let me know it with some regularity."

Something gave a little twist inside Blair's belly. "And that sucks. I'm going to tell you I'm sorry about that, because I know how it feels to get slammed down when you're doing your best."

"My best isn't altogether that good, is it? No, I'm not looking for sorry," she said before Blair could speak. "It's hard to be told you're lacking, but that's what I am — for now. So I come up here in the mornings, early, and lift these bloody things the way you showed me. I won't be the weak one, the one the rest of you have to worry about."

"You don't have much muscle yet, but you've got some speed. And you're a frigging genius with a bow. If you weren't so good with it, things wouldn't have turned out the way they did last night."

"Work on my weaknesses, and on my strengths, on my own time. That's what you said to me — and it made me angry. Until I saw the wisdom of it. I'm not angry. You're good at training. King was . . . He was more easy on me, I think, because he was a man. A big man at that," Moira added with sorrow in her eyes now. "Who had affection for me, I think, because I was the smallest of us."

Blair hadn't met King, Cian's friend who'd been captured, then killed by Lilith. Then turned, and sent back as a vampire.

"I won't be easy on you," Blair promised.

By the time she'd finished a session with the weights and grabbed a quick shower, Blair had worked up that appetite. She decided to go for one of her favorites, and dug up the makings for French toast.

She tossed some Irish bacon into a skillet for protein, selected Green Day on her MP3 player. Music to cook by.

She poured her second cup of coffee before breaking eggs in a bowl.

She was beating the batter when Larkin strolled in the door. He stopped, stared at her player. "And what is it?"

"It's a —" How to explain? "A way to whistle while you work."

"No, it's not the machine I'm meaning. There are so many of those, I can't keep them all in my brain. But what's the sound?"

"Oh. Um, popular music? Rock — of the hard variety."

He was grinning now, head cocked as he listened. "Rock. I like it."

"Who wouldn't? Not going for eggs, this morning. Doing up French toast."

"Toast?" Disappointment fell over his face, erasing the easy pleasure of the music. "Just cooked bread?"

"Not just. Besides, you get what you get when I'm manning the stove. Or you forage on your own."

"It's kind of you to cook, of course."

His tone was so long-suffering, she had to swallow a laugh. "Relax, and trust me on this. I've seen you chow down, cowboy. You're going to like it as much as Rock, especially after you drown it in butter and syrup. I'll have it going in a minute. Why don't you flip that bacon over?"

"I'm needing to wash first. Been mucking out the stall and such, and I'm not fit yet to touch anything."

She lifted a brow as he strolled right out. She'd seen him slip out of all manner of kitchen duties already. And she had to admit, he was slick about it.

Resigned, she turned the bacon herself, then heated a second skillet. She was about to dunk the first piece of bread when she heard voices. The newlyweds were up, she realized, and added to the batter to accommodate them.

Effortless style. It was something Glenna had in spades, Blair thought. She wandered in wearing a sage green sweater and black jeans with her bold red hair swinging straight and loose. The urban take on country casual, Blair supposed. When you added the pretty flush of a woman who'd obviously had her morning snuggles, you had quite a package.

She didn't look like a woman who would rush a squad of vampires while she bellowed war cries and swung a battle-ax, but she'd done just that.

"Mmm, French toast? You must have read my mind." As she moved to the coffeepot, Glenna gave Blair's arm an absent stroke. "Give you a hand?"

"No, I got this. You've been taking the lion's share of KP, and I'm better at breakfast than dinner. Didn't I hear Hoyt?"

"Right behind me. He's talking to Larkin about the horse. I think Hoyt's a little put out he didn't get to Vlad before Larkin did. Coffee's good. How'd you sleep?"

"Like I'd been knocked unconscious, for a

couple hours." Blair dipped bread, then laid it to sizzle. "Then, I don't know, too restless. Wired up." She slanted Glenna a look. "And nowhere to put the excess energy, like the bride."

"I have to admit, I'm feeling pretty loose and relaxed this morning. Except." Wincing a little, Glenna massaged her right biceps. "My arms feel like I spent half the night swinging a sledgehammer."

"Battle-ax has weight. You did good work with it."

"*Work* isn't the word that comes to mind. But I'm not going to think about it — at least not until I've gorged myself." Turning, Glenna opened a cupboard for plates. "Do you know how often I had a breakfast like this — fried bread, fried meat — before all this started?"

"Nope."

"Never. Absolutely never," she added with a half laugh. "I watched my weight as if the, well, as if the fate of the world depended on it."

"You're training hard." Blair flipped the bread. "You need the fuel, the carbs. If you put on a few pounds, I can guarantee it's going to be pure muscle."

"Blair." Glenna glanced toward the doorway to ensure Hoyt hadn't started in yet.

"You've got more experience with this than any of us. Just between you and me, for now, anyway, how did we do last night?"

"We lived," Blair said flatly. She continued to cook, sliding fried bread onto a plate, dunking more. "That's bottom line."

"But —"

"Glenna, I'll tell you straight." Blair turned, leaning back on the counter for a moment while bread sizzled and scented the air. "I've never been in anything like that before."

"But you've been doing this — hunting them — for years."

"That's right. And I've never seen so many of them in one place at one time, never seen them organized that way."

Glenna let out a quiet breath. "That can't be good news."

"Good or bad, it's fact. It's not — never been in my experience — the nature of the beast to live, work, fight in large groups. I contacted my aunt, and she says the same. They're killers, and they might travel, hunt, even live together in packs. Small packs, and there might be an alpha, male or female. But not like this."

"Not like an army," Glenna murmured.

"No. And what we saw last night was a squad — a small slice of an army. The thing is, they're willing to die for her, for Lilith. And that's powerful stuff."

"Okay. Okay," Glenna said as she set the table. "That's what I get for saying I wanted it straight."

"Hey, buck up. We lived, remember? That's a victory."

"Good morning to you," Hoyt said to Blair as he came in. Then his gaze went straight to Glenna.

They shared coloring, Blair thought, she and her however-many-times great-uncle. She, the sorcerer and his twin brother, the vampire, shared coloring, and ancestry, and now this mission, she supposed.

Fate was certainly a twisty bastard.

"You two sure have the glow on," she said when Glenna lifted her face to meet Hoyt's lips. "Practically need my shades."

"They shield the eyes from the sun, and are a sexy fashion statement," Hoyt returned and made her laugh.

"Have a seat." She turned off the music, then brought the heaping platter to the table. "I made enough for an army, seeing as that's what we are."

"It looks a fine feast. Thank you."

"Just doing my share, unlike some of us who're a little more slippery." She met Larkin's perfectly timed appearance with a shake of her head. "Right on time."

His expression was both innocent and affable. "Is it ready then? It took me a bit longer to get back as I stopped to tell Moira there was food being cooked. And a welcome sight it is."

"You look, you eat." Blair slapped four slices of French toast on a plate for him. "And you and your cousin do the dishes."

CHAPTER 2

Maybe it was the post-battle itches, but Blair couldn't settle. After another session with Glenna, everyone's injuries were well on the mend, so they could train. They *should* train, she told herself. Maybe the sweat and effort would work off the restlessness.

But she had another idea.

"I think we should go out."

"Out?" Glenna checked her chart of household duties and noted — God help them — Hoyt was next up on laundry detail. "Are we low on something?"

"I don't know." Blair scanned the charts posted prominently on the refrigerator. "You seem to have the supply and duty lists under control — Quartermaster Ward."

"Mmm, Quartermaster." Glenna sent Blair a twinkling look. "I like it. Can I get a badge?"

"I'll see what I can do. But when I say we

should go out, I'm thinking more a little scouting expedition than a supply run. We should go check out Lilith's base of operations."

"Now there's a fine idea." Larkin turned from the sink, where soap dripped from his hands, and he was not at all happy. "Give her a bit of a surprise for a change."

"Attack Lilith?" Moira stopped loading the dishwasher. "Today?"

"I didn't say attack. Throttle back," Blair advised Larkin. "We're outnumbered by a long shot, and I don't think the locals would understand a bloodbath in broad daylight. But the daylight's the key here."

"Go south to Chiarrai," Hoyt said quietly. "To the cliffs and caves, while we have the sun."

"There you go. They can't come out. Nothing they can do about us poking around, taking a look. And it'd be a nice follow-up to routing them last night."

"Psychological warfare." Glenna nodded. "Yes, I see."

"That," Blair agreed, "and maybe we gather some intel. We see what we see, we map out various routes going and coming. And we make a point of letting her know we're there. Or were there."

"If we could lure some of them out. Or go

in just far enough to give them some trouble. Fire," Larkin said. "There should be a way to set a fire in the caves."

"Not altogether a bad idea." Blair thought it over. "Bitch could use a good spanking. We'll go prepared for that, and armed. But we go quiet and careful. We don't want some tourist or local calling the cops — then having to explain why we've got a van loaded with weapons."

"Leave the fire to me and to Glenna." Hoyt pushed to his feet.

"Why?"

In answer, Glenna held out her hand. A ball of flame shimmered in her cupped palm.

"Pretty," Blair decided.

"And Cian?" Moira continued to deal with the dishes. "He wouldn't be able to leave the house."

"Then he stays back," Blair said flatly. "Larkin, if you're done there, let's go load up some weapons."

"We have some things in the tower that might be useful." Glenna brushed her fingers over Hoyt's arm. "Hoyt?"

"We can't just leave him without letting him know what we're about."

"You want to wake up a vampire this time of day?" Blair shrugged. "Okay. You go first."

■ ■ ■ ■

Cian didn't care to be disturbed during his rest time. He figured a closed and locked bedroom door would be a clear signal to anyone that he wanted his privacy. But such things never seemed to stop his brother. So he sat now, awake in the dim light, and listened to the plan for the day.

"So, if I have this right, you woke me to tell me you're going out, down to Kerry to poke at the caves?"

"We didn't want you to wake, find us all gone."

"My fondest dream." Cian waved that lazily away. "Apparently, the good, bloody fight last night isn't enough for the hunter."

"It's good strategy, going there."

"Didn't work out so very well, did it, the last time we went there?"

Hoyt said nothing for a moment, thinking of King, and the loss of him.

"Nor, for you or me, the time before that," Cian added. "You ended up barely able to walk away, and I took a fucking header off a cliff. Not one of my happiest memories."

"Those times were different altogether, and you know it. It's daylight now, and this time she won't know we're coming. And being it's daylight, you'll have to stay behind."

"If you think I'll sulk about that, you'd be wrong. I've plenty to keep me busy. Calls and e-mails, which I've largely neglected these past weeks. I still have businesses that need my attention, which might as well be tended to since you've pulled me out of bed in the middle of the damn day. Let me add it'll be a pure pleasure to have five noisy humans out of the house a few hours, that I can promise you."

He rose, walked to his desk and wrote something on a notepad. "Since you'll be out and about, I'll need you to go here. There's a butcher in Ennis. He'll sell you blood. Pigs' blood," Cian said with a bland smile as he handed his brother the address. "I'll ring him up, so he knows someone's coming. Payment's not a problem as I have an account."

His brother's writing hand had changed over all this time, Hoyt noted. So much had changed. "Doesn't he wonder why . . ."

"If he does, he's wise enough not to ask. And he's no doubt pleased to pocket the extra euros. That's the coin here now."

"Aye, Glenna explained it to me. We'll be back before sunset."

"Better hope you are," Cian warned when Hoyt left him.

■ ■ ■ ■

Outside, Blair tossed a dozen stakes in a plastic bucket. Swords, axes, scythes were already on board. All of the fiery variety. It was going to be interesting explaining things if they got stopped, but she didn't scout out a vampire nest without going fully loaded.

"Who wants the wheel?" she asked Glenna.

"I know the way."

Blair checked the need to take control, climbed in the back, took the seat behind Glenna as the others joined her. "So, Hoyt, have you ever been in the caves? I don't figure that kind of thing changes much in a few hundred years."

"Many times. But they're different now."

"We've been in them," Glenna explained. "Magically. Hoyt and I did a spell before we left New York. It was intense."

"Fill me in."

Blair listened, one part of her brain marking the route, landmarks, traffic patterns.

In any part, she saw what Glenna described. A labyrinth of tunnels, chambers blocked with thick doors, bodies stacked like so much garbage. People in cages like penned cattle. And the sounds of it — Blair could hear that in the back of her mind —

the weeping, the screaming, the praying.

"Luxury vamp condo," she murmured. "How many ways in?"

"I couldn't say. In my time the cliffs were riddled with caves. Some small, barely big enough for a child to crawl through, others big enough for a man to stand. There were more tunnels, wider, taller than I remember."

"So, she excavated. She's had plenty of time to make it all homey."

"If we could block them off," Larkin began, and Moira turned to him in horror.

"There are people inside. People held in cages like animals. Bodies tossed aside without even the decency of burial."

He covered her hand with his and said nothing.

"We can't get them out. That's what he's not saying to you." But it had to be said, Blair thought. "Even if a couple of us wanted to try a suicide run, that's just what it would be. We'd die, they'd die. A rescue isn't an option. I'm sorry."

"A spell," Moira insisted. "Something to blind or bind, just until we free those who've been captured."

"We tried to blind her." Glenna flicked a glance in the rearview to meet Moira's eyes. "We failed. Maybe a transportation spell."

She looked at Hoyt now. "Would it be possible for us to transport humans?"

"I've never done it. The risks . . ."

"They'll die in there. Many have already." Moira scooted up in her seat to grip Hoyt's shoulder. "What greater risk is there than death?"

"We could harm them. To use magicks that may harm —"

"You could save them. What choice do you think they would take? What choice would you?"

"She's got a point." If they could do it, Blair thought, if they could save even one, it would be worth it. And it would be a good hard kick in Lilith's ass. "Is there a chance?"

"You need to see what you move from one place to another," Hoyt explained. "And it's more successful if you're close to the object. This would be through rock, and we'd be all but blinded."

"Not necessarily," Glenna countered. "Let's think about this, let's talk it through."

While they talked — argued, discussed — Blair let it all stew around in the back of her mind. Pretty day, she thought absently. The sun shining on all that green. The lovely, long roll of land with cows grazing lazily. Tourists would be out, taking advantage of the weather after yesterday's storm. Shopping in the towns, or driving out to gawk at the Cliffs of Mohr, getting their snapshots and videos of the dolmen in The Burren.

She'd done the same thing herself, once upon a time.

"So, does Geall look anything like this?"

"Quite a bit really," Larkin told her. "It's very like home, except, well, the roads, the cars, most of the buildings. But the land itself, aye, it is. It's very like home."

"What do you do back there?"

"About what, exactly?"

"Well, a guy's got to make a living, right?"

"Oh. We work the land, of course. And we've horses, for breeding, selling. Fine horses. I've left my father shorthanded. He may not be too pleased with me right at the moment."

"Odds are he'll understand if you end up saving the world." She should have known he worked with his hands, Blair realized. They were strong and hard, and he had the look, she supposed, of a man who spent the bulk of his time outdoors. All those sun-streaks in his hair, the light golden haze on his skin.

Whoa, settle down, hormones. He was just another member of the team she'd been pulled into. It was smart to learn all you could about who was fighting beside you.

And stupid to let yourself get little tingles of lust over them.

"So you're a farmer."

"At the bottom of it."

"How does a farmer know how to use a sword the way you do?"

"Ah." He swiveled around to face her more directly. For a moment, just a short moment, he lost his trend. Her eyes were so deep and blue. "Sure we have tournaments. Games? I like to play in them. I like to win."

She could see that as well, though it was probably more Hollywood than Geallian. "Yeah, me, too. I like to win."

"So then, do you play games?"

There was a teasing, playfully sexy undercurrent in the question. She'd have had to have been brain-dead to miss it. Brain-dead for a month, she decided, not to feel the little buzz.

"Not so much, but I win when I do."

He draped an arm over the back of her seat in a casual move. "In some games, both sides are the winner."

"Maybe. Mostly when I fight, I'm not playing around."

"Play balances out the fighting, don't you think? And our tournaments, well, they'll have served as a kind of preparation for what's to come. There are many men in

45

Geall, and some women besides, who have a good hand with a sword or a lance. If the war goes there, as we're told it will, we'll have an army to meet these things."

"We'll need it."

"What do you do? Glenna says that women must work for a living here. Or that most do. Are you paid in coin to hunt demons?"

"No." He wasn't touching her, and she couldn't say he was putting moves on her. But she felt as if he were. "It's not the way it works. There's some family money. I mean we're not rolling in it or anything, but there's a cushion. We own pubs. Chicago, New York, Boston. Like that."

"Pubs, is it? I like a good pub."

"Who doesn't? Anyway, I do some waitressing. And some personal training."

His brows knit. "Training? For battle?"

"Not really. It's more for health and vanity. Ah, helping people get in shape, lose weight, tone up. I don't need a lot of money, so it works out okay. Gives me some room, too, to take off when I need to."

She glanced over. Moira was staring out the side window like a woman in a dream. In the front, Hoyt and Glenna continued to talk magic. Blair leaned closer to Larkin, lowered her voice.

"Look, maybe our magical lovebirds can

pull this transportation bit off, maybe not. If they can't, you're going to have to handle your cousin."

"I don't handle Moira."

"Sure you do. If we've got a shot at executing a little cave-in, or firing up those caves, we have to take it."

Their faces were close now, their voices down to whispers. "And the people inside? We burn them alive, or bury them the same way? She won't accept it. Neither can I."

"Do you know what torment they're in now?"

"It's not of our doing."

"Caged and tortured." She kept her eyes on his, and her voice was low and empty. "Forced to watch when one of them's dragged out of the cage, and fed on. Terrified, or well beyond that while they wonder if they'll be next. Maybe hoping they will just so it ends."

There was no playfulness now, in his face, in his tone. "I know what they do."

"You think you know. Maybe they don't drain them, not the first time. Maybe not the second. They just toss them back in the cage. It burns, the bite. If you live through it, it burns. Flesh, blood, bone, a reminder of the impossible pain when those fangs sank into you."

"How do you know?"

She turned her wrist over, so he could see the faint scar. "I was eighteen, pissed off about something and careless. In a cemetery up in Boston, waiting for one to rise. I went to school with the guy. Went to his funeral, and heard enough to know he'd been bitten. I had to find out if he'd been turned, so I went, and I waited."

"He did this?" Larkin traced a finger over the scar.

"He had help. No way a fresh one would've managed it. But the one who sired him came back. Older, smarter, stronger. I made some mistakes, and he didn't."

"Why were you alone?"

"Hunting alone is what I do," she reminded him. "But in this case, I was out to prove something to someone. Doesn't matter, except that it made me careless. He didn't bite me, the older one. He held me down while the other one crawled over toward me."

"Wait. Can you tell me, is that the way of it with a sire? To provide . . ."

"Food?"

"Aye, that would be the word for it, wouldn't it?"

It was a good question, she decided, good that he wanted to understand the phychol-

ogy and pathology of the enemy. "Sometimes. Not always. Depends, I'd say, on why
the sire chose to change instead of just drink.
They can form attachments, or want a hunting partner. Even just want a younger one
around to do the grunt work. You know, sort
of work for them."

"I see that. So the sire held you down so
the younger could feed first." And how terri-
fying, he thought, would that have been? To
be restrained, probably injured. To be eighteen and alone, while something with a face
you'd once known came for you.

"I could smell the grave on him, he was
that fresh. He was too hungry to go for the
throat, so he got me here. That was the mistake, for both of them. The pain woke me up.
It's unspeakable."

She said nothing for a moment. It threw
her off her stride, the way he laid his fingers
on that scar now, as if to ease an old wound.
She couldn't remember the last time anyone
had touched her to comfort.

"Anyway. I got a hand on my cross, and I
jabbed it right into that bastard's eye, the
one holding me down. Christ, did he
scream. The other one's so busy trying to
eat, he doesn't worry about anything else.
He was an easy kill. They were both easy
after that."

"You were just a girl."

"No. I was a demon hunter, and I was stupid." She looked Larkin in the eye now, so he would see that comfort, sympathy couldn't stand in front of sense and strategy. "If he'd gone for the throat, I'd be dead. Yeah, probably, I'd be dead and we wouldn't be having this conversation. I know what I felt when I saw that thing coming for me. In the good black suit his mother had picked out for him to be buried in. I know what those people inside those caves feel, at least I know a part of it. If they can't be saved, death's kinder than what's waiting for them."

He closed his hand over her wrist, completely covering the scar, surprising her with the gentleness of the touch. "Did you love the boy?"

"Yeah. Well, the way you do when you're that age." She'd almost forgotten that, nearly forgotten how sad she'd been, even through the pain. "All I could do for him was take him out, and take out the one who'd killed him."

"It cost you more than this." Larkin lifted her hand, brushed his lips over the scar. "More than the pain and the burn."

She'd nearly forgotten, too, she realized, what it was like to have someone understand. "Maybe it did, but it taught me something important. You can't save everyone."

"That's a sad lesson. Don't you think, even when you know you can't, you should try anyway?"

"That's amateur talk. This isn't a game or a contest. Somebody beats you in this, you die."

"Well, Cian's not here to dispute the matter, but would you want to live forever?"

She let out a short laugh. "Hell, no."

There were others along that lonely stretch of cliff and sea. But not as many as Blair had expected. The views were amazing, but she supposed there were others, equally dramatic, and more easily accessible.

They parked, and took what weapons and tools they could most easily conceal. Someone might spot her sword in its back sheath under the long leather coat, Blair decided. But they'd have to be looking. And then, what were they going to do about it?

She studied the lay of the land, the road, the other cars parked along it. A middle-aged couple had climbed to some of the tabletop rocks at the base of the cliff, where it now met the road. Looking out to sea — and completely oblivious to the nightmare that lived below.

"Okay, so it's over the seawall and down.

Gonna get wet," she concluded, looking down at the narrow strip of shale, then the teeth of the rocks where the water swirled and plumed. She glanced back at the others. "Can you handle this?"

As an answer, Larkin rolled over the wall. She started to shout at him to wait, to wait one damn minute, but he was already heading down the jagged drop that faced the sea.

He didn't change into a lizard, she observed, but he could sure as hell climb like one. She had to give him A's for balls and agility.

"Okay, Moira. Take it slow. If you slip, your cousin should break your fall." As Moira went over, Blair looked at Glenna.

"Never did any rock climbing," Glenna muttered. "Never could figure out the damn point until now. So, I guess there's always a first time."

"You'll be fine." But Blair watched Moira's progress, and was relieved she was proving nearly as agile as her cousin. "The drop's not that bad from here. It won't kill you."

She didn't add that bones would be broken. She didn't have to. Hoyt and Glenna went over together, and Blair followed.

There were some reasonably good handholds, she discovered — as long as you weren't worried about your manicure. She concentrated on getting the job done, ignored the cold spray as she worked her way down.

Hands gripped her waist, lifted her down the last couple of feet. "Thanks," she told Larkin, "but I've got it."

"A bit awkward with the sword." He glanced up to the road, grinned. "Fun though."

"Let's keep the party moving. They probably have guards. Maybe some human servants — though it has to be tough keeping humans on tap if there's as many vampires in there as you said."

"I didn't see anyone alive outside of cages," Glenna told her, "not when we looked before."

"This time it's live and in person, so if they've got any, that's who they'll send out. Hoyt you'd better take point, since you know the area."

"It's different, you see it's different than it was." Some of what he was feeling leaked into his voice, the emotion and the sorrow. "Nature and man have done it. That road above us, and the wall, the tower with the light."

Looking up, over, he saw his cliffs, the ledge that had saved his life when he'd fought with what Cian had become. Once, he thought, he'd stood up there and called the lightning as easily as a man calls his hound.

It had changed, he couldn't deny it. But still, in the heart of it, it was his place. He made his way through the rocks, over them, through the spray. "There should be a cave here. And there's nothing but . . ."

He laid his hands on the earth and rock. "This is not real. This is false."

"Maybe you're a little turned around," Blair began.

"Wait." Glenna made her way over to him, put her hands next to his. "A barrier."

"Conjured," Hoyt agreed, "to look and feel like the land, but it isn't the land. This isn't earth and rock. It's illusion."

"Can you break it down?" Larkin thumped a fist against the rock, testing.

"Hold on." Frowning, Blair slicked back her damp hair. "She's got enough mojo for this, or has someone in there with enough, we don't know what else she has. This is smart." Blair tested the wall herself. "Really smart. Nobody gets in unless she wants them in. Nobody gets out unless she wants them out."

"So we just walk away?" Larkin demanded.

"I didn't say that."

"There are more openings, pockets in the wall. Were," Hoyt corrected. "This is a powerful spell."

"And nobody's curious — people who come here, live here — about what happened to them." Blair nodded. "That's powerful, too. She wants her privacy. We're going to have to disappoint her."

Hands on hips, she turned around, searching. "Hey, Hoyt, can you and Glenna carve a message into that big rock over there?"

"It can be done."

"What's the message?" Glenna asked her.

"Gotta think of one, since Up Yours, Bitch seems a little too ordinary."

"Tremble," Moira murmured, and Blair gave her a nod of approval.

"Excellent. Short, to the point, and just a little cocky. Take care of that, will you? Then we'll get started on the rest."

"What is the rest?" Larkin wanted to know. He gave the wall a frustrated kick. "A stronger message would be to break this spell."

"Yeah, it would, but right now I'm thinking she doesn't know we're out here. That could be an advantage." She heard something like a small blast of gunpowder, and turned to see the word *Tremble* deeply carved into the rock. Below it was another carving, of what she assumed was Lilith. With a stake through her heart.

"Hey, nice job. I really like the artwork."

"A little flourish." Glenna dusted off her hands. "I paint, and I couldn't resist the dig."

"What do you need to try the transportation spell?"

Glenna blew out a breath. "Time, space, focus, and a hell of a lot of luck."

"Not from here." Hoyt shook his head. "The cliffs are mine. The caves are hers. However much time has passed, the cliffs are still mine. We'll work the spell from above." He turned to Glenna. "We have to see first. We can't transport what we can't see. It's likely she'll sense us, and do whatever she can to stop us."

"Maybe not right away. We won't be looking for her this time, but for people. She may not realize what we're doing, and give us the time we need. Hoyt's right, it's better done on the cliffs," Glenna told Blair. "If we can get anyone out, we wouldn't want to bring them out here in any case."

"Good point." Maybe they wouldn't get any solid intel out of this trip, Blair mused, but they might not walk away empty-handed. "So, what do we do with them if it works?"

"Get them to safety." Glenna lifted her hands. "One step at a time."

"I can try to help you. I haven't much magic," Moira added, "but I could try to help."

"Every little bit helps," Glenna said.

"Okay, the three of you go up. Larkin and I will stay here, in case . . . well, in case. Anything that comes out this way to give us trouble has to be human. We'll handle it."

"It could take a while," Glenna warned her.

Blair studied the sky. "Plenty of daylight left."

She waited until they'd started up before she spoke to Larkin. "We can't go in. If this magic deal opens up the caves, we can't go in. I mean it." She punched his arm. "I can see what you're thinking."

"Oh, can you now?"

"Rush in, grab a maiden in distress or two, run out the hero."

"You're wrong about the hero end of it. That wouldn't be what I'm looking for. But now a pretty maiden in distress is hard for a man to resist."

"Resist it. You don't know the caves, you don't know where she's holding the prisoners, and you don't know their numbers or how they're equipped. Listen, I'm not saying a part of me wouldn't like to go charging in there if it opens up, do some damage, maybe save some lives. But we'd never make it out alive, and neither would anyone else."

"We have the swords Hoyt and Glenna charmed. The fire swords."

She struggled with frustration. It was so damn irritating to have to explain basic strategy. "And we'd take some vamps with us, no question. Then they'd have us and the swords."

"I know the sense of what you're saying, but it's hard to stand by and do nothing."

"If the magic team pulls this off, it won't be nothing. You're too good in a fight for us to lose you trying something that can't work."

"Oh, a compliment. Not many of those spill out of your lips." He grinned at her while drops of sea spray glinted in his hair. "I won't go in. I give you my word on it." He held out a hand for hers. When she took it, he gave it an easy squeeze. "But there wouldn't be anything stopping us from slapping some fire in the hole should this bloody rock open. It would be what you call making a statement, wouldn't it?"

"Guess it would. Just don't get cocky, Larkin."

"Sure I was born that way, I'm afraid.

What's a man to do, after all?"

He turned to face the wall, and leaned back on one of the wet rocks as the spume sprayed. And looked relaxed enough, Blair noted, that he might have been sitting in the parlor by the fire.

"Well, likely we've got some time on our hands just now. So, tell me, how did you first know you'd be a demon hunter?"

"You want the story of my life? Now?"

He moved his shoulders. "Might as well pass the time. And I'll admit to some curiosity about it. Before I left Geall, I wouldn't have believed any of this, not at the heart of it. And now, well . . ." He stared thoughtfully at the wall of rock and sod. "What's a man to do?" he repeated.

He had a point she decided. She moved over to join him, angling her body so that she could scan one sweep of the cliff face while he took the other. "I was four."

"Young. Young to have any understanding of matters that dark. That they're real, I'm saying, and not just the shadows a child imagines are monsters."

"Things are a little different in my family. I thought it would be my brother. I was jealous. I guess that's natural enough, the sibling rivalry." She slid her hands into the pockets of her coat, idly toying with the plastic bottle of holy water she'd shoved in there before they'd left. "He'd have been six — six and a half. My father'd been working with him. Simple tumbling, basic martial arts and weaponry. Lots of tension in the house back then. My parents' marriage was falling apart."

"How?"

"It happens." Maybe in his world the sky was rosy pink and love was forever. "People get dissatisfied, feelings change. Added to it my mother was sick of the life, the things that took my father away. She wanted normal, and it was her mistake she'd married someone who'd never give it to her. So she was busy picking fights with my father, and he was busy ignoring her and working with my brother."

Which would mean, Larkin thought, that no one was paying attention to her. Poor little lamb.

"So I was always after my father to train me, too, or trying to do some of the stuff my brother was doing."

"My younger brother trailed after me like a shadow when we were children. This is the same in all worlds, I suppose."

"Bug you? Bother you?" she amended.

"Oh, drove me mad some of the time. Others, I didn't mind so much. If he was close by, it was easier to devil him. And others yet, well, it wasn't so bad as company."

"So pretty much the same as with me and my brother. Then this one day they were down in the training area — a space most people would have a family room." But you had to have a family to rate a family room. "We had equipment — weights, a pommel horse, uneven bars, rings. One whole wall was mirrored."

She could still see it, perfectly, and the way they'd reflected her father and her brother, so close together, while she'd been off to the side. And alone.

"I watched them in the mirrors; they didn't know I was there. My father was giving Mick — my brother — a rash of grief because Mick just couldn't get this move. Back flip," she murmured, "dive, shoulder roll, throw the stake into the target. Mick just couldn't get it, and my father was dead set he would. Finally, Mick got pissy himself, and he threw the stake across the room."

It had almost brushed her fingers, she remembered. As if it had been meant for her hand.

"It rolled right to me. I knew I could do it. I just wanted to show my father I could do it. I just wanted him to look at me. So I did. I called his name: 'Watch me, Daddy,' and I

61

did it, the way I'd watched him do it over and over trying to get Mick to understand the rhythm."

She closed her eyes a moment because she could still see herself, still feel it in her. As if the world had stopped, and only she was in motion for those few seconds.

"Hit the heart. Mostly luck, but I hit the heart. I was so happy. Look what I did! Mick's eyes just about fell out of his head, then . . . there was this little smile in them — just a little. I didn't know what it meant then, I thought he'd just gotten a kick out what I did, because we mostly got along pretty well. My father didn't say anything, not for a few seconds — seemed like an hour — and I thought he was going to yell at me."

"For doing something well?"

"Getting in the way. And, not yell, really. He never raised his voice; that's all about control. I figured he was going to tell me to go back up with my mother. You know, dismiss me. But he didn't. He told Mick to go upstairs, and it was just him and me. Just me and my father, and he was finally looking at me."

"He must have been very proud, very pleased."

"Hell no." Her laugh was short and without any humor. "He was disappointed.

That's what I saw when he finally looked at me. He was disappointed that it was me and not Mick. Now he was stuck with me."

"Surely he . . ." Larkin trailed off when she turned her head, met his eyes. "I'm sorry. Sorry his lack of vision hurt you."

"Can't change what you are." Another lesson she'd learned hard. "So he trained me, and Mick got to play baseball. That was the smile. Relief, joy. Mick, he'd never wanted what my father wanted for him. He's got more of my mother in him. When she left, filed for divorce, I mean, she took Mick, and I stayed with my father. I got what I wanted, more or less."

She stiffened when Larkin put an arm around her shoulders, but when she would have shifted away he tightened his grip in the comfort of a one-armed hug. "I don't know your father or your brother, but I do know I'd rather be here with you than either of them. You fight like an avenging angel. And you smell good."

He surprised a laugh out of her, a genuine laugh, and with it, she relaxed against the wet rock, with his arm around her shoulders.

CHAPTER 3

On the cliffs, the circle was cast. Now and again, there was the sound of a car passing on the road below. But no one walked here, or snapped their pictures, or stood on his headland.

Perhaps, Hoyt thought, the gods did what they could.

"It's so clear today." Moira looked skyward. "Barely a cloud."

"So clear, you can see across the water all the way to *Gaillimh.*"

"Galway." Glenna stood, gathering strength and courage. "I've always wanted to go there, to see the bay. To wander along Shop Street."

"And so we will." Hoyt took her hand now. "After Samhain. Now we look, and we find. You're sure of the location where we'll send any if we can transport?"

Glenna nodded. "I'd better be." She took

Moira's hand in turn. "Focus," she told her. "And say the words."

She felt it from Hoyt, that first low rumble of power, the reaching out. Glenna pushed toward it, pulling Moira with her.

"On this day and in this hour, I call upon the sacred power of Morrigan the goddess and pray she grant to us her grace and prowess. In your name, Mother, we seek the sight, ask you to guide us into the light."

"Lady," Hoyt spoke. "Show us those held beneath this ground, against their will. Help us find what is lost."

"Blind the beasts that seek to kill." Moira struggled to focus as the air began to swirl around her. "That no innocents will pay the cost."

"Goddess and Mother," they said together, "our power unite, to bring into day what is trapped in the night. Now we seek, and now we see. As we will, so mote it be."

Darkness and shadows and dank air, fetid with the foulness of death and decay. Now a shimmer of light, glimmers of shapes in the shadows. There was the sound of weeping, so harsh, so human, and the moans and gibbering of those who had no tears left to shed.

They floated through the maze of tunnels, felt the cold as if their bodies walked there.

And even the mind shuddered at what they saw.

Cages, stacked three deep, four high, jammed into a cave washed in a sickly green light. But their minds saw through the gloom of it, to the blood pooled on the floor, to the faces of the terrified and the mad. Even as they watched, a vampire unlocked one of the cages, dragged the woman inside it out. The sound she made was a kind of keening, and her eyes seemed already dead.

"Lora's bored," it said as it pulled her across the filthy floor by the hair. "She wants something to play with."

In one of the cages, a man began to beat the bars and scream. "You bastards! You bastards!"

The tear that spilled down Glenna's cheek was cold.

"Hoyt."

"We'll try. Him, the one who's shouting. He's strong, and it may help. See him. See nothing else."

Because she needed the words as well as the sight, Glenna began to chant. Moira's voice joined her.

And the ground trembled.

Larkin was singing. Something about a black-haired maid from Dara. Blair didn't mind listening; he had a clear, easy voice. The sort, she thought, of a man used to raising it in a pub, or while he walked the fields. And it was calming to have the tune, the steady roar of the sea, and the warm beam of the sun.

Added to it, the simple companionship was a change for her. Usually when she waited, she waited alone.

"You wouldn't have the little thing? The little thing with the music in it with you?"

"No. Sorry. Next time I get a chance, I'm buying myself a pair of those Oakley Thumps, got the MP3 player built in. Sunglasses." She mimed the shape of them over her face — and it occurred to her Larkin would look damn hot wearing a pair himself. "With the little thing with the music inside them."

"You can wear the music?" His whole face lit up. "What a world of miracles this is."

"I don't know about miracles, but it's jammed with technology. Wish I'd thought to bring the player along." Music would be easier than all this conversation. She was used to waiting alone, damn it. Not hanging around with a companion, exchanging small talk and life stories.

It was making her itchy.

"Well, that's all right. Be nice if I had my pipe."

"Pipe." She turned her head. Couldn't quite fit the idea of a pipe with that gilded Irish god face. "You smoke a pipe?"

"Smoke? No, no." He laughed, shifted his weight as he lifted his hands in front of his mouth, wiggled his fingers. "Play. The pipe. Now and again."

"Oh, okay." His eyes were the color of good, dark honey. Might look hot in a pair of Oakleys, she mused, but it would be a shame to put lenses over those eyes. "That works."

"Do you play anything? Musically?"

"Me? No. Never had time to learn. Unless you count beating out a tattoo on vampires." She mimed again — it seemed they did a lot of charades between them — punching her fists in the air.

"Well now, your sword sings, that's for certain." He gave her a friendly little shoulder bump. "Don't know as I've heard the like of it. And this would be a fine place for a battle, I'm thinking." He tapped fingers rhythmically on the hilt of his sword. "The sea, the rocks, the bright sun. Aye, a fine spot."

"Sure, if you like not having an escape route, or losing your footing on slick rocks. Drowning."

He gave her a pitying look and a sigh. "You're not considering the atmosphere, the dramatic tone of it all. Can vampires

68

drown?" he wondered.

"Not so much. They . . . Did you feel that?" She pushed off the rock as the ground under her vibrated.

"I did. Maybe the spell's breaking down." He drew his sword, scanned the cliff wall. "Maybe the caves behind it will appear now."

"If they do, you're not going in. You gave your word."

"I keep my word." Irritation flickered over his face. This was the soldier now, she noted, and not the pipe-playing farmer. "But if one of them sticks its head out, just a bit . . . Do you see anything? I'm not seeing anything different than it was."

"No, nothing. Maybe it's the magic trio on the cliffs. Seems like they've had enough time to do something." She kept her hand on the stake in her belt as she worked her way as far toward the crashing surf as she dared. "Can't see from here. Can you, like, be a bird? Like a hawk or something? Take a look up there?"

"I can, of course. I don't like to leave you alone down here."

Irritation rippled down her spine. Here she was explaining herself again. "I'm in the sun, vamps can't come out. Besides, I've worked alone for a long time. Let's get a status report on magic time. I don't like not knowing where we stand."

He could do it quickly, he thought. He could be up and back in a matter of minutes. And from the sky, he could see her, and anything that came at her, as well as the group on the cliffs.

So he passed Blair his sword and thought of the hawk. Of its shape, of its vision, and of its heart. The light shimmered into him, over him. In that change, as arms became wings, as lips formed a beak, as talons sprang and curled, there was a sudden and breathless pain.

Then freedom.

He soared up, a gold hawk that took the air, and circled once over Blair with a cry like triumph.

"Wow." She stared up, watching his flight, the sheer power and majesty of it. She'd seen him change before, had ridden on his back when he'd taken the shape of a horse into battle. And still, she was dumbstruck.

"That is so sexy."

While the ground continued to shake, she gripped Larkin's sword, drew her own. And with the sea roaring at her back, faced the blank wall of the cliff.

Overhead, the hawk swept through the air over the cliffs. He could see keenly enough to pick out individual blades of grass, the petals of the rugged wildflowers that forced their way through fissures in rock to seek the sun. He saw the long ribbon of the road, the wide plate of the sea, and all the way to where the land met it again.

The hawk yearned to fly, and to hunt. The man inside it pitted his will against that yearning even as he skimmed the sky.

He could see them below, his cousin, the witch and the sorcerer, hands linked as they stood on the quaking ground. There was light, wild and white, in them, around them, a spinning circle that rose up in a tower to shake the air even as the ground.

The wind caught at him, plucked at his wings like greedy fingers. In it he could hear their voices, blended together as one, and could feel their power, a hot stream that washed the whirling air.

Then that wind slapped at him, and sent him into a rolling, spinning dive.

Blair heard the hawk cry, saw it spiral. Her heart rolled up into her throat, lodged there as Larkin tumbled through the air. It stayed there, a hot, hard ball even as the hawk sheered up, wings spread. Then dived to land gracefully at her feet.

For a moment, she saw the melding of them, hawk and man. Then Larkin stood facing her, his breathing labored, his face pale.

"What the hell was that? What the hell happened? I thought you were going to splat. Your nose is bleeding."

Her voice was tinny to his ears so he shook his head as if to clear it. "Not surprising." He swiped at the blood. "Something's happening up there, something very big from the feel of it. The light damn near blinded me, and the wind's a bloody wicked one. I couldn't tell, not for certain, if they're in trouble. But I think we'd best go up and make certain."

"Okay." She started to hand him his sword, and the ground heaved. Off-balance, she pitched forward. He managed to catch her, but the momentum threw him back against the rock, and nearly sent both of them into the water.

"Sorry, sorry." But it was brace against him or fall. "You hurt?"

"Knocked the bleeding breath out of me again is all."

The next spume of surf soaked them both. "Screw this. We'd better get out of here."

"I'm for that. Steady now."

They linked their arms around each other's waists, struggling to stay upright. Rock and sod began to spill down the cliff face, making the idea of climbing up it again unappealing if not impossible.

"I can get us up to the others," he told her. "You'll just have to hold on, and I'll —"

He broke off as the wall itself began to waver, to change. To open.

"Well now," he murmured, "what have we here?"

"Spell broke down, or was broken down. Could be trouble."

"I'm hoping."

"Right there with you."

Even as he spoke, they rushed out. Big and burly, and armed with swords.

"How can they —"

"Not vamps." Blair pushed away from Larkin, planted her feet. She figured the quaking ground was as much a problem for the enemy as it was for her and Larkin. "Fight now, explain later."

She swung her sword up, blocked the first blow. The force rippled down her arm even as the ground buckled under her feet. She used it, going down, blocking again as she snatched one of the stakes out of her belt.

She jammed it through his leg. He stumbled, howled, and she came up with her sword.

One down, she thought, and refused the pity. She pivoted, nearly went down as the ground came up, and clashed steel with the one who sprang behind her.

Out of the corner of her eye, she saw Larkin taking on two at once. "Bear claw!" she shouted.

"There's an idea." His arm thickened, lengthened. With the keen black claws that curled out, he swiped even as his sword swung in his other hand.

They were holding their own, Blair thought, but no more than that. There was no room to maneuver, not when a wrong step could have them tumbling into the sea.

Bashed on the rocks, swept away. Worse than the sword. Still, they couldn't climb, not now. There was no choice but to stand and fight.

She fell, rolled, and the sword plunged into the rocky ground an inch from her face. She kicked up, pumping hard, and sent her opponent into the sea.

Too many of them, too many, she thought as she gained her feet and staggered. But it could be worse. It could . . .

The light changed, dimmed. With the false twilight came the first splatters of rain.

"Christ, Jesus Christ. She's bringing the dark."

With it, vampires began to slink out of the cave. The sea, and a hard, drowning death

74

suddenly seemed the better alternative.

Calculating quickly, she sent fire rippling down her blade. They could block them with fire, hold some back, destroy others. But too many would get through.

"We can't win this, Larkin. Make like a hawk, get to the others. Get them out of here. I'll hold them off as long as I can."

"Don't be foolish. Get on." He threw her his sword. "Hold on."

He changed, but it wasn't a hawk that stood beside her. The dragon's gold wings spread, and as it reared back, its tail sliced down the first that came out of the caves.

She didn't think, just leaped on its back, locking her legs around its serpentine body. She sliced out to the left, hacking at one that charged. Then she was rising up, streaming through the gloom and the mist.

And she couldn't help it, couldn't stop it. She let out a wild cry of sheer delight, throwing back her head as she stabbed the swords into the sky. And set them both to flame.

The wind rushed by her, and the ground rushed away. She sheathed one sword so that she could run a hand over the dragon. The scales, glimmering gold, felt like polished jewels, sun-warmed and smooth. Looking down, she saw earth and sea, and swirling pockets of mists that blanketed the jaws of the rocks.

Then she saw, on the high cliff, three figures sprawled on the tough, wet grass.

"Get down there. Get down there fast!" She knew he could hear and understand her, in any form, but she might have saved her breath.

The rush of speed slapped her back as he arrowed toward the ground. She was jumping off even as he landed, and began to change back.

The fear was bright silver in her belly, but she saw Hoyt push himself up to sit, saw him reach for Glenna. His nose was bleeding, as hers was. When Larkin reached Moira, turned her over, Blair saw blood on her lips.

"We've got to move, we've got to go. They could follow us, and if they want to, they can move fast." She pulled Glenna to her feet. "Let's move faster."

"I'm woozy. Sorry, I . . ."

"Lean on me. Larkin —"

But he'd already chosen his own way. She shoved at her wet hair as she pushed Glenna toward the horse he'd become. "Get up. You and Moira. Hoyt and I are right behind you. Can you walk?" she asked Hoyt.

"I can." If his legs were shaky, he still moved, and quickly as Larkin galloped off.

"So much time passed. It's dusk."

"No, she made it. Lilith did it. She's got more power than I figured."

"No. No, not her." Hoyt was forced to brace a hand on Blair's shoulder for balance. "She has someone, something with the power to do this."

"We'll figure it out." She half carried, half dragged him to the van where Larkin was already helping the other women inside "Glenna, keys. I've got the wheel."

Glenna fumbled them out of her pocket. "Just need a minute, a few minutes to recover. That was . . . it was rugged. Moira?"

"I'm all right. Just a bit dizzy is all. And a bit sick in the stomach. I've never . . . I've never touched anything like that."

Blair drove, fast enough to cover some distance, and kept an eye on the rearview for a tail. "Earthquakes, false dusk, a little lightning. Hell of a ride." She slowed as the sun began to break through again. "Looks like she gave up on us. For now. Nobody's hurt? Just shook up?"

"Not hurt, no." Hoyt gathered Glenna against him, brushed the tears from her face with his lips. "Don't. *A ghra,* don't weep."

"There were so many. So many of them. Screaming."

Blair took two careful breaths. "Don't do

this to yourselves. You tried, you gave it your best. It was always a long shot you'd be able to get anyone out of there."

"But we did." Glenna turned her face into Hoyt's shoulder. "Five. We got five out, then we couldn't hold it any longer."

Stunned, Blair pulled off to the shoulder, turned around. "You got five out? Where are they?"

"Hospital. I thought . . ."

"Glenna, she thought if we could get them out, we could transport them to a place where they would be safe, and be cared for." Moira looked down at her empty hands.

"Smart. Really smart. It gets them medical attention fast, and keeps us from having to answer awkward questions. Congratulations."

Glenna lifted her head, and her eyes were ravaged. "There were so many of them. So many more."

"And five people are alive, and safe."

"I know, you're right, I know." She straightened, rubbed her face dry with her hands. "I'm just shaken up."

"We did what we came to do. More than."

"What were they?" Larkin asked her. "What were they you and I fought back there? Not vampires, you said."

"Half-vamps. Still human. They've been

78

bitten, probably multiple times, but not drained. And not allowed to mix blood; not changed."

"Then why would they fight us?"

"They're controlled. The best term, I guess, is *thrall*. They're under a thrall, and do as they're ordered. I counted seven, all big guys. We took out four. She probably doesn't have any more, or not many. It's got to be tough to keep them under control."

"There was a fight?" Glenna asked.

Blair pulled back onto the road. "The caves opened. She sent out the first wave, the half-vamps. Then she did her little weather trick."

"You thought I would leave you there," Larkin broke in. "You thought I would leave you to them."

"First priority is to stay alive."

"That may be, but I don't desert a friend, or a fellow soldier. What manner of man do you think I am?"

"That's a question."

"The answer isn't a coward," he said tightly.

"It's not, and a long way from it." Would she have left him? No, she admitted. Couldn't have, and would have been insulted to be told to go. "It was all I could think of to keep the rest of us alive, to keep her from winning. How was I supposed to know you had a dragon on your repertoire?"

In the back seat, Glenna choked. "A *dragon?*"

"Sorry you missed it. It was wild. But, Jesus, Larkin, a dragon? Someone must have seen it. Of course, everyone else will think they're nuts, but still."

"Why?"

"Why? Because, you know, dragon, and how they don't exist."

Fascinated now, he swiveled in his seat. "You don't have dragons here?"

Blair shifted her gaze toward him. "No," she said slowly.

"Sure that's a pity. Moira, did you hear that? They've no dragons here in Ireland."

Moira opened her tired eyes. "I think she's meaning they don't have them anywhere in this world."

"Well, that can't be. Can it?"

"No dragons," Blair confirmed. "No unicorns or winged horses, no centaurs."

"Ah well." He reached over to pat her arm. "You have cars, and they're interesting. I'm starved," he said after a moment. "Are you starved? That many changes, it just empties me out. Could we stop somewhere, do you think, buy some of those crisps in the bag?"

■ ■ ■ ■

It wasn't exactly a victory feast, munching on salt-and-vinegar chips and chugging soda from a bottle, but it got them home.

When they arrived, Blair stuck the keys in her pocket. "You three go inside. Larkin and I can take care of the weapons. You're still pretty pale."

Hoyt lifted the bag holding the blood he'd bought at the butcher's. "I'll take this up to Cian."

Blair waited until they were inside. "We're going to have to talk to them," she told Larkin. "Set up some parameters, some boundaries."

"Aye, we are." He leaned on the van as he looked toward the house. It was good, he thought, and somewhat curious, how they understood each other at times with no words. "Are we agreed? They can't use that kind of magic, at least not often, not unless there's no choice."

"Nosebleeds, queasiness, headaches." She pulled weapons out of the cargo area. You had a team, she thought, you had to worry about its members. No choice. "I could just look at Moira and see the headache. It can't be good for them, that kind of physical toll."

"I thought, at first, when I saw them on

the ground, I thought . . ."

"Yeah." She let out a long, unsteady breath. "So did I."

"I've come to feel a great deal for Hoyt and Glenna, Cian, too, come to that. It's stronger, deeper even than friendship. Maybe it's even more than kinship. Moira . . . She's always been mine, you know. I don't know how I could live if anything happened to her. If I didn't stop it."

Setting the weapons aside, Blair boosted herself up on the rear of the van. "It can't be like that. That if the worst happened to her, to any of us, that you didn't stop it. It's up to each of us to do what we have to do to survive, and to do all we can to watch each other's backs. But —"

"You don't understand." His eyes were fierce when they met hers. "She's part of me."

"No, I don't understand, because I've never had anyone like that in my life. But I think I understand her well enough to know she'd be hurt, maybe even pissed off if she thought you felt responsible for her."

"Not responsible. That makes it an obligation, and it's not. It's love. You know what that is, don't you?"

"Yeah, I know what that is." Annoyed, she started to jump down, but he moved, turn-

ing his body until it blocked hers. "Do you think I felt nothing for you, nothing, when we stood with our backs to the sea and those demons coming out of the dark? Did you think I felt nothing, so would go, would save myself, because you said to?"

"I didn't know you were going to pull a dragon out of your hat, so —"

She broke off, went rigid when he reached out, gripped her chin in his hand. "Did you think I felt nothing," he said again, and his eyes were deep and gold and thoughtful. "Feel nothing now?"

And hell, she thought. She'd boxed herself in.

"I'm not asking about your feelings," she began.

"I'm telling you whether you ask or not." He moved in a little closer, his legs planted on either side of hers, his eyes on her face. Curiously. "I can't say I know what I feel as I don't think I've felt it before. But there's something when I look at you, now. When I see you in battle. Or when I watched you, just this morning watched you, moving like magic in the mist."

As she'd felt something, she admitted, when she'd ridden on his back into battle. When she'd watched him light up over music. "This is a really bad idea."

"I haven't said I had an idea as yet. But I've feelings, so many of them I can't seem to pick one out from the others and have a good look at it. And so . . ."

Her head jerked back as his bowed to hers. Her hand slapped on to his wrist.

"Oh, be still a moment," he said with a half laugh. "And let me have a try at this. You can't be afraid of something as easy as a kiss."

Not afraid, but certainly wary. Certainly curious. She sat as she was, the fingers of one hand curled loosely on the back edge of the van, the others around his wrist.

His lips were soft on hers, just a whisper of contact. A brush, a rub, a light and teasing nip. She had a moment to think he was very good at this particular game before the mists floated over her mind.

Strong, he thought. He'd known there'd be strength, and it was a lovely jolt to the system. But there was sweetness as well; he hadn't been sure of that. So that kissing her was like having wine running through his blood.

And there was need, what seemed to be a deep, simmering well of need in him. He hoped in her.

The kiss deepened so he heard the sound of her pleasure purr in her throat. So he felt that wonderful body of hers press, press and yield to his.

When he would have laid her back, back beside the swords, the axes, she put a hand to his chest and held him away.

"No."

"I hear it plain enough, but no isn't what I felt."

"Maybe not, but it's what I'm saying."

He traced a finger from her shoulder to her wrist while his eyes searched her face. "Why?"

"I'm not sure why. I'm not sure, so it's no."

She turned, began to gather weapons.

"I'm wanting to ask a question." He smiled when she glanced over her shoulder. "Do you wear your hair so short so I'll be enchanted by the nape of your neck. The way it slopes there, it make me just want to . . . lick at it."

"No." Just listen to the way he uses that voice, she thought. The women of Geall must scamper after him like puppies. "I wear it short because it doesn't give the enemy much to grab and pull if he wants to fight like a girl." She turned back. "And it looks good on me."

"It does, that it does. Like a faerie queen. I always thought, if they existed, they'd have strength and courage in their faces."

He leaned toward her again, and she laid the blade of a sword against his chest.

He looked down at it, up at her. This time his smile was full of fun. "That's a good bit more than no. I was just going to kiss you again. I wouldn't ask for anything else. Just one more kiss."

"You're awful damn cute," she said after a minute. "And I'd be lying if I said I wasn't tempted. But because you're awful damn cute and tempting, we're going to leave it at one."

"All right then, if that's the way it has to be." He reached past her, picked up an ax, the bucket of stakes. "But I'm just going to be thinking about another one. And so are you."

"Maybe." She started toward the house, arms loaded with weapons. "A little frustration will give me a nice edge."

He shook his head as he looked after her. She was, he thought, the most fascinating of women.

CHAPTER 4

Blair went straight up to put the weapons in the training area, then went down the back stairs to the kitchen. Larkin could clean the swords, she decided. Work off some of that sexual energy.

She found Glenna there, and the kettle on.

"I'm making some tea, a blend that should take the edge off the day."

"I've heard alcohol does that." And considering it, Blair opened the refrigerator for a beer.

"That's for later — for me. My system's a little twisted up yet. Hoyt went up to see Cian, fill him in."

"Good. We need to talk, Glenna."

"Could I take you through the steps and stages of the spells later, if you need them? It's all a little too hard and bright just now."

"No, I don't need them — that's your territory." Blair boosted herself onto the table, watched Glenna keep her hands busy. "I mean that. When it comes to this area, I'm a civilian. There are some magically inclined, and fairly skilled people, in my family. But nowhere near what you guys have."

"I have more than I did before. Maybe I'm more open to it now." Taking a few pins out of her pocket, Glenna efficiently bundled her hair up. "Maybe it's the connection with Hoyt, the connection we all have to each other. But whatever it is, I'm finding power inside me I never imagined."

"Looks good on you, too. You need to know, to accept, to understand, what the three of you did today was amazing, and it was powerful, and it saved lives. And regardless of that, you have to know, accept and understand it isn't something you can do again. At least not anytime soon."

"We could get more, I think," Glenna said without turning around. "Maybe only one or two at a time. We were greedy, we wanted to get all we could, and we burned it all too long."

"Glenna, it's your territory, like I said. But I'm the one who was looking at the three of you after the serious whammy went down. The fact is, both Larkin and I thought, for a minute there, you were dead. What you were was all but emptied out."

"Yes, that's exactly right. Exactly the right term for it."

"You may not come back from it the next time."

"Isn't that why we're here?" Glenna's hands were steady now as she measured the tea leaves. "To risk it all? Isn't it true that any one of us might not come back each time we walk out the door, each time we pick up a weapon? How many times have you picked up a weapon and the gift you have and risked it all?"

"I couldn't count the times. This is different. You know it. Larkin and I . . . we need you. We need the rest of you strong and healthy."

"You nearly died today, didn't you?"

"Thanks to dragon-boy —"

"Blair." Glenna turned, took the steps over and closed her hand tight over Blair's.

Connections, Glenna had said, and Blair felt it now. You didn't evade the truth, Blair decided, with someone you were so closely connected to.

"Okay, yeah, it was bad — bad enough I wasn't sure we'd get out of it. But it could've been worse. We all did our jobs, and now I'm having a beer and you're making tea. Good for us."

"You're better at this than I am," Glenna murmured.

"No, I'm not. Just more used to it. Being used to it, I can have a beer because I know we not only beat her today, Glenna. We insulted her, and that feels tingly right down to my toes. And you know what I'd like?"

"I think I do. I think you'd like to go back there and do it all again."

"Bet your ass I would. Nothing better, that's the pure truth. But it would be stupid, self-indulgent, and it would probably get us all killed. Take the victory, Glenna, 'cause you sure as hell earned it. And accept you may not be able to do it just that way again."

"I know it." Glenna walked back to the stove when the water began to boil. "I know you're right. It's hard to accept you're right. In the past few weeks, I've held magicks stronger than anything I ever dreamed existed. It thrills — and it costs. I know we'll need more time, more preparation if we try to do what we did today again."

She poured the water into the pot. "I thought we'd lost Moira," she said quietly. "I felt her falling away, slipping. She's not as strong magically as I am, certainly not as strong as Hoyt." As the tea steeped, she turned back to face Blair. "We let her go. We let her go, only an instant before it exploded.

I don't know what would have happened to her if we'd held her in with us."

"Would you have gotten so many out without her?"

"No, no we needed her."

"Take the victory. It was a good day. One question though. How did you know where to send them? Not the magic stuff, just the logistics."

"Oh, I had a map." Glenna smiled a little. "I'd already calculated the quickest routes to hospitals, in case any of us needed one. So it was just a matter of, well, of following the map."

"A map." After a laugh, Blair took a deep drink. "You're something, Glenna. You are something else. Vampire bitch had you on her team, I think we'd be sunk. Hell of a day," she said with a sigh. "I rode on a freaking dragon."

"It was cute, wasn't it, how surprised he was we didn't have any." Chuckling now, easier now, Glenna got down cups and saucers. "What did he look like? I paint them sometimes."

"Like you'd expect, I guess. He was gold. Long, wicked tail — took a couple of them out with it. And the body's more sinuous than snakelike. Yeah, long and sinuous, the body, the tail, the head. Gold eyes. God, he was beautiful. And the wings, wide, peaked, translucent. Scales big as my hand, that went from pale gold to dark, and all the shades between. And fast? Holy God, he's fast. It's like riding the sun. I was just . . ."

She trailed off when she saw Glenna leaning back against the counter, smiling.

"What?"

"I was just wondering if you have that look in your eye over the dragon or over the man."

"We're talking dragon. But the man's not half bad."

"Gorgeous, fairly adorable, and with the heart of a champion."

Blair raised her eyebrows. "Hey, didn't you recently get married — to somebody else?"

"It didn't strike me blind. Just FYI? Larkin gets that look in his eye, now and again, when he turns in your direction."

"Maybe he does, and maybe I'll think about taking him up on it one of these days. But right now . . ." She slid off the table. "I'm going to go upstairs and take a really long, really hot shower."

"Blair? Sometimes the heart of a champion is tender."

"I'm not looking to bruise hearts."

"I was thinking of yours, too," Glenna

replied when she was alone.

Blair heard voices from the library as she passed, and veered just close enough to identify them. Satisfied that Larkin was speaking with Moira, she rerouted for the steps to head upstairs. She wanted nothing more than to wash away the sea salt, the blood and the death.

She paused at the top of the steps when she saw Cian in the shadows of the hallway. She knew her fingers had reached down to skim over the stake in her belt, and didn't bother to pretend she hadn't. It was knee-jerk. Hunter, vampire. They'd both have to accept it, and move on.

"A little early for you to be up and around, isn't it?"

"My brother has no respect for my sleep cycle."

There was something preternaturally sexual, she thought, about a vampire staring out from the cloaked light. Or there was with this one. "Hoyt had a rough one."

"So I could see for myself. He looked ill. But then . . ." The smile was slow and deliberate. "He's human."

"Do you work on that kind of thing? The silky voice, the dangerous smile?"

"Born with it. Died with it, too. Are we going to come to terms, you and me?"

"I think we have." She saw his gaze slide down to her hand, and the stake under it. "Can't help it." But she lifted the hand away, hooked her thumb in her belt. "It's ingrained."

"Do you enjoy your work?"

"I guess I do, on some level. I'm good at it, and you have to like doing what you're good at. It's what I do. It's what I am."

"Yes, we are what we are." He stepped closer. "You look as she must have when she was your age. Younger, I suppose, she'd have been younger, our Nola, when she looked as you did. Women wore down faster then."

"A lot of times vampires look to family for their first kills."

"Home's the place you go where they have to take you in. Do you think any of the others in this house would be alive if I wanted them otherwise?"

"No." So it was time for honesty. "I think you'd have played along with them for a few days, maybe a week. Get some jollies out of it. And wait until they trusted you, let their guards down. Then you'd have slaughtered them."

"You think like a vampire," he acknowledged. "It's part of your skill. So, why haven't I slaughtered the lot of them?"

She kept her eyes on his, struck suddenly

by the fact it was nearly like looking into her own. Same color, same shape. "We are what we are. I guess that's not what you are, or not anymore."

"I killed my share in my day. But excepting that I once tried to kill my brother, I never touched my family. I can't say why except I didn't want their lives. You're family, whether either of us is comfortable with that. You come from my sister. You have her eyes. And once I loved her, quite a lot."

She felt something — not pity, it wasn't something he asked for. But she felt a kind of understanding. Following the feeling, she drew the stake out of her belt, keeping the point toward her, and handed it to him. A look of bemusement passed over his face as he studied it.

"I'm not going to have to start calling you Uncle Cian, am I?"

He managed to grin and looked pained at the same time. "Please don't."

They parted ways, with Cian going downstairs, then into the kitchen. He found Glenna fussing with tea trays. She looked a little hollowed out, he thought, and shadowed around the eyes.

"Have you ever considered having someone else play mother?"

She jerked at his voice, clattering the cup

she was holding onto the tray. "Guess I'm jumpy." She reset the cup carefully in its saucer. "What did you say?"

"I wonder why one of the others can't deal with food now and then."

"They do. Well, Larkin's slippery, but the others do. Anyway, it keeps me busy."

"From what I'm told you've been busy with things nondomestic."

"Hoyt spoke to you."

"He seems to enjoy waking me in the middle of the day. Which is why I want coffee," he added as he moved to the counter to make it. When he saw her frowning at the stake he set beside the pot, he shrugged. "A sort of peace offering, you could say, from Blair."

"Oh, well, that's good, isn't it?"

He shifted, caught her chin in his hand. "Go lie down, Red, before you fall down."

"That's what the tea's about. It's a restorative. We need it. Batteries dead low here." She managed a smile, but it faded quickly. "She brought a storm, Cian. She has someone with her who has enough power to call a storm, to block the sun, so we need to recharge those batteries. Hoyt and I have to work, and we need to work with Moira. We need to pull out what she has, help her hone it."

She turned back, began to arrange cookies on pretty little plates, anything to keep her hands moving. "We were separated today, the three of us on the high cliffs, Blair and Larkin below. They could've been killed, and we couldn't have helped them, couldn't have stopped it. We didn't see it coming because we were so focused on the transportation spell. And when it came, when the power whipped around and slapped us down, we were already tapped out."

Suffering for it now, he thought. Humans always would suffer for what they'd done, and for what they hadn't. "Now you have a better idea of your limits."

"We're not allowed to have limits."

"Oh, bugger that, Glenna." He snatched up a cookie. "Of course you have limits. You've expanded them, and likely you'll push the box a bit wider before you're done. She has limits as well, and that's what you're forgetting. Lilith has weaknesses, and is neither invulnerable nor omnipotent. Which you proved today by slipping five of her trophies out from under her."

He bit into the cookie as he got down a mug.

"I know I should think of the five we saved. Blair said to take the victory."

"And she'd be right."

"I know. I *know.* But oh God, I wish I didn't see the ones we left behind. I wish their faces, their screams weren't in my head. We can't save them all, and I said as much to Hoyt when we were in New York. It was easy to say it then."

She shook her head. "And you're right, I need some rest. I have to take this tray up, see that the others get some of it inside them. You could do me a favor."

"I probably could."

"You could take this one into the library. Moira's in there."

"She'll likely think it's poisoned if I take it into her."

"Oh stop."

"All right, all right. But don't blame me if she pours it down some drain." He hefted the tray, muttering to himself as he left the kitchen. "I'm a vampire, for God's sake. Creature of the damn night, drinker of blood. And here I am playing butler to some erstwhile Geallian queen. Mortifying is what it is."

And *he'd* wanted to pass some time in the library, with a book and the fire.

He stepped in, leading with his irritation, and a scathing comment rolling up to the tip of his tongue.

Which would have been wasted, he decided, as she was curled up on one of the sofas, sleeping.

Now what the hell was he supposed to do? Leave her be, wake her and pour the damn tea into her?

Undecided, he stood where he was, studying her.

Pretty enough, he thought, with a potential for true beauty if she put any effort into it. At least when she slept it didn't seem as though her eyes would swallow her face, and whoever she aimed those long, large gray beacons toward with it.

There was a time he'd have found it entertaining to corrupt and defile her kind of innocence. To peel it away slowly, layer by layer, until there was nothing left of it.

These days he preferred the simplicity of the more experienced, women who were in it for no more than he was. A few hours of heat in the dark.

Creatures like this took a great deal of effort. He couldn't remember the last time he'd been stirred enough to play with one.

In the end he decided to leave the tray on the table. If she woke, she'd drink it. If she didn't, well, sleep itself would go a long way to restoring her.

Either way, he'd have done the chore.

He moved to the table, laid the tray down

with barely a click of china on wood. But she stirred, nonetheless. A low moan, a little tremor. He backed away, his eyes on her face — and was careless enough to step into a thin slant of sunlight.

The quick, searing pain in his shoulder had him cursing under his breath even as he moved quickly out of the beam. Annoyed with Glenna, with himself, with the sleeping queen, he turned to go.

She began to twitch in her sleep, small sounds of fear gurgling in her throat. Her body rolled up into a tight ball as she shuddered. And in sleep, she began to speak breathlessly.

"No, no, no." Again and again, until she fell into unintelligible Gaelic.

She thrashed, rolling to her back, going stiff as she bowed up, exposing the line of her throat.

He moved quickly, stepping between the couch and the table, and leaning down, gave her a hard shake.

"Wake up," he ordered. "Snap out of it now, I haven't the patience for this."

She moved fast — and he faster — slapping the stake she stabbed out with from her hand. It clattered on the floor ten feet away.

"Don't do that." He gripped her wrist, felt her pulse striking like an anvil against his fingers. "Next time you do, I'll snap this like a twig, I promise you."

"I — I — I —"

"Very succinct. Are you understanding me?"

Her eyes, huge and glassy with fear darted around the room. "She was here, she was here. No, no, not here." Moira came up to her knees, gripping his arm with her free hand. "Where is she? Where? I can still smell her. Too sweet, too heavy."

"Stop." He released her wrist to take hold of her shoulders. Another shake had her teeth chattering. "You were asleep, you were dreaming."

"No. I was . . . Was I? I don't know. It's not dark. It's not dark yet, but it was . . ." She put her hands on his chest, but instead of pushing him away as he expected, she simply dropped her head there. "I'm sorry. I'm sorry. I need a moment."

He caught himself reaching back to stroke her hair — that long thick braid the color of dark oak. He dropped his hand to the side.

"You fell asleep here on the couch," he said in a flat, almost businesslike voice. "You had a dream. Now you're awake."

"I thought Lilith . . ." She reared back. "I nearly staked you."

"No. Not even close."

101

"I didn't mean — I wouldn't have meant." She closed her eyes in an obvious effort to find some composure. When she opened them, her eyes were clearer, and very direct. "I'm very sorry, but why are you here?"

He stepped to the side, gestured. Now it was simple shock that moved over her face. "You . . . You made me tea and biscuits?"

"Glenna," he corrected, surprisingly embarrassed at the very thought. "I'm just the delivery boy."

"Um. It's very kind of you all the same. I didn't mean to sleep. I thought I would read after Larkin went upstairs. But I . . ."

"Have your tea then. You'll likely be the better for it." When she only nodded, made no move, he cast his eyes to the ceiling. Then he poured out a cup of tea. "Lemon or cream, Your Highness?"

She tipped her head to look at him. "You're annoyed with me, and who could blame you for it? You brought me tea, and I tried to kill you."

"Then don't waste my time or the bloody tea. Here." He pushed the cup into her hands. "Drink it down. Glenna's orders."

Still watching him, she took a sip. "It's very nice." Then her lips trembled, her eyes filled.

His belly tightened. "I'll leave you with it

then, and with your tears."

"I wasn't strong enough." The tears didn't fall, just glimmered in her eyes like rain over fog. "I couldn't help them hold the spell, I couldn't do it. So it broke away, it shattered, and it was like shards of glass ripping through us. We couldn't get any of the others, any of the others from the cages."

He wondered if he should tell her that Lilith would only replace the ones they took. Likely twice the number in her fury.

"Now you waste your own time, blaming yourself, and feeling sorry for yourself with it. If you could've done more, you would have."

"In the dream, she said she wouldn't bother to drink me. Being the smallest, the weakest, I wouldn't be worth the trouble."

He sat on the table facing her, helped himself to one of her biscuits. "She's lying."

"How do you know?"

"Creature of the night, remember? The smallest is very often the sweetest. A kind of appetizer, if you will. If I were still in the habit of it, I'd bite you in a heartbeat."

She lowered the tea cup to frown at him. "Is that, in some strange way, a kind of flattery?"

"Take it as you like."

"Well. Thank you . . . I suppose."

"Finish off your tea." He got to his feet. "Ask Glenna for something to block the dreams. She's bound to have it."

"Cian," she said as he started toward the doorway. "I am grateful. For everything."

He only nodded and continued out. A thousand years, he thought, and he still didn't really understand humans — and women in particular.

Blair drank Glenna's tea, and decided she'd stretch out for an hour with her headphones. Ideally, the music would rest her mind, give it time to clear and recharge. But it all circled around with Patty Griffin's soulful voice.

The sea, the cliffs, the battle. That moment, when the sky darkened, of absolute certainty that she'd come to the end. And that tiny cold seed of relief inside her that it would, finally, be over.

She didn't have a death wish, she thought. She *didn't.* But there was that small, secret place in her that was tired, so horribly tired of being alone, of having what she was and what she had to do dictate she would stay alone.

Alone with blood and death and endless violence.

It had cost her the love of a man she'd wanted so much, and the future she'd believed they would have together. Was that when it had started? she wondered. Was that when that little seed had planted itself inside her? The night Jeremy had walked away from her?

Pitiful, she thought and pulled off the headphones. Pathetic. Was she going to let her psyche be twisted up by a man — and one who hadn't been man enough to deal with her? Would she come to accept death just because he hadn't accepted her for who and what she was?

That was just bullshit. She turned to her side, hugging her pillow as she studied the fading light through the window.

She only thought of Jeremy because Larkin had gotten her juices going again. She didn't want to go soft again for a man, to feel herself being taken over and swept off by all that emotion.

Sex was okay, sex was fine, as long as it didn't mean anything more than relief and release. She couldn't go through the pain again, and that awful feeling of abandonment that left the heart a quivering, bleeding mass inside the chest.

No one stayed, she thought as she closed her eyes. Nothing was forever.

She drifted off, the music from the headphones she'd neglected to turn off tinny and distant.

It filled her head, the music that was her own excited blood pumping. It was nearly dawn, the night's work over. But she was so full of energy, so fired up, she knew she could go for hours yet.

She looked down at herself as she walked the last block toward home. She'd ruined another shirt. The job, she thought, was hell on the wardrobe. It was torn and bloody, and her left shoulder was a mass of bruises and throbbing pain.

But she was so juiced!

The suburban street was quiet and pretty — everyone tucked up in bed and safe. And as the sun came up, the dogwoods and tulip trees were so showy and pink. She could smell hyacinths and took a deep breath of soft, sweet spring.

It was the morning of her eighteenth birthday.

So she was going to clean up, rest up, then spend a lot of time making herself irresistible for a very hot birthday date.

As she unlocked the front door of the house where she lived with her father, she slung her bag off her good shoulder, dumped it. She needed to clean her weapons, but first she wanted about a gallon of water.

Then she spotted the suitcases sitting near

the door, and the leading edge of thrill dropped away.

He came down the steps, already wearing his coat. He was so handsome, she thought. Tall and dark, that chiseled face and bold eyes. Just the slightest glint of silver in his hair. A world of love and misery opened inside her.

"So you're back." He glanced at her shirt. "If you're going to let them bloody you, take a change of clothes. You'll draw attention to yourself walking around like that."

"No one saw me. Where are you going?"

"Romania. To research, primarily."

"Romania? Couldn't I go? I'd really like to see —"

"No. I've left a checkbook. There should be enough to run the house for several months."

"Months? But . . . when are you coming back?"

"I'm not." He picked up a small carry-on bag, slung it over his shoulder. "I've done all I can for you. You're eighteen, you're of age."

"But — you can't — Please, don't just go. What did I do?"

"Nothing. I've put the house in your name. Stay, or sell it. Go where you like. It's your life."

"Why? How can you just walk out on me

this way? You're my father."

"I've trained you to the best of my ability, and yours. There's nothing else I can do for you."

"You could stay with me. You could love me, just a little."

He opened the door, picked up the suitcases. It wasn't regret she saw on his face, but an absence. He was, she understood, already gone.

"I have an early flight. If I need anything else, I'll send for it."

"Do I mean anything to you?"

He looked at her then, full in the face. "You're my legacy," he said, and walked out the door.

She wept, of course, stood there alone with spring wafting in on the pretty breeze.

She cancelled her date, spent her birthday alone in the house. A few days later, she sat, alone again, in the cemetery, preparing to destroy what the boy she'd cared for had become.

For the rest of her life she would wonder if she'd kept that date, would he have lived?

Now she stood in the bedroom of her Boston apartment, facing the man in whom she'd poured all her love, and her hopes. "Jeremy, please, let's sit down. We need to talk about this."

"Talk?" There was still dull shock in his eyes as he shoved clothing into a duffle. "I can't talk about this. I don't want to *know* about this. Nobody should know about this."

"I did it wrong." She reached out, had him shrug her away in a gesture so sharp and dismissive she felt it cut her to the bone. "I shouldn't have taken you out, shown you. But you wouldn't believe me when I tried to tell you."

"That you kill vampires? What was I thinking, not believing you?"

"I had to show you. We couldn't get married if you didn't know everything. It wasn't fair to you."

"Fair?" He whirled toward her, and she saw it clearly on his face. Not just the fear, not just the rage. Disgust. "This is fair? You lying and deceiving me all this time?"

"I didn't lie. I omitted, and I'm sorry. God, I'm so sorry, but it wasn't something I could tell you when we first . . . and then I didn't know how to tell you what I was, what I do."

"What you are is a freak."

She jerked her head back as if he'd slapped her. "I'm not a freak. I know you're upset, but —"

"Upset? I don't know who you are, what you are. Christ, what I've been sleeping with all these months. But I know this. I want you to stay away from me, away from my family, my friends."

"You need time. I get that, but —"

"I've given you all the time you're going to get. It makes me sick to look at you."

"That's enough."

"It's past enough. Do you think I could be with you, that I could touch you again after this?"

"What's wrong with you?" she demanded. "What I did saved lives. It would have killed people, Jeremy. It would have hunted and killed innocent people. I stopped it."

"It doesn't exist." He dragged the duffle off the bed they'd shared for nearly six months. "When I walk out of here, it doesn't exist, and neither do you."

"I thought you loved me."

"Looks like we were both wrong."

"So you walk out," she said quietly, "and I cease to be."

"That's right."

Not the first time, she thought, no, not the first. The only other man she'd loved had done the same. Slowly, she drew the diamond from her finger. "You'd better have this back."

"I don't want it. I don't want anything that's touched you." He strode to the door, glanced back once. "How do you live with yourself?"

"I'm all I've got," she said to the empty room. Then she set the ring on the dresser, lowered to the floor and wept.

Men are vile creatures, really. Using women up, casting them aside. Leaving them alone and broken. Better to leave them first, isn't it? Better yet to pay them back, and leave them bleeding.

Sick and tired of being the one left behind, aren't you? And all the fighting, all the death. I can help you with that. I'd so like to help you.

Why don't we talk about it, you and me? Just us girls. Let's have a few drinks and trash men, why don't we?

Aren't you going to ask me in?

Blair stood at the window, and the face behind the dark glass smiled at her. Her hands went to the window, started to lift it.

Hurry now. Open up. Ask me in, Blair. That's all you have to do.

She opened her mouth, the words already in her mind.

Then something flew at her from behind, sent her sprawling across the room.

111

CHAPTER 5

There was a scream of rage from what floated outside the window. The glass seemed to vibrate from it, almost to bow in from the pressure.

Then it was gone, a blur of motion. Blair felt the room spin.

"Oh no, you don't. There'll be none of that." Larkin took a firm grip on Blair's shoulders, pulled her up to her knees. "What the bloody hell were you doing?"

His face shimmied in and out of focus. "I'm going out. Sorry."

The next thing she knew she was coming to on her own bed, with Larkin tapping her cheeks. "Ah, there you are. Stay with us this time, will you, *muirnin*? I'm going to fetch Glenna."

"No, wait. Give me a minute. I just feel a little sick." She swallowed hard, pressed a hand to her shaky stomach. "Like I've had entirely too many margaritas. I must've been dreaming. I thought I . . . Was I dreaming?"

"You were standing at the window, about to open it. She was outside, somehow standing out there. The French one."

"Lora. I was going to ask her in." She turned horrified eyes to Larkin. "Oh my God, I was going to ask her in. How can that be?"

"You looked . . . wrong. I'd have said you were asleep, but your eyes were open."

"Sleepwalking. A trance. They got into my head, and they did something. The others!"

He pressed her back down when she started to jump off the bed. "Downstairs, the lot of them. In the kitchen where Glenna's put a meal together, God bless her. She asked if I'd fetch you. I knocked, but you didn't answer." He looked toward the window now, and his face went grim. "I nearly went away again, thinking you were sleeping and could probably use that as much as food. But I thought I heard . . . I heard her talking to you."

"If I'd let her in . . . I've never heard of them being able to do mind control if you haven't been bitten. Something new. We'd better get down, tell the others."

He brushed lightly at her hair. "You're

shaky yet. I could carry you."

"Bet you could." It made her smile. "Maybe next time." She sat up, leaned toward him, touched her lips to his. "Thanks for the save."

"You're very welcome." He took her hand to help her off the bed, then wrapped his arms around her when she swayed.

"Whoa. Head rush. They worked something on me, Larkin. They used memories and emotions. Private stuff. That seriously pisses me off."

"You'd be more so if she'd managed the invitation."

"Good point. Okay, let's go down and . . ." She wobbled again, cursed.

"My way then after all." He scooped her off her feet.

"Just need another minute. Need to find my balance."

"You feel balanced enough to me." He looked down, smiled slowly. "You've a lovely shape to you. I like that the clothes you wear don't hide it away. And just now you've got a pretty scent to go with it. A bit like green apples."

"Are you distracting me from the fact I nearly invited a vampire in for dinner?"

"Is it working for you?"

"A little."

"Let's try for a little more then." He stopped, lowered his head and covered her mouth with his.

A quick jolt. Not so playful as it had been before, and she realized there was a great deal of anger and fear in him for her. She didn't know the last time anyone had been afraid for her. She responded to it before she could stop herself, turning into him, tangling her fingers in his hair. Filling up with him that aching loneliness that had followed her out of the dream.

"Fairly effective," she murmured when he lifted his head again.

"Well, sure it put some of the color back in your cheeks, so that's fine for now."

"You'd better put me down. If you carry me in there, it'll scare them. They'll be scared enough when we tell them what happened."

He shifted her so her feet touched the ground, but kept his arms around her. "Steady enough?"

"Yeah, better, really."

Still he kept a hand on her arm as they walked the rest of the way to the kitchen.

"If this can be done, why is it they haven't done it before?" Hoyt sat at the head of the table in the dining room, the fire crackling at his back. He looked down the length of it to Cian.

"I've never heard of it being done before." With a shrug, Cian sampled the fish Glenna had prepared. "With a personal connection between the vampire and the human, yes, an invitation can be seduced or cajoled. But that's most often due to the human's instinctive denial of what it sees. This is a different matter, and from what both you and Larkin said, you were sleeping."

"First time for everything." With no appetite, Blair ate because she needed fuel. "We've got magical types on our team. So, obviously, does she. Some sort of spell."

"I fell asleep in the library, and . . ." Moira sipped water to wet her throat. "There was something. Not what happened to you, Blair, not exactly. But it was as if she was there with me. Lilith. More, that I was with her and it wasn't in the library, at all. We weren't in the library. She was with me in my bedchamber, at home. In Geall."

"What happened?" Blair asked her. "Do you remember?"

"I . . ." Moira's gaze stayed on her plate as her color came up. "I'd been asleep, you see, and it seemed she was just there, as real as you are. She climbed into the bed with me.

116

She . . . touched me. My body. I felt her hands on me."

"That's not unusual." Blair toyed with her fish. "The dream, the clarity of it, maybe, but the content. Vampires are sexual creatures, and very often bisexual. It sounds like she was testing things out with you, playing at it."

"I had an experience right after we came here," Glenna said. "Afterwards, I took precautions, protected myself in sleep. It was stupid, *stupid* of me not to think to protect everyone else."

"Well, that's going on your permanent record." Blair wagged her fork in Glenna's direction. "Glenna doesn't think of everything."

"I appreciate the save by levity, but I should have thought of this."

"We'll figure it out now, because there's no way they're going to put the whammy on one of us and waltz in this house."

"They have someone of power. Not a vampire." Moira glanced toward Cian for confirmation, and got a slight nod. "I've read that there are some vampires who can cause a trance, but they must be there, physically there, with their victim. Or have bitten them before. This bite causes a connection, a bond, between them so that person, the human may be put under the vampire's control."

"Clear of bites here," Blair pointed out.

"Aye. And you were sleeping, as I was — as Glenna was before. You couldn't be caught in their eyes while you slept."

"It takes a lot of juice for a vamp to whammy a human. A lot of energy," Blair explained. "And practice."

"True enough," Cian confirmed.

"So they've turned a witch or sorcerer," Hoyt said.

"No." Moira bit her lip. "I think not. If what I've read is the truth. The vampire can gain power by drinking blood of power, but it becomes diluted. And if this person of power is turned, he would lose most, if not all, of his magic. It's the price for the immortality. The demon he becomes loses the gift, or retains only the dregs of it."

"So it's more likely she has witches or whatever on her payroll, so to speak." Blair considered it as she ate. "Someone who'd already turned to the dark side, we'll say. Or someone she has in thrall. A half-vamp. A potent one."

"I don't know if that has to be." Unlike the others, Larkin had already cleared his plate and was going for more. "I've been listening to all of this."

"How can your ears work when your mouth is so busy?" Blair wondered.

He only smiled as he scooped up more fish, more rice. "It's good food," he said to Glenna. "If I don't eat it, how would you know I appreciated it?"

"I'd like to know where you put all that appreciation. But you were saying," Blair added, gesturing.

"These things happened in sleep, so it would seem to me the spell doesn't work on the conscious mind. Wouldn't it take more power to . . ." He fell back on Blair's term. "To whammy someone when they were awake and aware?"

"It would." Hoyt nodded. "Of course, it would."

"And not just sleeping, not this day. Moira was all but ill with exhaustion from what she was part of today. Blair was worn through as well. I don't know what it was like when it happened to you Glenna, but —"

"I was beat — worn out, upset. It was one of the reasons I didn't think to take any precautions before I fell into bed."

"There you have it then, I'm thinking. Not just sleep, but sleep when the body is weak and the mind at its most vulnerable. So it seems to me that whatever, whoever, she might be using isn't as strong as what we have right here at this table."

"You have been listening." Blair considered him. "Dragon-boy here makes a good point. She hit us when our defenses were down, and she came damn close to getting lucky. What do we do about it?"

"Hoyt and I will work on protection. I've been using the most basic shield to this point." Glenna looked at Hoyt. "We'll pump it up."

"Be good if we could do something for the house, too," Blair pointed out. "Some sort of general woo-woo so they can't get inside, even with an invite."

"You can't block an invitation." Cian sat back with his wine. "You can withdraw it, with the right spell, but it can't be blocked."

"Okay, maybe not. Maybe something that extends the perimeters, creates a safe area around the house itself."

"We've tried." Hoyt laid his hand over Glenna's. "We haven't been able to find the way."

"Something to work on. It would be another layer. The more layers they have to get through the better. Think vamp-free zone."

"Perhaps I should move into a nice B and B," Cian suggested, and had Blair frowning at him until she understood.

"Oh. Oh, right. Sorry. Forgot. Can't have

a vamp-free zone with a vamp in residence."

"We haven't been able to find a way to exclude him from it," Glenna explained. "We have a few ideas. More like concepts than actual ideas," she admitted. "And Hoyt's been working for some time on conjuring a kind of shield for you, Cian, so that you could go outside during the day. In the sun."

"Others have tried and failed on that. It can't be done."

"People used to believe the world was flat," Blair pointed out.

"True enough." Cian shrugged. "But I'd think if it could be done it would have been in the thousands of years since our existence. And experimenting with it at this point isn't the best use of time."

"It's my time," Hoyt said quietly.

"We could have used you today." Glenna spoke after a long beat of silence. "In Kerry, at the cliffs. It's worth the time. We think we'd have more success if we had some of your blood."

"Oh?" Cian said dryly. "Is that all?"

"Think about it. Still, our first priority will be protection. Hoyt and I will put that together." She gave his hand a squeeze. "Why don't we get started?"

"Meanwhile, nobody sleeps until we have protection. I've got some extra crosses, some holy water, in my gear." Blair got to her feet. "Cian, unless you're planning to go out, I'd like to set up basic precautions at doors and windows."

"Have at it. But those kind of trinkets won't supercede an invitation."

"Layers," Blair said again.

"I'll help you." Larkin pushed his plate aside. "There's a lot of doors and windows."

"All right, so it looks like we split into teams. Hoyt and Glenna, magic time. Larkin and I will do what we can to block entrances. That leaves Cian and Moira on KP."

It wasn't that she didn't trust Hoyt and Glenna — she did as much as she'd ever trusted anyone. It wasn't that she wasn't open to magic. She had to be.

But even with the charm under her pillow, the candle lit, and the second charm hanging with the cross at her window, Blair slept fitfully that night.

And the night after.

The training helped, the sheer physical exertion of it, and the purpose. She pushed, and pushed hard. No one, including herself, ended any day without bruises and sore muscles. But no one, including herself, ended any day without being just a little stronger, just a little faster.

She watched Moira blossom — or thought of it that way. What Moira didn't have in strength she made up for in speed and flexibility. And sheer determination.

There was no one who could compete with her when she had a bow in her hands.

Glenna polished the skills she already had — the canniness, the solid instincts. And she was coming along with a blade and an ax.

Hoyt brought an intensity to everything. Whether he fought with a blade, with a bow or with his own hands, he had an almost unwavering focus. She thought of him as the most reliable of soldiers.

And Cian as the most elegant, and vicious. He had the superior strength of his kind, and the animal's cunning, but he added style to it all. He would kill, Blair thought, with violent grace.

She thought of Larkin as the utility player. In hand-to-hand, he was a scrapper, and simply didn't give up. He lacked Hoyt's intensity and Cian's elegance with a sword, but he fought tirelessly until he downed his opponents, or they simply dropped from exhaustion. He had a good eye with the bow — not Moira's, but who did?

And you never knew when he'd pull out one of his little tricks, so you'd end up battling with a man who had the head of a wolf, or the claws of a bear, the tail of dragon.

It was handy, and effective.

And damn sexy.

There were times he made her impatient. He was a bit too impulsive, and often showy. Errol Flynning it, she thought. And showoffs often ended up in the ground.

But when it came down to it, if she had to pick the people she'd want fighting beside her in the battle to save the world, she wouldn't have chosen differently.

But even soldiers in the war to end wars needed to eat, to do laundry, and take out the trash.

Blair took the supply run because she wanted, desperately, to get out of the house. Two days of rain had limited outdoor activities, and made her edgy. If one person, just one, said that the rain is what made Ireland green, she'd split their head open with an ax.

Added to it, since the night of her close encounter with Lora, there'd been no sign of the enemy. The lull ruffled that edge and added twitchy.

Something was brewing. Bound to be brewing.

She had preferred to go alone, to have a couple of hours to herself, with her own thoughts, her own company. But she hadn't been able to argue it was an unnecessary risk.

But she'd drawn the line at giving Larkin a driving lesson on their way into Ennis.

"I don't know why I couldn't do it," he complained. "I've watched Glenna drive the thing. And she's taught Hoyt."

"Hoyt drives like an old blind man from Florida."

"I don't know what that means, except it's an insult of some kind. I could do better than he does, with this, or the beauty Cian keeps in the stable."

"Garage. You keep cars in a garage, and Cian's made it clear he'll bite and drain anyone who touches his Jag."

"You could teach me on this one." He reached over to trail his finger down the side of her neck. "I'd be a fine student."

"Charm won't work." She flipped on the radio. "There, listen to the music and enjoy the ride."

He cocked his head. "That sounds a bit like home."

"Irish station, traditional music."

"It's wonderful, isn't it, that you can have music at the snap of a finger. Or move so fast from one place to another in a machine."

"Not in Chicago traffic. You do a lot of sitting and cursing instead of moving."

"Tell me about your Chicago."

"It's not my Chicago. Just where I've been

based the last couple of years."

"It was the Boston before that."

"Yeah." But Boston was Jeremy, and she'd had to get away from it. "Chicago. It's, ah, it's a city. Major city in the Midwest of the U.S. On a lake — big-ass lake."

"Do you fish in it, this lake?"

"Fish? Me? No. I guess people maybe do. Ah . . . they sail on it. Water sports and stuff. It's wicked cold in the winter, wind like you wouldn't believe. Lake effect, a lot of snow, bone-chilling cold. But, I don't know, it's got a lot happening. Restaurants, great shopping, museums, clubs. Vampires."

"A big city? Bigger than Ennis?"

"A lot bigger." She tried to think what he'd make of the El, and just couldn't.

"How is it that if it's such a large city with so many people, they haven't banded together to fight against the vampires?"

"They don't believe in them, or if some do, they pretend they don't. If somebody gets attacked, or gets dead, they put it down to gangs, or sick bastards. Mostly the vamps keep a low profile — or they did until recently. Prey on the homeless or runaways, transients. People other people don't miss."

"There were legends in Geall of creatures that haunted the night, preyed on humans long ago. I never believed them, until the queen — my aunt — was killed by them. And even then . . ."

"It's hard to believe what you've been taught is fantasy, or the impossible. So you put up the shield. It's natural."

"But not you." He studied her profile. It was strong, yes, but with such a pretty curve of cheek, and that dark, dark hair such a lovely contrast to the white of her skin. "You've always known. Do you ever wish it otherwise? That you were one of the people with the shields. Who never knew?"

"No point in wishing for what you can't have."

"What's the point of wishing for what you can and do?" he countered.

He had a point, Blair decided. He usually did if you listened long enough.

She found a spot in a car park, dug out the money for the ticket. Larkin just stood, hands in the pockets of the jeans Glenna had bought him on some earlier trip, looking at everything.

It was a relief not to be asked a dozen questions. She knew he'd been to town before, but imagined every visit was a little like a walk through Disney World for him.

"Just stick close, okay? I don't want to have to go hunting for you."

"I wouldn't leave you." He took her hand,

127

tightening his grip a little when she started to shake him off. "You should hold on to me," he said with absolute innocence in his eyes. "I could get lost."

"That's bullshit."

"Not in the least." He linked fingers with hers and set out at a stroll. "Why with all these people, and the street, and the sounds and sights, I could lose my way any moment. At home, the village isn't nearly as big as this, and there aren't so many in it. On market day now, it can be crowded and colorful. But I know what I'm about there."

"You know what you're about everywhere," she said under her breath.

He had good ears, and his lips twitched at the comment. "On market day, people come into the village from all over the land. There's wonderful food —"

"Which would be your first priority."

"A man has to eat. But there's cloths and crafts and music. Lovely stones from the mountains, and shells from the sea. And you bargain, you see, that's the fun of it. When we're at home again, I'll buy you a gift on market day."

He stopped to study the souvenirs and jewelry in a shop window. "I have nothing here to trade, and Hoyt tells me we can't use the coin I brought with me. You like baubles." He flicked a finger at one of the drops in her ears. "So I'll buy you a bauble on market day."

"I think we might be too busy to shop for baubles. Come on." She gave his hand a tug. "We're here for supplies, not shiny things."

"There's no need to hurry. We can have a bit of fun while we're about it. From what I see, you don't have enough fun."

"If we're still alive in November, I'll do cartwheels in the street. I'll do naked cartwheels."

He shot her that quick grin. "That's a new and important reason for me to fight. I haven't thought of the cartwheels, but I have thought about you naked a time or two. Oh, look there. Cakes!"

Sex and food, she thought. If he'd tossed in a beer and a sporting event, he'd be the ultimate guy. "No." She rolled her eyes, half-heartedly dug in her heels as he pulled her across the street. "We're not here for cakes either. I've got a list. A really long list."

"We can see to it soon enough. Ah, would you look at that one? See the long one, with the chocolate."

"Eclair."

"Eclair," he repeated, making the word sound like a particularly pleasurable sex act. "You should have one of those, and so should I." He turned those long, tawny eyes on her. "Be a darling, won't you, Blair? I'll pay you back."

"You ought to be fat as a pig," she muttered, but she went inside the bakery to buy two eclairs.

And came out with a dozen cupcakes as well.

She had no idea how he'd talked her into them, or the detour into half a dozen shops to browse. She was usually — hell, she was *always* — stronger than that.

Then she noticed the way the female clerks, other browsers, women on the street looked at him. Tough to be stronger than that, she decided.

He managed to nudge her into whittling away more than an hour doing nothing before she dragged him with her to finish the supply list.

"Okay, that's it. Foot firmly down. We haul this stuff straight back to the car and head for home. No more window shopping, no more flirting with shop girls."

"Sure it was shameful the way you poured your charm over that dear woman."

Blair gave him a bland look. "You're a real card." She gestured with her chin. "That way. No detours."

"You know, the way this village is built —

I'm meaning the way the roads are, it's very like my own. And how the shops are huddled up together. And here, this is very like home, too."

Before she could stop him, he'd opened the door of a pub. "Ah, there's a familiar smell. And there's music. So we'll stop for a moment."

"Larkin, we need to get back."

"So we will. But we should have a beer first. I like beer."

Since her arms were loaded, she didn't put up much resistance when he nudged her inside. "It's nice," he said, "after all the walking to sit and have a tankard. It's not a tankard," he remembered.

"A pint. They usually say a pint here." It was the walking, she decided that made her give in. The man was exhausting. And exhilarating.

She dumped purchases on and around one of the chairs at a low table, sat. "One beer." She held up a finger. "And that's it. I don't want any more trouble from you."

"Have I been trouble to you?" He took her hand, lifted it to kiss her fingers. "Sure I don't mean to be."

Her eyes narrowed. "Wait a minute, wait a minute. Have you been playing me? Is this whole thing been your idea of a date?"

His brows drew together. "I don't know the date. I can't keep track of the days."

"No, I meant . . . never mind. Pint of Guinness," she told the waitress who came over. "Glass of Harp."

"And how's it all going then?" he asked the waitress, and had her beaming him a smile.

"Very fine, and thank you. And for you?"

"A lovely day it's been. Do you live in the village?"

"In Ennis, I do, yes. Are you visiting?"

"We are. My lady is from Chicago."

"Oh, I have cousins there. Well then, welcome to Ireland. I hope you're enjoying your stay. I'll get your beer right away."

Idly, Blair tapped a finger on the table as she studied him. "You don't even have to turn it on, do you? It's just there, all the time."

"I don't understand what you're meaning."

"No, you probably don't. Do the girls back home lap up your cream that way? Blush and flutter?"

He put his hand over hers. "No need at all to be jealous, darling. I've no thought for any woman but you."

"Save it." She had to laugh. "I wouldn't fall for that one even if it wasn't possibly the end of the world."

"There's no one here, or back home, who's caught my eye as you've caught it. I wonder if any will now that I've seen you. You're not like the women I know."

"I'm not like women anyone knows."

The easy smile faded. "You think that's a flaw in you, a fault, or . . . a barrier," he decided. "Something that makes you less appealing than other women. That's false. When I say you're not like other women, I mean you're more interesting, more exciting. More alluring. Stop."

The sudden and unexpected irritation in his voice put her back up. "Stop what?"

"You put that face on. The one that says *bullshit*. I like charming the ladies, for it doesn't do a bit of harm." He waited, and this time Blair could see he had to put some effort into smiling at the waitress when she served them. "Thanks for that." Then he lifted the pint glass, took a long, slow sip.

"You're pissed," she murmured, recognizing the glint in his eye. "What have you got to be pissed about?"

"I don't like the way you demean yourself."

"Demean my — are you whacked?"

"Just be quiet. I said I like charming the ladies, and I do. I enjoy a flirt here and there, and a tumble when I can get one. But I don't hurt women, not with my hands, not with my words. I don't lie. So when I tell you how I see you, it's the simple truth of it. I think you're magnificent."

He drank again, nodding when she only stared at him. "Well, that put the cork back in you right enough. Magnificent," he repeated. "In face and form, in your heart and your mind. Magnificent because of what you do every day, and have done for years, since you were all but a babe. I've never known another like you, and never will. I'm telling you that if a man looks at you and doesn't see what a wonder you are, it's his vision that's at fault, and not a bit of you."

CHAPTER 6

They fell back into routine, training, strategizing. From the rumbles and flashes coming from the tower, Blair knew there was magic in the work as well.

But what they were doing, under it all, she thought, was waiting.

"We have to make a move." She plowed rapid punches into the heavy bag they'd hung at one end of the once-grand ballroom. "We're caught in a loop, and it's time to do something. Shake things up."

"I'm for that." Larkin watched her, wondering how many levels of frustration she worked through by beating up a big hanging sack. "A daylight attack on the caves is what I was thinking."

"Been there." She pummelled — left, left, right. "Done that."

"No, we went there, but we didn't do the attacking now, did we?"

Annoyed because he was right — worse because he wasn't mentioning the fact she'd been the one to be so nearly used after the mission to Kerry — she shot him a glance. "We go in, we're dead. Or most of us."

"That may be, but we're likely to die in any case before the end of this thing."

Hard truth, she thought. She had to respect it. "Yeah, odds are."

"So there could be a way to give them something to think about without actually going inside and hastening that eventuality. Though I'd like a chance at that — deviling them on their own ground for a change." He picked up a stake, hurled it at the practice dummy.

She understood the sentiment, and felt the same. But knew better. "Whenever possible, you don't fight on their terms, or their turf. The caves are suicide."

"Could be for them, if we lit them up."

She pulled the next punch, turned to him. "Lit them up?"

"Fire. But it would have to be the two of us. The others, Moira in particular, would never agree to it."

Intrigued, she began to unwrap her hands. "I meant to ask you before. The dragon suit. You breathe fire?"

He goggled at her. "Breathe fire?"

"Yeah. Dragons breathe fire, right?"

"No. Why would they want to do that? How could they?"

"That begs the question how can a man turn into one, but okay, another fantasy crushed. So how do you intend to fire up the caves?"

He lifted a sword. "It would only take one of us to get close enough, a few feet in. I'd enjoy that. But . . ." He set the sword down again. "A more practical manner would be flaming arrows."

"Shooting flaming arrows into caves in broad daylight. Well, that shouldn't draw too much attention. I'm not shutting you down," she added before he could speak. "An earthquake and a dragon flight barely made anyone blink. People have blinders. But there's another factor. There are still people in there."

"I know it. Can we save them?"

"Highly unlikely."

"If I were locked in a cage, waiting to be a meal for one of those things, or changed into one, I'd rather burn. You said the same before."

"I don't think you're wrong, but we'd need a full-on attack to make a dent. And you're not wrong either when you say we'd never talk the others into it." She walked over to study his face. "And you're saying it, but you couldn't do it. Not when it came down to it."

He strode over to yank the stake from the dummy. He *wanted* to be able to do it, in his head. But in his heart . . . that was another thing altogether. "Could you?"

"Yeah, I could. Then I'd have to live with it, and I would. I've been fighting this war all my life, Larkin. You don't get through it without casualties. Innocent casualties — collateral damage. If I thought we could end it this way, or put a serious hurt on Lilith, I'd have already done it."

"And you think I can't."

"I know you can't."

"Because I'm weak?"

"No. Because you're not hard."

He pivoted, hurled the stake, hit the heart of the practice dummy. "And you are?"

"I have to be. You haven't seen what I've seen, and for all you know, you still don't know what I know. I have to be hard. What I am makes me hard."

"What you are, a warrior, a hunter, is a gift and a duty. To harden around it, that's a choice. I can do what needs to be done, and if this was the way, this sacrifice of men, I would live with it. It would hurt me, and it would weigh on me, but I would do what needed to be done."

Enough weight, she thought as he left her, you get hard, or you break under it.

And this is why she worked alone, she reminded herself. Why she was alone. So she didn't have to explain herself, or justify herself. Why she'd accepted, after Jeremy, that the only way to do what she'd been born to do, was to stay alone.

She heard a muffled boom from overhead in the tower, glanced up. Sure some people found it — that intimacy, that unity — and made it work. But they had to understand each other first, and accept all the dark places. To not just tolerate them, but embrace them.

And that, when it came to her and her life, just wasn't in the cards. She rewrapped her hands, and went back to pummelling the heavy bag.

"Someone you know?" Cian asked from the doorway.

She barely spared him a glance. She was using her feet now as well as her hands. Side kicks, back kicks, double jumps. She'd worked up enough of a sweat that her breath was short and choppy. "Tenth-grade algebra teacher."

"I'm sure she deserves a good hiding. Ever found a use for that? The algebra business."

"Not a one."

139

He watched her get a running start, and hit the bag with a flying kick that nearly snapped it off its chain. "Nice form. Oddly, I see Larkin's face on that bag." He smiled a little when she stopped to catch her breath and gulp down water. "I just passed him going down. He looked annoyed — a rarity for him, as he's an affable sort, isn't he?"

"I bring annoyance out in people."

"True enough. He's a likable boy."

"I like him okay."

"Hmm." Cian crossed over to pick up several knives, then began to throw them at the target across the room. "When you've been around humans as long as I have you recognize traits and signals. And, if you're me, you have a curiosity about their choices. So I wonder why the two of you don't just have at each other. Dangerous times, possible end of days, and so on."

Her back went up, she could literally feel the shift in her spine. "I don't just roll with any guy who's handy — if it's any of your business."

"Your choice, of course." He walked over, tugged out the knives. When he came back, he handed them to her in an easy, almost companionable gesture. "But I think it's a bit more than him being in the vicinity and available."

She gave the knife a testing toss in the air, then hurled it at the target. Hit dead center. "Why this sudden interest in my sex life?"

"Just a study of human reactions. My brother walked out of his world and into this one. The goddess pointed the direction, and he followed."

"He didn't just follow the goddess."

"No," Cian said after a moment. "He came to find me. We're twins, after all, and the attachment runs deep. Added to it, he's by nature dutiful and loyal."

This time she walked over to retrieve the knives. "He's also powerful and courageous."

"He is, yes." Cian took them, threw them. "The odds are I'll watch him die. That's not something I'd choose. Even if he survives this, he'll grow old, his body will shut down, and he'll die."

"Cheery, aren't you? It could be peacefully in his sleep, after a long full life. Maybe after a last bout of really great sex."

Cian smiled a little, but it didn't reach those cool blue eyes. "Whether it's by violence or nature, the result is the same. I've seen more death than you, more than you ever will. But still, you've seen more than most humans have or will. And that separates us, you and me, from the rest."

"We don't have any choice about that."

"Of course we do. I know a bit about loneliness, and what can chase it back, even for the short run."

"So I should jump Larkin because I'm lonely?"

"That would be one answer." Cian retrieved the knives again, and this time replaced them. "The other might be to take a closer look at him, and at what he sees when he looks at you. Meanwhile, the tension and repression gives you a nice edge. Want to go a round or two?"

"Wouldn't say no."

She felt better. Bruised but better. Nothing like a good grapple with a vampire — even one who didn't want to kill you — to clear the head. She'd just go down and grab something to eat before the evening training session.

But first she was going to stop by her room and rub some of Glenna's magic cream into the bruises.

She walked into her room, and onto the rise above the Valley of Silence.

"Oh crap. Crap, crap. I don't need to see this again."

"You do." Morrigan stood beside her, pale blue robes fluttering in the wind. "You need to know it, every rock, every drop, every blade of grass. This is your battleground. This will be the stand of humankind. Not the caves in Kerry."

"So we just wait?"

"There will be more than waiting. You are hunter and hunted now. What you do, what you choose to do, brings you closer to this."

"One battle." Suddenly weary, Blair raked a hand through her hair. "Everything else is just another skirmish leading here. It's all about this. Will it end it?"

Morrigan turned those emerald eyes to Blair's. "It never ends. You know this, in every part of you, you know this single truth. But if she defeats you on this ground, worlds will be tossed into chaos. There will be suffering, death and torment for a time beyond imagining."

"Got that. What's the good news?"

"Everything you need to take this ground is within you. Your circle has the power to win this war."

"But not end it." Blair looked over the ground again, the misery of it. "It's never going to end for me."

"The choice is yours, child, has always been yours."

"I wish I could walk away. Some days I wish that, and others . . . Others I think wow, look what I'm doing, what I can do.

And it makes me feel, well, righteous, I guess. Right, anyway. But some days when I go home after a hunt and there's no one there, it all seems too hard, and too empty."

"You should have been cared for, and were not," Morrigan said, gently now. "And still, all that came before, all that comes now has made you. You have more than one battle to win, more than one quest. And always, child, more than one choice."

"Turning away isn't a choice for me. So we'll come here, and we'll win. Because that's what we have to do. I'm not afraid to die. Can't say I look forward to it, but I'm not afraid."

She looked back at the ground, the way the mists filled the pockets in the earth, the way the rocks speared up through it. Now, as always, the look of it shuddered through her. Now, as always, she saw herself lying bloody there. Ended.

She nearly asked if what she saw was truth or imagination, but knew the god wouldn't answer.

"So if I go," Blair decided, "I'm taking a hell of a lot of them with me."

"In one week, you, the circle of six, will go to the Dance of the Gods, and from there to Geall."

Blair turned away from the drop now to

look into Morrigan's face. "One week."

"One week from this day. You've done what needed to be done here. You've gathered together, and now, together, you'll make this journey to Geall."

"How?"

"You'll know. In one week. You must trust those with you, and what you hold inside you. If the circle doesn't reach Geall, and come to this place at the appointed time, this world, yours, and all the others are plunged into the dark."

The sun went out. In the black, Blair heard the screams, the howls, the weeping. The air suddenly stank with blood.

"You're not alone," Morrigan told her. "Not even here."

She snapped back, and stared into Larkin's eyes. She felt his fingers digging into her shoulders.

"There you are, there you are now." She was too stunned to evade when he pulled her into his arms, wrapped them around her like bands as he pressed his lips to her hair. "There you are," he repeated. "Was it the vampire?"

"No. Wow. You need to turn me loose."

"In a minute or two. You're shaking."

"I don't think so. I think that's you."

"It may be. I know you scared six lives out

of me." He drew her back, barely an inch. "You were just standing there, just standing, staring. You didn't hear me when I spoke to you. Didn't see me when I was right in front of you. And your eyes . . ." He pressed his lips to her forehead now, firmly, the way she imagined parents checked a child for fever. "So dark, so deep."

"It was Morrigan. She took me on a little excursion. I'm okay."

"Do you want to lie down, to rest? Steady yourself a bit. I'll stay with you."

"No, I said I'm fine. I thought you were mad at me."

"I was — am a bit. You're a frustrating creature, Blair, and I've never had to put so much work into wooing a woman."

"Woo?" Something snapped shut in her throat. "I don't like the whole woo thing."

"That's clear enough, but I do. And a man has to please himself as well as the woman who's caught his eye, doesn't he? But in any case, whether or not I'm annoyed and frustrated, I wouldn't leave you alone."

They always do, a little voice whispered in her head. Sooner or later. "I'm okay. Just a little wigged out at getting a message from the land of the gods."

"What is the message?"

"Better get everyone together and deliver

it all at once. In the library," she decided. "It's the best setup."

She paced, waiting for Hoyt and Glenna. Apparently, magic couldn't be interrupted even by messages from gods. Struggling against impatience, she toyed with the two crosses around her neck. One, she'd worn nearly all her life. It had come down through her family, through Nola, and all the way back to Hoyt. Morrigan's Cross, one of those given to him at the onset of this battle while he was still in his own time.

The second, he and Glenna had forged with silver and fire and magic. A team emblem, she supposed, as much as a shield, which each of them — but Cian — wore at all times.

The first had saved her life once, she remembered. So magic, she supposed, had priority over impatience.

Still, when Moira offered her tea, she shook her head.

Already she was going over in her mind what had to be done — and she didn't like most of it. Still, it was movement, and that's what they wanted. What they needed.

"There are two outside," Moira said quietly. "We haven't seen any for days, but there are two out there now, just at the edge of the trees."

Blair moved to the window beside her, scanned. "Yeah, I see them. Just barely."

"Should I get my bow?"

"That's a long shot in the dark." Then Blair shrugged. "Sure, why not? Even if you don't hit one, it'll show them we're not sleeping."

Blair glanced around as Moira went out. Cian was sprawled in a chair with a glass of wine and a book. Larkin sat on the couch, sipping at a beer and watching her.

She didn't want the tea Moira had brought in, didn't want to be soothed by it. Nor did she want alcohol to dull the edge.

So she paced a little more, stood at the window again. She saw the vampire on the left poof. She hadn't even seen the arrow, but she saw the second vamp fade back into the trees.

No, we're not sleeping, she thought.

"Sorry that took so long, but we couldn't leave that in the middle. Tea. Perfect." Glenna went directly to the table when they came in, poured a cup for herself and for Hoyt. "Is something up?"

"Yeah. Moira will be right back. She just went up to take out one of the vamps outside."

"Oh." Glenna let out a little gush of breath as she sat. "So they're back. Well, it was nice while it lasted."

"I could only get one." Moira came in with her bow. "It was too dark to see the second, and I'd have likely wasted an arrow." But she propped the bow and her quiver by the window, in case she had another chance.

"Okay, we're all here. Morrigan paid me a visit — or had me pay her one. However it works."

"You had a vision?" Hoyt demanded.

"I had whatever it is. At the battleground. It was empty. Just wind and fog, her. A lot of cryptic god stuff, the bottom line being she said we're to leave for Geall a week from today."

"We go back?" Moira stepped to Larkin, squeezed a hand on his shoulder. "We go back to Geall."

"That's what the lady said," Blair confirmed. "We've got a week to get ready for it. To figure out what we need, pack it up, finish up what's going on up in the magic tower. We go to the stone circle, the way you got here," she said, nodding at Larkin and Moira. "The way Hoyt came through. I don't know how it works, but —"

"We have keys," Moira told her. "Morrigan gave me a key, and one to Hoyt."

"I'd say travel arrangements are up to you guys. We'll take all the weapons we can carry. Potions, lotions — whatever Hoyt and Glenna figure we can use best. Major glitch that I see is that for Cian to get there, we have to hope for a cloudy day or leave the house after sunset. Since we've got watchers again, they'll know we're on the move. They'll try to stop us, no question."

"And they'll tell Lilith we've gone," Glenna added.

"She'll know where. When we go to Geall, we take her there." Moira's hand tightened on Larkin's shoulder. "I'd bring that plague to my people."

"It can't be helped," Blair began.

"You say that because you've grown used to living with this. I want to go home," Moira said. "I want to go home more than I can say, but to bring something so evil with me. What if the battle didn't take place? If we found her portal, sealed it off somehow. We could change destiny."

Destiny, in Blair's opinion, wasn't something you messed around with. "Then the battle takes place here, where it's not meant to. And I'd have to say our chances of winning drop."

"Moira." Larkin rose, moving around the

couch until he faced her. "I don't love Geall less than you, but this is the way. It's what was asked of you, and what you asked of me."

"Larkin."

"The plague you speak of has already infested Geall. It took your mother. Would you ask me to leave my own now, to break this trust. To risk all?"

"No. I'm sorry. I'm not afraid for myself, not any more. But I see the faces of those people in cages, and they take on the faces of those I know, from home. And I'm afraid."

She steadied herself. "It's more than Geall, I know. We'll go, in one week."

"Once we're there we'll raise an army." Hoyt looked at Moira. "You'll ask your people to fight, to unify under this circle."

"They'll fight."

"It's going to involve a lot of training," Blair pointed out. "And it's going to be more complicated than what we've been doing. We're just six. We'd better be able to pull together hundreds, and it's not just putting a stake in their hands. It's teaching them how to kill vampires."

"With one exception." Cian lifted his glass in half salute.

"No one will lay hands on you," Moira

told him, and he answered with a lazy smile.

"Little queen, if I thought otherwise, I'd toss some confetti and wish you all bon voyage."

"Okay, here's another thing." Blair passed by the windows again, just to see if any vampires had chanced coming toward the house. "For all we know Lilith may be on the move, too. She may even get there before we do. Anyway, can we rig up the circle — some spell — so we'll know if it's been used to . . . open the door?"

"There should be." Glenna looked at Hoyt. "Yes, I think we can work that."

"You wouldn't have to. She can't use the Dance of the Gods." Larkin reached for his beer again. "Didn't you say, Moira, when we came through that a demon couldn't enter the circle?"

"It's pure," she agreed. "What they are can't enter the ring, much less use it to go between worlds."

"Okay, bigger problem."

Cian acknowledged Blair's comment with another lift of his glass. "Looks like I'll be tossing that confetti after all."

"That's a kick in the arse, isn't it. I'd forgotten." Larkin pursed his lips before drinking again. "So we'll find a way around it. As I understand it, we six must go, so there must be a way to do it. We just need to find it."

"We go together," Hoyt said and set his tea aside, "or we don't go at all."

"Aye." Larkin nodded in agreement. "We leave no one behind. And we're taking the horse this time." He remembered himself, smiled easily at Cian. "If it's all the same to you."

"We work the problem. Any magical solutions spring to mind?" Blair asked Hoyt.

"The goddess must intercede. She must. If we attempt, Glenna and I, to open this ourselves to let Cian through, we could change it all, disrupt the power, close it altogether so no one gets through — or out again."

"Every time you change the nature of something," Glenna explained, "you risk repercussions. Magic has a lot in common with physics, really. The circle is a holy place, sacred ground, and we can't mess with that. But at the same time, Cian's meant to go, and at the goddess's behest. So we'll work on the loophole."

"If there's another way, another portal that Lilith needs to use, maybe Cian's supposed to use that." Blair frowned at him. "It'd be my second choice. I don't like separating, especially on moving day."

"Added to the fact," he reminded her, "that I don't know where in the bloody hell that portal or window might be."

"Yeah, there's that. But maybe we can find out."

"Another search spell?" Glenna reached for Hoyt's hand. "We can try."

"No, I wasn't thinking of spells. Not exactly." Blair angled her head, studied Larkin. "Any living thing, right?"

He set down his beer, smiled slowly. "That's the way of it. What do we have in mind?"

"You're sure you want to do this?" Blair stood in the tower with Larkin. "I know it was my idea, but —"

"And a fine one it is. Ah, now, are you worried for me, *a stor*?"

"Sending you out into a fortified vamp nest, one with magical shields — sending you unarmed. No. What's to worry about?"

"I won't need a weapon, and it wouldn't be easy to carry one the way I'm going."

"Anything seems off, you get out. Don't be a hero."

"I was born to be a hero."

"I'm serious, Larkin, no grandstanding." Her stomach was already jittering. "This is just for information. Any signs she's getting ready to move, numbers if you can get a clear idea, a look at their arsenal —"

"Sure you've been over this with me already, a time or two. Do I strike you as being addle-brained?"

"We should wait for the morning, then we could drive you as far as the cliffs. We'd be there if you ran into trouble."

"And it's more likely than not they've got the caves blocked off again during the daylight hours, as you said yourself. They'd be less likely to expect anything like this at night. As *I* said so myself. If I'm to be a soldier in this war, Blair, I have to do what I can do."

"Just don't do anything stupid." Giving in to the need, to the worry, she grabbed his hair with both hands, yanked his face to hers.

She kept her fear out of the kiss. It wasn't fear she wanted to send with him. Instead she poured out hope and heat, and held on to him as the punch of the kiss vibrated down to her toes.

"Not so fast," he said when she started to back away. And spun her around so her back was pressed to the tower wall. "Not all of us are done as yet."

This was what he'd looked for, this fire. Like liquid flames that sparked from her to run into his blood. He let it scorch him as he gripped her hips, then ran his hands up her body, down again. So he could take the shape of her with him.

"Cian lured them to the front of the . . ." Moira stopped short, eyes going wide at the sight of her cousin and Blair locked in each other's arms. "I'm sorry."

"It's not a problem. Just getting myself a fine kiss goodbye." He cupped Blair's face in his hands. "I'll be back by morning." Then he turned, opened his arms to Moira.

She rushed into them. "Be careful. I couldn't lose you, I couldn't bear it, Larkin. Remember that, remember we're all waiting for you, and come back safe."

"By first light." He kissed each one of her cheeks. "Keep a candle burning for me."

"We'll be watching." Blair made herself turn and open the window. "In Glenna's crystal, for as long as we can."

"I wouldn't mind having that French toast when I return." He looked straight into her eyes.

They changed first. She hadn't noticed that before, Blair realized. His eyes changed first, pupil and iris, then came the shimmer of light.

The hawk looked at her, as the man had. Then it flew into the night, silent as the air.

"He'll be fine," Blair said under her breath. "He'll be fine."

Moira reached for her hand, and together they watched until the hawk flew out of sight.

CHAPTER 7

He soared. With his height and the hawk's vision he could see the things that slunk around the house. He counted eight — a small party then, and likely just watchers as Blair had said. Regardless, he took another circle to be sure it was a scouting expedition and not an attack force.

Widening the circle, he spotted the van at the end of the lane, just beyond the turnoff. Of course, he thought, they would need a way to get back and forth from the caves, wouldn't they? But it was nervy, and a bit insulting come to that, for them to leave their machine so close to the house.

He circled again, considering the situation, then dived for the ground.

He remembered what Glenna had said about how the van worked, how a key was needed to spark the — what was it? Ignition. Wasn't it a shame they hadn't left it hanging in there, in the lock of the thing.

But he remembered, too, that she'd explained that the wheels it rolled on were filled with air. If the wheel was punctured, and the air got out, and then the wheel was called a flat. It was a pain in the ass, she'd said.

He thought it would be fruitful, and fun as well, to give the vampires a pain in the ass.

He changed to a unicorn, with a pale gold wash over its white hide. And lowering his head, plunged his keen-tipped horn into the tire. There was a satisfying little pop, then the hiss of escaping air. Wanting to be thorough, he pierced it a second time.

Pleased, Larkin trotted around the van, puncturing each tire until he saw the van sat on four flat wheels. Let's see you try to get this machine to roll now, you bastards, he thought.

Then he rose up again on wings and flew south.

There was enough moonlight to guide him, and a cool wind to aid his speed. He could see the land below, the spread and roll of it. The rise of hills, the patchwork of fields.

Lights glimmered from the villages, and the larger towns.

He thought of the lively pubs, with the music playing, with the scents of beer and pretty women. The voices in conversation and the rise of laughter. One evening, when all this was done, he wanted to sit in a pub with his friends, those five who were so vital to him, and lift a pint with all those voices, all that music around them.

It was a good image to hold on to during a long flight to a nest of monsters.

Below, he saw the long, lovely sweep of river they called Shannon.

It was beautiful land, he thought, as green as home, and with the sea close. He could hear the rumble of it as he angled southwest.

The dragon would be faster, he knew, but it was the hawk he'd agreed to. He wished he could fly here again, in the dragon, with Blair on his back. She could tell him the names of what he saw below, the towns and the ruins, the rivers and lakes. Would she know the name of that waterfall he soared over, the one as high and powerful as his own Faerie Falls back home?

He remembered the feel of her legs locking around him as they rose up into the air. The way she'd laughed. He'd never known another like her, warrior and woman, with such strength and vulnerability. A ready fist and a tender heart.

He liked the way she talked, quick and confident. And the way her lips quirked up on one side, then the other when she smiled.

There was a longing in him for her, which he thought as natural as breath. But there was something tangled with it, something sharp that he didn't recognize. It would be interesting to find out what it all meant.

He winged over the waterfall, and a dense forest that framed it. He skimmed over the quiet glimmer of lakes with starshine glinting on the water. And he aimed for the slicing beam of the lighthouse on the cliffs.

He flew down, silent as a shadow.

On the narrow strip of shale, he saw two figures. A woman, he realized, and a young boy. Alarm tightened his heart inside his chest. They would be captured wandering here near the caves in the dark. Imprisoned, then used, then killed. And he had no weapon to defend them.

He landed in the shadow of rock, and nearly changed into a man to do what he could. But the woman turned to laugh at the child, and the cold white moonlight struck her face.

He had seen her only once before, standing on the high cliffs. But he would never forget her face.

Lilith. The self-proclaimed queen of the undead.

"Please, Mama, *please,* I want to hunt."

"Now, Davey, remember what I told you. We don't hunt near our home. We've plenty of food inside, and since you've been so good . . ." She bent down to tap a finger to his nose, a gesture of amused affection. "You can have your pick."

"But it's no fun when they're just *there*."

"I know." She sighed, ruffled his glossy gold hair. "It's more like a chore than a thrill. But it won't be much longer. When we move on to Geall, you can hunt every night."

"When?"

"Soon, my precious lamb."

"I'm tired of being here." Voice petulant, he kicked at the shale.

Larkin could see he had the face of a little imp — round and sweet.

"I wish I had a kitty. Please, can't I have a kitty cat? I wouldn't eat it like last time."

"That's what you said about the puppy," she reminded him with a quick, gay laugh. "But we'll see. But how about this? I'll let one out for you, and it can run through the caves. You can chase it down, hunt it down. Won't that be fun?"

When he grinned, moonlight sent the dusting of freckles on his chubby cheeks into relief. And glinted on his fangs. "Can I have two?"

"So greedy." She kissed him, and not,

Larkin saw with a sick revulsion, in the way a mother kisses a son. "That's what I love about you, my own true love. Let's go inside then, and you can pick out the ones you want."

Behind the rock, Larkin changed. A sleek, dark rat darted inside the caves behind the sweep of Lilith's long skirts.

He could smell death, and see the things that moved in the dark. Things that bowed when Lilith glided by.

There was little light — only a scatter of torches clamped to the walls here and there. But as they moved deeper there was a faint green tinge to the light he felt was unnatural. Magic, he knew, just as he knew this magic wasn't clean and white.

She drifted through the maze of it, holding the boy's hand as he trotted at her side. Vampires scuttled up the walls like spiders, or hung from the ceiling like bats.

He could only hope they weren't overly interested in snacking on rat blood.

He followed the swish of Lilith's robes, and kept to the dark corners.

The sounds of unspeakable human suffering began to echo.

"What sort do you want, my darling?" Lilith swung his arm with hers as if they were on an outing to a fair and a promised treat. "Something young and lean, or perhaps something with a little more flesh?"

"I don't know. I want to look in their eyes first. Then I'll know."

"Clever boy. You make me proud."

There were more cages than he'd imagined, and the sheer horror had him struggling to stay in form. He wanted to spring into a man, grab a sword from one of the guards, and start hacking.

He would take down a few of them, and that might be worth dying for. But he would never get any of the people out.

Blair had warned him, but he hadn't fully believed.

The boy had dropped his mother's hand and now strolled, hands behind his back, pacing up and down the length of the cages. A child eyeing treats at the baker's, Larkin thought.

Davey stopped, pursing his lips as he studied a young woman huddled in the corner of a cage. She seemed to be singing, or perhaps she was praying, for the words were unintelligible. But Larkin could see her eyes were already dead.

"This one wouldn't be any fun to hunt." Even when Davey poked at her through the bars, she sat passively. "She's not afraid anymore."

"Sometimes they go mad. Their minds are weak, after all, like their bodies." Lilith gestured to another cage. "What about this one?"

The man in it was rocking a woman who was either asleep or unconscious. There was blood on her neck, and her face was pale as wax.

"Bitch. You bitch, what have you done to her? I'll kill you."

"Now this one's got some life left in him!" With a broad grin, Lilith tossed back her gilded mane of hair. "What do you think, my sweetie?"

Davey cocked his head, then shook it. "He won't run. He won't want to leave the female."

"Why, Davey, you're so perceptive." She crouched down, kissing his cheeks with obvious pride. "Such a big boy, and so wise."

"I want this one." He pointed at a woman who'd pressed herself to the back of the cage. Her eyes darted everywhere. "She's afraid, and she thinks that maybe, maybe, she can still get out so she'll run, and run and run. And him." Davey gestured up. "He's mad, he wants to *fight*. See the way he shakes the bars."

"I think those are excellent choices." She snapped her fingers at one of the guards, both of whom wore light armor and skull-caps. "Release those two, and pass the word. Except for preventing them from leaving the caves, they're not to be touched. They belong to the prince."

Davey jumped up and down, clapped his hands. "Thank you, Mama! Do you want to play with me? I'll share with you."

"That's so sweet, but I have some work to see to now. And remember to wash up when you're finished eating." She turned to one of the guards again. "Tell Lady Lora I want her to join me, in the wizard's cave."

"That one first." Davey pointed to the woman.

She screamed and struggled as the guard dragged her out of the cage, while another guard beat back at the ones with her who tried to pull her back inside.

Everything inside Larkin strained to do something. Anything.

Davey bent down, sniffing at the shuddering woman to imprint her scent. "You're mine now, and I get to play with you as long as I want. Isn't that right, Mama?"

"That's right, my darling."

"Let her go," Davey ordered the guard. Then his eyes flashed red as he looked at the woman. "Run. Run, run! Hide-and-seek!" he shouted when she stumbled out.

He leaped onto the wall, clung there as he shot a grin over his shoulder at Lilith. And he slithered out into the dark.

"It's nice to see him having such a good time. Turn the other loose in, oh, fifteen minutes. I'll be with the wizard for the time being."

He could come back, Larkin told himself. Once he'd done what he'd come to do, he could go back, create a diversion, unlock the cages. At least give the prisoners a fighting chance to escape. To survive.

But now, blocking out the moans and screams along with his own needs, he followed Lilith.

The prison was separated from what he supposed were living quarters, storage and work areas, by a long tunnel. She'd built a kind of mansion under the ground, he realized. Chamber flowed after chamber, some of them richly furnished, some sealed off with doors and guarded.

Two, a man and female both in black jeans and sweaters, carried fresh linens down the tunnel. Obviously servants, he decided, and thought they were likely human servants. Both stopped as Lilith approached, bowed deeply.

Lilith glided on as if they weren't there.

He heard the sounds of combat and

paused to looked down a tunnel. A training area, not that dissimilar from what they used at Cian's. Here the creatures, male and female, practiced with sword or mace, dagger, or bare hands.

Two prisoners, unarmed and shackled, were being used much as he and his circle used practice dummies.

He saw the one called Lora clashing steel with a male of superior size. They wore no protective gear, and the swords, he saw, were honed to a killing edge.

Lora leaped up and over her sparring partner, the movement so fast it was merely a blur. Even as he pivoted, she ran the sword through his chest.

And as he fell, she leaped on him. "You miss that one every time." She leaned down, playfully lapped at the blood. "If you were human, *mon cher,* you'd be dead."

"No one can best you with a sword." His breathing was ragged, but he reached up to stroke a hand down her cheek. "I don't know why I try."

"If Lilith didn't need me, we'd go another round." She trailed a finger down his check, licked the blood from it.

"Perhaps later . . . toward dawn."

"If the queen doesn't want me, I'll come to you." She leaned down again, and the kiss was long, ferocious.

She sheathed the bloody sword and strode out, with Larkin behind her.

She barely paused as the woman who'd been freed to run fell in front of her weeping. Lora merely stepped over her, glanced up to the pair of red eyes glowing in the dark. "Playing tag, Davey?"

"I wanted to play hide-and-seek, but she keeps falling down. Make her get up, Lora! Make her run some more. I haven't finished the game yet."

Lora let out a long-suffering sigh. *"Ca va."* She crouched down, lifted the woman's head by the hair. "If you don't run and keep our darling Davey amused, I'll cut off your fingers, one at a time. Then your toes." She got up, dragging the woman with her. "Now, *allez!* Scamper."

When the woman ran off weeping, Lora looked back up at Davey. "Why don't you give her more of a head start? It's more sporting and the game will last longer."

"It'd be more fun if you played. It's always more fun with you."

"And there's nothing I'd like better, but your mother wants me now. Perhaps later we can have another game." She blew him a kiss and continued on.

Sick to the depths, Larkin followed her.

She entered a chamber. Larkin felt the ripple of magic even as he darted in after her. The door shut with a hollow thud.

"Ah, Lora. We've been waiting for you."

"I was finishing up a bout with Lucius, then I ran into Davey. He's having such a good time."

"He's been pining for a game." Lilith held out a hand. Lora walked over, slipped hers into it. Together, nearly cheek-to-cheek, they looked at the man who stood in the center of the room.

He wore black robes edged in red. His hair was a thick mane of silver around a face that boasted eyes dark as onyx, a long, hooked nose, a thin, unsmiling mouth.

There was a fire behind him that burned without hearth or log or turf. Suspended above it was a cauldron that spilled out pale green smoke, the same color as the light that glowed sickly through the caves. Two long tables held vials and jars. Whatever swam in them looked viscous, and alive.

"Midir." Lilith gestured toward the man with a wide sweep of her arm. "I wanted Lora with us when we had this discussion. She keeps me calm. As you know I've needed time to compose myself after that disaster a few days ago."

She wandered over, picked up a carafe,

poured the red liquid from it into a glass. Sniffed. "Fresh?" she asked him.

"Yes, my lady. Tapped and prepared for you."

She sipped, offered the glass to Lora. "I should ask if you're fully recovered from your injuries."

"I am well, my lady."

"I'd apologize for losing my temper, but you disappointed me, Midir. Extremely. Your punishment would have been more severe if Lora hadn't cooled that temper. They snatched those *cows* out from under my nose. They left an insulting message on my very doorstep. It was for you to protect my home from such matters, and you failed, miserably."

"I am prostrate, my lady." He knelt, bowed his head. "I was not prepared for the attempt, nor for the force of the power they held. It will never happen again."

"It certainly won't if I give you to Lora. Do you know how long she can keep a man alive?" She glanced over at her companion with a soft and knowing smile.

"There was the one in Budapest," Lora recalled. "I kept him six months. I could have gone longer, but I got bored with him. I don't think Midir would bore me for years. But . . ."

Lora ran her hand up and down Lilith's back. "He's of use, *chérie*. He has great power, and he's bound to you, *n'est-ce pas?*"

"He made me promises, a great many promises. Don't speak," she snapped when Midir lifted his head again. "Because of those promises, he's yet to feel my bite. But you're my dog, Midir, and never forget it."

Slowly now, he raised his head. "I serve you, Majesty, and only you. I sought you out, my lady, to give you the portal, so you may walk between worlds, and rule them all."

"And so you can walk between them, wizard, plucking power like daisies with my army at your back. And still this power broke when struck by what the mortals wielded."

"They should never have gotten by him, it's true." Again, Lora soothed. "He allowed them to humiliate you, and that is unforgivable. Still, we are more with him than without him. With him, we'll have all by Samhain."

"See? She keeps me calm." Lilith took the goblet back from Lora as they stood, arms circling each other's waists. "You're alive because of what she said — as I agree with her. And because you at least had the good sense to bring on the dark once we understood we had been breached. Oh, stand up, stand up."

He rose. "My lady, may I speak?"

"I left the tongue in your mouth."

"I have pledged my power and my life to you, and have dedicated that life and power for more than two hundred years to you. I have made this place for you, as you commanded, under the ground, and cloaked it from the human eye. It is I who carved the portal so that you and your army may travel between worlds, so that you, my queen, may go to Geall and ravage, and reign."

She angled her head and a pretty smile curved her mouth. "Yes. But what have you done for me lately?"

"Even my power has limits, my lady, and it takes a great deal to hold the cloak. The magic these others hold is strong, and still, in the end, I felled them."

"True, true. But after they picked my pockets."

"They are formidable, my lady." He folded his hands so they disappeared within the wide sleeves of his robes. "Less would hardly be worthy of you. And your triumph will be only greater when you destroy them."

"Sweet talker."

"He did nearly get me into the house," Lora said. "So close, I could almost taste her. It was a good spell, a strong one to bend the hunter's will. We could try it again."

"We could," Midir agreed. "But it is only

two weeks until we reopen the portal. I will need my strength for that, Majesty. And another sacrifice."

"Another?" Lilith rolled her eyes. "How tedious. And a virgin again, I assume."

"If you would, my lady. In the meanwhile, I have a gift which I hope pleases you."

"More diamonds?" She tapped a hand in front of her mouth in a delicate yawn. "I grow weary."

"No, my lady, not diamonds. More precious, I think." He picked a small hand mirror by its bone handle, offered it.

"Do you toy with me? Such a trinket only . . ." She let out a gasp as she twirled it by the handle. "Is this my face!" Stunned, she touched a hand to her own cheek, stared into the glass.

It was as if she looked through a thin mist, but she could see the shape of her face, her eyes, her mouth. The joy of it brought tears to her eyes.

"Oh. Oh, I can see who I am. I'm beautiful. See, my eyes are blue. Such a pretty blue."

"Let me —" Lora squeezed close, her eyes widening as she saw herself in the little glass with Lilith. "Oh! *C'est magnifique! Je suis belle.*"

"Look at us, Lora. Oh, oh, see how wonderful we are!"

"So much better than a photograph or a drawing. See, we move! Look how our cheeks press together."

"I am here," Lilith murmured. "So long ago, before I was given the gift, I saw my face in polished glass, in the clear water of a lake. The shape of it, and how my hair tumbled down to frame that shape."

She touched her hair now, watching her fingers move through it. "The way my lips, my cheeks would move with a smile, the way my eyebrows will lift and fall. And last, the last time I saw this face, it was in the eyes of the one who sired me. Two thousand years have passed since I've looked into my own eyes." A tear trickled down her cheek, and its reflection enchanted her. "I'm here," she said quietly, a voice thick with emotion. "I'm here."

"You're pleased, Your Majesty?" Midir lowered his folded hands to his waist. "I thought it your fondest wish."

"I have never had such a gift. Look! How my mouth moves when I speak. I want a great one, Midir, a big one so I can see the whole of me at once."

"I believe it can be done, but it would take time and power. The portal . . ."

"Of course, of course." Lilith angled the mirror from overhead to try to see more of herself. "I'm as greedy as Davey, demanding more even as I hold a treasure in my hands. Midir, you've pleased me beyond measure. I'll have what you need brought to you."

When he bowed she walked to him, touched his cheek. "Beyond measure," she repeated. "I won't forget that you troubled to touch my heart."

Larkin scurried out after them. Since they spoke of nothing now but the mirror and their own beauty, he veered off to look for their arsenal, to get a clearer idea of their numbers.

He streaked down darkened tunnels, squeezed under doors. In one chamber he found three vampires feasting on a man. When the man moaned, Larkin's shock made him careless. One of them spotted him, and lifted its bloody face in a smile.

"Wouldn't mind a little rat for dessert."

As he pounced, Larkin shot under the doorway again, and across to the next, streaking between the feet of the guard and under.

Into the arsenal.

Weapons for a thousand, he realized. For a thousand and more. Sword and lance, bow and ax, all stored with a military precision that told him this was indeed an army, and not just a pack of animals.

And this they would take to Geall to destroy it.

Well, he'd give them some trouble first.

Turning into a man, he took the single torch from the wall to set the tables, the chests, the cabinets to light.

Distraction and destruction, he thought, tossing the torch aside before turning back into the rat again.

As fast as he could, he went back to the area where the prisoners were kept. He saw the man the boy had chosen was no longer in his cage. So he was too late to save him or the woman. But there were others, more than twenty others, and he would give them a chance at least.

There was only one guard now, leaning up against the wall and despite the moans and pleas, he seemed to be half dozing.

It would take speed and it would take luck, Larkin thought. He was counting on having both. He changed into a man, grabbed the sword at the vampire's side, swung it hard.

As the dust exploded, the screams from the cages were deafening.

"You have to run." He grabbed the keys from the hook on the wall and began to unlock cages. He shoved the sword into the hands of a man who looked at it blankly.

"You can hurt them with that," Larkin said quickly. "Kill them if you cut off the head. Kill them with fire. There are torches in the tunnels. Use them. Here." He shoved the keys into another pair of hands. "Unlock the rest. Then run. Some of you may get out. I'm going to do what I can to keep the way clear."

Though he knew he risked draining his energy, he changed once more as the chaos whirled around him. Into a wolf that sprang out of the doorway.

He veered left, hoping to buy time and charged the first vampire he saw. He took it by surprise, ripped out its throat. Muzzle dripping, he ran.

He'd hoped the fire he'd set in the arsenal would keep many of them busy. But he heard no alarm as yet.

He saw two carrying bodies to a stack of more dead. Tossed, he thought, like offal. As he ran, he changed, and as he changed he reached for a sword.

He took them both with one blow.

There was shouting now, not the human screaming, but sounds of alarm and fury. Once more he changed into the wolf to use its speed. He could do no more than he had done.

He swung down a tunnel, and he saw the boy.

He was crouched on the ground, feasting on the man who'd been in the cage. The child's shiny hair was streaked with blood, and it dripped from his fingers, from his lips.

The low growl that rumbled out of Larkin's throat had the boy looking up. "Doggie!" Davey grinned, horribly. "None for you until I'm finished. I'm done with that one, so you can have it if you want."

He gestured toward the woman who lay facedown a few feet away.

"She wasn't as much fun as this one, so I finished quick."

Beyond rage, Larkin bunched to spring.

"Davey, there you are!" The one who'd sparred with Lora clipped quickly down the tunnel. "Your mother wants you in your chambers. Some of the humans are loose, and they've managed to set a fire."

"But I haven't finished yet."

"You'll have to finish later. Are these both your kills?" He crouched down to give Davey a congratulatory pat on the back. "Good for you. But if you eat any more, you'll just get sick. I'll send someone down, have these taken to the heap, but for now, you need to come with me."

He glanced over as he spoke, eyeing Larkin. "One of your mother's wolves? I thought she'd sent them all —"

Larkin saw the change on its face, the sudden bracing of its body. He leaped, but missed the throat as the vampire blocked the charge. The force of the blow hurled Larkin against the wall, but he was up quickly, charging again before the thing could clear its sword.

There was screaming, horrible screaming and his own snarls and snaps. The part of him that was wolf lusted for blood as much as the man inside it lusted for vengeance.

He sank his claws into the thing's shoulder, its chest.

Then there was pain, unspeakable pain as the child leaped on his back and used his fangs.

With a howl, Larkin reared back, managed to shake the boy off. But he was up quickly, and the one on the ground was reaching for its sword.

The wolf was done, and Larkin prayed he had enough left in him to get out, and away.

His light sparked, shimmered weakly. There was more pain, and with it now a dragging weakness. But he became the mouse, small and quick, slipping into shadows and hunting the sound of the sea.

The fire in the back of his neck burned to the bone. The caves echoed with screams, running feet. He was nearly trod on as his strength and his speed wavered, but continued to head toward the thin wash of moonlight, the roar of the sea.

There were people running, clawing their way up the cliff wall. Some carried the weak, the wounded. Larkin knew if he attempted a change again, he'd need to be carried himself.

He could do nothing more. With what he had left, he dragged his small body to a rock, wedged himself behind it.

The last thing he saw was the flicker of stars going out as dawn crept closer.

CHAPTER 8

"He should have been back by now." From the window in the parlor, Blair watched dawn break through the long night. "On his way back anyway. Maybe you should start again." She turned around to Hoyt and Glenna. "Just start again."

"Blair." Glenna crossed over, ran a hand up and down Blair's arm. "I promise you, as soon as he can be seen, we'll see."

"It was a stupid idea. Reckless and stupid. What was I thinking? I sent him in there."

"No." Now Glenna gripped both of her arms. "He went in, and we all agreed. We're all equal in this. None of us bears all the burden."

"He went in there without a weapon, without a shield." She closed her hand over her crosses.

"He could hardly fly or crawl or slither around a nest of vampires with a cross around his neck," Cian pointed out. "A beacon like that? He wouldn't have lasted five minutes."

"So what? He lasts ten going in naked."

"He's not dead." Moira spoke quietly, and continued to sit on the floor, staring at the fire. "I'd know. I think we'd all know. The circle would be broken." She looked over her shoulder at Hoyt. "Isn't that so?"

"I believe it is, yes. It may be as simple as he needed to rest. Maintaining other shapes must take considerable energy and concentration."

"It does. That's why he eats like a plow horse." Scooting to face the room, Moira managed a weak smile. "And he's never, that I know, held a shape above two or three hours."

Another nightmare, Blair thought. To imagine him skulking around the caves as the rat they'd agreed on, then, whoops, he's a human without so much as a Popsicle stick to defend himself.

Alive, she could hold on to that. It made sense that they'd feel it if he'd been killed. But he could be in a cage, hurt, being tortured.

"I'm going to go make some food." Glenna gave Blair's shoulder a comforting pat.

"I'll do it. I should practice more with the cooking," Moira said as she got to her feet. "And I need something to do besides sit and worry."

"I'll give you a hand." Glenna draped an arm over Moira's shoulders. "I'll bring out some coffee in a few minutes."

"I'm going out." Hoyt pushed himself out of the chair. "It may be I can draw something, sense something, outside the confines of the house."

"I'll go with you."

But he shook his head at Blair. "I'd do better alone."

What was she supposed to *do?* She wasn't used to standing and waiting. She was the one who went out, did the job, risked her skin. She wasn't supposed to stand and wring her hands while someone else was on the line.

"Would you mind closing those other drapes? Light's coming in from that side."

Baffled, she looked back. Cian was sprawled lazily in a chair — and the slant of light coming in the east windows was barely a foot from the tips of his boots.

She imagined most of his kind would have been scampering back in a fast hurry from that spread of light. Not Cian. She doubted they'd get a scamper out of him if they gave him a boot in front of a sunny window.

"Sure." She moved over, drew them, and plunged the room into gloom. She didn't bother with a lamp. Just then the dark was a comfort.

"What will they do to him? Don't lie, don't soften it. If they have him, what will they do to him?"

You know, Cian thought. You know already. "She'll have him tortured. For the entertainment value and for the practical purpose of getting information."

"He won't tell her —"

"Of course he will." Impatience whipped into Cian's voice. It was infuriating that he was attached enough to Larkin to worry about the boy.

"She can do things to a man no human being can withstand — and keep him just this side of alive while she's at it. He'll tell her anything. So would you, so would any of us. And does it matter?"

"Maybe not." She came over, gave in to her weak legs and sat on the table in front of his chair. He was giving her the truth, naked and without sentiment. It was what she needed. "She'll change him, won't she? That's the big coup, siring one of us."

"That would be two of us."

"Right. Right." She dropped her head in

her hands because it felt sick. As sick as her gut, as sick as her belly. "Cian. If . . . we'll have to . . ."

"Yes, we will."

"I don't think I can stand it. I don't think I could go on with this. If he's just dead, I can, because otherwise it would be like we wasted his life. But if she sends him back here changed, and we have to . . ." She lifted her head now, rubbed her hands over her damp cheeks. "How did you get through it? After King? Glenna told me you and King were tight, and you had to end him. How did you get through it?"

"I got piss-faced for a couple of days."

"Did it help?"

"Not particularly. I grieved and I drank, then I let the anger in. It's because of what was done to King, more than any other reason, that I'll see this through to the end." He angled his head, studying her. "You've fallen for him."

"What? It's not — I care about him, of course. All of us. We're a unit."

"Humans are so strange, their reactions to what they feel. The expressions of emotions. For you it seems to be embarrassment. Why is that? You're both young, healthy, and caught in a situation filled with passion and jeopardy. Why shouldn't you form an attachment?"

"It's not that simple."

"Not for you, apparently." He glanced over as Hoyt strode back in, and Blair sprang to her feet.

"There's a van on the lane there. The wheels are all ripped. There are some weapons in it."

Blair didn't bother with a jacket, but went out, jogged down the lane. The driver's door was open, she noted, with the key dangling from the ignition, as if someone had tried to start it, then abandoned it in a hurry.

There were a couple of swords and a cooler holding several packets of blood in the cargo area.

"Well, it's theirs," she said to Hoyt. "No question of that. And the chances of all four tires going flat come in at zero." She hunkered down, stuck her finger in the wide hole in the rubber. "Larkin did this, somehow."

"They must have abandoned it, taken to the woods, I'd think, to hide from the sun."

"Yeah." Her smile showed grim purpose. "At last I have something to do. I'll go get armed."

"I'll go with you."

She went into the forest with crossbow and stake, seeking out the shadows, moving like one. At the fork of a path, she and Hoyt separated, each moving deeper into light that was dappled and dim.

She found one cowering, curled on mossy ground in deep shade. A boy, she noted, no more than eighteen when he died. From his clothes — holey jeans and a faded sweatshirt, she imagined he'd probably been a student doing the backpacking thing.

"Sorry about this," she told him.

He hissed at her, crawled over to hide behind the trunk of a tree.

"Oh come on, like I can't still see you? Don't make me come up there."

She didn't hear the one coming behind her, but sensed it. Blair did a half pivot, lowered her right shoulder, so when it leaped at her back, she flipped it over.

This one was about the same age, a girl, and looked a lot more frisky.

"You two a couple? That's cute, and really bad luck."

The female charged, and Blair lowered the crossbow. She didn't just want a kill, she realized, she wanted a fight.

She dodged the kick, taking the brunt of it on the side of the hip, and the second in the small of the back. There was enough force to pitch her forward. She landed on her hands, sprang over, and planted the heel of her boot in the vampire's face.

"Kickboxing classes, huh?" She saw something in the eyes when it came back at her, when they traded blows. It hadn't fed, she realized, remembering the cooler in the van. It was desperate.

And prolonging the kill was only torturing it. This time when it charged, Blair pulled her stake and put it through the heart.

"Bitch. Stupid bitch." The one behind the tree shouted it out, and the heavy dose of New Jersey in the voice nearly amused her.

"Which one of us?"

When he leaped up, she rolled to her toes. But he began to run away. "Oh, for God's sake." She snatched up the crossbow, and put an arrow in him. "Coward."

She whirled at the sound behind her, then relaxed when she saw Hoyt coming along the path. "Only one," he told her.

"Two here. There may be more, but they'll have gone deeper. We should get back, see if there's any word on Larkin."

"I couldn't sense anything, but neither could I sense his death. He's a clever man, Blair, resourceful, as you can see by what he did with the wheels on the van."

"Yeah. He's nobody's jackass, even if he can change into one."

"I know what it is to care about someone, and to worry for their life." As they walked, Hoyt's eyes tracked through the trees, alert and watchful. "We can defend each other in this, but we can't protect each other. Glenna taught me the difference."

"I never had to worry about anyone before. I don't think I'm very good at it."

"I can tell you that the skill of it comes entirely too easily."

When they stepped out of the woods Moira was running out of the house as if it had burst into flame. The light of absolute joy on her face had all the fear inside Blair dropping away.

"He's coming back!" she shouted. "Larkin, he's coming home."

"There now." Hoyt put at an arm around Blair's shoulders as relief shook them. "So you needn't use that worry skill any more today."

It took everything he had to stay the hawk, to stay in the air. Pain and fatigue warred inside him, each threatening to break through and shatter the strength he had left. He'd lost blood, he knew that, but how much he couldn't say. He only knew the bite at the back of his neck was a constant searing fire.

There had been no one — human or vampire — in sight when he'd come to, after dawn, in his own shape. There'd been blood on the shale, not all his own. Not enough, he comforted himself, not enough of it to mean all he'd freed had been slaughtered.

Surely some had made it. Even one . . .

He felt himself falter, felt his wing try to tremble itself into an arm. He bore down, calling the hawk to hold him.

There the river, he thought. There the Shannon. He was well toward home now.

He brought Blair's face into his mind, that two-pointed smile, the strong blue of her eyes, the quick music of her voice. He would make it, he would make these last miles.

He could feel his heart — the hawk's — racing, too fast. Even breathing was a vicious strain, and his vision was no longer sharp. There was something else inside him, something the demon in a child's form had put in him. Inside him, pumping into his own blood, poisoning it.

A weakness, the dark of it, whispered slyly that he should just let go.

Then he heard something else, stronger.

You're almost home, bird-boy. Keep going, you're almost back. We're waiting for you. Going to make you the breakfast of champions — all-you-can-eat buffet. Come on, Larkin, come home.

Blair. He held on to the sound of her voice, and flew.

There were the woods, and the pretty

stream, and the stone house and stables. And beyond them, the graveyard where he was damn well determined not to end up now that he was so close.

There! There was Blair, outside the house with her face tipped up to the sky so he could see it. Her eyes. And there was Moira, his sweetheart, and the others save Cian. He gave one heartfelt prayer of thanks to all the gods.

Then his strength simply dissolved. He fell the last ten feet to the ground as a man.

"Oh God, oh God!" Blair sprinted to him, reaching him a full stride before the others. "Wait, be careful. We have to see if he broke anything."

She began to run her hands over him even as Glenna did the same. Then she felt the raw skin at the back of his neck, and slowly brushed his hair aside.

She stared up into Moira's brimming eyes. "He's been bitten."

"Oh God, sweet God. But he's not changed." Moira lifted one of his limp hands to her lips. "He couldn't be out in the sun if he'd been changed."

"No, not changed. And not broken. Banged up pretty good. His pulse is really thready, Glenna."

"Let's get him inside."

"He needs food." Moira hurried ahead as Hoyt and Blair lifted Larkin. "It would be like one of us going without food for days. Food and liquids. I'll get something."

"The sofa in the parlor," Glenna ordered. "I'll go get what I need."

Once they'd laid him on the sofa, Blair crouched by his head. He was white as death, and bruises were already gathering. "It's okay, you're home now. That's what counts. You're home."

"Cian — Cian said to start with this." Moira rushed in with a large glass of orange juice. "To get the fluids and the sugar into him."

"Yeah, good. Gotta bring him around. Come on, fly-boy."

"Here, let me try this." Glenna knelt at the side of the sofa. She dipped her thumb into a jar of balm, smeared it first on the center of his forehead. "On the chakras," she explained as she worked. "A little chi balancing. Moira, take his other hand, push some of your strength out. You know how. Blair, talk to him again, the way I told you to when he was flying. It'll reach him. Hoyt?"

"Yes." Hoyt laid his hands on either side of Blair's head. "Tell him to come back."

"Come on, Larkin, you've got to wake up.

Can't just lie around all day. Besides, break-fast is ready. Please wake up now. I've been waiting for you." She pressed his hand to her cheek. "Watching for you. His fingers moved! All the way out, Larkin, that's enough damn drama for the day."

His eyelids fluttered. "Why are women al-ways nagging a man?"

"Guess that's just what it takes," she man-aged.

"Here we are now, here." Moira moved around the couch to lift his head, to hold the glass to it.

He drank like a camel, then managed to smile at her. "There's my sweetheart. Look at this, what a picture. Three beautiful faces. I'd give you all my worldly goods and a life-time of devotion if you'd get me something to eat."

It was Cian who stepped in, holding a small plate with two pieces of dry toast. "You'll need to start slow." He exchanged a look with Blair. She met it, then squeezed her eyes shut. Nodded.

"Don't bolt it down," she warned.

"Just bread. Can't I have meat? I swear I could eat a whole side of venison. Or that lovely dish you make, Glenna, with the balls of meat and the noodles."

"I'll make it tonight."

"You need to have just enough to take the edge off," Blair began, "to get a little strength back. You eat a full meal, you'll just boot it — vomit," she explained, "when we're taking care of the bite."

"It was the little one, her boy. Little bastard. I was a wolf at the time, so it didn't go as deep as it might have."

"Glenna has balm. She used it on me when I was bitten." Moira stroked Larkin's hair. "It's a terrible burn, I know, but the balm cools it."

"You weren't bitten," Cian said flatly. "A scrape, not a puncture."

"What difference does it make?"

"Quite a bit." Blair straightened. "There's infection, and there's also considerable risk of the one who bit you having some control over you."

"Aye." Larkin frowned, closed his eyes. "I felt something working in me. But —"

"We'll take care of it. It needs to be purified with holy water."

"That's fine. Then if I could have the lovely balm Moira spoke of, and a meal, I'd be good as new — but for the fact every bone of my body feels as if it's been hit with a hammer."

Straight truth, Blair thought. Straight, hard truth. "Do you know the burn you felt when it sank into you? The burn you're feeling now?"

"I do."

"This will be a lot worse. I'm sorry." She walked out, hurried up the steps. And Moira rushed out behind her.

"There must be another way. How can we hurt him again? He's still so weak, and already in pain. I can see the pain in his eyes."

"You think I can't?" She swung into her room. "There is no other way."

"I know it says there isn't in the books. I've read them. But with Glenna and Hoyt —"

Blair pulled a bottle of holy water from her kit, and her face was set when she whirled around. "There *is* no other way. He's infected. That puts him and all of us at risk." She shot out her arm, turned up her wrist to show the scar. "I know what it's like. If there was another way, don't you think I'd try it?"

Moira shuddered out a breath. "What can I do?"

"You can help hold him down."

She took down towels, bandages. She made herself walk to Larkin, look straight into his eyes. "This is going to hurt."

"It's going to hurt," Cian added, "like a motherfucker."

"Oh well." Larkin licked his lips. "That's heartening."

"I might be able to block some of the pain," Glenna began.

"I don't think you can, or should." Blair shook her head. "It's part of it. It's the way it's done. Here, we need to get him on the floor, facedown. Get those towels under him. Cian, you'd better take his feet. Wouldn't want any to splash on you."

Larkin winced as they shifted him. "What would he need to take my feet for?"

"We're going to hold you down," Blair told Larkin.

"I don't need —"

"Yes, you will."

He met her eyes again, saw what was in them. "You do it then. I trust you to see it through."

With Cian at his feet, Hoyt on one side and both women on the other, Blair opened the bottle. She brushed his hair clear, exposed the raw bite.

"Under these circumstances, it's not considered unmanly to scream. Brace yourself," she warned him, and poured the blessed water on the wound.

He did scream. And his body arched up, bucked. The wound itself seemed to boil, and she let the viscous liquid that bubbled out run as she continued, ruthlessly, to douse it with water.

She flashed back to the night she'd had to go to her aunt, less than a week after her father had left her. And how her aunt's tears had run down her face as she poured the water over the bite on Blair's wrist.

How it had felt as if the flesh, the bones were being seared with a burning knife.

When the wound ran clear and he was gasping for breath, she used towels to wipe it clean, to dry it. "The balm would probably help now."

White as a sheet, Glenna fumbled for the jar. Now her tears fell on him. "I'm sorry, Larkin. I'm so sorry. Can I help him sleep now? Even for an hour?"

Blair swiped the back of her hand over her mouth. "Sure, it's done. He could use a little sleep."

Again, she rushed upstairs. She dashed into her room, slamming the door behind her. Then she dropped down on the floor at the foot of her bed, wrapped her arms around her head and sobbed.

She cringed away when an arm came around her, but it only wrapped tighter. "You were so brave," Moira crooned, like a mother lulling a child. "So strong and so brave. I try to be, and it's so very hard. I want to believe I could have done what you did, for I love him so much."

"I'm sick, I feel sick."

"I know, so do I. Can we hold on to each other for a bit, do you think?"

"I can't feel like this. It doesn't help."

"I think it does. To care, even to hurt. Cian fixed him juice and toasted bread. I couldn't have imagined it. But he cares. It's impossible not to care for Larkin. And if you love him —"

Blair lifted her head, brushed at tears. "I don't want to go there again."

"Well, if you were to love him, you'd have a happy and unusual life. Would you show me how to make the French toast? He'd be pleased to have it when he wakes up."

"Yeah. Yeah, sure. I'll just go splash some water on my face, and be right down." They got up. "Moira? I can't be good for him. I'm not good for anyone."

Moira paused at the door. "That would be up to him, wouldn't it, as much as you?"

He was still pale when he woke, but his eyes were clear. He insisted on eating at the table, within easy reach, he said, of food.

He plowed through French toast, eggs, and bacon with a slow and studied pace. As he ate, he told them what he'd done and seen and heard.

"So many changes, Larkin. You know you shouldn't —"

"Now, don't scold me, Moira. It's all come out all right, hasn't it? Could I have more of the Coke?" He sent a sweet, charming smile with the request.

"It wasn't a rescue mission." Since she was closer, Blair yanked open the refrigerator, grabbed another bottle of Coke. "We specifically talked about that."

"You'd have done the same. Oh, don't shake your head and glower at me." He snagged the bottle. "I had to try, and any of us would have done the same. You didn't see, you didn't hear. It couldn't be walked away from, not without some attempt to help. And the truth of it is, I've been wanting to light a blaze in there for some time."

He looked at Cian now. "Since King."

"He'd have appreciated the gesture."

"It nearly killed you," Blair pointed out.

"War's meant to kill, isn't it? I should have left the boy be — what looked like a boy. But what it was doing . . . I lost the sense of it then, no denying that, and only wanted to end him. That was useless and stupid." He reached around to touch his fingers to the bandage at the back of his neck. "And I won't forget what it cost me."

Then he shrugged, scooped up more eggs. "So . . . She wasn't happy with this wizard, this Midir."

"I know the name," Hoyt put in. "He was infamous — before my time," he added. "Black magicks, raising demons to do his bidding."

Larkin guzzled Coke from the bottle. "He's doing her bidding now."

"It was said he was devoured by his own power. In a way, I suppose he was."

"I think she intended to punish him, or to let the other one — Lora — have a go at him. But when he gave her the mirror, the magic one — she went all soft and dazzled. She and the other one, mesmerized they were by their own faces."

"There's considerable vanity there," Cian told him. "It would be a great thrill to see their reflections after so long."

"It wasn't what I was expecting, their — well, human reaction, or so it seemed. And the, ah, affection between the women seemed genuine."

"He's being delicate," Cian said. "Lilith and Lora are lovers. They both take others, of course, often at the same time, but they're mates, and sincerely devoted to each other. The relationship isn't without its dysfunction, but has held for four hundred years."

"How do you know?" Blair asked him.

"Lora and I had — what should we call it? A fling? This would have been, hmm, in the early 1800s, in Prague, if memory serves. She and Lilith were having one of their spats. Lora and I enjoyed ourselves for a few nights. Then she tried to kill me, and I threw her out the window."

"Tough breakup," Blair murmured.

"Ah, well, she's Lilith's creature, whoever else she might play with from time to time. I knew it before she tried to stake me. As for the boy, I don't know about him. A more recent addition to her cadre, I'd say."

"Family," Larkin corrected. "I know there's something deviant between them, but in some way, she thinks of him as a son, and he of her as his mother."

"That makes them weaknesses." Hoyt nodded. "The boy and the French woman."

"Davey. It's what she called him," Larkin added.

Hoyt nodded. A name was always useful. "If we could capture or destroy either of them, it would be a blow to her."

"She's not leaving for Geall as soon as we are," Blair mused. "Maybe we can set up some traps. We can't know where they'll come out on the other side, not exactly, but we may be able to do something. Anyway, we've got a few days to think about it."

"And we will. Now we're all tired. We all need some sleep." Glenna laid her hands on Larkin's shoulders. "You need to get your strength back, handsome."

"I'm feeling more myself. Thank you. But it's the pure truth I could use a bed." He got to his feet. "There, it seems my legs will hold me now. Would you come up with me, Blair? I'd like to have a word."

"Yeah, all right." She went up the back way with him. She wanted to keep her hands in her pockets, but he seemed a little unsteady on the stairs. So she took his arm, pulled it around her shoulder. "Here, lean on me."

"I wouldn't mind. I wanted to thank you for taking care of me."

"Don't." It made her stomach clench. "Don't thank me for that."

"You tended to me, and I will thank you. I heard your voice. When I was flying home, and I wasn't sure I could make it, I heard your voice. And I knew I could."

"I thought she had you. I imagined you in a cage, and that was worse than thinking you might be dead. I don't want to be that scared, I don't want to feel that helpless."

"I don't know how to keep that from happening." He was out of breath when they reached his room, grateful for the help to his bed. "Would you lie with me?"

She managed to get him down, then gaped at him. "What?"

"Oh, not that way." With a laugh, he took her hand. "I don't think I've got that in me just yet, but it's a lovely thought for another time. Wouldn't you lie here with me, *a stór,* sleep with me for a while?"

After the pain she'd given him, she'd assumed she'd be the last person he'd want to be with. But here he was, holding out a hand for hers.

"Just sleep." She laid down beside him, turned in so she could see his face. "No fooling around."

"Is having my arm around you fooling around?"

"No."

"And one kiss?"

"One." She touched her lips to his. "Close your eyes."

He did, on a sigh. "It's good to be home again."

"Are you in any pain?"

"Not really. A bit sore is all."

"You're lucky."

He opened his eyes again. "Couldn't you say I was skilled and courageous?"

"Maybe that, too. And I can add smart. Unicorn horn versus Goodyear. I really like that one."

She laid her hand on his heart, closed her eyes. And slept.

CHAPTER 9

It was the stiffness in his own bones that woke him. Larkin lay there a few minutes wondering if this was how he'd feel every blessed morning when he was an old man. Sort of whifty in the head and heavy in the body. Maybe it was such a gradual thing that the mind adjusted so you forgot what it was to feel young and spry.

He swore he creaked when he rolled over.

Of course she was gone. He probably couldn't have managed to make love with her if she'd stayed — if he'd been able to talk her into it. She was a puzzler, Blair was. So strong, all but steely, and a goddess in battle. But there were all these layers inside, soft ones, bruised ones.

A man just wanted to peel off that hard edge and get to the heart of the matter.

And she was so interesting to look at. The hair like a soft cap, so dark against her white skin. Those deep eyes of magic blue that looked right at you. No coyness at all. Sometimes he just liked to watch her mouth move whatever words were coming out of it, to see all the shapes it could make.

Then there was her form, all lean and tight. Sleek, really. He couldn't say he minded overmuch her trouncing him in hand-to-hand, not when he had that body bumping up against his. Long legs and arms, those strong shoulders that were often bare during training. Those lovely firm breasts.

He'd thought quite a bit about her breasts.

And now he was stirring himself up with no place to go with it.

He got up, wincing. He supposed, all things considered, he was lucky to have gotten off just sore and bruised. He had Glenna to thank for that, and maybe he'd seek her out, see if she could do a bit more now that he was rested.

He took a shower, giving into the luxury of running the water hot as he could stand. He would miss this, that was the sheer truth. He wondered if Moira, who was clever with figuring how things worked, could build one in Geall.

Once he was dressed, he wandered out. The house was quiet enough he wondered if the others were still sleeping, and considered going down to the kitchen. He was hungry again, and no surprise there.

But he doubted he'd find Blair in the kitchen. He thought he knew well enough where she'd be.

He heard her music before he reached the training room. It wasn't the same music as she'd been playing in the kitchen the other day. There was a woman singing now, in a rough, fascinating voice about wanting a little respect when she came home.

Well, it didn't seem too much to be asking, in Larkin's opinion.

And there was Blair, stripped down to the little white shirt and the black pants that sat low on her hips — a personal favorite of his, truth be known.

She was tumbling, he noted. And using most of the big room to do it. Handsprings, kicks and flips. At one point, she rolled to a sword that lay on the floor and began to fight what must have been a multitude of invisible opponents.

He waited until she gave a last thrust, her body posed in a deep warrior position.

"Well, you slaughtered the lot of them."

Only her head moved first, turning until her eyes met his. Then she brought her feet together, lowered the sword. "Nothing but dust."

She walked over to set down the sword, turned the music down, then picked up a bottle of water. Drinking, she took a good long look at him. His face was bruised, scraped along the temple — which for some reason didn't make him less of a looker, she decided.

In any case, his color was good.

"How're you doing?"

"Well enough, though I'd've been better if you'd been beside me when I woke."

"Didn't know how long you'd need to sleep. How's the bite?"

"Barely know it's there." He moved to her, took her hand, turned up her wrist. "We'll both have our scars now."

"Your hair's wet."

"I got in the shower. My bones were aching, and I think I smelled fairly ripe after my night of it."

"You'll have soaked the bandage." She frowned as she nudged him around. "Let me have a look."

"Itches mostly," he said, enjoying having her fingers in his hair, on his skin.

"It's healing fast. Glenna's magic balm. Boy, I wish I'd had some of that after my round. Guess you'll do."

"Will I?" He turned, gripped her waist, then boosted her up so she sat on the table.

"Careful there, Bunky, you're not off the disabled list."

"I don't know what you're talking about. Doesn't matter so much. I was thinking before how I like watching your mouth move." He rubbed his thumb over her bottom lip. "It's got such energy."

"Didn't you wake up all frisky? I think you'd better —"

It was as far as she got before her mouth was very busy.

He didn't just taste this time but feasted. Didn't just sample, but possessed. This was more hunger, more demand than she'd been prepared for, the sort that swamped mind and body and left her floundering with need.

She hadn't put her defenses up, not in time. Now it was too late to do anything but meet the assault.

She'd yielded, just a little, just enough, then the heat flooded back into her. He could feel it, pouring out and up, and through him, a glorious scorching. He ran his hands over her, touching, finally touching, up the lean torso, over firm breasts, along strong shoulders and back again.

He felt her shudder of response, heard the moan of it catch in her throat, and knew she'd belong to him.

But she pressed her hands to his chest.

"Wait. Wait. Let's step back a minute."

Her voice was thick and breathy, and made him want to lap her up like cream. "Why?"

"I don't know, but I'll think of a reason in a minute, as soon as my IQ goes back up above the level of a turnip."

"I don't know what your eye queue might be, but the rest of you is perfect."

She managed a laugh but kept her hands firm so his mouth wouldn't take hers again and fry her brain a second time. "I'm not. Not nearly perfect. And it's not that I don't think diving into this would feel really good. *Really* good. More than likely we're going to end up doing just that eventually. But it's complicated, Larkin."

"Things are as simple or as complicated as you make them."

"No. Sometimes things just are. You don't even know me."

"Blair Murphy, demon hunter. That's what you'd think of first — that's what you've been taught to think of first. But it's not nearly the whole of you. Strong, for certain, and full of courage."

She started to interrupt, but he laid a finger on her lips. "But there's more in you than valor and duty. You've soft places in your heart. I saw them when Glenna and Hoyt handfasted. You fussed with the flowers and the candles because you wanted them to have their moment. You knew they loved, and that it's important. There was sweetness in that."

"Larkin —"

"And you've been hurt. The bruises are all inside, all wrapped up where no one should see them. Hurting makes you think you're alone, that you need to be. But you're not. I know you've fought your whole life against something horrible, and you've never turned away from it. And even so, you can smile, and laugh, and get dewy-eyed when two people in love make promises to each other. I don't know your favorite color or what book you last read when you had a moment of leisure, but I know you."

"I don't know what to do about you," she said when she could speak again. "I really don't. That's not the way it's supposed to be for me. I'm always supposed to know."

"And no surprises? I'm happy to change that for you. Well, since I don't think I'm going to be getting the clothes off you right at the moment, why don't we have a walk."

"Ah . . . Hoyt and I did a sweep through the woods this morning. Took out three."

"I didn't say a hunt. A walk. Just a walk. There's plenty of light left in the day."

"Oh. Ah —"

"You'll need a shirt, or a jacket. We'll go down through the kitchen, grab one for you. That way we can get ourselves a box of biscuits."

Just how strange was it, she wondered, to go walking over fields with a man in the late-afternoon sun? With no real purpose but to walk — no mission, no scouting, no hunt. Armed with sword and stake, and sugar cookies.

"Did you know, Hoyt will be staying here with Glenna after this is all done?"

She bit into a cookie, frowned at him. "Here, in Ireland? How do you know?"

"We talk of things, Hoyt and I, when we tend the horse. Here in Ireland, yes. In this place. Cian made them a gift of the house and land."

"Cian gave them the house?" She ate more cookie. "I can't figure him either. I know some vampires — or I've heard — go off the juice. Human juice. There are rumors, legends mostly, of some living among us, passing for human, going off the kill. I never really believed any of it."

"Passing as human doesn't make them so. And yet, Cian's one I'd trust more than most men. I wonder if living so long a life has something to do with it."

"Tell that to Lilith. She's got twice his years."

"Demons would have choices, wouldn't they? Go this way or that. I don't know the answers there. And when this is done, you'll go back to your Chicago?"

"I don't know." There was an itch between her shoulder blades at the thought of it. "Somewhere else, I think. Maybe New York for a while."

"Where Glenna lived. She showed me pictures of it. It's a marvel. Maybe you'll stay in Geall for a while. Like a holiday."

"Holiday in Geall." She shook her head. "Talk about marvels. Maybe. A few days anyway." It wasn't like she had anyone waiting for her to get back.

They walked to the cemetery, and the ruined chapel. Flowers still bloomed here, and the breeze whispered in the high grass.

"These are my people. It's so weird to know that. If it had been traced back this far, no one ever told me."

"Does it make you sad?"

"I don't know. A little I guess. Hoyt brought me here to show me where I came from. That's Nola's grave." She gestured to a stone where the flowers she'd laid days before were faded and dying. "She was the beginning of the family legacy. The start of it. One of her children would have been the first hunter. I don't know which one, and guess I'll never know. But at least one of them."

"Would you change it, if you could?"

"No." She looked over at him when he draped his arm over her shoulder. "Would you give up what you can do?"

"Not for all the gold in the Green Mountains. Especially now. Because it makes a difference now. When you have your holiday in Geall," he said as they walked on, "I'll take you to the Faerie Falls. We'll have a picnic."

"And back to food." She dug out a cookie, stuffed it in his mouth.

"We'll swim in the pool — the water's clear as blue crystal, and warm as well. After I'll make love to you on the soft grass while the water tumbles down beside us."

"And on to sex."

"Food and sex. What could be more pleasant to think about?"

She had to admit, he had a point. And couldn't deny that the simplicity of an afternoon walk had been an unexpected gift, more precious than she would have imagined.

"It's blue," she said. "My favorite color's blue."

He shot her a grin, took her hand so they walked linked over the hill, and down. "Look there. That's a pretty sight."

She saw Glenna and Hoyt in the herb garden, caught in an embrace. The garden thrived around them; the sun showered down. Glenna held a basket of herbs she'd harvested, and her free hand lay on Hoyt's cheek.

"Hear the mockingbird call?" Larkin asked, and she did, the happy little trill of it.

There was a quiet intimacy to the moment, something that couldn't be captured and preserved yet was enduring and universal. A miracle to find this, she thought, this normality, this heart against heart in all the horror.

She realized until she'd come here, she hadn't believed in miracles.

"This is why we'll win," Larkin said quietly.

"What?"

"This is why they can't beat us. We're stronger than they are."

"Not to spoil the moment, but physically they've got it all over the average human."

"Physically. But it's not all about brute strength, is it? It never is. They look to destroy, and we to survive. Survival's always stronger. And we have this." He nodded toward Hoyt and Glenna. "Love and kindness, compassion. Hope. Why else would two people make promises to each other at such a time, and mean to keep them? We won't give all this up, you see. We won't have it taken from us. We'll band together for this, and we'll never stop."

He heard Glenna laugh, and the sound of it reached into him, into that hope as she and Hoyt walked toward the house.

"You're thinking neither will they. Neither will they stop, but that doesn't change it, Blair. In the caves, I saw them in the cages. Some were beaten down, too tired, too frightened to do more than wait to die. But others rattled those cages and they cursed those bastards. And when I let them out, I saw more than fear, even more than hope in some of the faces. I saw bloody vengeance."

When he turned to look at her, Blair saw all of that in his face.

"I saw the stronger helping the weaker," he continued, "because that's what humans do. Terrible times do one of two things to us, they bring out the worst or the best."

"You're counting on the best."

"We've already started on that, haven't we? We're six of us."

She let that play through her mind as they walked on. "The way I was trained," she began, "was to depend on one thing. Yourself. No one else. You're in the battle alone, beginning to end — and it never ends."

"So you're always alone? What would be the point, then?"

"Winning. Coming out of the battle alive, and your enemy dead. Black and white. No grandstanding, no mistakes, no distractions."

"Who could live that way?"

"My father could. Did. Does. After he . . . after I was on my own, I spent some time with my aunt. She had a different philosophy. Sure it's about winning, because if you don't win you're dead. But it's also about living. Family, friends. Going to the movies, sitting on the beach."

"Walking in the sun."

"Yeah. It works for her, for her family."

"You're her family."

"And she always made me feel that way. But it's not the way I was trained. Maybe that's why it's never worked as well for me. I . . . there was someone once, and I loved him. We made some promises to each other, but we couldn't keep them. He couldn't be with me. I couldn't make it work, because what I am didn't just shock and frighten him. It disgusted him."

"Then he wasn't the man for you, or, in

218

my thinking, any kind of a man at all."

"He was just normal, Larkin. A normal, average guy, and I thought I wanted — thought I could have that. Normal, average."

She was made for better, he thought. She was made for more.

"You could say Jeremy — that was his name — taught me I couldn't have that. It's not that I don't have a life outside of what my father calls 'the mission.' I have some civilian friends. I like to shop, eat pizza, watch TV. But it's always in there, the knowing what comes out after sundown. You can't shake it. We're not like other people."

She looked up. "Sun's getting low. Better go in, set up for a training session." She gave him a quiet look. "Playtime's over."

It wasn't a hardship, Larkin thought, to sit and have a beautiful woman tend to you — especially when the woman smelled lovely and had hands like an angel.

"How's this?" Glenna gently kneaded his shoulder, down the arm and back again.

"It's good. It's fine. You can stop anytime in the next hour or two."

She chuckled, but worked her way across his back to his other shoulder. "You took some hard knocks, pal. But you're coming right along. It wouldn't hurt for you to skip training tonight."

"I think it's best I keep up with it. Time's short enough."

"A few days, and we leave." She looked over his head, out the window as she continued to work his back and shoulders. "Strange how quickly this has become home. I still miss New York, but it's not home anymore."

"But you'll go back from time to time."

"Oh yeah, I'll need my fix. You can take the girl out of the city, but . . ." She walked around him, played her fingers over the bruising on the side of his ribs. And made him jolt.

"Sorry. I'm a bit ticklish."

"Suck it in and think of Geall. I'll be quick."

It was torture really, fearing at any minute he might giggle like a girl. "You'll like Geall. At the castle, there are fine gardens, and herbs — oh Jesus, you're killing me. And the river, where it runs behind the castle is nearly wide as a lake. The fish all but jump out into your hands, and . . . Thank God, is that all of it?"

"You'll do. Put your shirt on."

He rolled his shoulders first, circled his head on his neck. "It's better. Thanks for that, Glenna."

"All in a day's work." She walked to the sink to wash balm from her hands. "Larkin, Hoyt and Cian have been talking."

"That's good, seeing as they're brothers." He got up, pulled on his shirt. "But you're not meaning light family conversations."

"No. Logistics, strategies. Hoyt's good with logistics — he doesn't miss details, but Cian's better with strategy, I suppose. Anyway." She turned, drying her hands on a towel. "I asked that they not discuss all this over dinner, so we could just have a meal. A normal . . . well, as normal as you can have with weapons everywhere."

"And a fine meal it was. I saw you and Hoyt earlier, kissing in the herb garden."

"Oh."

"And that was normal. The walk I took with Blair, or Moira cuddled up with a book somewhere. We need all that, so you shouldn't worry I'm offended that I haven't been part of a discussion on logistics and strategy."

"You make it easy. Thanks. The thing is, we're working out not only how to get weapons and the supplies we'll need from here to the Dance, but from here to Geall, and from the Dance in Geall to wherever we're going once we're there."

"The castle would be the place for it."

221

"The castle." Glenna gave a quiet laugh. "Off to the castle. The transportation might be a bit tricky, and we'd need you and Moira to help with that. Meanwhile, only you and Moira know your way around once we're there. How are you at drawing maps?"

"This would be the whole of Geall." In the library, Larkin drew it out. "This being the shape of it as I've seen on the maps at home. A sort of ragged fan, with these dips being inlets and bays and harbors. And here would be the Dance."

"In the west," Hoyt murmured, "as it is here."

"Aye, and a bit inland. Though if it's a clear day you can see the coast, and out to sea. There's a forest, as there is here, but it spreads just a bit more to the north. The Dance is on a rise, and the Well of the Gods here. And here, ah, about here, would be the castle."

He marked it, drawing a kind of rook and flag. "It's a good hour's ride, if you're going easy, along this road. There'd be forks here, and again here. To this way, you'd go into the village — Geall City. And this way down to Dragon's Lair, and onto Knockarague. My mother's people came from there, and there are plenty who would come to fight."

"And the battleground?" Hoyt asked him.

"Here, near the center of Geall. These, the mountains, in a kind of half ring running north, curving east, and down to the south. The valley is here. It's wide, and it's rough land, pocked with caves, layered with rock. It's called *Ciunas.* Silence, as a man could wander there, lost, for hours. And no one would hear. In all of Geall, to my knowing, it's the only place nothing lives but the grass and the rocks."

"No point in having an apocalypse in a meadow," Cian commented. "Five days' march, isn't that what Moira said?"

"Hard march, yes."

"Tricky for me, even if I managed to get that far."

"There are places along the way. Shelters, cabins, caves, cottages. We'll see you don't go up like a torch."

"You're a comfort to me, Larkin."

"A man does what he can. There are settlements closer to the valley," he continued, sketching them in. "Men can be called on there as well. But I think there needs to be some fortification done. The enemy would find those locations handy for their own shelter and preparations."

"Boy's got a brain," Cian commented. "She'd attack these." Cian tapped his finger on the map. "Decimate the population, turn those she felt would serve her best, use the rest for food supply. Those would be her first strike."

"Then those will be our first defense." Hoyt nodded.

"You'd be wasting valuable time and effort."

"We can't leave people undefended," Hoyt began.

"Get them out. Leave her without the food source or fresh recruits, at least in that area. I'd say burn the settlement to the ground, but I'd be wasting my time and effort."

"But you'd be right." Blair stepped into the room. "Leave her with no shelter, no supplies, nothing but ash. It's the cleanest, quickest and most efficient method."

"You're talking of people's homes." Larkin shook his head at her. "Of people's homes and lives and livelihoods."

"Which they won't have when she's done in any case. But they won't do it," she said to Cian. "And if they did, or tried, people would rebel, and we'd be fighting two fronts. So clear out the population, move the old, the weak, those who can't or won't fight to the castle or other fortifications."

"But you agree with him," Larkin insisted. "On the surface of it. Burn it down, the homes, the farms, the shops."

"Yes, I do."

"There are other ways." Hoyt held up a hand. "Glenna and I haven't been able to do a spell to repel the vampires from around this house because of Cian. But we could try one to protect these areas, to keep them out of the homes there. Their wizard may be able to break through that, but it would take time — and have his focus and energies tied up."

"That could work." But she exchanged a look with Cian, understood he was thinking the same as she. So they wouldn't burn the settlements. Lilith would.

"So, this is Geall." She leaned over the map. "And this is the place. Landlocked, slapped up against the mountains. Lots of caves, lots of hiding places, and desolate for all that. A goat would have a hard time beating a retreat out of there."

"We won't be running," Larkin said tightly.

"I was thinking of them. Without other shelter during the day, they'll use the caves. That gives us the high ground, but gives them ambush advantage. It'll be night, another advantage for them. We'll use fire, big advantage us. But before we get there, I've got some ideas about some surprises along the way. Now we don't know where she's going to come out, but we have to figure the odds are it's within this area."

Blair placed a hand on the map. "Battle-ground, shelter, castle. She's not going to nip behind a rock during the day — not her style, so she's got it worked that she comes in at night and moves with some speed to shelter. Most likely, she'll send an advance to these settlements, get it all taken care of for her arrival. So we need to know the quickest routes from these points to these."

They worked, debated, discussed. She could tell Larkin had backed off from her, stepped away on some basic level. She told herself it couldn't be helped. Told herself she wouldn't be hurt.

What was between them was illusion anyway. Something framed in fantasy, as transient as innocence. The passion was fine, it helped fill voids — temporarily. She knew very well that passion flickered out and died when things got tough. However cold the comfort, she held it to her. Kept it close when she went to her room alone.

Moira bided her time. All through training she could see there was something wrong between Blair and Larkin. They barely spoke, and if they did it was like strangers. When most of the night was gone, she caught him by the arm before he could leave the training room.

"Come on with me, would you? There's something I want to show you."

"What?"

"In my room. It'll take a minute. We'll be home in a few days," she said before he could object. "I wonder if all this will seem like a dream."

"A nightmare."

"Not all of it." Recognizing his poor mood, she bumped him affectionately with her hip. "You know not all of it. Time's moving so fast now. For a while, it seemed we'd been here forever. Now it's flying, and it's like we only arrived."

"I'll feel better when I get there. When I know where I am, what I'm about."

Oh yes, she thought, something was wrong. She opened the door to her room, and didn't speak again until they were both inside, and the door shut.

"What's gone wrong between you and Blair?"

"I don't know what you'd be talking about. What did you want to show me?"

"Not a thing."

"You said —"

"Well, I lied, didn't I? I've seen the two of you together for a while now, and just today out walking, hand-in-hand — and a look in your eye that I'm not mistaking."

"And what of it?"

"Tonight, the air frosted between you every time one of you opened your mouth to the other. You quarreled?"

"No."

She pursed her lips. "Maybe you need to quarrel."

"Don't be foolish, Moira."

"What's foolish about it? She made you happy. She brought something into you I've never seen, and it seemed to me you were bringing the same to her."

He toyed with some of the pretty stones she'd taken from the stream and put on the bureau. "I think you're wrong. I think I was wrong."

"Why is that?"

"She said today I didn't really know her. I didn't believe her, but now . . . Now I wonder if she didn't have the right of it."

"Maybe she does, maybe she doesn't, but it's no question to me she's done or said something to upset you. Are you just going to leave it to lie there? Why don't you kick it to pieces, or at least kick it back at her?"

"I don't —"

"And don't make excuses to me," she snapped, impatient. "Whatever it is can't be bigger than what we're facing. Anything else is petty now. Anything else, I swear, can be fixed. So, go and fix it."

"Why is it up to me to fix things?"

"You might as well because you'll just be sulking and brooding instead of sleeping until you do. And before you get to the sulking and brooding, I'll be badgering you about it until your head's aching."

"All right, all right. You're a true pain in the arse, Moira."

"I know." She touched his cheek. "It's because I love you. Go on now."

"I'm going, aren't I?"

He used his irritation with Moira to carry him out of the room and down to Blair's. He knocked, but didn't wait for an invitation. He opened the door, saw her sitting at the desk at the little computer thing.

He shut the door firm behind him.

"I'll have a word with you."

CHAPTER 10

She knew that tone — when I want to have a word with you really meant I want to have a *fight* with you. And that was fine, that was great. She was in the perfect mood for a quick, nasty brawl.

But that didn't mean she'd make it easy for him.

She kept her seat. "Obviously, you've missed the fact I'm busy."

"Obviously, you've missed the fact I don't give a bleeding damn."

"My room," she said coolly, "my choice."

"Toss me out then, why don't you?"

She swiveled toward him, stretched out her legs casually in what she knew was an insulting gesture. "Think I couldn't?"

"I think you'd have considerable trouble with it right at the moment."

"From the look of you, you came looking for trouble. Fine." She crossed her feet at the ankles — just a little *more* insulting body language, she thought. Idly, she picked up a bottle of water to gesture with. "Have your word, then get out."

"From the sound of you, *cara,* you've been expecting trouble."

"I know you've got a problem with me. You made that clear enough. So spit it out, Larkin. We haven't got time, and I haven't got the patience for petty grievances."

"Is it petty to talk so callously of destroying people's homes, their life's work, everything they've built and sweated for?"

"It's a legitimate, and proven, strategy in wartime."

"I'd expect to hear that from Cian. He is what he is, and can't help it. But not from you, Blair. And it wasn't just the strategy, but the way it was spoken, and how you talked of those who would defend those homes — rebel as you put it — as a nuisance."

"They would be, creating a liability we couldn't afford."

"But otherwise, you could *afford* to burn them out."

She knew, too well, the look and sound of angry revulsion on a man. All she could do was harden herself against it. "Better to lose brick and wood than flesh and blood."

"A home's more than brick and wood."

"I wouldn't know, I never had one. But that's not the point. In any case, it's moot. It's not being done. So if that's it —"

"What do you mean you never had a home?"

"We'll say I never developed an emotional attachment to the roof over my head. But if I had, I'd rather see it go than me, or anyone I cared about." The muscles in the back of her neck had tightened like wire, shooting a headache straight up into her skull. "And this is a ridiculous discussion because we're not burning down anything."

"No, because we're not the monsters here."

She lost her color at that. He could see it just sink out of her face. "Meaning you're not, Hoyt's not, but Cian and I are another matter. Fine. It's not the first time I've been compared to a vampire."

"That's not what I'm doing."

"You expect it from him, but not from me," she repeated. "Well, expect it. No, strike that, don't expect anything. Now, get out."

"I'm not finished."

"I am." She rose, started for the door. When he stepped in front of her, took her arm, she yanked free. "Move, or I make you move."

"Is that your solution? Threaten, push, shove?"

"Not always."

She hit him. Her fist came up, connected, before the thought of doing it clicked in her brain. It knocked him down, and left her stunned, shocked and shamed. Losing control with another person, physically harming another person, was simply not allowed.

"I'm not going to apologize because you asked for it. But that was crossing the line. The fact that I did means I'm already over the line, and this conversation has got to be over. Here, get up."

She offered a hand.

She didn't see it coming, another mistake, the yank on her hand, the sweep of his leg knocking her feet out from under her. When she hit the floor, he rolled on top of her before she countered.

She had an instant to think he'd been training very well.

"Is that how you win arguments?" he demanded. "A fist to the face?"

"I was done arguing. That was punctuation. You're going to want to get off me, Larkin, and fast. I've got a slippery hold right now."

"Bugger that."

"Bugger *you.*" She flipped him off, then

233

sprang to a crouch to block anything he might throw at her. "I won't be played like this. It's all so easy when it's walks in the sunshine, and talking about picnics, but when things get hard, when I have to be hard, then you're revolted. I'm a fucking monster."

"I never called you that, and I'm not revolted. I'm sodding mad is what I am." He dived at her, and they hit the floor again, rolled. Their bodies rammed into a table, tipping it over so the blown glass bowl on it shattered.

"If you'd stop trying to bruise and bloody me for five bloody seconds we could finish this."

"If I wanted you bloody, you'd be pumping from an artery. I don't need you passing judgment on me, or giving me the big chill because I've shocked your sensibilities. I don't need this *bullshit* from you or —"

"What you need is to shut the hell up."

He crushed his mouth to hers in an angry, frustrated kiss even as her elbow found its way into his gut. He had to lift his head to wheeze back in the air she stole.

"Don't tell me to shut up." She grabbed his hair with both hands, yanked his mouth back down to hers.

Just as angry, just as frustrated. Just as

needy. The hell with it, she thought. The hell with right and wrong, with sense, with safety. Screw control.

There were times you just took, and let yourself be taken.

Didn't mean anything, she told herself as she dragged at his shirt. It was only flesh, it was only heat. She wanted to weep and rage as much as she wanted to consume.

She shoved him over, straddled him as she pulled her shirt over her head. But he reared up, clamping his arms around her as his mouth found her breast. So she held on, letting her head fall back, letting him plunder.

Now he was riding the dragon, he thought, flying on the power of it. She was like trying to hold flame, so the sheer burn of her made him delirious. He used teeth and tongue, gorging himself as her fingers dug into his shoulders, his back, his sides. Then she was under him again, her hips grinding up while their mouths clashed.

He pulled the loose pants she wore down her hips, and there was nothing beneath them but woman, hot and wet. Hotter and wetter when his hand found her. Her harsh, throaty moan seared across his lips.

When the orgasm ripped through her, she could only think, God, thank God. But the greed whipped back, spun through like a cyclone that had her biting, scratching, tearing. She would give no quarter here, and ask none, but only clamped strong legs around him. Held on to that exquisite shock when he plunged into her.

And drove her like a mad thing, thrust upon urgent thrust, until they were both burned out.

What had she done? She'd just had crazed, kick-your-ass sex without a single thought of self-preservation, of consequences, of . . . anything. No thought, none at all, just brutal, primal need.

He was still inside her, and if felt as though their bodies had melted together in the heat. How would she separate herself again? How could she come out of this whole?

She wasn't supposed to feel like this. She wasn't supposed to want something — someone — so much she forgot herself. Let herself be taken even as she took, and in blind, feral passion.

She hadn't stopped it. She hadn't been able to stop it. And now she would pay.

He murmured something; she couldn't make it out. Then he nuzzled — a kind of nose in the neck like a puppy — before he rolled aside.

The simple sweetness of the gesture after the ferocity all but broke her into pieces.

"Crushing you." He grabbed a couple of ragged breaths. "Well, that was fairly amazing, and not at all the way I'd had it all planned out. Are you all right then?"

Careful, she warned herself. Careful and cool. "No problem."

She sat up, reached for her pants.

"Hang on a minute." He patted her arm. "My head's still spinning here. And I barely took the time to look at you seeing as we were both in a rush."

"Got the job done." She hitched on her pants. "That's what counts."

He pushed himself up, reached her shirt before she did. "Look here at me, would you?"

"I'm not big on postgame analysis, and I've got things to do."

"I don't remember a game. A battle, perhaps. I thought we'd both come out on the winning side of it."

"Yeah, so like I said, no problem." She would start to tremble in a minute, any minute. "I need my shirt."

He studied her face. "Where did you go? You have so many little hiding places."

"I don't hide." She ripped the shirt out of his hand.

"Aye, you do. Someone gets too close, you go sliding off into one of your shadows."

"Okay, why do you want to piss me off?" She dragged on her shirt. "We had sex — really good sex. It's been coming on for a while, and now it's done. We can put the focus back where it belongs."

"I don't think things are so very different here than in Geall that what we just had between us would be just sex."

"Look, cowboy, if you want romance —"

He got to his feet, slowly. It was the look in his eyes that warned her his temper was back. That was fine, in fact, that was good. They'd swipe at each other, and he'd go.

"There wasn't anything romantic about it. I thought there would be the first time we came together, but things took a different turn, and no complaints. Now you're trying to shove me away, knock me back, the way you did before with your fist. Let me say that the fist was more honest than this."

"You got what you were after."

"You know better. You know it wasn't only this."

"What's the point in anything else? What's the goddamn point? It's got nowhere to go."

"Have you been looking into Glenna's crystal? You see tomorrow now, and the day after?"

238

"I know things like this are doomed before they start. Cian's not the only one who is what he is, Larkin."

"Ah, now we come to it."

"Just —" She lifted her hands, shoved at the air, turned away. "Let it go. If the occasional grope in the dark isn't enough for you, look somewhere else."

So, he'd hurt her along the way, he realized. He was hardly the first, and couldn't quite decide if he was sorry for his part of it as yet. "I don't know what's enough for me when it comes to you." He scooped up his pants, yanked them on. "But I know I care for you. I know you matter."

"Oh please." She grabbed the water from her desk, gulped some down. "You don't even like me."

"Where does that fly from? Why would you say something so foolish and so false?"

"You seem to have forgotten what started this whole thing, what you came in here for in the first place."

"I haven't, but I don't see what that has to do with how I feel about you."

"Well, for God's sake, Larkin, how could you feel anything for someone when you're standing on the other side of a basic line?"

He considered his words now. He was, he knew, being compared to the Jeremy she'd spoken of before. Someone who'd been unable — or unwilling — to love and accept who she was."

"Blair, you're a hardheaded woman, and I've my own streak of stubbornness. My own stands and thoughts and — what did you call it? — sensibilities. And so what?"

"So. You, me." She pointed to him, tapped her own chest, then swiped a finger between them. "Line."

"Oh, bollocks. You think I can't disagree with you, and passionately, come to that, and care for you? Respect you, admire you, even knowing inside my heart you're wrong about the thing we're arguing over? The same, I wager as inside yours you believe I'm wrong. I'm not," he said with the barest hint of a smile, "but that's another matter. If everyone has to believe the same, if there's never any passionate differences, how do people come together in your world?"

"They don't," she said after a moment. "Not with me."

"Then you're just stupid, aren't you? And narrow in your thinking," he added when she gaped at him. "Hard in the head as well, as I believe I've already mentioned."

She took another careful sip of water. "I'm not stupid."

"Just the rest of it then." He nodded as he

240

took a step toward her. "Blair, it's not always where you end up, is it, that's the most important thing? It's the journey itself, and what you find, what you do along the way. Now I've found you, and that's an important thing."

"Where we're going matters."

"It does. But so does where we are. I have feelings for you, feelings I've never had for anyone. They don't always fit comfortably inside me, but I have a way of shifting things around until I find the fit."

"You maybe. I'm not good at this."

"As I am, you'll just have to follow my lead."

"How did you manage to turn this around on me?"

He only smiled, then kissed her cheek, her brow, her other cheek. "I just managed to get you faced toward me. That's the right direction."

She had to keep her mind focused on the job, the work. If she didn't, Blair found it tended to wander in that direction Larkin had spoken of. Then she'd catch herself daydreaming, smiling for no reason, or remembering what it was like to wake up beside a man who looked at her in a way that made her feel so much like a woman.

There was too much to do to take time indulging in fantasies.

"You have to be practical, Glenna. We all do. Now." Blair tapped Glenna's storage chest with her foot. "What's essential in here?"

"All of it."

"Glenna."

"Blair." Glenna folded her arms. "Are we or are we not going into battle against über evil?"

"Yes, we are. Which means we go in lean, stripped down, mobile."

"No, which means we go in loaded. These are my weapons." Glenna swept out a hand, a bit, Blair thought, like one of those game show models showing off fabulous prizes. "Are you leaving your weapons behind?"

"No, but I can also carry mine on my back, which you can't do with this two-ton chest."

"It doesn't weigh two tons. Seventy-five pounds, tops." Glenna's lips trembled at Blair's long, cool stare. "Okay, maybe eighty."

"The books alone —"

"May make all the difference. Who's to say? I'll worry about the transport."

"This better be a damn big stone circle," Blair muttered. "You know you're taking more than the rest of us combined."

"What can I say? I'm a diva."

Blair rolled her eyes, stalked to the tower window to stare out into the rain.

There was little time here left, she thought. Nearly moving day. And while she could sense — nearly see — a few of Lilith's forces in the trees, there'd be no movement toward the house. No attack.

She'd expected something. After what Larkin had pulled off, the sheer balls of it, she'd expected a reprisal. It seemed impossible Lilith would take such an insult, such a loss, without slapping back.

"Maybe she's too busy gearing up for Geall, too."

"What?"

"Lilith." Blair turned back to Glenna. "Nothing out of her for days now. And Larkin's infiltration had to sting. Jesus, when you think about it, one man — unarmed — not only getting in, but getting prisoners out. It's a kick in the face."

Glenna's eyes glinted. "I wish that was literal as well as figurative."

"Get in line. But anyway, maybe she's too busy preparing to move her front to bother harassing us right now."

"Very likely."

"I'm going to head down to the war room.

We need to work out the fine details of the traps we want to set."

"Will it make a difference?"

"What do you mean?"

"I've been thinking about it, all of it. What we've done, what they've done." Glenna rubbed a hand over the top of her chest. "But the time and the place are set. Nothing we do will change that time, that place."

"No, Morrigan made that clear in our last little chat. But what we do, how we handle the time between now and then will set the tone for that time and place. She was saying that, too. Hey, pal, it's okay to be nervous."

"Good." With brisk efficiency, Glenna set vials she'd replenished back in her healing case. "I called my parents today. I told them I'd probably be out of touch for a few weeks. Told them what an incredible time I'm having. I couldn't tell them about any of this, of course. I haven't even told them about Hoyt yet because it's too hard to explain."

She closed the case and turned. "It's not that I'm not afraid to die. I am, of course — maybe more now than I was when this began. I have more to lose now."

"Hoyt, and happy ever."

"Exactly. But I'm prepared to die if that's what it takes. Maybe more now than when this began, for those exact reasons."

"Love sure can twist you up."

"Oh boy," was Glenna's heartfelt agreement. "And I wouldn't change a single moment since I met him. Still, it's so hard, Blair. I have no way of telling my family how or why if I don't make it through this. They'll never know what happened to me. And that weighs on me."

"Then don't die."

Glenna gave a half laugh. "A better idea."

"I'm sorry. I don't mean to make light of it."

"No, it's kind of bolstering, actually. But . . . if anything happens to me, would you take this to my family?" She held out an envelope. "I know it's a lot to ask," she began when Blair hesitated.

"No, but . . . Why me?"

"You and Cian have the best chance of coming through this. I can't ask him to do it. They won't understand, even with this, but at least they won't spend the rest of their lives wondering if I'm alive or dead. I don't want to put them through that."

Blair studied the envelope, the artistic flare of the handwriting forming her parents' names and address. "I tried to contact my father, twice, since this started. E-mail, because I don't actually know where he is. He hasn't answered me."

"Oh, I'm sorry. He must be out of reach for —"

"No, probably not. He just doesn't answer me, that's fairly typical. And I really need to get over it. It isn't that he wouldn't care. Big vamp war — he'd care. And if I died, he'd be sorry. Because he trained me not to, and going down would be a reflection on him."

"That sounds harsh."

"He is." She looked into Glenna's face, clear-eyed. "And he doesn't love me."

"Oh, Blair."

"Time to suck that up, too. Past time. You've got something else here." She tapped the letter. "And it's important."

"It is," Glenna agreed. "But they're not my only family."

"I get that. What we've got, the six of us? It's one of the good things I've picked up along the way."

With a nod, Blair tucked the envelope into the back pocket of her jeans. "I'll give this back to you, November first."

"That'd be good."

"See you downstairs."

"Soon. Oh, and Blair? It's nice, you and Larkin. It's nice to see."

"See what?"

Now Glenna let out a genuine laugh. "What, am I blind? Added to that I have the super X-ray vision of a newlywed. I'm just saying I like the way you are together. It seems like a nice fit."

"It's just — It's not . . . I'm not looking for the big, Hollywood finish, the one where the music crescendos and the light goes all pink and pretty."

"Why not?"

"Just not the way it is. I'll take it a day at a time. People like me look too far down the road, they end up falling into the big hole somebody dug right in front of them."

"If they don't look far enough or hard enough, they don't see what they were really looking for."

"Right now, I'll settle for avoiding the hole."

She headed out. No way to explain, she thought, not to a woman still floating on the wings of new love, that there were some people who just weren't built for it. Some people didn't have that strolling hand-in-hand with the man of their dreams into the sunset in their destiny.

When she strolled into the sunset, she went alone, she went armed and she went looking for death.

Not exactly the stuff of romance and hopeful futures.

She'd tried it once, and it had been a disaster that had blown up in her face. Larkin was no Jeremy, that was for damn certain. Larkin was tougher, and stronger, and sweeter for that matter.

But that didn't change the basics. She had her duty — the mission — and he had his world. Those weren't the elements for a long-term connection.

Her particular branch of the old McKenna family tree would die out with her. She'd made up her mind to that when she'd scraped herself up after Jeremy.

She started to swing toward the stairs, but the music stopped her. Cocking her head, she strained to hear, to recognize. Was that Usher?

Jeez, was Larkin up in the training room fooling around with her MP3? She'd have to kill him.

She jogged up the stairs. It wasn't that she couldn't appreciate the fact he enjoyed her music. But she'd spent a lot of time downloading and setting up that player. He didn't even know how the damn thing worked.

"Listen, cowboy, I don't want you —"

The room was empty, the terrace doors firmly shut. And music poured through the air.

"Okay, weird." She set her hand on the stake she always carried in her belt, and side-stepped slowly toward the weapons. The lights were on full; nothing could hide in shadows. But she closed her hand over the handle of a scythe.

The music shut off; a switch flicked.

Lora stepped through the wall of mirrors.

"Hello, *cherie*."

"Nice trick."

"One of my favorites." Turning a circle, she seemed to study the room. She wore heeled boots, snug black pants with a fitted jacket that showed a flirty bit of frothy lace between the deep plunge of lapels.

"So, this is where you spar and sweat, and prepare to die."

"This is where we train to kick your ass."

"So tough, so *formidable*." She floated around the room with the spiked heels of those boots gliding just above the floor.

Not here, Blair told herself. Not really here, just the illusion of her. But to prove it, she hurled a stake. And watched it pass right through Lora's figure to embed itself into the wall.

"That was rude." Lora turned with a little pout. "Hardly a way to welcome a guest."

"You weren't invited."

"No, we were interrupted the last time, before you could invite me in. But still, I brought you a present. Something picked just especially for you. I went all the way to America for it. All the way to Boston."

She did a long, sweeping turn with her eyes bright as suns. "Wouldn't you like to see? Or would you like to guess? Yes, yes, you must guess! Three guesses."

To show complete lack of interest, Blair stood hip-shot, a hand hooked in the pocket of her jeans. "I don't play games with the un-dead, Fifi."

"You're just no fun, are you? But one day we'll have fun, you and I." She floated closer, running her tongue over fangs before she smiled. "I have so many plans for you. Men have let you down, haven't they? Poor Blair. Withheld their love, and you crying out for it inside."

"The only thing I'm crying out for is an end to this conversation before it makes me sick."

"What you need is a woman. What you need . . ." She trailed a finger in the air, a breath away from Blair's cheek. "Yes, *bien sur,* you need the power and the pleasure I'd give you."

"I don't go for cheap blondes with silly French accents. Plus the outfit? It's so last week."

Lora hissed, her head snapping forward as if to bite.

"I'll make you sorry, and I'll make you grovel. Then I'll make you scream."

Deliberately, Blair widened her eyes. "Golly. Does that mean you don't want to date me anymore?"

With a laugh, Lora spun away. "I like you, I really do. You have, ah . . . flair. That's why I brought you such a special present. I'll just go get it. Wait one minute."

She stepped backward, through the mirrors.

"Fuck this," Blair muttered. She grabbed a crossbow, armed it. With the bow in one hand, the scythe in the other, she began to move cautiously toward the door.

This was Glenna's area, not hers. Time to call in the witch.

But Lora slid through the wall again, and what she pulled with her had Blair's blood freezing.

"No. No, no, no."

"He is handsome." Lora slid a tongue down Jeremy's cheek as he struggled against her hold. "I can see why you feel for him."

"You're not here." Oh God, his face was bleeding. His right eye swollen nearly shut. "It's not real."

"Not here, but real. Say hello, Jeremy."

"Blair? Blair? What's going on? What are you doing here? What's happening?"

"It was so easy." Lora clamped a hand on his throat, choking him as she lifted him an inch off the floor. And laughing when Blair charged them, flew through them and ran hard against the wall. "I just picked him up in a bar. A few drinks, a few suggestions. Men are deceivers ever. That's Shakespeare. 'Why don't we go to your place?' was all I needed to whisper into his ear. And here we are."

She brought him down so his feet touched the ground, but kept her hand around his neck. "I would have fucked him first, but it seemed that would take the shine off the gift."

"Help me." He choked it out, wheezing each breath. "Blair, you have to help me."

"Help me," Lora mimicked and threw him to the ground.

"Why are you wasting your time with him?" Blair felt her stomach twist as Jeremy crawled toward her. "You want me, come for me."

"Oh, I will." Lora leaped, falling on Jeremy. Dragging him to his back, she straddled him. "This weak — yet attractive — human broke your heart. Isn't that so?"

"He dumped me. What do I care what you do to him? You're wasting your time with him when you should be dealing with me."

"No, no, it's never a waste of time. And caring, *chérie,* is what you do." Lora clamped a hand over Jeremy's mouth as he started to scream, then watching Blair, scraped her nail down his cheek to draw fresh blood. She licked it from her fingertip. "Hmm. Fear always gives it such a nice kick. Beg for him. If you beg, I'll let him live."

"Don't kill him. Please, don't kill him. He means nothing to you. He's not important. Leave him there, just leave him, you got my attention. I'll meet you, alone, wherever you want. Just you and me. We'll settle this. The two of us. We don't need men getting in the way. Don't do this. Ask for something in return. Just ask."

"Blair." Lora offered her a sweet, sympathetic smile. "I don't have to ask. I just take. But you begged very well, so I'll . . . Oh don't be ridiculous. We both know I'm going to kill him. Watch."

She sank her teeth into him, sliding her body down his as it convulsed in an awful parody of sex. Blair heard herself screaming and screaming. And screaming.

CHAPTER 11

When Larkin rushed in all he saw was Blair stabbing a stake over and over into the floor. She was weeping as she did it in wild, screaming sobs, and there was a madness on her face.

He ran to her, but when he grabbed for her, she struck out in a blow that bloodied his lip.

"Get away, get away! She's killing him!"

"There's nothing there." He gripped her wrist, and would have taken another punch if Cian hadn't dragged her back.

She kicked, twisted to attack. Cian slapped her, twice. Hard enough to make the crack of it echo. "Stop. Hysterics are useless."

Enraged, Larkin leaped to his feet. "Take your hands off her. You think you can strike her?" He might have charged, but Hoyt pinned his arm.

"Hold on a bloody minute."

Larkin's answer was to rear back, smash his head into Hoyt's jaw even as Glenna sprinted over to stand between Larkin and Cian. "Just calm down." Glenna held up her hands. "Just everyone calm down."

But there was shouting, accusations, and Blair's helpless sobbing.

"*Ciunas!*" Moira's voice cut through the mayhem with a cold authority. "Quiet, all of you. Larkin, he did what needed to be done, so stop this nonsense. Let go of her, Cian. Glenna, get her some water. We need to find out what's happened here."

When Cian released her, Blair simply melted to the floor. "She's killed him. I couldn't stop her." She brought up her knees, wrapped her arms around her head as she lowered it. "Oh God, oh my God."

"You have to look at me now." Moira crouched down, firmly took Blair's arms and brought them down again. "You have to look at me, Blair, and tell me what happened here."

"He never believed, not even when I showed him. It was easier to push me away, to throw me away than to believe it. Now he's dead."

"Who is?"

"Jeremy. Jeremy's dead. She brought him

here, so I would see her do it."

"There's no one here, Blair. No one here, and no one in the house but the six of us."

"There was." Glenna passed down the water. "I can feel it." She looked at Hoyt for confirmation.

"A smear on the air." He nodded. "A heaviness to it that comes from black magic."

"She came through the wall, and I thought, now we'll fight. You and me, French bitch." Though Blair fought to steady it, her voice continued to hitch. "I threw a stake, but it went right through her. She wasn't really here. She . . ."

"Like on the subway. It happened to me," Glenna explained. "In New York. A vampire on the subway, but no one else could see it. He spoke to me, it moved, but it wasn't really there."

"Boston." Sick to the soul of her, Blair got to her feet. "She went to Boston. I used to live there. It's where I met him — Jeremy. They were in his apartment. She told me where she was. Cian, do you have contacts there?"

"I do."

She gave him an address. "Jeremy Hilton. Someone needs to check. Maybe she was just messing with me. But if . . . They have to make sure she didn't change him."

"I'll take care of it."

She looked down to where she'd hacked and drilled the steak into the floorboards. "Sorry about the floor."

"That'd be Hoyt's and Glenna's problem now." Cian touched her shoulder briefly before he left the room.

"We should go down. You should lie down," Glenna said. "Or sit at least. I can give you something that will help."

"No. I don't want anything." She scrubbed the useless tears away with the heels of her hands. "I knew she'd come back at us, but I never considered, I never thought. Glenna, your family —"

"They're protected. Hoyt and I saw to that. Blair, I'm so sorry we didn't do something for your . . . for your friend."

"I never thought of him. Never considered they would . . . I'm, ah, I'm going to take a few minutes before we get back to work."

"All you need," Glenna told her.

Blair looked at Larkin. "I'm sorry. I'm sorry I hit you."

"It's nothing." Letting her go, letting her go alone, was more painful than any blow.

She didn't weep again. Tears wouldn't help Jeremy, and they certainly wouldn't do her any good.

She contacted her aunt, relayed the details. She could count on family to protect family. In any case, she doubted Lilith, or Lora, any of them would go after people who were prepared, who knew them. And could defend themselves.

They'd chosen the helpless for a very good reason.

It didn't waste time or effort, was low-risk, and very, very effective.

She was absolutely calm when she armed herself, sliding the sword into the sheath on her back, the stake into the one on her belt. Her mind, her purpose were clear as glass when she went outside.

There wouldn't be many, she thought. It was poor strategy to waste more than a handful at this stage. Which was a pity.

They would expect her to be broken, to be shaking and weeping under the covers. That was a mistake.

She watched the two come toward her, from the right and from the left. "Hello, boys. You looking for a party?"

The sword came out of its sheath with the slick sound of metal on metal. She whirled; a quick, two-handed swing. And decapitated the one coming at her from behind.

"Came to the right place."

When they charged, she was ready. Slicing, piercing, blocking with a sword that sang like vengeance. She took the nick on her forearm. She wanted to feel it, that sting.

They were clumsy, she thought. Young and poorly trained. Fat and soft in the lives they'd led before they'd been turned. Not defenseless, not like Jeremy, but far from seasoned.

She flipped out the stake, eliminated one.

The one that was left dropped its sword, began to run.

"Hey, hey, not done yet." She chased it, took it down with a flying tackle. Then holding the stake to its heart, stared into eyes filled with fear.

"Got a message for Lora. You know her? The French pastry? Good," she said when it nodded. "Tell her she was right about one thing. It will be her and me, and when I end her, it's going to be . . . Oh never mind, I'll tell her myself."

She plunged the stake down. Rising, she tunneled her fingers through her dripping hair. Then picked up the scattered weapons, and started back to the house.

The door swung open before she reached it, and Larkin stormed out. "Have you gone mad?"

"They weren't expecting it." She tossed him one of the swords, moved by him into the house. "Only three anyway. Probably clears the ones she's stationed near the house." She laid the other confiscated swords on the kitchen counter. "And those were lightweights."

"You'd go out alone? Risk your life this way?"

"I went out alone most of my life," she reminded him. "And risking my life is part of the job description."

"It's not a job."

"A job's exactly what it is." She poured herself a large mug of coffee. Hands still steady, she noted. Mission accomplished. "I'm going to go dry off."

"You had no right to take a chance like that."

"Minimal risk," she countered as she walked out. "Excellent results."

When she'd changed her clothes, she joined the others in the library. She could see from their expressions Larkin had informed the rest of the group of her little sortie.

"They were stationed close to the house," she began. "Likely to try to hear or see something they could pass on. That won't be a problem now."

"It would have been a problem if there'd been more of them." Hoyt spoke quietly, but it didn't disguise the steel beneath the words. "It would have been a problem if they'd killed or captured you."

"Didn't happen. We have to be ready to take opportunities. Not only the six of us, but the people we're going to be sending into battle. They have to be trained, how to kill, when to kill. Not just with sword and stake, but with their bare hands, or whatever comes to hand. Because everything's a weapon. And if they're not trained, if they're not ready, they're just going to stand there and die."

"Like Jeremy Hilton."

"Yeah." She nodded at Larkin, absorbed his anger along with the weight in her heart. "Like Jeremy. Cian, were you able to find anything out?"

"He's dead."

She closed off the part of her that wanted to moan. "Could he have been changed?"

"No. There was too much trauma to the body for that."

"It's still possible he —"

"No." Cian bit off the word to cut her off. "She ripped him to pieces. It's one of her signatures. He's just dead."

She let herself sit. Better to sit, she decided, than to fall over.

"There was nothing you could do, Blair," Moira told her gently. "Nothing you could have done to stop it."

"No, there was nothing. That was her point — look what I can do, right in front of you, and you're helpless. We were engaged, Jeremy and I, a couple years ago. So I had to tell him — in the end I had to show him — what I am, what I do. He walked out, because he wasn't going to believe it, wasn't going to be part of it. Now it's killed him."

"She killed him," Larkin corrected. "Who you are didn't kill him." He waited until she shifted her gaze, met his eyes. "She wants, very much wants, you to blame yourself. Will you give her that victory?"

"She won't win anything from me." Tears stung her eyes again, but she willed them back. "I'm sorry, all around. This messes me up, and I have to live with it awhile on my own before I can put it away."

"We'll put off the meeting." Glenna glanced around at the others for agreement. "You can take some time."

"Appreciate it, but work's better. Thinking's better." If she went upstairs now, were alone now, Blair knew she'd just fall apart again. "So okay. If we're going to set traps on the other side, we'll need to calculate the best locations, and determine how many we'll need on those details."

"We have more immediate concerns," Hoyt interrupted. "The transportation to

262

Geall itself. If Cian's barred from the Dance, he can't reach the portal."

"There must be an exception." Moira laid a hand on Blair's shoulder, gave it one hard squeeze before moving aside. "Morrigan chose us, all of us."

"Maybe she's finished with me." Cian shrugged. "Gods are fickle creatures."

"You're one of the six," Moira insisted. "Without you in Geall, the circle's broken."

"I could go back to the caves. From the air." Larkin paced in front of the windows. How could he sit at such a time? "Scout. I might be able to find where they're going through."

"We can't separate. Not this close to deadline. We stick together now." Glenna scanned faces, lingering on Blair's. "We stay whole."

"There's another thing, I think I should mention." Moira glanced toward Cian. "When Larkin and I went to the Dance in Geall, it was barely midday. It seemed to happen so quickly, the way we were swept up and away. But when we came out here, it was night. I don't think we can know how long it takes, or if time's the same. Or . . . or if we leave at night as we planned, if it would still be night when we come to Geall."

"Or high bloody noon." Cian cast his eyes up. "Isn't that just perfect?"

"There has to be a way to protect him if there's sunlight."

"Easy for you to say, Red." Cian rose to get a glass of whiskey. "Your delicate skin may burn a bit in strong sunlight, but you don't go to ash, do you?"

"Some sort of block, Hoyt," Glenna began.

"I don't think SPF-forty will do the trick," Cian countered.

"We'll figure it out," she snapped back. "We'll find a way. We haven't come this far to give up, to leave you behind."

Blair let them talk, argue, debate. The voices just buzzed around her. She didn't comment, didn't contribute. When Hoyt finally harangued Cian into giving him a sample of blood, she left them to their magic.

He didn't try to sleep. A half dozen times he started to go to her room. To offer what? he wondered. Comfort she didn't want, anger she didn't need?

She had suffered a terrible loss, and a hard, hard shock to her heart. She hadn't, perhaps couldn't turn to him. Not even, he thought now, as a fellow warrior.

He couldn't soothe hurts she refused to let him see, or reach wounds she closed in to herself.

She had loved the man, that much was clear. And there was a small part of himself, an ugliness he could despise, that was jealous of the brutalized dead.

So he stood at the window, watching the sun rise on his last day in Ireland.

When someone knocked, he assumed it was Moira. *"Bi istigh."*

He didn't turn when the door opened, not until Blair spoke. "My Gaelic's pretty crappy, so if that was go to hell, too bad." She hefted the bottle of whiskey she held in one hand. "I raided Cian's supply. Going to get a little drunk, have a wake for an old friend. Want to join me?"

Without waiting for an answer, she walked over to sit on the floor at the foot of the bed, resting her back against it. She opened the bottle, poured a generous two fingers into each of the glasses she'd brought in.

"Here's to just being dead." She lifted the glass, tossed back the contents. "Come on, have a drink, Larkin. You can be pissed at me and still have a drink."

He walked over, lowered to the floor to sit across from her. "I'm sorry you're hurting."

"I'll get over it." She handed him the second glass, poured more whiskey in her own. *"Sláinte."* She tapped the glasses together, but this time she sipped instead of gulped.

"Attachments, my father taught me, were weapons the enemy could use against you."

"That's a hard and cold way to live."

"Oh, he's good at hard and cold. He walked out on me on my eighteenth birthday. Done." She leaned her head back and drank. "You know, he'd hurt me so many times before, cut my heart out, I thought, just by not loving me. But it was nothing, nothing that happened — didn't happen — before came close to what it did to me when he walked away. That's how I got this."

She turned her wrist over, examined the scar. "Going out while I was still reeling, trying to prove I didn't need him. I did need him. Too bad for me."

"He didn't deserve you."

She smiled a little. "He'd completely agree with that, but not the way you mean. I wasn't what he wanted, and even if I had been, he wouldn't have loved me. Took me a long time to come around to that. Maybe he'd have been proud. Maybe he'd have been satisfied. But he never would've loved me."

"And still you loved him."

"Worshiped him." For a moment, Blair closed her eyes as she let that part of her go. That part was over. "I just couldn't rip that out and turn it to dust. So I worked, really hard, until I was better than he'd ever been.

But I still had that need inside me. To love somebody, to have them love me back. Then there was Jeremy."

She poured more whiskey for both of them. "I was working at my uncle's pub. My aunt, my cousins and I took shifts. Hunting, or working the bar, waiting tables, just taking the night off. My aunt called it having a life. Work as a family, share the burden, have some normal."

"Sounds like a sensible woman."

"She is. And a good one. So I'm riding the stick — working the bar — when Jeremy comes in with a couple of friends. He's just copped this big account, and they're going to hoist a few. He's a stockbroker." She waved that away. "Hard to explain. Anyway, he's good looking. Great looking, actually. So, he hits on me —"

"He *struck* you?"

"No, no." Finding that wonderfully funny, she snorted out a laugh. "It's parlance, slang. He flirted with me. I flirted back because he gave me the buzz. You know what I mean? That little *zzzz* you get inside?"

"I do." Larkin brushed a hand over hers. "I know that buzz."

"He hung around till closing, and I ended up giving him my number. Well, we don't need every detail. We started seeing each other — going out together. He was fun, sweet. Normal. The kind of guy who sends you flowers the day after your first date."

Her eyes misted over, but she shook her head, downed more whiskey. "I wanted normal. I wanted a chance at it. When things got serious between us, I thought yeah, yeah, this is the way it's supposed to be. The job doesn't mean I can't have somebody, be part of somebody. But I didn't tell him what I did on those nights we weren't together, or what I did some nights after he was asleep. I didn't tell him."

"Did you love him?"

"I did. And I told him that. I told him I loved him, but I didn't tell him what I was." She drew a deep breath. "Honestly? I don't know if that was sheer cowardice or ingrained training, but I didn't tell him. We were together eight months, and he never knew. There had to be signs, there had to be *clues.* Hey, Jeremy, don't you wonder how I got these bruises? Why my clothes are trashed? Where the hell this blood came from? But he never asked, and I never let myself wonder why."

"People, you said, have blinders. Love, I think, can thicken them."

"Bet your ass. He asked me to marry him. Oh God, he pulled out all the stops. The wine, the candles, the music, all the right words. I just rode on it, the big, shiny fantasy of it. Still, I didn't say anything, not for days. Until my aunt sat me down."

She pressed the thumb and finger of one hand to her eyes. "You have to tell him, she said to me. You have to make him believe it. You can't have a life, can never build one with him, not with lies or half-truths or without trust. Dragged my feet another couple of weeks, but it ate at me. I knew she was right. But he loved me, so it would be all right. It would all work out fine. Because he loved me, and he'd see I was doing not just what I had to do, but what was right."

Holding her glass in both hands, she closed her eyes. "I explained it to him as carefully as I knew how, taking him through the family history. He thought I was joking." She opened her eyes now, met Larkin's. "When he realized I wasn't, he got hostile. Figured it was my sick way of breaking the engagement. We went round and round about it. I badgered him into going to the cemetery with me. I knew one was supposed to rise that night, and hey, a picture's worth a thousand. So I showed him what they were, what I was."

She drank again, one long sip. "He couldn't wait to get away from me. Couldn't wait to pack his things and get away. To walk out on me. I was a freak, and he never wanted to see me again."

"He was weak."

"He was just a guy. Now he's a dead guy."

"So it's your fault, is it? Your fault that you cared enough to share what you are with him. To show him not only that there are monsters in the world, but that you're strong enough, courageous enough to fight them? Your fault that he wasn't man enough to see the wonder of you?"

"What wonder? I do what I'm trained to do, follow the family business."

"That's bollocks, and worse, it's self-pity."

"I didn't kill him — you were right about that. But he's dead because of me."

"He's dead because a vicious, soulless demon killed him. He'd dead because he didn't believe in what was in front of his eyes, and didn't hold on to you. And none of that is your doing."

"He left me, like my father left me. I thought that was the worst. But this . . . I don't know what to do with the pain."

He took her glass, set it aside. Reaching out he pulled her into his arms, pressed her head onto his shoulder. "Put a bit of it here for now. Shed your tears, *a stór*. You'll feel better having given them to him."

He held her, stroking her hair and soothing, while she wept for another man.

She woke tucked into his bed, still dressed, and grateful she was alone. The hangover wasn't the clanging bell of a night of foolish indulgence, but the dull gong that came from using whiskey as a cushion.

He'd drawn the drapes so the sun wouldn't wake her, she noted, and checked her watch for the time. The fact that it was already noon made her groan as she threw back the covers to sit on the side of the bed.

Too much to do, she told herself, to coddle a half-assed hangover and a raging case of sorrow. Before she could gather the fortitude to stand, Larkin walked in. He carried a glass that held something murky and brown.

"I'd say good morning, but it likely doesn't feel as such to you."

"It's not too bad," she told him. "I've had worse."

"Regardless, it isn't the day for having a head. Glenna says this will help it."

She looked dubiously at the glass. "Because drinking it will make me throw up everything in my system?"

"She didn't say. But you'll be a brave girl

271

now and take your medicine."

"I guess." She took the glass, sniffed at the contents. "Doesn't smell as bad as it looks." She took a deep breath, downed all of it. Then shuddered right down to her toes. "Tastes a lot worse. Not just eye of newt, but the whole damn newt."

"Give it a minute or two to settle."

She nodded, then stared down at her hands. "I wasn't at my best last night, to put it extremely mildly."

"No one expects you should be at your best at all times. Certainly not me."

"I want to thank you for the ear, and the shoulder."

"Those seemed to be the parts of me you needed most." He sat beside her. "Were you clear-headed enough to understand what I said to you?"

"Yeah. It's not my fault. In my head I know it's not my fault. There are other parts of me, Larkin, that have to catch up with my head on this."

"They wasted you, these men. I won't." He pushed to his feet again when she stared at him. "Something else for you to catch up with. Come down when you're ready. We've a lot of work."

She kept staring even after he'd gone out and closed the door behind him.

■ ■ ■ ■

It helped to have the work. They would carry
— the old-fashioned way — as much of the
supplies and weapons as possible to the circle. Hoyt and Glenna would continue to
work on a shield of some kind for Cian.

With Larkin in the form of a horse, Blair
loaded him while Moira loaded Cian's stallion.

"Sure you can ride that thing?" Blair asked
her.

"I can ride anything." Moira glanced toward the tower window. "It's the only way to
get this done. They need to concentrate on
what they're doing. We can't risk trying to
carry everything we're taking the full distance after sunset."

"Nope." Blair swung onto Larkin's back.
"Keep your eyes open. We may have company in the woods."

They started out, single file. "Can you really smell them?" Moira called out.

"It's more that I sense them. I'll know if
one gets close." She scanned the trees, the
shadows. Nothing stirred but birds and rab-
bits.

Sunlight, she thought, and birdsong. It
would be a different matter taking this route
at night. She and Moira, she decided, on

Larkin, with Hoyt and Glenna on the stallion. Cian, she thought, could move nearly as fast as a horse at a gallop if necessary.

It was a twisting and at times a barely trod path. And at times the shadows over it were deep enough to have her fingers twitch toward the crossbow.

She felt the ripple of Larkin's muscles between her thighs, nodded. So he could sense them, too, she thought. Or the horse he was inside could sense them. "They're watching. Keeping their distance, but watching."

"They'll understand what we're about." Moira glanced back. "Or get word to Lilith, and she will."

"Yeah. Pick up the pace a little. Let's get this done."

They came out of the woods, crossed a short fallow field. On the rise of it stood the stone Dance.

"It is big," Blair murmured. Not Stonehenge big, she thought, but impressive. And like Stonehenge, even before she moved into the shadow of the stones, she felt them. Almost heard them.

"Strong stuff." She dismounted.

"In this world, and in mine."

Moira slid off the stallion, then laid her head against Larkin's. "It's our way home."

"Let's hope so." Within the Dance, Blair

began to off-load weapons. "You're sure vamps can't come inside the circle?"

"No demon can pass between the stones and step on the sacred ground. It's that way in Geall, and from everything I've read on it, that way in this world as well."

Moira looked as Blair did, toward the woods. But she thought of Cian and what would become of him if they were forced to leave him behind.

"We'll figure it out."

Moira glanced over. "You're worried, too."

"It's a concern. We've got to get him there, keep him from frying — so make that two really major concerns. Handy this is a safety zone, and we're not going to come back in a few hours and find they've raided our weapons stash, but Cian's the downside."

Without thinking, she rubbed Larkin's flank. When he turned his head, eyed her, she dropped her hand. "Hoyt and Glenna are on it. We all go, that's the deal. So we'll figure it out."

The swish of Larkin's tail slapped her in the butt. "Hey."

"He's a playful sort," Moira commented. "In almost any form."

"Yeah, he's a real jokester. Ought to be careful, one of these days he might stick in one of the four-legged varieties." She came around to his head. "Then where will you be?"

He slurped his tongue from her jaw to her cheekbone. "Eeww."

Moira's laugh bubbled out as she stacked the last of the weapons. "He makes me laugh, even in the worst of times. Ah well," she said when Blair scowled and swiped the slobber from her cheek. "You don't seem to mind his tongue on you when he's a man."

The sound Larkin made was as close to a laugh as a horse could manage. Moira just grinned and swung back onto the stallion. "It's hard to miss when two people are eager to get their hands on each other. I once had a crush on him myself." She reached over, tugged Larkin's mane. "But then I was five. I've gotten well over it now."

"It's the quiet ones you've got to watch out for," Blair muttered. "You." She jerked her head toward Moira as she mounted Larkin. "Quiet type, into the books, little shy around the edges. I wouldn't have figured you'd take the idea of me banging your cousin so casually."

"Banging?" Moira pursed her lips as they rode through the stones. "That would be a term for sexual relations? It fits, doesn't it because . . ." She draped the reins over Vlad's neck so she could slap her hands together. And this time, Blair laughed.

"You're just full of surprises."

"I know what happens between a man and a woman. Theoretically."

"Theoretically. So you've never —" She caught Moira's wincing glance toward Larkin. "Oh, sorry. Big horses have big ears."

"Well, I suppose it's a small thing, considering all the rest. No, I've never. If I'm to be queen, I'll need to marry. But there's time. I'd want to find someone who'd suit, and who understands me. I'd like best to love as my parents loved each other, but at least, I'd want to care for him. And I'd hope he'd be skilled at banging."

This time the sound Larkin made was a kind of mutter.

"Why should you be the only one?" Moira slid her foot from the stirrup to give him a light kick with her boot. "Is he good at it then, our Larkin?"

"He's an animal."

Beneath her, Larkin broke into a fast trot.

Yes, Blair thought, it was good to laugh, even in the worst of times.

CHAPTER 12

Cian fingered the rough black material with mild distaste. "A cloak."

"But it's a magic cloak." Glenna tried a winning smile. "With hood."

Black cloaks and vampires, he thought with an inward sigh. Such a cliche. "And this . . . thing is supposed to prevent me from going up in flames in direct sunlight."

"It really should work."

He sent her a mildly amused look. "*Should* being the operative word."

"Your blood didn't boil when we exposed it," Hoyt began.

"There's cheery news. It happens I'm made up of more than blood."

"Blood's the key," Hoyt insisted. "Blood's the heart of it. You've said so yourself."

"That was before my flesh and bone were on the line."

"We're sorry there's no time to test it."

Glenna pushed a hand through her hair. "It took so long, and until we were reasonably sure, we couldn't ask you to put it on and step outside."

"Considerate of you." He held it up. "Couldn't you have made it a bit more stylish?"

"Fashion wasn't our primary concern." Hoyt didn't quite snap out the words, but it was close. "Protecting your sorry self was."

"I'll be sure to thank you for it if I'm not a pile of inarticulate ash at the end of the day."

"And so you should." Moira condemned him with one quiet look. "They worked through the night, and all through this day with only you in mind. And while you've slept the rest of us have been working as well."

"I had work of my own, Your Highness." He dismissed her simply by turning his back. "Well, it's unlikely to be an issue as your stone circle rejects my sort."

"You have to trust in the gods," Hoyt told him.

"I'm forced to remind you, yet again. Vampire. Vampires and gods aren't drinking buddies."

Glenna stepped up to Cian, laid a hand over his. "Wear it. Please."

"For you, Red." He tipped her face up,

kissed her lightly on the lips. Then he stepped back, swirled it on. "Feel like a bloody B movie extra. Or worse, a sodding monk."

He didn't look like a monk, Moira thought. He looked dangerous.

Blair and Larkin came in. "We're as secure as we're going to be," Blair said, then lifted her eyebrows at Cian. "Hey, you look like Zorro."

"I beg your pardon?"

"You know, that scene where he's in the chapel with the girl, and he's pretending to be the priest. Only, jeez, the kind of priest we used to call Father What a Waste. Anyway, sun's down. If we're going to go, we'd better."

Hoyt nodded, looked at Cian. "You'll stay close."

"Close enough."

Blair might have wished they'd taken time to practice the maneuver, but it was too late for wishes. No more talk, she thought. No more discussion — and no dress rehearsals. It was now or never.

After a quick nod, a quick breath, she and Larkin went through the door first. Even as he changed, she was leaping up, then reaching a hand down to help Moira vault behind her.

They rode away from the stables at a hard run, with the hope of drawing any that waited in ambush. She barely saw Cian streak out. He was at the stable doors in seconds, releasing the stallion.

Then he was gone again, and Hoyt and Glenna were on Vlad's back.

With barely a glimmer of moonlight to guide them, a gallop was risky once they reached the trees. Blair kept Larkin to a trot, trusting him to watch the path as she scanned the woods.

"Nothing yet, nothing. If they're around they're hanging back."

"Can you see Cian?" With her bow ready, Moira tried to look everywhere at once. "Sense him?"

"No, there's nothing." Blair shifted in the saddle to look over Moira's shoulder at Hoyt. "Watch the flank. They may come at us from behind."

They rode in absolute silence, with only the sound of hooves on the path. And that, Blair thought, was a problem. Where were the nightbirds? Where were all the little rustles and peeps of the small animals in a night woods?

Demon hunters, she knew, weren't the only creatures who could sense vampires.

"Be ready," Blair said under her breath.

She heard it then, the clash of steel, a sudden scream. She didn't have to urge Larkin on with words or a nudge of her heels. He was already at a gallop.

She sensed them seconds before they charged out of the trees. Foot soldiers this time, she judged, with some seasoning and wearing light armor. She sliced down with her sword even as Moira's arrows began to fly.

Hooves struck out, and trampled whatever fell beneath them. But the enemy came from everywhere, blocking the circle, and barring the path to the Dance. Blair kicked out, knocking one back as it clawed at her leg. Too many, she thought. Too many to make a stand.

Better, she thought, better to charge, break the line, and get to the stones.

Then the one that leaped down from a branch above her nearly unseated her, knocking her back as she rammed up an elbow to block it. Moira pitched to the ground. With a cry of rage, Blair smashed back with a fist. She'd nearly jumped down when Cian flew across the path.

He swooped Moira up, all but threw her back on Larkin. "Go!" he shouted. "Go now."

She charged the line, the flames from her

sword cutting a burning path. She could only hope Cian was out of harm's way as a ball of fire whizzed by her. She felt Larkin vibrate beneath her, and the form of him shift.

Then she was soaring up on the dragon's back, with his claws raking across the line of vampires, slashing out with his tail as Hoyt and Glenna galloped through the gap.

She could see the stones now. Though clouds covered the moon they glowed like polished silver, shining against the dark. She would have sworn even with the rush of wind, the cries of battle, she heard them singing.

As Hoyt and Glenna flew through them and into the circle, Larkin dived.

She leaped from his back, favoring the leg the vampire had scored. "Get ready," she ordered.

"Cian —"

She squeezed Moira's shoulder. "He'll come. Hoyt?"

He drew out his key; Moira did the same. "We don't say the words until Cian's with us." As with the stones themselves, power seemed to pulse from Hoyt as he took Glenna's hand. "We don't say the words until we're a circle again."

Blair nodded. Whatever the stones held, whatever Hoyt and Glenna had been born with, the full force of the power came from unity. They'd wait for Cian.

She turned to Larkin. "Nice riding, cowboy. How bad is it?"

He pressed a hand to his bleeding side. "Scratches. You?"

"Same. Clawed up a little. Everybody else?"

"We'll do." Glenna was already stanching a gash in Hoyt's arm.

"He's coming," Moira murmured.

"Where?" Hoyt clamped a hand on her arm. "I see nothing."

"There." She pointed. "He's coming."

He was a blur coming out of the trees, a swirl of black up the rise.

"Wasn't that entertaining? They're regrouping, for all the good it will do them." There was blood on his face, and more running down from a slice in his thigh.

"Come." Hoyt held out a hand to him. "It's time."

"I can't." Cian lifted his own hand and pressed it against the air between the stones. "It's like a wall to me. I am what I am."

"You can't stay here," Hoyt insisted. "They'll hunt you down. You'll be alone."

"I'm not such easy prey. Do what you're meant to do. I'll stay to make certain it works."

"If you stay we all stay." Larkin stepped to the gap between two stones. "If you fight, we all fight."

"The sentiment's appreciated," Cian told him. "But this is bigger than one of us, and you have somewhere to be."

"The other portal," Larkin began.

"If I find it, you can buy me a drink in Geall. Go." He met Hoyt's eyes. "What's meant is meant. So you've always believed, and so — in my way — have I. Go. Save worlds."

"I'll find a way." Hoyt reached through the stones to grip Cian's hand. "I'll find a way, I swear it to you."

"Good luck to you." Cian saluted them with his sword. "To you all."

With a heavy heart showing clearly in his eyes, Hoyt stepped back, lifted the crystal. Light beamed in it, and from it.

"Worlds wait. Time flows. Gods watch."

Tears glimmering on her cheeks, Glenna took his hand and repeated the words.

"It's not right." Larkin spoke softly. "It's not right to leave one of us."

"Maybe we can — Oh shit," Blair murmured as the ground began to rumble. The wind swirled up, and light began to pulse.

"Slan, mo cara." With one last look at Cian, Larkin gripped her hand. "It's a hell of

a ride," he told her. "Best hold on to me. Moira?"

She held her crystal; she spoke the words. And she stared into Cian's eyes as she felt the world shift. Then she reached out, grabbed his hand. "We are one force, one power. *This* is meant!"

And pulled him into the circle.

It was like being sucked into a tornado, Blair thought. Impossible wind that seemed to pull you away from the earth, spin you in mad circles while the light blasted your eyes.

Would there be munchkins on the other side?

She could see nothing but that wild white light, the spinning whirl of it. Could find no footing, no solid ground, so anchored herself with Larkin's hand.

Then there was dark, and utter stillness. She rubbed her hand over her face, tried to catch her breath. And she saw now there was moonlight, silver streams of it that speared down and struck the standing stones.

"Is this our stop?"

"Oh my *God!*" Glenna's voice was giddy. "What a rush. What a . . . wow. And Cian." Putting both her trembling hands on either side of Cian's face, she kissed him soundly. "How did you do it?" she asked Moira.

"How did you bring him inside?"

"I don't know. I just . . . It was meant. You were meant to be here," she said to Cian. "I felt it, and . . ." Moira seemed to realize she was still clutching his hand, and pulled hers away. "And well, here you are."

She pushed at hair that had come loose from its braid. "Well then, *fàilte a Geall*. Larkin." She made a laughing leap into his arms. "We're home."

"And handily enough, it's night." If Cian was shaken, he hid it well — merely glancing around him as he shoved back his hood. "Not that I don't trust your magical powers."

"There's still the matter of getting ourselves, and all this stuff where we're going." Blair gestured widely to encompass the chests, the weapons and cases.

"We can send men for most of it in the morning. I think we carry what we need most," Moira suggested.

"Weapons then. We don't know what we're walking into. Sorry," Blair added. "But you've been gone well over a month. We can't know."

"I can carry three, take the air." Larkin tugged Moira's disordered braid. "I could see if there's anything to worry about. And you can take one on the horse."

"My horse," Cian reminded him before he

looked at Moira. "I can take you on my horse."

"Sounds like a plan. Let's get it in motion." Blair slung on her own duffle, then grinned at Hoyt and Glenna. "You guys are going to love this."

Across Geall they flew, with the stallion and its two riders galloping below. As the moonlight dripped like magic, hills and wedges of forest were edged with silver; the river gleamed on its wandering journey through them. Blair saw cottages with thin smoke spiraling from chimneys, the dots that were cattle or sheep lolling in fields. The roads below were narrow and dirt, and empty of travelers but for Cian and Moira.

No cars, she thought, no lights but for the occasional glimmer that might have been a candle or lantern. Just land, she realized, left to roll and spread, and rise to the silhouettes of mountains.

A land, she reminded herself, that until a few weeks ago, she'd believed a fairy tale.

She turned her head, saw the coast with its high, steep cliffs that flowed down to graceful inlets. The sea spread out, velvet black, and cupped a trio of rough little islands on its journey to the horizon.

She heard Glenna give a quick gasp behind her, and looked over again.

The fantasy rose from the high hill, a wide curl of river at its back. Its stones gleamed like jewels in the moonlight, rising up into towers and turrets, stretching out into crenelated walls.

A castle, Blair thought, dumbfounded. And what castle would be complete without a drawbridge, or peaked caps on towers that held silky white flags?

A claddaugh on one, she noted as they waved in the breeze. A dragon on the other.

Glenna leaned forward to speak in her ear. "A hell of a lot to take in, for a couple of twenty-first-century girls."

"I thought nothing was going to surprise me." There was wonder in her voice; Blair could hear it herself. "But wow, a freaking castle."

Larkin circled it so they could keep the horse and riders in view below. Then he glided down to a wide courtyard.

Instantly, Blair found herself surrounded by men in light armor, swords already drawn. She held her hands up in plain sight as she and her companions slid to the ground.

"Your name and your purpose." One of the guards stepped forward.

Larkin shed the dragon. "That's hardly a warm welcome, Tynan."

"Larkin!" The guard sheathed his sword, then grabbed Larkin in a one-armed hug. "Thank the gods! Where the devil have you been all these weeks? We'd all but given up on you. And the princess, where —"

"Open the gates. The princess Moira is waiting to come home."

"You heard Lord Larkin," Tynan snapped. He lacked an inch or two of Larkin's height, but his voice boomed with command. "Raise the gate. You must tell all. Your father will want to be waked."

"There's much to tell. Wake the cook while you're about it. Give welcome to my friends. The warrior Blair, Glenna the witch, Hoyt the sorcerer. We've traveled far today, Tynan. Farther than you can know."

He turned, reaching up to lift Moira down from the horse.

The men bowed, Blair noted, when Moira's feet touched the ground.

"Tynan, your face is a welcome sight." She kissed his cheek. "This is Cian, and this fine fellow is his Vlad. Would you have one of the men take him to the stables, see he's housed and tended?"

"Me or the horse?" Cian murmured, but she pretended not to hear.

"Have my uncle told we've come home, and we wait upon him in the family parlor."

"At once, Highness."

Moira led the way through the courtyard toward a wide archway. The doors were already open for them.

"Nice summer house you've got here," Blair murmured. "*Lord* Larkin."

He shot her a grin. " 'Tisn't much, but it's home. In truth, my own family home isn't far from here. My father would be acting as ruler until Moira is crowned."

"If it's meant," Moira said over her shoulder.

"If it's meant," he agreed.

Torches were being lit in the great hall, so Blair assumed word of the return was already spreading. In the floor, fashioned of some sort of tile, the two symbols from the flag here inlaid so that the claddaugh seemed to float over the dragon's head.

They flew again in the glass dome curved into the high ceiling.

She had the impression of heavy furnishings, of colorful tapestries, caught the scent of roses as they started up a curve of stairs.

"The castle has stood more than twelve hundred years," Larkin told her. "Built here, at the order of the gods, on this rise known as Rioga. Royal. All who have ruled Geall since have ruled from here."

Blair glanced back at Glenna. "Makes the

White House look like a hovel."

Blair wouldn't have called the room they entered any sort of parlor. It was huge and high-ceilinged, backed by a hearth tall and wide enough for five men to stand in. The fire already roared inside, and over it was a mantel of lapis blue marble.

Overhead, a mural depicted what she assumed were scenes of Geallian history.

There were several long, low seats with jewel-toned fabrics. Chairs with high, ornate backs stood at a long table where servants were already placing tankards and goblets, bowls of apples and pears, plates of cheese and bread.

Paintings and tapestries covered the walls while patterned rugs spread over the floor. Candles flamed in chandeliers, in tall stands, in silver candleabras.

One of the servants, a curvy one with a long spill of gold hair curtseyed in front of Moira. "My lady, we thank the gods for your return. And yours, my lord."

There was a glint in her eye when she looked at Larkin that had Blair's eyebrows raising.

"Isleen. I'm happy to see you." Moira took both her hands. "Your mother is well?"

"She is, my lady. Already weeping with joy."

"Will you tell her I'll see her soon? And we need chambers prepared for our guests." Moira took her aside to explain what she wanted.

Larkin was already heading for the table, and the food. He broke off a hunk of bread, hacked off a wide chunk of cheese, then mashed them together. "Ah, this tastes like home," he said with his mouth full. "Here now, Blair, have some of this."

Before she could object, he was stuffing some in her mouth. "Good," she managed.

"Good? Why it's brilliant as starshine. And what's this?" He lifted a tankard. "Wine, it is? Glenna, you'll have some, won't you?"

"Boy, won't I."

"Little changes," came a voice from the wide doorway. The man who stood there, tall, well built, his dark hair liberally threaded with gray, stared at Larkin. "Surrounded by food and pretty women."

"Da."

They met halfway across the room, and with bear hugs. Blair could see the man's face, the emotion that held it. Then she could see Larkin in the eyes of tawny gold.

The man caught Larkin's face in his big hands, gave his son a hard kiss on the mouth. "I didn't wake your mother. I wanted to be sure before I lifted her hopes."

"I'll go to her as soon as I can. You're well. You look well. A bit tired."

"Sleep hasn't come easy these past weeks. You're injured."

"It's not to worry. I promise."

"No, it's not to worry. You're home." He turned, and he smiled — and again, Blair saw Larkin in him.

"Moira."

"Sir." Then her breath hitched and she was running to him. Her arms clamped around his neck as he lifted her off the ground.

"I'm sorry, I'm sorry I took him from you. I'm sorry I worried you so."

"You're back now, aren't you? Safe and whole. And you bring guests." He set Moira back on her feet. "You're welcome here."

"This is Larkin's father, and the brother of my mother. Prince Riddock. Sir, I would present my friends to you, the best I've ever known."

As Moira introduced them, Larkin stood behind his father's back, signalling the others that they should bow or curtsey. Blair went with the bow, feeling foolish enough.

"There's so much to tell you," Moira began. "If we could sit. Larkin, the doors please? We should be private."

Riddock listened, interrupting occasionally to ask Moira to repeat or expand. Now and then he directed a question to his son, or to one of the others.

Blair could almost see the weight of the words press down on his shoulders, and the grim determination with which he bore it.

"There have been other attacks, at least six, since —" Riddock hesitated briefly. "Since you left us. I did what I could to heed what you wrote to me, Moira, to warn the people to stay in their homes after sunset, to not welcome strangers in the dark. But habits and traditions die hard. As did those who followed them these weeks."

Riddock studied Cian across the long table. "You say we must trust this one, though he is one of them. A demon inside a man."

"Trust is a large word." Idly, Cian peeled an apple. "Tolerate might be smaller, and more easily swallowed."

"He fought with us," Larkin began. "Bled with us."

"He is my brother. If he isn't to be trusted," Hoyt said flatly, "neither am I."

"Nor any of us," Glenna finished.

"You've banded together these weeks. This is to be understood." Riddock took a small sip of his wine as his gaze remained watchful on Cian. "But to believe a demon could and would stand against his own kind, to — tolerate — such a thing, is more than a swallow."

Cian only continued to peel his apple, even as Hoyt started to his feet.

"Uncle." Moira laid a hand over Riddock's. "I would be dead if not for him. But beyond that, he stood with us within the Dance of the Gods, traveled here by their hands. Chosen by them. Will you question their will?"

"Every thinking man questions, but I will abide by the will of the gods. Others may find it more difficult."

"The people of Geall will follow your orders, sir, and your lead."

"Mine?" He turned to her. "The sword waits for you, Moira, as does the crown."

"They will wait awhile longer. I've only just come home, and there's much to be done. Much more important matters than ceremony."

"Ceremony? You speak of the will of the gods one moment, and dismiss it the next?"

"Not dismiss. Only ask that it waits. You have the trust and the confidence of the people. I'm untried. I don't feel ready, not in my heart or in mind." Her eyes were grave as they searched her uncle's face. "Awhile longer, please. I may not be the one to lift the sword, but if I am, I need to know I'm ready to carry it. Geall needs and deserves a ruler of strength and confidence. I won't give it less."

"We'll talk further on it. Now you're weary. You must all be weary, and a mother waits to see her son." Riddock got to his feet. "We'll speak more in the morning, and we'll do all that needs to be done in the coming days. Larkin."

He rose at his father's bidding. "I wish you good night," Larkin said to the others. "And soft dreams on your first night in Geall."

He looked briefly at Blair, then followed his father from the room.

"Your uncle's an imposing man," Blair commented.

"And a good one. With him we'll raise an army that will send Lilith back to hell. If you're ready, I'll show you to your chambers."

It was a little hard to settle down and sleep, Blair decided, when she was spending the night in a castle. And in a room that was suited to royalty.

Before they'd arrived, she'd been expecting something a little more Dark Ages, she supposed. Tough stone fortress on a windy hill. Smoky torches, mud, animal droppings.

Instead she got something closer to Cinderella's castle.

Instead of a cramped room, something like a barracks with rushes — whatever they were, exactly — on the floor and a lumpy cot, she had a spacious chamber with whitewashed walls. The bed was big, soft and draped in a blue velvet canopy. The thick rug had images of peacocks worked into its soft wool.

A check out the windows showed her she looked down on a garden with a pretty spurting fountain. The window seat was padded with more velvet.

There was a small writing desk. Pretty, she thought, not that she'd be making much use of the crystal inkwell or the quill.

The fire was simmering, and its surround was blue-veined white marble.

It was all so fine she could nearly overlook the lack of modern plumbing. The closest the place came to it was the chamber pot tucked behind a painted screen.

She had a feeling she'd be making use of the great outdoors in that area quite a bit.

She stripped down to her underwear and used the basin of water provided to clean the scratches on her leg before dabbing on some of the balm Glenna had given her.

She wondered how the others were doing.

She wished it were morning so *she* could be doing.

When the door opened, she picked up the dagger she'd set beside the basin. Then put it down again when Larkin stepped in.

"Didn't hear you knock."

"I didn't. I thought you might be sleeping." He closed the door quietly behind him, took a quick scan of the room. "Does this suit you then?"

"The room? It's rock star. Feel a little weird, that's all. Like I walked into a book."

"I understand that, as I felt the same not long ago. Your wounds, do they trouble you?"

"They're nothing. Yours?"

"My mother fussed over them. That made her happy, as did weeping all over me. She's anxious to meet you, all of you."

"I guess." Awkward, Blair thought. Why was it all so awkward? "I, ah, it never really computed before. You being royalty."

"Oh well, that's not much to do with me, really. It's more ceremonial than anything. Honorary, you could say." He cocked his head as he moved toward her. "Did you think I wouldn't come to you tonight?"

"I don't know what I thought. It's all pretty confusing."

"Confused, are you?" A smile flirted

around his mouth. "I don't mind that. I'll just confuse you a bit more, seduce you."

He traced his finger along the edge of her tank, just teasing the skin.

"You spend a lot of time on seductions? Say, working that on the blonde with the breasts? What was her name? Isleen."

"Flirtation, all in good fun, never seduction. It's not proper or fair to take advantage of one who serves you." He leaned to her, brushed his lips over her shoulder, nudged the strap down. "And while I might have dallied in the past, you weren't here. For it's the God's truth there's not another woman in Geall to compare to you."

He brought his lips to hers, just to nibble. "Blair Murphy," he murmured. "Warrior and beauty."

He played his hands down her back, deepening the kiss just a little. Then just a little more. And when his lips cruised over her face, along her throat, he all but crooned to her in Gaelic.

The sound of it, the feel of him nearly had her eyes rolling back in her head.

"I keep thinking this is a mistake. But it feels so damn good."

"Not a mistake." He caught her chin with his teeth while his thumbs slid up, circled her nipples. "Not at all."

Part of the journey, she told herself as she melted into him. They'd take something good, something strong for themselves along the way.

So she met his lips with hers now, sank herself into him, the warm, solid flesh. There was sweetness in those easy strokes of his hands, and a shivering thrill whenever they found her secrets.

When he lifted her into his arms, she didn't feel like a warrior. She felt conquered.

"I want you." She pressed her face into the curve of his throat as he lay her on the bed. And just breathed him in. "How can I want you so much?"

"It's meant." He lifted her hand, kissed the cup of her palm. "Ssh," he said before she could speak. "Just feel. For tonight, let's both of us just feel."

She could be so soft, he thought, so pliant, so giving. In surrender she made him feel like a king. Those eyes, the drowning blue, watched him as they moved together. They blurred with pleasure as he touched her, tasted her. Those hands, so firm on the hilt of a sword, trembled a little when she drew his shirt aside to find him.

Her lips pressed against his chest, against the heart that was already lost to her.

They took each other slowly, quietly, while

the firelight shimmered over their bodies. There were murmurs and sighs instead of words, and a long, lazy climb instead of the frantic race.

When he slipped inside her, he watched her face, watched her as they moved together. As everything in him gathered for that final leap, he watched her still.

And at the end of it, he thought he'd simply fallen into her eyes.

CHAPTER 13

The guy was a snuggler. He just curved in, body to body, with an arm hooked around her waist — the way she imagined a kid might hold on to a teddy bear.

Blair just wasn't used to having someone hang on to her at night, and couldn't decide if she liked it or not. On one hand, it was sort of sweet and sexy to wake up with him wrapped all over her. Everything was all warm and soft and cozy.

On the other, if she had to move fast, get to a stake or a sword, he was dead weight.

Maybe she should practice breaking loose, rolling out, reaching the closest weapon. And maybe she should relax. It wasn't as if this was a permanent situation.

It was just . . . convenient.

And that was a stupid attitude sunk in bullshit, she admitted. If she couldn't be honest inside her own head, her own heart, then where?

They were more than a convenience to each other, more than compatriots. More, she was afraid, than lovers. At least on her side.

Still, in the light of day she had to be realistic. Whatever it was they were to each other, it couldn't go anywhere. Not beyond this. Cian had spoken the pure truth in Ireland, outside of the Dance. The problems they faced were a lot bigger and more important than one person or their personal needs and wishes. And so their personal needs had to be, by definition, temporary.

After Samhain it would be over. She had to believe they'd win, that was essential, but after the victory dance, the backslapping and champagne toasts there would be hard facts to face.

Larkin — *Lord* Larkin — was a man of Geall. Once this was done and she'd completed the mission, Geall would be for her, in a very real sense, a fairy tale again. Sure, maybe she could hang around for a few days, have that picnic he'd talked about. Bask a little. But in the end, she'd have to go.

She had a birthright, she had a duty, she thought as she touched her fingers to Morrigan's cross. Turning her back on it wasn't an option.

Love, if that's what she was feeling, wasn't enough to win the day. Who knew better?

He was more than she'd ever expected to have, even in the short term, so she couldn't and wouldn't complain about her luck, or her destiny, or the cold will of gods. He accepted her, cared for her, desired her. He had courage, a bone-deep loyalty, and a sense of fun.

She'd never been with a man who possessed all that, and who still looked at her as if she were special.

She thought maybe — it wasn't impossible — he loved her.

For her, Larkin was a kind of personal miracle. He would never walk away from her without a backward glance. He would never shove her aside simply because of what she was. So when they parted, there could be no regrets.

If things were different they might have been able to make a go of it. At least give it a good, solid try. But things weren't different.

Or, more accurately, things were too different.

So they'd have a few weeks. They'd have the journey. And they'd both take something memorable away from it.

She kissed him, a soft and warm press of lips. Then she poked him.

"Wake up."

His hand slid down her back to rub lazily over her ass.

"Not that way."

" 'S the best way. Feel how firm you are, smooth and firm. I dreamed I was making love with you in an orchard in the high days of summer. For you always smell of tart, green apples. Makes me want to take a good bite of you."

"Eat enough green apples, you get a belly-ache."

"My belly's iron." His fingers trailed up and down the back of her thigh. "In the dream there was no one but us two, and the trees ladened with fruit under a sky painted the purest of blues."

His voice was all sleepy and slurry, she thought. Sexy. "Like paradise? Adam and Eve? An apple got them in big, bad trouble, if memory serves."

He only smiled. He'd yet to open his eyes. "You look on the dark side of things, but I don't mind that. In the dream, I gave you such pleasure you wept from the joy of it."

She snorted. "Yeah. In your dreams."

"And sobbed my name, again and again.

Begging me to take you. 'Use this body,' you pleaded, 'take it with your strong hands, with your skilled mouth. Pierce it with your mighty — ' "

"Okay, you're making that up."

He opened one eye, and there was such laughter in it her belly quivered in response. "Well, yes, but I'm enjoying it. And see there, you're smiling. That's what I wanted to see when I opened my eyes. Blair's smile."

Tenderness swamped her. "You're such a goof," she murmured, and rubbed her hand over his cheek.

"The first part of the dream was true. We should look for the orchard one day." He closed his eyes again, started to snuggle in.

"Hold on there. Shut-eye's over. We have to get started."

"In a hurry, are you? Well, all right then."

He rolled onto her. "I didn't mean —" And slipped into her.

The pleasure was so deep, so easy, that her breath caught even as she laughed. "I should've known your mighty would be up and ready."

"And always at your service."

After a later start than she'd planned, she pulled on clothes. "We need to talk about some basics."

"We'll break our fast in the little dining hall."

"I've never known you to have a fast to break. And I wasn't talking about food."

"Oh?" He looked mildly interested as he belted his tunic. "What else then?"

"To get really basic, bathroom facilities. Elimination, hygiene. The chamber pot deal's okay for emergencies, but I'm going to have a problem with it on a regular basis."

"Ah." Brows knit, he scratched his head over it. "There are toilets of sorts in the family wing, and latrines for the castle guards. But they're not what you'd be used to."

"I'll make do. Bathing?"

"The shower." He said it wistfully. "I miss it already. I can have a tub brought up, and water heated. Or there's the river."

"Okay, that's a start." She didn't need plush, Blair thought. She just needed, well, reasonable. "Now we have to talk about training."

"Let's talk about it over food." He took her arm, pulling her from the room so she wouldn't argue while his stomach was rumbling.

There were spiced apples Larkin seemed particularly fond of, and chunks of potatoes fried in, she assumed, the fat of the thick slices of ham that accompanied them. The tea was black as pitch, and nearly had the same kick as coffee.

"I miss the Coke as well," he commented. "Going to have to suck that one up."

While the room was smaller than the parlor had been, it was still large enough to fit the big oak table, a couple of enormous servers, and chests she imagined held linens and dishware.

"Does a drawbridge work like a door?" she wondered. "To keep them out," she explained when Larkin gave her a questioning smile. "Do they need an invitation to come into the castle compound? We'd better deal with that, cover our ass. Hoyt and Glenna should be able to come up with something."

"We have a few days."

"If Lilith sticks to the schedule. Either way, we've got our work cut out for us. Organizing, getting civilians transported from the battle area. Hoyt and Glenna might want to try that vamp-free-zone spell, but I have to say, I don't see it working. We're not talking about one house, or even a small settlement."

She shook her head as she ate. "Too much area, too many variables. And, most likely, a waste of their time and energies."

"That may be. Moving people to safety is

more important. My father and I spoke of it last night, before I came to you. Even now runners are out so the word spreads."

"Good. We're going to need to put most of our focus on training the troops. You've got guards and — knights, maybe?"

"Aye."

"They have your basic combat skills, but this is a different matter. Then your general population needs to be prepared to defend themselves. We need to get to work on setting those traps. And I'm going to want a firsthand look at the battleground itself."

Her mind clicked off its list while she plowed through breakfast. "We're going to need to set up multiple training areas — military and civilian. Then there's weapons, supplies, transportation. We probably need an area where Hoyt and Glenna can work."

"It will all be seen to."

Something in his tone, the calmness of it, reminded her this was his ground now. He knew it, and its people. She didn't.

"I don't know the pecking order. The chain of command," she said. "Who's in charge of what."

He poured them both more tea. For a moment he thought how nice it was — even if the talk was of war — to sit, just the two of them, over the morning meal.

"Until the sword is drawn from the stone, my father rules as the head of the first family of Geall. He isn't king. He will not be king, but Moira, I think, understands that the men . . . the military as you call it, trust him. They'll follow the ruler, the one whose hand lifts the sword, but . . ."

"This is giving them time. It's letting them follow orders, and absorb the idea of this war, from a man who's been proven to them. I get it. Moira's smart to wait a little longer to take command."

"She is, yes. She's also afraid."

"That she won't be the one to lift the sword?"

He shook his head. "That she will. That she'll be the queen who must order her people to war. To shed their blood, cause their deaths. It haunts her."

"It's Lilith who sheds their blood, causes their death."

"And it will be Moira who tells them to fight. The farmers and the shopkeepers, the tinkers and the cooks. For generations Geall has been ruled in peace. She'll be the first to change that. It weighs on her."

"It should. It should never be easy to send a world to war. Larkin, what if it's not her? What if she's not the one, through destiny, or just because she doesn't have it in her to pull that sword out of stone?"

"She was the queen's only child. There's no other in her line."

"So lines can shift. There's you."

"Bite your tongue." When she didn't smile, he sighed. "There would be me. My brother, my sister. My sister's children. The oldest is but four. My brother, he's hardly more than a boy himself, and it's the land that calls to him. My sister wants nothing more than to tend her babies and her home. They could never do this thing. I can't believe the gods would put this into their hands."

"But yours?"

He met her eyes. "I've never wanted it, to rule. War or peace."

"People would follow you. They know you, and they trust you."

"That may be. And if it comes to it, what choice would I have? But the crown isn't my wish, Blair." Nor was it his destiny, of that he was sure. He reached over, took her hand. "You must know what I wish."

"Wishes, dreams. We don't always get what we ask for. So we have to take what there is."

"And what's in your heart? In mine? I want —"

"I'm sorry." Moira stopped at the doorway. "I'm sorry to disturb you, but my uncle has spoken to the guards, and to the inner circle of knights. You're to come to the great hall."

"Then we'd better get started," Blair said.

She felt under-dressed in jeans and a black sweater. For the first time since Blair had met her, Moira wore a dress. A gown? Whatever the term it was simple and elegant, in a kind of russet tone that fell straight down her body from a high, gathered waist.

Her silver cross hung between her breasts, and a thin circlet of gold sat on her head.

Even Glenna seemed polished up, but then again, her favorite witch had a way of giving a casual shirt and pants an air of style and grace.

The cavernous room was heated by fires on either side and fronted by a wide platform, up two steps where a deep red carpet ran. On it stood a throne. An actual throne, Blair mused, in regal red and gold.

Riddock sat on it now, with Moira standing at his side.

To the other side sat a woman. Her blond hair was bound back in what Blair thought was called a snood. A younger woman, obviously pregnant, sat beside her. Two men stood at their backs.

The first family of Geall, Blair decided. Larkin's family.

And at a glance from his father, he touched Blair's arm, murmured: "It'll be fine." Then he left her to go up the steps and stand between his parents.

"Please." Riddock gestured. "Take your ease." He waited until they'd taken chairs at the base of the platform. "Moira and I have talked at length. At her request, I have spoken to the guards and many of the knights to tell them of the threat, and the coming war. It is Moira's wish that you, and the other who came with you, be given the authority of command. To recruit, to train, to forge our army."

He paused, studied them. "You are not Geallian."

"Sir," Larkin objected. "They are proven."

"This war is brought to our soil, and it will be paid in our blood. I ask why those from outside should lead our people."

"May I speak?" Hoyt got to his feet, waited until Riddock nodded. "Morrigan herself has sent us here, just as she sent two Geallians to Ireland, to us, so that we would gather into the first circle. We who have come here have left our worlds and our families, and have pledged our lives to fight this pestilence that comes to Geall."

"This pestilence murdered our queen, my sister, before ever you came." Riddock gestured toward them. "You are two women, a demon, and a man of magic. And you are strangers to me. I have seasoned men, who are proven to me. Men whose names I know, whose families I know. Men who know Geall and are unquestioned in loyalty. Men who I know will lead our people strong into battle."

"Where they'll be slaughtered like lambs." Though Riddock's stare at the interruption was frigid, Blair pushed to her feet. "Sorry, but that's the way it is. We can dance around it, play protocol, waste time, but the fact is your seasoned warriors don't know squat about fighting vampires."

When Hoyt laid a hand on Blair's arm, she shook it off. Testily. "And I didn't come here to be shuffled aside because I wasn't born here, or because I'm a woman. And I didn't come here to fight for Geall. I came here to fight for it all."

"Well said," Glenna murmured. "And ditto. My husband is accustomed to matters of court and princes. We're not. So you'll have to forgive us mere women. Mere women of power."

She held out a hand, and a ball of fire, then flicked the ball into the hearth on the side of the room. Testily.

"Mere women who have fought and bled, and watched friends die. And the demon you spoke of is my family. He's also fought and bled and watched a friend die."

"Warriors you may be," Riddock acknowledged with what could only be termed a regal nod. "But to lead takes more than magic and courage."

"It takes experience, a cool head. And cold blood."

Riddock glanced back to Blair with a slight lift of eyebrows. "These, aye, and the trust of the people you would lead."

"They have mine," Larkin said. "They have Moira's. Earned every hour of every day these past weeks. Sir, have I not earned yours?"

"You have." He said nothing for a moment, then again gestured to Hoyt, Glenna and Blair. "I would ask that you instruct, and that you take your commands from Lord Larkin and the Princess Moira."

"We can start with that," Blair decided. "Will you fight?" she asked Riddock.

Now the look in his eye had a kinship with a wolf. "To the last breath."

"Then you're going to need instruction, too, or that last breath's going to come sooner than you think."

Larkin cast his eyes heavenward, but laid a hand on his father's shoulder and spoke lightly. "Blair has a warrior's spirit."

"And an unruly tongue. The gaming area then," Riddock decided. "For our first instructions."

"Your father doesn't like me."

"That's not so." Larkin gave Blair a friendly elbow nudge. "He's merely working his way around to understanding you, and all of this."

"Uh-huh." She looked at Glenna as they walked outside. "Do you think we should tell Riddock how our people felt about kings?"

"I think we could let that one alone. But running up against what we did in there makes me realize it's not going to be a snap convincing a bunch of macho Geallian men that women should teach them how to fight a war."

"I've got some thoughts on that. And I think you should work with the women anyway."

"Excuse me?"

"Don't get a wedgie. You have more diplomacy and patience than I do." Probably, Blair thought, anyone did. "And the women will probably relate better to you. They have to be trained, too, Glenna. To defend themselves, their families. To fight. Someone has to do it. And someone has to know which ones should stay home, and which ones should go."

"Oh God."

"We're going to have the same deal with men. The ones who don't measure up have to be put to other use. Treating the injured, protecting the kids, the elderly, supplying food, weapons."

"And what do you suggest I do, Cian do," Hoyt asked, "while the two of you are so busy?"

"His nose is out of joint because we mouthed off to Riddock," Glenna murmured.

"My nose is fine and well, thanks all the same." Hoyt spoke with unwavering dignity. "He needed to be told, though there could have been considerably more tact. If we offended him, it only takes more time and effort to repair the damage."

"He's a reasonable man," Larkin insisted. "He wouldn't let a few breaches of protocol interfere with what needs doing." Frustrated himself, Larkin raked a hand through his hair. "He hasn't been in a position to rule before this. The queen was crowned very young, and he's had only the position as an adviser now and then."

He'd have to be a fast learner, Blair thought.

Men were already gathered in what Blair saw was an area they held their jousts, their tournaments and games. There was a long rope where colored hoops hung. Score-board, she decided. And the royal box, the rougher seats for the masses. Paddocks for horses, tents where competitors readied themselves for whatever sport was on the ticket.

"You ever see that movie, *Knight's Tale?*" Blair muttered.

"We will, we will rock you," Glenna responded and made Blair grin.

"Sure helps having you here. Coming up on show time. Pick out one you figure you can take."

"What? Why? What?"

"Both of you," Blair said, adding Hoyt. "Just in case."

Larkin stepped up to the lines of men. "My father has told you what it is we face, and what is coming. We have until Samhain to prepare, and on that day we must be in the Valley of Silence to do battle. We must win. To win you must know how to fight and how to kill these things that are not human. They are not men, and cannot be killed as men can be killed."

Hanging back as Larkin spoke, Blair studied the men. Most of them looked fit and able. She spotted Tynan, the guard both Larkin and Moira had greeted on arrival. He, Blair decided, looked not only fit and able. He looked ready.

"I have fought them," Larkin continued, "as the princess Moira has fought them. As those who came with us from outside this world have fought them. We will teach you what you need to know."

"We know how to fight." A man who stood beside Tynan called out. "What can you teach me I haven't taught you on this very field?"

"This won't be a game." Blair stepped forward. This one was a big bruiser, she noted. Looked cocky with it. Good strong shoulders, tough built, hard attitude.

Perfect.

"You won't get the consolation prize and a pat on the back if you come in second in this. You'll be dead."

His face didn't sneer at her, but his tone did. "Women don't instruct men on the art of combat. They tend the fires, and keep the bed warm."

He got some appreciative male laughter and a look of pity from Larkin.

"Niall," he said, with cheer, "you've

stepped full into the bog with that one. These women are warriors."

"I see no warriors here." With his hands on his hips, Niall elbowed toward the front of the line. "But two women dressed as men, and a sorcerer who stands with them. Or behind them."

"I'll go first," Blair murmured to Glenna. "I'll take you on," she told Niall. "Here and now. Your choice of weapons."

He snorted. "Do you expect me to spar with a girl?"

"Choose your weapon," Riddock ordered.

"Sir. At your command." He was snickering as he strode away.

Immediately the wagers began.

"Hey, now!" Larkin gave Blair a quick pat on the shoulder, moved into the men. "I'll have some of that."

Niall strode back with two thick fencing poles. Blair studied the way he held them, the way he moved. Full swagger now.

"This will be quick," he assured Blair.

"Yeah, it will. It's a good choice of weapon," she called out over the voices still calling out odds and wagers. "Wood kills a vampire, if you have the strength and the aim to get it through the heart. You look strong enough." She eyed Niall up and down. "How's your aim?"

He grinned, wide. "I've not yet had a woman complain of it."

"Well, let's see what you got, big guy." She gripped the pole lengthwise, nodded. "Ready?"

"I'll give you the first three hits, out of fairness."

"Fine."

She took him down in two, ramming the end of the pole in his gut, then sweeping down to crack it hard against his legs. Ignoring the laughter and whoops, she stood over him, the pole pressed to his heart.

"Now if you were a vampire, I'd put this right through you till it came out the other side. Then you'd be dust." She stepped back. "I think you should hold your bets, guys. That was just practice." She cocked her head at Niall. "Ready now?"

He got to his feet, and she saw the shock and embarrassment at being knocked down by a woman had lit a fire in him. He came in hard, the force of his pole against hers shooting up her arms. She leaped up and over when he aimed for her legs, then cracked her stick against his chest.

He fought well, she decided, and with a bullish strength — but he lacked creativity.

She used her pole like a vault, planting it in the ground, swinging up over her opponent. When she landed, she spun a kick into the small of his back, caught her pole. And tripped him with it.

This time she held it to his throat as he panted for breath.

"Three out of five?" she suggested.

He let out a roar, knocking at the pole. She let his forward motion carry her back, then pumped up with her feet to flip him over her. And flat onto his back again.

His eyes were still dazed as she pressed the pole to his throat again. The last fall had knocked the wind out of him, and stolen the color from his cheeks.

"I can do this all day, and you'll end up on your ass every time."

She got to her feet, and now planted her pole beside him to lean negligently against it. "You're strong, but so am I. Plus, you're heavy in the feet — and you weren't thinking on them. Just because you're bigger doesn't mean you'll win, and it sure as hell doesn't mean you'll live. I'd say you got close to a hundred pounds on me, but I knocked you flat three times."

"The first didn't count." Niall sat up, rubbed his sore head. "But I'll give you the two."

When he grinned at her, Blair knew she'd won.

"Larkin, come take this pole," Niall called out. "I'll fight you for her, for this one's a woman for certain."

Blair held out a hand. "He'd beat you, too. I helped train him."

"Then you'll teach me. And them?" He jerked his chin toward Hoyt and Glenna. "Can they fight like you?"

"I'm the best, but they're pretty damn good."

She turned to the group of men, waited while money finished changing hands. Tynan, she noted, was one of the few besides Larkin that collected any.

"Anyone else need a demonstration?"

"Wouldn't mind one from the redhead," someone called out, and had more laughter rolling.

Glenna fluttered her lashes, added a coy smile. Then drew her dagger from its sheath and shot a line of fire from it.

Men scrambled back, en masse.

"My husband's is bigger," she said sweetly.

"Aye." Hoyt swept forward. "Perhaps one of you would like a demonstration from me instead of my lovely wife. Sword? Lance?" He turned up his palms, let the fire dance above them. "Bare hands? For I don't stand behind these women, but I'm proud and honored to stand with them."

"Down boy," Blair murmured. "Fire's a weapon against them. Powerful weapon, as is wood, if used right. Steel will hurt them, slow them down, but it won't kill them unless you cut off the head. They'll just keep coming until they rip out your throat."

She tossed her fencing pole to Niall. "It won't be quick and clean like this little bout," she told them. "It will be bloody, and vicious, and cruel beyond the telling of it. Many of them, maybe most, will be stronger and faster than you. But you'll stop them. Because if you don't, they won't just kill you, the soldiers who meet them in combat. They'll kill your children, your mothers. Those they don't kill they'll change, they'll turn into what they are, or enslave them for food, for sport. So you'll stop them, because there's no choice."

She paused because now there was silence, now every eye there was on her. "We're going to show you how."

CHAPTER 14

Blair debated between the river and the tub.
The river was very likely freezing, and that
would be a bitch. But she just couldn't re-
sign herself to having some servant haul up
steaming buckets of water, to pour them into
what essentially would be a bigger bucket.
Then after she'd bathed, they'd have to repeat the whole deal in reverse.

It was just too weird.

Still, after several hours working with a
bunch of men, she needed soap and water.

Was that too much to ask?

"You did very well." Moira fell into step
beside her. "I know this must be frustrating
for you, like starting over. And with men
who feel, in some ways, they already know as
much — if not more — than you. But you
did very well. You've made a fine start."

"Most of those guys are in good to excellent shape, and that's a plus. But the bulk of

them still think it's a game, for the most part. Just don't believe. That's a big strike in the minus column."

"Because they haven't seen. They know of my mother, but many still believe — need to believe — it was some sort of wild dog. It might be if I hadn't seen myself what killed her, I could refuse to believe it."

"It's easier to refuse. Refusing is one of the reasons Jeremy's dead now."

"Aye. That's why I think people need to see, need to believe. We need to hunt down the ones that killed the queen, the ones that have killed others since that night. We need to bring at least one of them back here."

"You want to take one alive?"

"I do." Moira remembered how Cian had once pulled a vampire into the training room, then stood back so the rest of them would have to fight it. And understand it. "It will make a point."

"Not impossible to refuse what's in front of your face, but harder." Blair thought it through quickly. "Okay. I'll go out to-night."

"Not alone. Don't, don't," Moira said wearily when Blair started to argue. "You're used to hunting alone, capable of hunting alone. But you don't know the land here. They will by now. I'll go with you."

"You've got a point, and a strong one. But no, you're not the one for this hunt. I'm not saying you're not capable either. But you're not the best when it comes to close-in fighting. It'll have to be Larkin, and I'll need Cian."

In a gesture of annoyance, Moira tugged a blossom from a bush. "Now you have the strong point. I feel I've done nothing but matters of state since I've come home."

"You've got my sympathy. But I think that kind of thing has to be important, too. Statesmen — women — people — they raise armies. You've already taken steps to move people out of what's going to be a war zone. That's saving lives, Moira."

"I know it. I do. But . . ."

"Who's going to stir up the general population, fire them up into putting their lives on the line? We'll train them, Moira. But you've got to get them to us."

"You're right, I know."

"I'll get you a vampire — two if I can manage it. You get me people I can teach to kill one. But right now, I've got to wash up. A vamp could smell me a half a mile away."

"I'll have a bath readied for you, in your chambers."

"I was thinking I'd just use the river."

"Are you mad?" Finally, Moira's face relaxed into a smile. "The river's freezing this time of year."

It was never comfortable for Moira to speak with Cian. Not just because of what he was, as she'd reconciled herself to that. She thought of it, when she thought of him, as a condition; a kind of disease.

At their first meeting he had saved her life, and since had proven himself again and again.

His kind had murdered her mother, and yet he had fought beside her, had risked his life — or more accurately his existence — in doing so.

No, she couldn't hold what he was against him.

Still there was something inside her, something she couldn't quite see clearly, or study, or understand. Whatever it was made her uneasy, even nervy around him.

He knew it, or sensed it, she was sure. For he was so much cooler to her than the others. It was so rare that he would spare her a smile, or an easy word.

After the attack on their way to Geall, he'd swooped her up off the ground. His arms were the arms of a man. Flesh and blood, strong and real.

"Hold on," he'd said. And that was all.

She'd ridden with him to the castle, and his body had been that of a man. Lean and hard. And her heart had been raging for so many reasons, she'd been afraid to touch him.

What had he said to her then, in that sharp, impatient voice of his?

Oh yes: Get a grip on me before you fall on your ass again. I haven't bitten you yet, have I?

It had made her embarrassed and ashamed, and grateful he couldn't see the color flame into her cheeks.

Likely he'd have had something cutting to say about her virginal blushes as well.

Now she had to go to him, to ask him for help. It wasn't something she would pass off to Blair, or Larkin, certainly not to a servant. It was her duty to face him, to speak the words, ask the boon.

She would ask him to leave the castle, the comfort and safety of it, and go out into a strange land to hunt one of his own.

And he would do it, she knew, already she knew he would do it. Not for her — the request of a princess, the favor of a friend. He would do it for the others. For the whole of it.

She went alone. The women who attended her wouldn't approve, of course, and would consider the idea of their princess alone in a man's bedchamber unseemly, even shocking.

Such matters were no longer an issue for Moira. What would her ladies think if they knew she'd once fed him blood when he was wounded?

She imagined they would shriek and hide their faces — those who didn't swoon away. But they would have to look straight on at such things very soon. Or face much worse.

Her shoulders went tight as she stepped to the door of his chamber. But she knocked briskly, then stood to wait.

When he opened the door, the lights from the corridor washed over his face, and plunged the rest into shadow. She saw the faintest flicker of surprise come and go in his eyes as he studied her.

"Well, look at you. I barely recognized you. Your Highness."

It reminded her she was wearing a dress, and the gold mitre of her office. And remembering, she felt foolishly exposed.

"There were matters of state to attend to. I'm expected to attire myself appropriately."

"And fetchingly, too." He leaned lazily on the door. "Is my presence required?"

"Yes. No." *Why* did he forever make her clumsy? "May I come in? I would speak with you."

"By all means."

She had to brush against him to step inside. The room was like midnight, she thought. Not a single candle lit, nor the fire, and the drapes were pulled tight at the windows.

"The sun's gone down."

"Yes, I know."

"Would you mind if we had some light?" She picked up the tinderbox, fumbling a bit. "I can't see so well as you in the dark." The quick flare of light did quite a bit to calm her jumping stomach. "There's a chill," she continued, lighting more candles. "Should I light the fire for you?"

"Suit yourself."

He said nothing while she knelt in front of the hearth, set the turf. But she knew he watched her, and his watching made her hands feel cold and stiff.

"Are you comfortable here?" she began. "The room isn't so large or grand as you're used to."

"And separate enough from the general population so they can be comfortable."

Stunned, she turned, kneeling still while the turf caught flame at her back. She didn't flush. Instead her cheeks went very pale. "Oh, but no, I never meant . . ."

"It's no matter." He picked up a glass he'd

obviously poured before she'd come in. And now he drank deliberately of the blood with his eyes on hers. "I imagine your people would be put off by some of my daily habits."

Distress hitched into her voice. "It was never a concern. The room, it faces north. I thought . . . I only thought there would be less direct sun, and you'd be more comfortable. I would never insult a guest — a friend. I wouldn't insult someone who welcomed me into their home when they have come to mine."

She got quickly to her feet. "I can have your things moved, right away. I —"

He held up a hand. "There's no need. And I apologize for assuming." It was rare for him to feel the discomfort of guilt, but he felt it now. "It's a considerate choice. I shouldn't have expected less."

"Why are we . . . I don't understand why we seem to be so often at odds."

"Don't you?" he murmured. "Well, that's likely for the best. So, to what do I owe the honor of your presence?"

"You make fun of me," she said quietly. "You're so hard when you speak to me."

She thought he sighed, just a little. "I'm in a mood. I don't rest well in unfamiliar places."

"I'm sorry. And I'm here to impose again. I've asked Blair to hunt the vampires now in Geall, to bring at least one of them back here. Alive."

"Contradiction in terms."

"I don't know how else to express it," she snapped. "My people will fight because it's asked of them. But I can't ask them to believe — can't make them believe — what seems impossible. So they need to be shown."

It would be a good queen, he thought, who didn't expect to be followed blindly. And see how she stood there now, he noted. So still, so serious, when he knew a war raged inside of her.

"You want me to go with her."

"I do — she does. I do. God, I am forever stumbling with you. She asked that you and Larkin go with her. She doesn't want me. She feels, and so do I, that I'm of more use gathering the forces, helping lay the traps she devised."

"Ruling."

"I don't rule yet."

"Your choice."

"Aye. For now. I'd be grateful if you would go with her and Larkin, if you can find a way to bring back a prisoner."

"I'd rather be doing than not. But there's

the matter of knowing where to look."

"I have a map. I've already spoken with my uncle, and know where the attacks — the known attacks — took place. Larkin knows the land of Geall. You can have no better guide. And you know you can have no better companion, in leisure or in battle."

"I've no problem with the boy, or with a hunt."

"Then as soon as you're ready, if you'd come to the outer courtyard. I can have someone show you the way."

"I remember the way."

"Well. I'll go see to your mounts and provisions." She went to the door, but he was there before her — without seeming to have moved at all. She looked up into his face. "Thank you," she said and slipped quickly out.

Those eyes, he thought as he shut the door behind her. Those long gray eyes could kill a man.

It was lucky he was already dead.

But he could do nothing about the scent she'd left behind her, the scent of woodland glades and cool spring water. Not a bloody thing he could do about that.

"We'll be watching." Glenna laid a hand on Blair's leg when Blair mounted her horse. "If you get into trouble we'll know. We'll do what we can to help."

"Don't worry. I've got thirteen years of this under my belt."

Not in Geall, Glenna thought, but she stepped back. "Good hunting."

They rode through the gates, and turned south.

It was a good night for it, Blair thought. Clear and cool. It would be easier to track them by night when they were active than by day when they would have gone to nest somewhere. In any case, she wouldn't have Cian, which she considered an advantage, if they hunted by day.

She rode between the two men at an easy trot. "I didn't want to ask Moira," she began. "But her mother was the first attack reported."

"Aye, the queen was the first death we know of."

"And there were no other attacks that night? No one taken?"

"No." Larkin shook his head. "Again that we know of."

"Target-specific then," Blair mused. "They came for Moira's mother — we assume. We don't know how they got in."

"I've thought of it," Larkin admitted. "Before the queen's death, there would have been no reason to stop someone from coming in. A wagon of supplies, perhaps, or any reasonable bit of business. They would have been passed through."

"Plays." Blair nodded after a moment. "Come in shortly after sundown. Stay in a bolt hole until everyone settles in for the night. Lure the queen outside, kill her." She glanced at Larkin. "We don't have more specifics?"

"Moira won't speak of it, really. I'm not sure she remembers the details of it."

"Maybe it doesn't matter — for our purposes. So they kill the queen, then they stay. Maybe they can't get back through except at specific times. But they don't rampage," she pointed out. "A handful of deaths in all these weeks. That's pretty low profile for the breed."

"There will have been more," Cian commented. "Travelers, whores, those not as quickly missed as others. But they've been careful, and avoided what we're doing now. The hunt. I don't think they're only hiding from us."

"Who then?" Larkin glanced over and saw Blair was studying Cian thoughtfully.

"He means Lilith. You think they're trying to stay off her radar? Why?"

"Because it could be you're only half right

in your theory. Target-specific, yes," Cian agreed. "But I doubt the target was the queen. It's Moira who was chosen as a link in the first circle."

"Moira." There was alarm in Larkin's voice as he swiveled in the saddle to look back at the castle growing smaller with distance. "If they tried to kill her once —"

"They've tried to kill all of us, more than once," Cian pointed out. "Without success. She's as safe as she can be, where she is."

Blair outlined it in her mind. "You're thinking Lilith tried an end-run. Take one of us out before she was, essentially, one of us."

"It's a possibility, a strong one. Why waste the time and what must have been some effort to send a couple of assassins here? If you're going to buy in to the whole destiny business," Cian went on, "it's Moira and not Moira's mother who was the threat."

"They screwed up," Blair mused. "Took out the wrong target. So it may not be a matter of them not being able to get back, but not wanting to."

"Lilith isn't particularly tolerant of mistakes. Having a choice of being tortured and ended by her, or going to ground, snacking on the locals here, which would you do?"

"Door number two," Blair said. "And if you buy in to the whole destiny business, *her* first mistake was in turning you all those years ago. You're a more formidable enemy as a vampire than you might be as a man. No offense."

"None taken."

"Then you get Hoyt fired up, and start the whole Morrigan's Cross thing."

Thoughtfully, Blair fingered the two crosses she wore around her neck. "You've got Glenna connected to Hoyt — maybe, if you want the romantic — destined to find and love each other. And by doing so, exponentially increasing each other's power. You've got Larkin's connection to Moira, and due to it, his coming with her through the Dance and into Ireland."

"So makes a nice, tidy circle," Cian concluded. "Convoluted, but that's gods for you."

"She was meant to die. The queen." Larkin took a steadying breath. "Meant to die in Moira's place. If Moira comes to this herself, it will hurt her immeasurably."

"With her clever and questing mind, I'd be surprised if she wasn't already dealing with it. And dealing with it is what she'll do," Cian added. "What other choice is there?"

Larkin let it lie in his heart, on his head as they crossed a field.

"The next attack was here. I'm told the

man who farms this land thought wolves had been at his sheep. It was his boy who found him next morning. My father came here himself that day, to see the body, and it was as the queen's had been."

Blair shifted in the saddle. "About two miles, due south of the castle. No place to hide around here. Just open fields. But a couple of experienced vamps could cover a couple of miles fairly quickly. They can go in and out of the castle grounds as they've had an invite, but . . ."

"Not a good place to nest," Cian agreed. "Easy pickings, certainly, but too much exposure. No, it would be caves, or deep forest."

"Why not a house or cabin?" Larkin suggested. "If they chose with any care, they could find one out of the way, where it's not as likely someone would come by."

"Possible," Cian told him. "But the trouble with a cottage, a building, is daylight attack. Your enemy has one more weapon against you — and only has to pull a covering from a window to win the day."

"All right then." Larkin gestured across the field. "The next two attacks reported were just east of here. There's forest, but the hunting's good. There are plenty who track deer and rabbit there and might disturb a vampire's daytime rest."

"You know that," Blair told him. "They may not have. They're strangers here. It's a good place to start."

They rode in silence for a time. She could see sheep or cattle lolling in the fields — more easy pickings if a vampire couldn't take down a human. There were flickers of light she assumed were candles or lanterns in cottages. She could smell the smoke — the rich tang of peat rather than seasoned wood.

She smelled grass and animal dung, a deeper, loamy scent from fields planted and waiting for the coming harvest.

She could smell the horses, and Larkin, and knew how to separate Cian's scent from others like him.

But when they came to the edge of a wood, she couldn't be sure.

"Horses have been through here, and not long ago."

She looked at Larkin with eyebrows raised. "Well, listen to Tonto here."

"Tracks." He slid off his horse to study the ground. "Not shoed. Gypsies likely, though I don't see signs from a wagon, and they travel that way. They're leading out, in any case."

"How many?"

"It would be two. Two horses, coming out of the woods here to cross the field."

"Can you follow them in?" she asked him. "See where they came from?"

"I can." He mounted. "If they're on horseback, they could cover considerable distance. It would take the gods' own luck for us to track them down in one night."

"We backtrack the riders here, see what we see. The other attacks were east, right? Straight through these woods, out the other side."

"Aye. Another three miles at most."

"This would be a good hub." She looked at Cian as she spoke. "If they have decent shelter in here, it's a good spot to nest during the day, spread out for food at night."

"Leaves are still thick this time of year," he agreed. "And there'd be small game as well if they needed to make do."

Larkin took the lead, following the trail until the trees thickened to block the light. He dismounted again, tracking now on foot. By signs, Blair assumed she couldn't see.

Then again, she'd done the majority of her hunting in urban forests and suburban trails. But Larkin moved with the confidence of a man who knew what he was doing, pausing only to crouch down now and then, studying the tracks more carefully.

"Wait," she said abruptly. "Just wait. You get that?" she asked Cian.

"Blood. It's not fresh. And death. Older yet."

"Better get back on your horse, Larkin," she told him. "I think we've got some of the gods' luck after all. We can track it from here."

"I can't smell a thing but the woods."

"You will," she murmured, and drew her sword from the sheath on her back as they walked the horses down the path.

The wagon was pulled into the trees, off the path, and sheltered by them. It was a kind of small caravan, Blair thought, covered in the back with its red paint faded and peeling.

And the smell of death seemed to soak it.

"Tinkers," Larkin told them. And she'd been right, he could smell the death now. "Gypsies who travel the roads selling whatever wares they might make. The wagon's harnessed for two horses."

"A good nest," Blair decided. "Mobile if you need it to be. And you could drive around at night, no one would pay any attention."

"You could take it right into the village," Larkin said grimly. "Drive it up to someone's cottage and ask for hospitality. In the normal course of things, you'd get it."

He thought of the children who might run

343

outside to see if there would be toys for sale they could beg their parents to buy or trade for. And the thought sickened him even more than the stench.

He dismounted with the others, moved to the rear of the wagon where the doors were tightly shut, and bolted from the outside. They drew weapons. Blair slid the bolt free, tested the door.

When it gave, she nodded to her companions, mentally counted to three, then yanked it open.

The fetid air came first, crawling into the throat, pouring into the eyes. She heard the hungry hum of flies and fought against the need to gag.

It leaped out at her, the thing with the face of a pretty young woman whose eyes were red and mad. The stink rolled off her, where it was matted in her dark hair, streaked over her homespun dress.

Blair pivoted aside so it landed in the brush on its hands and knees, snarling like the animal it had become.

It was Larkin who swung his sword and ended it.

"Oh God, sweet Jesus. She couldn't have been fourteen." He wanted to sit, just sit there on the ground while his belly heaved. "They changed her. How many others —"

"Unlikely more," Cian said, cutting him off. "Then they'd have to compete for food, worry about keeping it under control."

"She didn't come through with them," Larkin insisted. "She wasn't one of them before. She was Geallian."

"And young, pretty, female. Food isn't the only need."

Blair saw when the full impact of Cian's words hit Larkin. She saw not just by the shock but the sheer outrage on his face.

"Bastards. Bloody fucking bastards. She was hardly more than a child."

"And this surprises you because?"

He whirled on Cian, and would, Blair was sure, have vented some of that horror and outrage. Perhaps Cian was giving him a target for it. But there wasn't time for indulgences.

She simply stepped between them and shoved Larkin back a full three paces. "Close it down," she ordered him. "Just settle it down."

"How can I? How can you?"

"Because you can't bring her back, or the ones that are in there." She jerked a chin toward the wagon. "So we figure out how to use this to capture the ones who did it."

Burying her own revulsion, she pulled herself up into the wagon. Into a nightmare.

What must have been the girl's parents were shoved together under a kind of bunk on one side of the wagon. The man had probably died quickly, as had the younger boy whose body lay under the bunk on the opposite side.

But the woman, they'd have taken more time there. No point in tearing off her clothes if you didn't intend to play with her first. Her hands were still bound, and what was left of her was covered in bites.

Yes, they'd taken time with her.

She could see no weapons, but one of the bunks was stained with blood fresher than what was staining the other bunk, the floor and the walls. That was where the girl had died, she assumed. And had waked again.

"The woman's only been dead a couple of days," Cian said from behind her. "The man and boy longer. A day or more longer."

"Yeah. Jesus." She had to get out, had to breathe. She climbed out of the back to draw in air she hoped would clear the smear in her throat, in her lungs.

"They'll come back for her." She bent over, bracing her hands on her thighs so the nausea, the dizziness would fade. "Bring her something so she can feed. She was new. Probably only woke tonight."

"We need to bury them," Larkin said.

"The others. They deserve to be buried."

"It has to wait. Look, be pissed at me if you have to, but —"

"I'm not. I'm sick in my heart, but I'm not angry with you. Or you," he said to Cian. "I don't know why it should be this way inside me. I saw what was in the caves back in Ireland. I know how they kill, how they breed. But knowing they made a monster of that girl only so they could use her between them, it makes my heart sick."

She didn't have any words, any real ones, to offer. She wrapped her fingers around his arm, squeezed. "Let's make them pay for it. They'll be back before sunrise. Well before if they can find what they're after quickly enough and get it back. They know she'll have risen tonight, and need to feed. That's why they —"

"That's why they left the bodies inside," Larkin said when she cut herself off. "So she'd have something until they could bring her fresh blood. I'm not slow-witted, Blair. They left her own family for her to feed on."

Nodding, she looked back toward the wagon. "So we close up the wagon, and we wait. Will they be able to smell us? The human?"

"Hard to say," Cian told her. "I don't know how old they are, how experienced.

Enough so Lilith thought they could handle this assignment. Which they bungled. But it's possible they'll catch the scent of live blood, even through all this. Then there's the horses."

"Okay, I've got that covered. Most likely they'll come back to the wagon from the same direction they left it. We'll take the horses farther into the woods, downwind. Tether them. All but mine. If I'm walking him when they see me, they'll figure he came up lame. And they'll be too happy with their luck of coming across a lone female to think beyond that."

"So, you think you're going to be bait," Larkin began, with a look on his face that warned Blair they were in for a fight about it.

"I'll just take the horses back while you two argue this out." Cian took the reins, melted into the trees.

Calm, Blair ordered herself. Reasonable. She should remember it was nice to have someone who actually cared enough to worry about her.

"If they see a man, they're more likely to attack. A woman, they're going to want me alive — temporarily. Gives them each a play-mate. It's the most logical way."

That was the end of her calm and reason-able. "And, here's what. If your ego has a problem with the fact that if I *were* out here alone I could still handle two of them, you'll just have to deal with it."

"My ego has nothing to do with the matter. It's just as logical for the three of us to lay back and wait, then move on them as one."

"No, because if they scent either you or me, we lose the element of surprise. Moira wants them — or at least one of them alive. That's why we're out here instead of having a nice glass of wine in front of a roaring fire. If we have to go full scale attack we'll probably have to kill them both. Surprise gives us a better chance of capture."

"There are other ways."

"Probably a dozen of them. But while they may not be back for five hours, they could also be back in five minutes. This will work, Larkin, because it's simple and it's basic. Because they wouldn't expect a woman by herself to be any kind of threat. I want to bag these two as much as you do. Let's make sure we do."

Cian slipped back out of the trees. "Have you settled it, then, or will we be debating this much longer?"

"It seems to be settled." Larkin brushed a hand over Blair's hair. "I've just been wasting my breath." Then he tipped back her chin. "If you have to speak to them to hold the illusion until we move in, they'll know you're not from Geall."

"Sure you think I can't manage a bit of an accent." She slathered on the brogue, and gave him a wide-eyed helpless look. "And give every appearance of being a defenseless female?"

"That's not altogether bad." He lowered his lips to hers. "But for myself, I'd never believe the defenseless part of it."

CHAPTER 15

An hour passed, then another. Then a third. There was little for her to do but eat some of the bread and cheese Moira had provided for them, wash it down with the water in her bag.

At least Larkin and Cian had each other for company, while all she had was her own head. She frowned when that thought passed through. She was used to hunting alone, to waiting alone in dark, quiet places.

Strange, it had only taken a matter of weeks for her to break that lifetime habit.

In any case, the waiting was taking longer than she'd hoped, and Blair hadn't factored in the boredom. It made her think of her first night in Ireland this time around, and the luck — fate — of getting a flat on a dark, lonely road.

There'd been three vampires that time, and the element of surprise had added to her advantage. Mostly, vamps didn't expect to get clocked with a tire iron, especially by a woman who was a hell of a lot stronger than they'd calculated.

They sure as hell hadn't expected her to pull out a stake and dust them.

These two — if they ever got back — wouldn't be expecting it either. Only she had to remember dusting them wasn't the mission. A tough one to swallow for a bred in the blood demon hunter.

Her father wouldn't approve of this little adventure, she mused. In his book you ended them, period. Quickly, efficiently. No flourishes, no conversation.

Of course, he'd have done his best to end Cian by now, she decided. Family connection and will of the gods be damned. He would never have worked with Cian or fought beside him, trained with him.

And one of them, possibly both of them, would be dead now.

Maybe that was why she'd been brought here instead of her father. Why she could admit now, as she waited on the rutted forest path, she hadn't told him about Cian. Not that her father bothered to actually read her e-mails, but still she hadn't brought up an allegiance to the undead in the ones she'd sent him.

There simply were no allegiances in demon hunting, not to her father's mind. It was you and the enemy. Black and white, live and die.

Only another reason she'd never earned his approval, she realized. It wasn't only because she wasn't his son, but because she'd seen the gray, and had questioned.

Because like Larkin she had felt, more than once, a pity and regret for the things she ended. She knew what her father would say. That an instant of pity or regret could mean an instant of hesitation. And an instant's hesitation could kill you.

He'd be right, she thought. But not completely, no, not absolutely, as there were shades of gray there, too. She could feel that pity and still do her job. She *had*.

Wasn't she standing here now, alive? And she damn well intended to stay alive.

She only wondered, for the first time since Jeremy, if it was possible to have a life along with a heartbeat. She'd stopped letting herself wish or want or ask if she could have someone to love her. Now there was Larkin, and she believed he did. Or close enough to love to care for and want.

In time maybe it could be love. The kind she'd never had before, the kind that crossed all the lines and accepted.

It was brutal, she thought, just brutal that there couldn't be enough time. There just wasn't enough of the commodity to span entire worlds.

But when she went back to her own, she would know there was someone who had looked at her, had seen who and what she was, and still had cared.

If she did make it back, if they won this thing and the worlds kept spinning, she would tell him what he'd given her. Tell him that he'd changed something inside her, so much for the better.

But she wouldn't tell him she loved him. Words like that would only hurt them both. She wouldn't tell him what she was finally able to admit to herself.

That she would always love him.

She *felt* the movement rather than saw it, and turned toward it, braced for attack. But it was Cian, the shape and scent of him, off the path and in the shadows.

"Heads up," he murmured. "Two riders starting into the woods. They're dragging a body behind them. Alive yet."

She nodded and thought: Curtain up.

She began to walk the horse slowly, in the direction of the wagon so they'd come up behind her. So it would seem, she thought, that she'd ridden into the woods before her horse had come up lame.

She felt them first, something that was beyond scent. It was more a knowledge, which covered all the senses. But she waited until she heard the hoofbeats.

She'd taken off her coat. She didn't think Geallian women walked around in black leather. Against the chill she wore one of Larkin's tunics, belted snugly enough to show she had breasts. Her crosses were tucked under the cloth, out of sight.

She looked like an unarmed woman, hoping for some help.

She even called out as the sound of the horses grew closer, making sure her voice was blurred with brogue and a little fear.

"Hello, the riders! I'm having a bit of trouble here — ahead on the path."

The hoofbeats stopped. Oh yeah, Blair thought, talk it over for a minute, figure it out. She called out again, increasing the quaver in her voice.

"Are you there? My horse picked up a stone, I'm afraid. I'm on my way to Cillard."

They were coming again, slowly, and she fixed what she hoped was a mixture of relief and concern on her face. "Well, thank the gods," she said when the horses came into view. "I thought I'd end up walking the rest of the way to my sister's, and alone in the dark for all that. Which serves me right, doesn't it, for starting out so much later than I should."

One dismounted. He looked strong, Blair judged, solidly built. When he pushed back the hood of his cloak she saw a tangle of white blond hair and a deep, V-shaped scar above his left eyebrow.

There was no sign of anyone being dragged behind the horses, so she assumed they'd dropped their prey off for the moment.

"You're traveling alone?"

Slavic, she thought. Just the faintest of accents. Russian, Ukrainian maybe.

"I am. It's not so very far, and I meant to leave earlier in the day. But one thing and another, and now this . . ." She gestured to her horse. "I'm Beal, of the o Dubhuir family. Would you be heading toward Cillard by chance?"

The second dismounted to hold the reins of both their horses.

"It's dangerous to be out in the woods, alone in the dark."

"I know them well enough. But you, you don't sound like you come from this part of Geall." She backed up a step as a frightened woman might. "Are you a stranger to the area then?"

"You could say that." And when he smiled, his fangs glimmered.

She gave a little shriek, decided such things couldn't be overplayed. He laughed when he grabbed for her. She brought her knee up hard between his legs, then topped it off with a solid roundhouse. When he went down to his knees, she kicked him full in the face, then planted her feet to meet the second attack.

The second wasn't as toughly built as the first, but he was faster. And he'd drawn his sword. Blair flipped back, landing on her hands to kick out at his sword arm. It gave her time and a little distance. When the first gained its feet, Larkin burst out of the woods.

"Let's see how you do against a man."

Blair took the fast running steps she needed to give the flying kick momentum. She hit the first mid-body as Larkin clashed swords with the other. She grabbed her sword from its sheath on her saddle as all three of the horses shied. Instinct had her whirling, bringing the blade up two-handed to block the down sweep of her enemy's sword.

She'd been right about his strength, she discovered, as the force of the blow rippled straight down to her toes. Because he had her in reach, she went in close. His advantage was she didn't want to kill him — but he didn't know that. She stomped hard on his instep, brought the hilt of her sword up in a vicious blow to his chin.

The hit knocked him back, into her mount. All three horses whinnied in alarm as they scattered.

He just kept coming, hacking and swinging until sweat rolled into her eyes. She heard someone — something — scream, but couldn't risk a look. Instead, she feinted, drawing his sword to the left, then plowed her foot into his belly. It took him down long enough for her to leap on him, hold her sword across his throat.

"Move and you're dust. Larkin?"

"Aye."

"If you're done playing around with that one, I could use a little help over here."

He stepped over. Then kicked the vampire in the head, in the face — several times.

"Yeah, that ought to do it." Breathless, she sat back on her haunches to look up at Larkin. Blood was spattered over his shirt, his face. "Is much of that yours?"

"Not a great deal of it. It would be his, for the most part." He stepped back, gestured so she could see the vampire he'd skewered into the ground with a sword.

"Ouch." She got to her feet. "We need to round up those horses, get these two in chains and . . ." She trailed off as Cian walked toward them, leading the horses.

He glanced at the vampires bleeding on the path. "Untidy," he decided. "But effective. This one's not in the best of shape." He nodded toward the bleeding man slung over one of the horses. "But he's alive."

"Nice work." She wondered, not for the first time, how hard it was for him to resist the smell of fresh human blood. But it didn't seem like the time to ask. "We'd better get these two contained. This one wakes up, he's trouble." Blair circled her aching shoulder. "That one's like a goddamn bull."

While the men chained the prisoners, she examined the unconscious man. He was bloodied and battered, but unbitten. Going to take him back to the wagon, she thought. Share him with the female. Have a little party.

"We need to bury the dead," Larkin said to her.

"We can't take the time now."

"We're not just leaving them."

"Listen, just listen." She gripped his hands before he could turn away. "That man's hurt, and hurt bad. He needs help as soon as we can get it for him, or he might not make it. Then we'd be digging another grave. Added to it, we need to get Cian back and inside before sunrise. We're going to be cutting it close as it is."

"I'll stay behind, deal with it myself."

"Larkin, we need you. If we don't make good time, Cian's going to have to go ahead, or go to ground, and that leaves me with two vampires and one wounded human. I could handle it alone if I had to, but I don't. We'll send someone back to bury them. I'll come back with you, and we'll do it ourselves if you'd rather. But we have to leave them for now. We have to go."

He said nothing, only nodded then strode to his horse.

"He's taking the female he ended to heart," Cian murmured.

"Some are harder than others. You have that cloak thing, right? In case."

"I do, but I'll be frank and tell you I'd rather not risk my skin on it."

"Can't blame you. If and when you have to ride ahead, you ride." She looked over where the two vampires were shackled, gagged and tied across one of their horses. "We can handle them."

"You could handle them on your own, we both know that."

"Larkin shouldn't have to deal with what's

back there in that wagon by himself." She swung onto her horse. "Let's get this done."

They rode in silence through the dark of the woods, across the fields dappled with pale moonlight. Once, just ahead, a white owl swooped over a gentle rise with only the whisper of wings. Blair thought, for an instant, she saw the glitter of its eyes, green as jewels. Then there was only the murmur of the wind through the high grass and the hushed silence of predawn.

She saw the vampire she fought lift its head. When its eyes met hers she saw the blood lust, and the fury. But over them both she saw the fear. He struggled against his chains, eyes wheeling toward the east. The one beside him lay weakly, and Blair thought the sounds he made behind his gag were sobs.

"They feel dawn coming," Cian said from beside her. "The burn of it."

"Go. Larkin and I can handle it."

"Oh, there's time yet, a bit of time yet."

"We should only be a couple miles out."

"Less," Larkin told her. "A bit less. The wounded man's coming around some. I wish he wouldn't."

The ride couldn't be doing him any good, Blair thought, but they couldn't afford to keep it slow and smooth any longer. The stars had faded out.

"Let's pick up the pace." She kicked her horse into a gallop, and hoped the man slumped over the horse she led would live another mile.

She saw the lights first, the flicker of them — candle and torch — through the rising mists. And there, the silhouette of the castle, high on the rise with its white flags waving against a sky that was no longer black, but a deep, dense blue.

"Go!"

The vampires bucked and jerked, making sounds far from human as the first streaks of red bled over the horizon behind the castle.

But Cian rode straight in the saddle, hair flying. "I so rarely see it from out of doors."

There was pain, the rip and the burn of it. And there was wonder, and a faint regret as he galloped through the gates and into the shadow of the keep.

Moira was there, her face tight and pale. "Go inside, please. Your horse will be tended. Please," she repeated, the strain cutting through the word as Cian slowly dismounted. "Be quick."

She gestured for the men with her to take the prisoners.

"Got a handy dungeon?" Blair asked her.

"We don't, no."

Riddock watched the men drag the chained prisoners away. "Arrangements have been made, as Moira requested. They'll be held in the cellars, and guarded."

"Leave the chains on them," Larkin ordered.

"Hoyt and Glenna are waiting inside," Moira told him. "We'll add magic to the chains. You're not to worry. You need food and rest, all of you."

"This one's human. And wounded." Blair stepped over, laid her fingers on the pulse in the man's throat. "Alive, but he needs attention."

"Right away. Sir?"

"We'll send for the physician." Riddock signalled to some men. "See to him," he ordered before turning to his son. "Are you hurt?"

"No. I have to go back, there are some we had to leave, back in the forest on the path to Cillard." Larkin's face was pale, and it was set. "They need to be buried."

"We'll send a party out."

"I have a need to see to it myself."

"Then you will. But come inside first. You need to wash, break your fast." He slung an arm around Larkin's shoulders. "It's been a long night for all of us."

Inside, Cian stood speaking with Hoyt and

Glenna. He broke off when the others entered and lifted a brow at Moira.

"You have your prisoners. What do you intend to do with them?"

"We'll speak of it, all of it. I've ordered food to the family parlor. If we could meet there, we have much to discuss."

She swept away with two of her women hurrying behind her.

Blair went to her own room where a fire was lit and fresh water waited. She washed away the blood, changing the borrowed tunic for one of her own shirts.

Then she braced her hands on the bureau and studied her face in the mirror.

She'd looked better, she decided. She needed sleep, but wasn't going to get it. Nor for a while yet. She'd have paid a lot for an hour in a bed, but that wasn't in the cards any more than a couple days at a nice spa.

Instead, she was going to take half the day to ride back out, bury three strangers. There wasn't time for it, not when she should have been working with the troops, devising strategies, checking on weapon production. A dozen practical and necessary tasks.

But if she didn't go, Larkin would do it alone. She couldn't let that happen.

He was already in the parlor when she walked in. And he was alone by the window, watching morning strike mist.

"You think I'm wasting valuable time," he said without turning around. "With something unnecessary and useless."

So he read her, she thought. And damn clearly. "It doesn't matter. You need to do it, so we'll do it."

"Families should be safe on the roads of Geall. Young girls should not be raped and tortured and killed. Should not be turned into something that must be destroyed."

"No, they shouldn't."

"You've lived with it longer than I. And perhaps you can face it more . . ."

"Callously."

"No." He turned now. He looked older, she thought, in the hard light, with the violence of the night still on him. "That wasn't the word, and would never be one I'd use for you. Coolly perhaps, practically for certain. So you must. I won't hold you to going with me."

Because he wouldn't, she knew she could do nothing else but go. "I said I would, and I will."

"Yes, you will, so thanks for that. Can you understand that I'm stronger for knowing you'll do this thing with me, that you'd understand my need to do it enough to take the time?"

"I think it takes a strong man to need to do what's human, and humane. That's enough for me."

"There's so much I have to say to you, so many things I want to say. But today isn't the day. I feel . . ." He looked down at his sword hand. "Stained. Do you know what I'm saying?"

"Yeah, I know what you're saying."

"Ah well. Come, we'll drink strong tea and wish it was Coke." He smiled a little as he walked to her. Then he laid his hands lightly on her shoulders, pressed his lips to her brow. "You are so beautiful."

"Your eyes must really be tired."

He eased back. "I see you," he told her, "exactly as you are."

He pulled her chair out for her, something she couldn't remember him doing before. As she sat, Hoyt and Cian came in. Cian flicked a glance toward the windows, then moved away from them to the table Moira had had set away from the light.

"Glenna will be along," Hoyt said. "She wanted to check on the man you brought in. The prisoners are secured." He looked at his brother. "And very unhappy."

"They haven't fed." Cian poured his own tea. "The castle boasts a fine wine cellar, which you didn't mention," he said to

366

Larkin. "A corner of it is nicely dark and damp enough to keep them. But unless your cousin simply intends to starve them to death, they'll need to be fed if they're chained in there above another day."

"I have no intention of starving them." Moira came in. She wore riding gear now, with a feminine flare, in forest green. "And neither will they be fed. They've had enough Geallian blood, animal and human. My uncle and I will ride out shortly, to rally the people and spread the word. As many as can manage will come here by sundown. And when the sun has set, what is in the cellars will be shown to them. Then destroyed."

She looked directly at Cian. "Do you find that hard, cold, with no drop of human emotion or mercy?"

"No. I find it practical and useful. I hardly thought you had us hunt them down to bring them here for counseling and rehabilitation."

"We'll show the people what they are, and how they must be killed. We're sending troops out now to lay the traps you want, Blair. Larkin, I've asked Phelan to take charge of the task."

"My sister's husband," Larkin explained. "Aye, he'd be up for that. You chose well."

"The man you brought back is awake,

though the physician wishes to dose him. Glenna agrees. He told us he went outside, hearing what he thought was a fox in his henhouse. They set upon him. He has a wife and three children, and shouted for them to stay in the house. It was all he could do, and we can thank the gods they obeyed. We're sending for them."

"Until Larkin and Blair return, Glenna and I can help with the training. And Cian perhaps," Hoyt added, "if there's somewhere inside."

"Thank you. I'd hoped that would suit you. Ah, we have the village smithy and two others forging weapons. We'll have more, but some who come will have their own arms."

"You've got trees," Blair pointed out. "You're going to want to start making stakes out of some of them. More arrows, lances, spears."

"Yes, of course. Yes. I need to go as my uncle and our party is waiting. I want to thank you for your night's work. We'll be back before sundown."

"She's starting to look like a queen," Blair said when Moira left.

"Worn out is what she looks."

Blair nodded at Larkin. "Being a queen's bound to be hard work. Add a war, and it's got to be brutal. Cian, you okay to fill the others in on our party last night?"

"I've already given them the highlights. I'll fill in the details."

"Then why don't you and I get started," she said to Larkin.

She went to the stables with him where he gathered the tools they'd need.

"I could fly us there quicker than we could ride. Would that suit you?"

"That'd be good."

He led the way around to the courtyard garden she recognized from her window. "The bag's heavy. Hang it round my neck once I've changed."

He passed it to her; became the dragon.

He dipped his head so that she could work the strap over it. Then she looked into his eyes, stroked his jeweled cheek. "You sure are pretty," she murmured.

He lowered so she could mount his back.

They were rising up, above the towers, the turrets, over the waving white flags.

The morning was like a gem of blue and green and umber, spreading around her. She tipped her head back, let the wind rush over her, let it blow away the fatigue of the long night.

She saw horses below on the road now, and carriages, wagons, people walking. The little village she'd yet to explore was a spread of pretty buildings, bright colors, busy stalls. The people who looked up raised caps or hands as they flew over, then went back about the business of the day.

Life, Blair thought, didn't just go on, it insisted on thriving.

She turned her face toward the mountains, with their mists and their secrets. And their valley called silence where in a matter of weeks there would be blood and death.

They would fight, she thought, and some would fall. But they would fight so life could thrive.

They reached the woods and circled before Larkin wove delicately through the trees to the ground.

She slid off him, took the bag.

When he was a man again, he took her hand.

"It's beautiful," she said. "Before we do this, I want to tell you Geall is beautiful."

Together they walked through the trees, then stopped to dig three graves in the soft, mossy ground. The work was physical, and mechanical, and they did it without conversation. Going back into the wagon, removing the bodies was a horror. Neither spoke, but simply did what needed to be done.

She felt the weariness dragging back into her bones, and the sickness that sat deep in the belly as they closed the ground over the bodies.

Larkin carried stones for each of the graves, then a fourth for the young girl he couldn't bury.

When it was done, Blair leaned on the shovel. "Do you want to, I don't know, say some words?"

He spoke in Gaelic, taking her hand as he said the words, then saying them again in English so she could understand.

"They were strangers to us, but to each other they were family. They died a hard death, and now we give them back to the earth and the gods where they will have peace. They will not be forgotten."

He stepped back, drawing her with him. "I'll pull the wagon into the field, away from the trees. We'll burn it."

Everything they'd owned, she thought as they set the wagon to light. Everything they'd had, these people who had no name for her. The idea of it was so sad, as the wagon burned and the smoke rose, that when she climbed onto the dragon's back again, she laid her head on his neck, closed her eyes and dozed as they flew over the ashes.

CHAPTER 16

She heard thunder, and thought groggily that they'd have to outrace a storm. Straightening, more than a little amazed she'd dozed off on the back of a dragon, she opened her eyes. Shook her head to clear it.

Not thunder, she realized and gaped at the towering fall of water that gushed over twin spires of rock into a wide blue pool.

There were trees here, still leafy and green, and the surprising tropical touch of palms. Lilies floated on the pool, pink and white, as if they'd been painted there. Beneath the surface of blue, she could see the dart of fish, bright and elegant as jewels.

The air smelled of flowers and clear water.

She was so stunned she stayed where she was when he landed. The dragon's head bent down so the strap of the bag slid off. And she was sitting piggyback on Larkin.

"What? We take a wrong turn?"

He turned his head to smile into her dazzled eyes. "I told you I would bring you here. Faerie Falls, it is. There's no picnic this time, but I thought . . . I wanted an hour, alone with you, somewhere there's only beauty."

"I'll take it." She jumped off his back, turned a circle.

There were starry little flowers in the grass, and a tangle of vines, blooming purple, winding right up the rocks, almost like frames for that plunge of water. The pool itself was clear as a mirror, blue as a pansy while the cups of lilies floated over it, and overhead the falls spilled fifty feet down.

"It's incredible, Larkin, a little slice of paradise. And I don't care how cold that water is, I'm having a swim."

She yanked off her boots, started on her shirt. "Aren't you?"

"Sure." He kept grinning at her. "I'll be right behind you."

She stripped, tossing her clothes carelessly on the soft ground. Poised on the bank, she sucked in her breath, braced for the shock. And dived.

When she surfaced, she let out a joyful yell. "Oh my God, it's *warm!* It's warm and it's silky and it's wonderful." She did a surface dive, came up again. "If I were a fish, I'd live here."

"Some say the faeries warm it every morning with their breath." Larkin sat, pulled off his own boots. "Others less fanciful talk of hot springs under the ground."

"Faeries, science, I don't care. It feels so damn good."

He jumped in, and as men were prone to do, hit the water hard so it would splash her as much as possible. She only laughed and splashed him back.

They went under together, tugging each other deeper or pinching bare flesh, playing like seals. She swam under, cutting through with strong strokes until she felt the vibration of water striking water. She sprang off the bottom and into the tumble.

It beat on her shoulders, the back of her neck, the base of her spine. She shouted out with a combination of relief and joy as it pummeled away the aches and fatigue. When he joined her, wrapped his arms around her, they laughed as the water plunged over them. The force pushed them back toward the heart of the pool where she could simply float with him.

"I was thinking earlier how much I'd like a couple days at a good spa. This is better." She sighed and let her head rest on his shoulder. "An hour here is better than anything."

"I wanted you to have something unspoiled. I needed, I think, to remind myself there are such places." Not only graves to be dug, he thought. Not only battles to be fought. "There isn't another woman I know, but Moira, who would have done what you did with me today. For me today."

"There aren't many men I know who would have done what you did today. So we're even."

He brushed his lips over her temple, her cheek, found her mouth. The kiss was soft and warm as the water. His hand that stroked over her as gentle as the air.

It seemed that nothing beyond this place, beyond this precious time existed. Here, for now, they could just be. While they drifted, she saw a white dove soar overhead, and circle. She saw the sparkle of its green eyes.

So the gods do watch, she thought, remembering the white owl. In the good times, and in the bad.

Then she turned her lips to his. What did she care for gods now? This was their time, this was their place. She sank into the kiss, letting the water and his arms carry her.

"I need you." His eyes were on hers as he took her mouth again. "Do you, can you know how much it is I need you? Take me in." He murmured it as he cupped her hips, slid into her.

They watched each other as they joined, fingers stroking faces, lips brushing lips.

It was more than pleasure that moved through her, more even than the joy of life. If it was truth, she thought, this need, this sharing, then she could live on it the rest of her life.

She wrapped herself around him, gave herself to that truth.

And knew the name of that truth was love.

It was probably possible to be more tired, to be more frustrated, but Glenna hoped she never found out. She'd done what Moira had asked and taken a group of women to one end of the gaming fields to try to give them the first basic lesson of self-defense.

They were more interested in gossiping and giggling, or trying to flirt with the men Hoyt worked with across the field than moving their asses.

She'd taken some twenty of the younger ones assuming they'd be more enthusiastic and in better physical shape. And that, she decided, might have been her first mistake.

Time, she thought, to get mean.

"Be quiet!" The sharp edge of her voice silenced the group into a single gasping breath. "You know, I like to ogle beefcake as much as the next girl, but we're not here so you can pick out your date for the harvest ball. We're here so I can teach you how to stay alive. You." She chose one at random, pointed at a pretty brunette who looked sturdy. "Step over here."

There were a few giggles, and the woman smirked as she strutted up to Glenna.

"What's your name?"

"Dervil, lady." Then she squeaked and stumbled back when Glenna's fist swung up and stopped a bare inch from her face.

"Is that what you're going to do when someone tries to hurt you, Dervil? Are you going to squeal like a girl, gulp like a fish?" She grabbed Dervil's arm yanked it up so that it blocked Dervil's face as Glenna shot her fist out again. Their forearms rammed together.

"That hurt!" Dervil's mouth fell open in shock. "You have no right to hurt me."

"Hurting someone isn't about rights, it's about intent. And a forearm block hurts less than a bare-fisted punch in the face. They'll like the look of you, Dervil. Block! No, don't throw your arm up like it's a dishrag. Firm, strong. Again!" She worked Dervil backward with each punch. "You've got some meat on you, and all that blood swimming in your veins. Squealing and flapping won't help you. What will you do when they come for you?"

"Run!" someone called out, and though there was some laughter at this, Glenna stopped and nodded.

"Running could be an option. There might be a time it's the only option, but you'd better be fast. A vampire can move like lightning."

"We don't believe in demons." Dervil thrust up her chin, rubbed her bruised forearm. From the mutinous set of her mouth, the glitter in her eyes, Glenna understood she'd made her first enemy in Geall.

So be it.

"You can bet they believe in you. So run. End of the field and back. Run like the demons of hell are after you. Goddamn it, I said *run.*" To get them moving, she spurted a little fire at their feet.

There were some screams, but they ran. Like girls, Glenna thought in despair. Waving arms, mincing feet, flapping skirts. And at least three of them tripped, which she considered an embarrassment for all females, everywhere.

Since she calculated she'd lose half of them if she made them run back, she jogged after them.

"Okay, from here. A couple of you actually have some speed, but for the most part, you're all slow and silly. So we'll run every day, one length of the field. You're going to have to wear, what are they? Tewes or leggings. Pants," she said, patting her own sweats. "Men's attire for training. Skirts are only going to trip you up, be in the way."

"A lady —" one of them began, only to freeze when Glenna lasered a stare at her.

"You're not ladies when I'm training you. You're soldiers." A different tack, she decided. "Who here has children?"

Several raised hands, so she chose one she thought was at least watching her with some interest. "You? Your name?"

"Ceara."

"What would you do, Ceara, if something came after your child?"

"I would fight, of course, I would. I would die fighting to protect my child."

"Show me. I'm after your baby. What do you do?" When Ceara looked blank, Glenna pushed down her own impatience. "I've killed your husband. He's dead at your feet, now the only thing that stands between me and your child is you. Stop me."

Ceara lifted her hands, fingers curled into claws, and made a halfhearted lunge at Glenna. And the breath went out of her as she was flipped over Glenna's shoulder to land on her back.

"How does that stop me?" Glenna demanded. "Your child's screaming for you. Do something!"

Ceara got into a crouch, sprang up. Glenna let herself be tackled, then simply flipped Ceara over, pressed an elbow to her throat.

"That was better, that was positive. But it was too slow, and your eyes, your body told me just what you were going to do."

When Glenna stood, Ceara sat up, rubbed the back of her head. "Show me," she said to Glenna.

By the end of the session, Glenna put her first students in two camps. The Ceara camp consisted of those who showed at least some interest and aptitude. Then there was the Dervil camp, which not only showed neither, but a strong resistance to spending time doing something that wasn't traditionally a woman's task.

When they were gone, she simply sat down on the ground. Moments later, Hoyt dropped down beside her, and she had the pleasure, at least, of resting her head on his shoulder.

"I think I'm a poor teacher," he told her.

"That makes two of us. How are we going

to do this, Hoyt? How are we going to pull this together, turn these people into an army?"

"We have no choice but to do it. But gods's truth, Glenna, I'm tired already and we've only begun."

"It was different when we were in Ireland, the six of us. We knew, we understood what we'd be facing. At least you're dealing with men, and some of them are already well trained with a sword or a bow. I've got a gaggle of girls here, Merlin, and most of them couldn't fight off a blind, one-legged dwarf much less a vampire."

"People rise when they have no choice. We did." He turned his head to kiss her hair. "We have to believe we can do this thing, then we'll do it."

"Believing counts," she agreed. "A lot of them don't believe what we're telling them."

He watched two of the guards carrying iron posts, watched as they began to hammer them into the ground. "They soon will." He got to his feet, reached for her hand. "We should see if the others are back."

Blair didn't know that she'd ever been sent for — unless you counted the occasional summons to the vice principal's office in high school. She doubted Moira intended to give her detention, but it was weird, being escorted to the princess.

Moira answered the door herself, and the smile she gave Blair was quiet and serious. "Thank you for coming. That will be all, Dervil, thank you. You should go now, secure your place in the stands."

"My lady —"

"I want you there. I want everyone there. Blair, please come in." She stepped back to allow Blair inside, then shut the door in Dervil's face.

"You sure come over all royal."

"I know it must seem that way." Moira rubbed a hand up and down Blair's arm before she turned to walk farther into the room. "But I'm the same."

She might have been wearing what Blair considered Moira's training gear — the simple tunic, pants and sturdy boots — but there was something different about her.

The room might have added to it. It was, Blair assumed, a kind of sitting room, and plush for all that. Cushions of richly worked tapestries, velvet drapes, the lovely little marble hearth with its turf fire simmering all spoke of position.

"I asked you here to tell you how the demonstration will be done."

"To tell me," Blair repeated.

"I don't imagine you'll like what I've chosen to do, but the decision is made. There's no other way for me."

"Why don't you tell me what you've chosen to do, then I'll tell you if I like it or not."

She didn't. And she argued. She threatened and she cursed. But Moira remained both implacable and immovable.

"What have the others said about this?" Blair demanded.

"I haven't told them. I've told you." Thinking they could both use it, Moira poured them each a glass of wine. "Put yourself in my position, please. These are the monsters who killed my mother. They murdered the queen of Geall."

"And the idea was — is — to show people they exist. What they are, how they need to be fought and destroyed."

"Aye, that's an essential point." Moira sat a moment, to sip wine, to settle. All through the worries of the night, the duties of the day, she'd been gathering herself for what was to come. "In a few days, I'll go to the stone. Again, before the people of Geall who've gathered there, I'll take hold of the sword. If I lift it, I will be queen. And as queen I'll lead my people into war — the first war in Geall. Can I send them into battle, can I send them to their deaths when I'm unproven?"

"Moira, you don't have to prove anything to me."

"Not to you, but to others. And to myself — do you understand? I won't take up sword and crown until I feel worthy of both."

"From where I'm standing you are. I wouldn't tell you that if I thought otherwise."

"You wouldn't, no. That's why I asked for you, and not one of the others. You'll speak to me plainly, and I can speak plainly to you. It matters that you think I'm ready for the sword and the crown. It matters a great deal. But I have to feel it, don't you see?"

"Yeah. Shit." Because she did see, Blair raked her hands through her hair. "Yeah."

"Blair, I'm afraid of what's been asked of me. Of what I need to do, of what's to come. I'm asking you to help me do this thing tonight, as a friend, a fellow warrior, and as a woman who knows how cold the path of destiny can be."

"And if I refuse, you'll do it anyway."

"Of course." Now a glimmer of a smile. "But I'd feel stronger and surer with your understanding."

"I do understand. I don't have to like it, but I can understand."

Moira set her wine aside, got to her feet to take Blair's hand. "That's enough."

They'd made it into a kind of party, Blair thought. Torches blazed, lining the field of play. Flames rose up toward the sky where the nearly full ball of moon beamed like a spotlight.

People crammed into the stands, jostled for position behind wooden barriers. They'd brought children, she noted, right down to babies — and the mood was festive.

She was armed — sword, stake, crossbow — and heard the murmurs as she passed through on her way to the royal box.

She slipped in next to Glenna.

"So what do you think the insurance would go for on a gig like this? Fire, wood, all this flammable clothing."

Glenna shook her head as she scanned the crowd. "They don't understand it. They're like fans waiting for the concert to begin. For God's sake, Blair, there are vendors selling meat pies."

"Never underestimate the power of free enterprise."

"I tried to get to Moira before we were brought here. We don't even know the plan."

"I do. And you're not going to like it." Before she could elaborate, there was a blare of trumpets. The royal family came into the box. "Just don't blame me," Blair said over the cheers of the crowd.

Riddock stepped forward, raising his hands to quiet the crowd. "People of Geall, you are here to welcome home Her Highness, the princess Moira. To give thanks for her safe return to us, and that of Larkin, lord of MacDara."

There were more cheers as Moira and Larkin stepped up to stand on either side of Riddock. Larkin shot Blair a quick, cocky grin.

He doesn't know, she thought, and felt her stomach twist.

"You are here to welcome the valiant men and women who accompanied them to Geall. The sorcerer Hoyt of the family Mac Cionaoith. His lady Glenna, *cailleach dearg.* The lady Blair, *gaiscioch dorcha.* Cian, of the Mac Cionaoith, and brother to the sorcerer. They are welcome to our land, to our home, to our hearts."

The cheers rolled. Give them a few hundred years, Blair thought, and there'd be little witch and wizard action figures. If the world survived that long.

"People of Geall! We have known a dark time, one of heartbreak and of fear. Our beloved queen was cruelly taken from us.

Murdered by what are not men, but beasts. On this night, on this ground, you will see what has taken your queen. They are brought here by order of her Royal Highness, and through the valor of Lord Larkin, the lady Blair and Cian of the Mac Cionaoith."

Riddock stepped back, and by the way his jaw tightened, Blair thought he knew the drill — and wasn't happy about it.

Moira moved forward, waited for the crowd to subside. "People of Geall, I have come home to you, but not to bring you joy. I come to bring you war. I have been charged by the goddess Morrigan herself to fight what would destroy our world, the world of my friends, all the worlds of humankind. I am charged, with these five whom I trust with my life, with my land, with the crown I may one day bear if the gods deem it, to lead you into this battle."

She paused, and Blair could see she was judging the tone of the crowd, the murmurs, pacing herself.

"It is not a battle for land or wealth, not for glory or vengeance, but for life itself. I have not been your ruler, I have not been a warrior, but a student, a dutiful daughter, a proud citizen of Geall. Yet I would ask you to follow me and mine, to give your lives for me, and for all that come after. For on the night of the feast of Samhain we will face an army of these."

The vampires were dragged onto the field. Blair knew what the people saw. They saw men in chains, murderers yes, but not demons.

There were shouts and gasps, there were calls for justice, there were even tears. But there was no true fear.

The guards fixed the chains to the iron posts, and at Moira's nod, left the field.

"These that killed my mother, that murdered your queen have a name. It is vampire. In her world, the lady Blair has hunted them, destroyed them. She is the hunter of this demon. She will show you what they are."

Blair let out a breath, turned briefly to Larkin. "Sorry."

Before he could speak, she vaulted out of the box and crossed the field.

"What is this?" Larkin demanded.

"You will not interfere." Moira gripped his arm. "This is my wish. More, this is my order. You won't interfere. None of you."

As Blair began to speak, Moira left the box.

"Vampires have one purpose. To kill." Blair circled them, letting them draw her scent, the scent that would stir the terrible

388

hunger. "They feed on human blood. They will hunt you, and drink you. If food is their only purpose you'll die quickly. In pain, in horror, but quickly. If they want more, they'll torture you, as they tortured the family Larkin, Cian and I found dead in the forest on the night we hunted these down."

The larger one tried to lunge at her. His eyes were red now, and those closest to the field would see the fangs he exposed.

"Vampires aren't born. They aren't conceived, they don't grow inside a womb. They're made. Made from humans. A bite from a vampire, if not fatal, infects. Some that are infected become half-vampires, slaves to them. Others are drained almost to the point of death, the very edge of life. Then they're fed the blood of their sire, and they die only to rise again. Not as a human, but as a vampire."

She continued to move, circling just out of reach.

"Your child, your mother, your lover can be turned like this. They won't be your child, your mother, your lover anymore. They'll be a demon, like these, with the blood lust that drives them to feed, to kill, to destroy."

She turned, and behind her the vampires strained against their chains, howling in frustration and hunger as she stood just out of range. "This is what's coming for you. Hundreds, maybe thousands of them. This is what you have to fight. Steel won't kill them. It hurts them."

She whirled, sliced the tip of her sword across the chest of the larger one. "They bleed, but they heal, and a wound like this will barely slow one down. These are the weapons that destroy a vampire. Wood."

She drew a stake, and when she feinted toward the smaller one, he cringed back, hunching to defend his chest. "Through the heart. Fire." She grabbed a torch, and when she flourished it in the air, both of them shrieked.

"They're night feeders because the direct light of the sun will end them. But they can lurk in the shadows, walk in the rain. Kill when the clouds block the sun. The symbol of the cross will burn them, and if you're lucky hold them back. Holy water burns them. If a sword is used it must cut through the neck, taking their head."

She, too, could judge the mood of the crowd, Blair thought. Excitement, confusion, those first whiffs of fear. And a great deal more disbelief. They still saw men in chains.

"These are your weapons, these are what you have along with your wits, your courage, against creatures that are stronger, faster and harder to kill than you are. If we don't fight, if we don't win, a little more than a month from now, they'll devour you."

She paused while Moira walked across the field to her. "Be sure," Blair murmured.

"I am." She gripped Blair's hand briefly then turned to the crowd where voices rippled with concern, confusion.

Moira lifted her voice over it. "Morrigan is called the queen of the warrior, yet it is said she has never fought in battle. Still, I bow to her command. This is faith. I cannot, will not ask that you have the faith in me that you would in a god. I am a woman, mortal as you are. But when I ask you to follow me into battle, you will follow a warrior. Proven. Whether or not I wear a crown, I will carry a sword. I will fight beside you."

She drew her sword, lifted it high. "Tonight, on this ground, I will destroy what took your queen and my mother. What I do here I do for her, by her blood. I do for you, for Geall, and all humankind."

She faced Blair. "Do it. If you have any love for me," she said when Blair hesitated. "Warrior to warrior, woman to woman."

"It's your show."

She chose the smaller of the two, though she judged he still had thirty pounds on

Moira. "On your knees," she ordered, holding her sword to his throat.

"Easy for you to kill when I'm in chains." He hissed it, but he dropped to his knees.

"Yeah, it would be. And I already regret I'm not getting a piece of you." She held the sword against his throat as she moved behind him. Then taking the key Moira had given her, unlocked the chains.

With pride and fear, she plunged the sword into the ground beside him, and walked away.

"What have you done?" Larkin demanded when Blair took her position in front of the box.

"What she asked me to do. What I'd want her to do for me if the situation were reversed." She looked up at him now. "If you can't trust her, why should they?" She reached up for his hand. "If we can't trust her, how can she trust herself?"

She released his hand, and facing the field, prayed she'd done the right thing.

"Pick up the sword," Moira ordered.

"With a dozen arrows pointed at me?" it demanded.

"None flies unless you try to run. Are you afraid to fight a human on equal ground? Would you have run that night if my mother had held a sword?"

"She was weak, but her blood was rich." His eyes slanted to the left, to his companion, still chained and staked too far away to be of any help. "It was meant to be you."

The knife from that had already been in her heart. The words only twisted it. "Aye, and you killed her for nothing. But now it could be me. Will Lilith have you back if you taste my blood tonight? You want it." Deliberately she cut a shallow slice across her palm. "It's so long since you fed."

She watched his tongue flick out to lick his lips as she held up her hand so the blood would drip down her arm and onto the ground. "Come. Strike me down and feed."

He yanked the sword free, and raising it, charged.

She didn't block the first blow, but pivoted aside, kicked out to send him sprawling.

A good move, Blair decided. Add some humiliation to the fear and the hunger. He came up, rushed Moira with that eerie, preternatural speed some of them possessed. But she was ready for him. Maybe, Blair thought, she'd been ready all of her life.

Sword struck sword, and Blair could see that while he had more speed, more strength, Moira had the better form. Moira drove his sword up, aside, then plunged her own into his chest. She danced back, once more took her stance.

Showing the crowd, Blair knew, that while such a wound might be mortal in a human, it barely broke a vampire's stride.

She ignored the screams, the shouts, even the sounds of panic and running feet and watched the combat on the field.

The vampire cupped a hand on his wound, brought the blood from it to his mouth. From behind her, Blair heard the sound of a body hitting the ground as someone fainted.

He came at her again, but this time he anticipated Moira's move. His sword nicked her arm, and he cracked the back of his hand across her face. She stumbled back, blocking the next blow, but was driven back toward the second vampire.

Blair lifted her crossbow, prepared to break her word.

Instead, Moira dived down, rolled aside. She came up with her legs pistoning in a hard double kick that simply made Blair's heart sing.

"Atta girl, atta girl. Now take him out. Stop fooling around."

But it had gone beyond that, beyond merely showing the people what a vampire was capable of withstanding in battle. Moira brought her sword down to cleave a gash in its shoulder, and still she moved back rather than strike a killing blow.

"How long did she live?" Moira demanded. "How long did she suffer?" She continued to block, to drive even when the hand that gripped the hilt of her sword was slick with her own blood.

"Longer than you will, or the coward who sired you."

He charged through her shock. She barely saw the move, would never know how she defended herself against it. There was pain, the sting as the sword grazed her side. There was her own scream as she swung her sword through the air, and took its head.

She went to her knees as much with the sudden tearing grief than from any wounds. She shook from it, and the roars of the crowd were like a distant ocean.

She gained her feet, turned to Blair. "Unlock the other."

"No. That's enough, Moira. It's enough."

"That's for me to say." She strode over, yanked the key from Blair's belt. "It's for me to do."

All sound dropped away as she started across the field. Moira saw the sudden light, a kind of glee in the vampire's eyes as she approached it. The hunger, and the pleasure of what was to come.

Then she saw the arrow whizz by, and strike its heart.

Moira whirled, the rage of betrayal ripping through her. But it wasn't Blair who held the bow. It was Cian.

He tossed it down. "Enough," was all he said before he walked away.

CHAPTER 17

Moira didn't think, she didn't wait. She didn't take her place back in the royal box to speak to her people again. As she rushed away, she could hear Larkin's voice lifted, strong and clear. He would stand in for her, and that would have to do.

She still carried her bloody sword as she sprinted after Cian.

"How dare you! How dare you interfere!"

He continued, reaching the courtyard now, moving across it. "I don't take orders from you. I'm not one of your subjects, not one of your people."

"You had no right." She spun ahead of him to block him from entering the castle. And seeing his face, saw cold rage.

"I'm not concerned about rights."

"Couldn't you stand it? Watching me fight one of them, torment it, destroy it. You couldn't stand by and see me beat down a second."

"If you like."

He didn't push past her but changed direction to continue across the courtyard and through an archway.

"You will not turn from me." This time when she rounded him, she laid the flat of her sword on his chest. Her rage wasn't cold, but hot, bubbling through her like the wrath of gods. "You're here because I wish it, because I permit it. You aren't master here."

"Didn't take long, did it, for you to drape on the mantle. But understand this, princess, I'm here because I wish it, and your *permission* is less than nothing to the likes of me. Now either use that sword or lower it."

She threw it aside so it clattered on the stones. "It was for *me* to do."

"For you to die in front of a roaring crowd? You're a bit small for the gladiator title."

"I would —"

"Have given a hungry vampire his last meal," Cian snapped. "You couldn't have bested the second of them. Maybe, just maybe, you'd have stood a small chance against him if you were fresh and not wounded. But Blair chose the smaller of them to begin with because it was your best chance at proving your point. And so you did, be satisfied with that."

"You think you know what I can do?"

He simply squeezed a hand to the cut on her side, releasing it when she went dead white and swayed back against the wall. "Yes. And so did he. He'd have known exactly where to come at you." Cian lifted the bottom edge of her tunic, wiped the blood from his hand. "You wouldn't have lasted above two minutes before you were as dead as the mother you're so hell-bound to avenge."

Her eyes went from fog to smoke. "Don't speak of her."

"Then stop using her."

Her lips trembled once before she firmed them. "I would have beaten him because I had to."

"Bollocks. You were done, and too proud, too stupid to admit it."

"We can't know, can we, because you ended it."

"You think you could have stopped him from sinking his teeth into this?" Cian skimmed a finger down the side of her throat, barely lifting an eyebrow when she slapped his hand aside. "Stop me then. You'll need more than a peevish slap to manage it."

He stepped back, picked up the sword she'd tossed down. Smiled grimly when she winced at the pull in her side as he threw it to her. "There, you have a sword, I don't. Stop me."

"I've no intention of —"

"Stop me," he repeated, and moved quickly to give her a light shove back against the wall.

"You won't put your hands on me."

"Stop me." He shoved her again, then simply batted the sword aside.

She slapped him, hard across the face before he gripped her shoulders, pressed her back against the wall. She felt something that might have been fear, that might have been, as his eyes held hers transfixed.

"For God's sake, stop me."

When his mouth crushed down on hers, she felt everything. Too much. It was dark and it was bright, it was hard, and unbearably soft. All that was inside her rushed toward it, reckless and crazed.

Then he was standing aside, a foot away from her, and it seemed all the breath had left her body.

"That's not the way he'd have tasted you."

Cian left her trembling against the wall before he compounded an already enormous mistake.

He scented rather than saw Glenna. "She needs to be seen to," he said and continued away.

Inside, Blair sat in front of the fire in the family parlor, trying to get her bearings. "Just don't start on me," she warned Larkin. "She wheedled my word out of me, and the fact is, I understood why she needed to do it."

"Why didn't you tell me?"

"Because you weren't *there*. Because she left it for the last minute. Ambushed me. Which was damn good strategy, if you want my opinion. I argued with her, and maybe I could have argued harder, but she was right. Mostly right. And, Jesus, she made her point, didn't she? In spades."

He handed her a cup of wine, crouched in front of her. "You think I'm angry with you. I'm not. With her, a bit. With her because she didn't trust me with this. Because it wasn't just her mother those things killed, but my aunt. And I loved her. It wasn't just her people she sought to rally with this business tonight, but mine. And I can promise you, Moira and I will speak of it."

"Okay. Okay." She drank, looked at Hoyt. "Have you got two cents to put into this?"

"If you're meaning do I have an opinion

on it, I do. She shouldn't have taken this on herself. She's too valuable to risk, and we're meant to be a circle. No one of us should make such important decisions without the others."

"Well, if you're going to be logical." Blair sighed. "You're not wrong, and if there'd been time, I'd have insisted she bring everyone in on it. We wouldn't have stopped her, but we'd have all been prepared. She went all queen on me." Sighing again, Blair rubbed at the tension at the base of her neck. "Man, she took some hits."

"And Glenna will tend to her," Hoyt answered. "She would have taken more if Cian hadn't acted."

"I wouldn't have let it happen. I'm not going to kick at him for jumping in, grabbing the crossbow out of my hands, but I wouldn't have let her take on number two. She was finished." She drank again. "But I'm not sorry she's tearing the skin off his hide instead of mine."

"His is thick enough." Idly Hoyt poked at the fire. "We'll have our army now."

"We will," Larkin agreed. "None can doubt what we'll come to face. We're not a people of war, but we're not cowards. We'll have an army come Samhain."

"Lilith will be here any day," Blair pointed

out. "We've got a lot of work ahead of us. We'd better get some sleep, get an early start on it tomorrow."

But as she started to get up, Dervil came to the doorway. "I beg your pardon, but I'm sent for the lady Blair. My mistress wishes to speak with her."

"Another command performance," Blair muttered.

"I'll wait in your chambers." Larkin laid a hand on her arm. "You'll come, tell me how she is."

"I'll let you know." Blair started out, glanced at Dervil. "I know the way now."

"I'm asked to bring you."

At the door of Moira's chambers, Dervil knocked. It was Glenna who answered, let out a breath of relief when she saw Blair. "Good, thanks for coming."

"My lady." When Glenna lifted a brow, Dervil cleared her throat. "I would apologize for my poor behavior today, and ask at what time you wish to have the women gathered for instruction."

"An hour past dawn."

"Can you teach me to fight?"

"I will teach you," Glenna corrected.

Dervil's smile was hard and tight. "We'll be ready."

"Something I missed?" Blair asked Glenna

when Dervil left them.

"Just part of a very long day. Something else you missed." She kept her voice low. "I found Moira arguing with Cian at the edge of the courtyard."

"Not a big surprise."

"It was when he finished the argument with his lips."

"Come again?"

"He kissed her. Hard, steamy, passionate."

"Ho boy."

"She was pretty shaken." Glenna glanced over her shoulder. "And not, in my opinion, due to insult and outrage."

"I repeat: Ho boy."

"I'm telling you because I don't want to be worried about this all by myself."

"Thanks for sharing."

"What are friends for?" Glenna stepped back. "Finish that potion, Moira," she said, lifting her voice now to conversational level. "I mean it."

"I am. I will. You've fussed enough."

Moira sat near the fire. She wore robes now, with her hair loose down her back. The bruising on her face stood out against her pallor. "Blair, thank you for coming. I know you must be tired, but I didn't want you to go to bed before I thanked you."

"How are you holding up?"

"Glenna's fussed and tended and dosed me." She held up the cup, drank the contents down. "I feel well enough."

"It was a good fight. You had some nice moves out there."

"I toyed with him too long." Moira lifted her shoulders, then winced as the wound in her side objected to the movement. "That was foolish and prideful. More foolish, more prideful to tell you to release the second. You were right not to."

"Yeah, I was." Blair came over to sit on the hassock at Moira's feet. "I'm not going to tell you I know anything about being a queen. But I do know that being a leader doesn't mean doing it all yourself. Being a warrior doesn't mean fighting when the fight isn't necessary."

"I let my needs cloud my judgment. I know that. I won't do so again."

"Well, all's well that ends." She patted Moira's knee.

"You're the best friends I've known, save Larkin. And the closest women to me but my mother. I saw by your faces when you stood in the door that Glenna told you what she saw between me and Cian."

Unsure how to answer, Blair rubbed her hands on her thighs. "Okay."

"I think we might have some wine." When

Moira started to rise, Glenna laid a hand on her shoulder to stop her.

"I'll get it. I didn't tell Blair to talk behind your back, or gossip."

"I know that as well. It was concern, as a friend, as another woman. There's no need for concern. I was angry. No, enraged," Moira corrected as Glenna came back with the wine. "That he would take it upon himself to end what I wanted to do."

"He only beat me to it by a couple seconds," Blair told her.

"Well. Well. I went after him when it was my duty to stay, to speak to my people. But I went after him, and I deviled him. He'd done what he did to stop me from making a foolish and perhaps fatal mistake. And he told me as much, but I wasn't ready to listen, to accept. He showed me as much, and it's all of a piece, what happened at the end of it. He only showed me that I wasn't strong enough to stop any sort of attack. It meant nothing more than that."

"Okay . . ." Blair searched for words. "If you're satisfied with that."

"It's difficult for a woman to be satisfied when she's kissed in such a way, then coldly rejected." Still Moira lifted a shoulder. "But it was done in anger on both sides. I won't apologize to him, nor do I expect he will to me. We'll simply go on, remembering there are more important things than pride and temper."

"Moira." Glenna stroked a hand over Moira's hair. "Do you have feelings for him?"

As if to search inside herself, Moira closed her eyes. "There are times it seems I'm nothing but feelings. But I know where my duty lies. I've agreed to go to the stone, take hold of the sword. Not tomorrow. There's much to do tomorrow. But by week's end. I've shown my people they have a warrior in me. Soon, if the gods' will it, I'll show them a queen."

When they stepped out, Moira remained in the chair, watching the fire.

"What I gave her will help her sleep, and soon, I hope." Blowing out a breath, Glenna dug her hands into her pockets.

"This could get complicated."

"What *isn't?* I should have seen something like this coming."

"Time to turn in your crystal ball on a newer model?"

"Oh well." They walked together toward their own rooms. "Should we talk to Cian about this?"

"Sure. You go first."

With a half laugh, Glenna shook her head.

"Okay, we leave it alone. Stay out of it — at least for now. You know, I'm a firm believer in full disclosure in relationships. But I'm not going to say anything to Hoyt about this."

"If you think I'm going to blab to Larkin, think again. We've all got enough on our minds."

The morning was soggy and cold, but there were a flock of women on the gaming field. Most of them wore pants — what the locals called *braes* — and tunics.

"More than twice the turnout I had yesterday," Glenna told Blair. "That's Moira's doing."

"She sure as hell drove the point home last night. Look, I'll give you an hour, get them started. Then I'm going to want to get my pet dragon up in the air."

Whether it was the gloom of the morning or the dregs of the tension from the night before, Blair was antsy. "I want to check out the battlefield firsthand, make sure those settlements near it are cleared out. And I want to swing by, make sure the traps are up and running."

"Just another day in paradise. Well, I guess we ought to move this indoors." Hands on hips, Glenna turned a circle. "See if there's a space we can work with."

"Why?"

"In case you haven't noticed, it's raining."

"Yeah, I got that with all the water dripping off my hair. Point is, we don't know what conditions will be like on Samhain. For that matter, we don't know what they'll be like if any of these women have to tangle with a vamp before that. Might as well get used to fighting dirty, so to speak."

"Crap."

"Buck up, soldier." Blair gave her a friendly punch in the arm.

At the end of an hour, Blair was filthy, mildly bruised and in the best of moods. A little down-and-dirty training had gone a long way toward smoothing down the restlessness.

She started across the courtyard with the goal of finding Larkin, then stopped short when she recognized his mother and sister coming her way.

Perfect, she thought. Aces. She was covered with mud and sweat, and about to cross paths with the mom of the guy she was sleeping with. Just her lucky day.

Since there was nowhere to duck out of sight, she toughed it out. "Good morning."

"And to you. I am Deirdre, and this is my daughter, Sinann."

Blair nearly extended a hand before she remembered herself. Since she didn't think she could pull off a curtsey under current conditions, she simply nodded. "It's nice to meet you. I've, ah, been training some of the women."

"We watched." In the way of pregnant women, Sinann folded her hands over the mound of her belly. "You have skill — and energy."

She smiled when she said it, so Blair ordered herself to relax. "They're coming along."

"My son speaks well of you."

"Oh." Blair looked back at Deirdre, cleared her throat. Relax, hell. "That's good to know. Thank you. I was just looking for him. We need to do a little scouting."

"He's in the stables." Deirdre gave Blair a long, quiet look. "Do you think I don't know he shares your bed?" Before Blair could speak, could think to speak, Sinann made a sound that might have been muffled laughter.

"I'm his mother, after all," Deirdre continued in that same mild tone. "I'm aware he's shared beds of other women before you. But he's never spoken to me of them, as he speaks of you. So that changes the matter. I'll beg your pardon. From what he's said, I believed you'd prefer plain speaking."

"I do. I would. Oh boy, I'm sorry. I've just never had a conversation like this, and not with someone like you."

"A mother?"

"For starts. I don't want you to think I just share my bed with anyone who's . . ." Could this be more embarrassing? Blair wondered as Deirdre simply continued to study her with what looked like amused interest. "He's a good man. He's, well, he's an amazing man. You've done your job very well."

"No compliment is dearer to a mother's heart, and I certainly agree with you." The amusement faded now. "This war comes to us, and he'll do battle. I've never faced such a thing, so I have to believe, deep in my heart, that he does what he must, and will live."

"I believe it, if that helps."

"It does. I have other children." Deirdre touched a hand to her daughter's arm. "Another son, the husband of my daughter who is a son to me. I'll have the same faith in them. But my daughter can't fight like the women you teach."

"The child is to be born before the yule," Sinann told Blair. "My third. My children are too young to fight, and this one not yet born. How do I protect them?"

Blair thought of the crosses Hoyt and Glenna had made. She believed the others would agree Larkin's pregnant sister should have one. "There's a lot you can do," Blair assured her. "I'll help you."

Now she turned to Deirdre. "But you shouldn't worry about your daughter, your grandchildren. Your sons, your husband, my friends and I will never let what's coming here get this far."

"You give me peace of mind, and I'm grateful. We may not be able to fight, but we won't be idle. There are many things women who are no longer young, and women who carry life, can do. We'll do them. Now, you have work so we won't keep you longer. Good day to you, and gods protect."

"Thank you."

Blair stood a moment, watching them walk away. Women with spine, she thought. Lilith was going to be so out of her league.

Satisfied, she hunted Larkin down in the stables where he was stripped down to the waist, slicked with sweat, and helping forge weapons.

Her mood only improved. What could be better than watching a half-naked, great-looking guy beat hot steel into a sword?

She could see they'd made a good start

from the number of weapons set aside to cure. The anvil rang with hammer strokes, and smoke billowed as a red-hot blade was plunged into a vat of water.

Was it a wonder, she asked herself, that her mind clicked over to sex?

"Can I get one of those engraved?" she called out. "Something like: 'To the woman who pierced my heart.' Corny, yet amusing."

He looked up, grinned. "You look like you've been rolling in the mud."

"Have been. I was about to go clean up."

He handed his hammer off to one of the other men, then picked up a cloth to scrub the sweat from his face as he walked to her. "We'll have every man and woman in Geall armed by Samhain. Cian's remark some time ago about beating the plowshares into swords isn't that far off. Word's gone out."

"Good. It needs to. Can you break away from here?"

He used his finger to rub some of the mud from her cheek. "What did you have in mind?"

"A couple of flybys. Weather's crappy, I know, but we can't wait for sunshine and rainbows. I need to see the battlefield, Larkin. I need a firsthand look."

"All right then." He grabbed the tunic he'd discarded earlier and called out a quick stream of Gaelic to the men working behind them.

"They'll push on well enough without me."

"Have you seen Moira this morning?"

"Aye. We had a discussion, with considerable heat. Then cooled off and made up. She's gone into the village to speak to people, the merchants. To bargain for more horses, wagons, supplies, whatever it is she's scribbled down on her list of things we'll need in the coming weeks."

"It's good thinking. And smart to make sure she's seen after last night. Anyone who wasn't there would have heard by now. The more visible she is, the better."

In the coming weeks, Blair thought as she went inside to clean up, the shopping, list-making, supply-gathering were all something women like Deirdre and Sinann could deal with. Keep them busy, she mused. And keep the royal family visible.

She scraped off the mud, changed into a reasonably fresh shirt, then strapped on her standard weapons.

When she met Larkin in the courtyard, she took the sheaths for his sword, his stakes. "Got something for you." She picked up the harness she'd set on the ground, slid the sheaths into the loops. "Put this together for you so you can carry your weapons when you're zipping around up there."

"Well, isn't this fine!" He grinned like a kid presented with a shiny new red wagon. "This was thoughtful of you, Blair." He leaned over to give her a kiss.

"Do your thing, and we'll try it out."

"I owe you a gift." He kissed her again.

When he'd become the dragon, Blair looped the harness over his body, gave it a quick cinch. "Not bad, if I do say so myself." She vaulted onto him. "Let's fly, cowboy."

She'd never get used to it. Even in the rain it was a thrill to feel the wonder of what was beneath her, and rise up and up. Into mists now, drenched with wet, that curtained the land below. It was like flying inside a cloud, she thought, where the sound was muffled and there was nothing but the flight.

She decided she'd never be satisfied with anything as ordinary as an airplane again.

The rain thinned, and as the sun struggled to carve beams through the clouds, she saw the rainbow. It arched, a bleeding blur of delicate colors that seemed to drip through the rain. With a lazy sweep of wings, Larkin turned so that the arch glimmered like a doorway ahead. And the colors deepened, seemed to shine like wet silk. As shafts of sunlight cut through the clouds, the rain and those soft, arching colors turned the sky to wonder.

There was a trumpeting call, a kind of joyful blare. Then the sky was filled with dragons.

She lost her breath, literally felt it whiz out of her lungs as beautiful winged beasts soared beside her, in front of her, behind. In more colors than the rainbow, she realized, with their emeralds and rubies and sapphires. She felt Larkin's body ripple as he answered their call, and grinned like a fool when he turned his head and fixed a laughing gold eye on her.

She was flying with a flock of dragons. Herd? Pack? Pod? What did it matter? The wind from their wings blew over her face and hair, sent her coat billowing as they soared through the rainbow sky. The other dragons circled, looped, somersaulted in playful dances. Anticipating, she gripped the harness, shouted for Larkin to: "Do it! Do it!"

And screamed with excitement as he dived and rolled. Hanging upside down as he soared belly-up, she could see the mists tear and reveal the sparkling green and deep, deep brown of the land of Geall.

He skimmed the treetops, dipped over the rush of a river, then climbed, climbed, climbed into air that gleamed now with the strengthening sun.

They flew on, past rainbows and jeweled wings, until it was only the two of them and the sky. Overcome, she lowered to him, laid her cheek on his neck. He'd said he'd owed her a gift, she remembered. He had given her one beyond price.

They flew through sunlight now, and occasional and surprising showers of rain. Below she could see small villages or settlements, the rough roads that joined them, the tangle of streams or narrow rivers, tough little knuckles of forest.

But ahead lay the mountains, dark and mist-shrouded and somehow foreboding.

She could see the edge of the valley that lay at their feet, broken land scarred with rock. The first shudder rippled down her spine as she looked down on what she'd too often seen in dreams.

The sun didn't sparkle here. It was as if the light was absorbed, just sucked away into the dark belly of gullies and chasms, rejected by the dull grass that fought with the spears and juts of weather-pocked rock.

The land dipped and rose, tightened in on itself into folds. And the looming mountains cast great shadows across it, shadows that seemed to cause the land itself to move and shift.

It was more than a shudder that ran through her now. It was an unreasonably, atavistic fear. A fear that this hard and forbidding land would be her grave.

As Larkin veered off, she closed her eyes and let the fear have its way for a moment. Because it couldn't be beaten off, she thought, couldn't be battered down by fists or weapons. It had to be recognized, and accepted.

Once it had, she could control it. If she were strong enough, she could use that fear to fight, and to survive.

When he touched down, she slid off. Legs a little shaky, she admitted to herself. But they held her up, and that's what counted. Her fingers might have felt stiff, but they worked, and she used them to uncinch the weapon harness.

Then Larkin stood beside her.

"It's an evil place."

It was almost a relief to her to hear him say it. "Yeah, oh yeah, it is."

"You can almost feel that evil rising up out of the ground. I've been there before, and it always seemed to me to be a place out of Geall. Not quite a part of it. But it never felt as it did today, as though the ground itself wanted to open up and swallow you whole."

"Oh boy. It got to me, I've got to be honest. Turned my blood cold." She rubbed her hands over her face, then glanced around. "Where are we?"

"Just a ways off from it. I didn't want to set down there. It's an easy walk from here, and I wanted a few moments first."

"I'll take them."

He touched her cheek. "A long way from rainbows here."

"The wrong side of them, I'd say. And I want to say something else, before we head back and face that place. That flight — the rainbow, the other dragons, the whole ball of it, it was the most incredible experience of my life."

"Is that the truth of it?" He cocked his head. "I thought the most incredible experience of your life would be making love with me."

"Oh yeah, right. Well, next to that."

"All right then." He tipped up her chin to kiss her. "I'm glad you enjoyed it."

"It was more than enjoyment. It was just flat down amazing. The best gift anyone's ever given me."

"Handy for me, that rainbow. Dragons can't resist one."

"Really? They're so gorgeous. I thought my eyes would pop out of my head."

"Happens you've seen a dragon before," he reminded her.

"And you're the most gorgeous and handsome of them, blah blah, but honestly, Larkin, they're extreme. All those colors, and the power . . . Hold on — do people ride them, the way I've been riding you?"

"No one rides like you, *a stór.* And they don't, no. They're not horses, after all."

"But if they could. You talked to them."

"It's not what you'd call conversation. It's a kind of communication to be sure. A sort of expression of thought of feeling. And something I can only do when I'm in the dragon, so to speak."

"Aerial warfare would give us a big, fat advantage. I want to think about this."

"They're gentle creatures, Blair."

"So, for the most part, are the women Glenna and I are training to fight. When worlds are on the line, pal, you use everything that comes to hand." She could see the resistance clearly enough on his face. "Let me just play with it in my head awhile. It's this way, right?"

"It is."

They walked the narrow road, framed in hedges and lined with spears of orange lilies. He bent, plucked one, then passed it to her.

Blair stared down at it, delicate petals in a

strong and vibrant color. Something wild and lovely.

She talked of war, she thought. And he gave her a flower.

Maybe it was foolish — maybe both of them were — but she slid its stem into one of the buttonholes of her coat. And she breathed in its sweet scent as they walked toward the battleground.

CHAPTER 18

They'd walked only minutes when Blair heard the sound of horses, and a rattle she assumed was a wagon or cart. When they cleared the curve in the road, she saw she'd been right. There were two wagons, both loaded with people and possessions. There were riders on horseback as well, some no more than children.

Mules were tethered to the back of each wagon and clopped along with a look she could only describe as extreme irritation.

The first wagon pulled up, with the man driving it lifting his cap to Blair, then addressing himself to Larkin.

"It's the wrong way you're traveling," he said. "For by orders of the royal family all in this province are to go into Dunglas, or farther, even into Geall City itself if they can manage it. There are demons coming, it's said, and war with them."

Beside him, the woman clutched the baby she carried closer to her breast. "It won't be safe here," she told them. "All are leaving their homes behind. The princess Moira herself has decreed that every citizen of Geall must be indoors by sunset. You're welcome to a seat in the wagon, and to ride with us as far as my cousin in Dunglas."

"It's kind of you, mistress, and thank you for the offer of hospitality, but we're on business here for the royal family and for Geall. We'll make our way."

"We had to leave our sheep, our crops." The man looked behind him. "But the riders who came from the castle said there was no choice in it."

"They'd be right."

The man turned back to study Blair. "And it's said, too, that warriors and wizards have come from beyond Geall to fight this war and drive the demons out of the world."

"It's truth." But Larkin saw both fear and doubt. "I've gone out of this world, and back into it. I'd be Larkin, lord of Mac Dara."

"My lord." Now the man removed his cap altogether. "It's our honor to speak with you."

"This is the lady Blair, a great warrior from beyond Geall."

The boy who sat on horseback beside the

wagon all but bounced in the saddle. "Have you killed demons, then? Have you fought and killed them, Lady?"

"Seamas." The woman, obviously his mother, spoke sharply. "You haven't been given leave to speak, much less to pester with questions."

"It's all right." Blair stroked a hand over his horse. The boy had a wide-open face, she thought, where freckles had exploded like ginger over cream. He couldn't have been more than eight. "I have fought them, and killed them. So has Lord Larkin."

"And so will I!"

She hoped not. She hoped to God he was safely tucked into bed by nightfall, and every night after. "A strong boy like you has another job. To stay inside, every night until the war's over, guarding his mother, his brothers and sisters. Keeping them safe will take courage."

"No demon will touch them!"

"Best make your way now, and safe travels," Larkin said.

"And to you my lord, my lady."

He clicked to the horses, snapped the reins. Blair watched them until both wagons had rumbled by. "That's a lot of faith in your family, to pack up, leave your home. That's another strong weapon, that kind of faith."

"You spoke well to that boy, made him see that staying inside with his mother was a duty. Lilith's whelp was about that age — a bit younger, actually." Larkin reached under his hair, traced the scar on the back of his neck with his fingers. "Sweet-faced, too. He was some mother's son before she turned him into a monster."

"She'll be paying for that, and a lot more. That bite give you any trouble?" she asked as they started to walk again.

"It doesn't. Not something I forget though, that's for certain. As I'm sure you know for yourself." He lifted her hand, turned her wrist over and kissed her scar. "Still pissed, as you say, that the little bugger got a taste of me. Hardly more than a baby, and damn near killed me."

"Kiddie vampires aren't any less lethal than the full grown variety. And actually, in my opinion, more creepy."

The hedgerows dropped away, and the Valley of Silence lay before them.

"And speaking of creepy," she murmured. "It's no less goosebumping from down here. I'm no sissy, but I wouldn't be insulted if you held my hand."

"I wouldn't be insulted if you held mine."

So they stood, clutching hands, on what seemed to Blair to be the end of the world.

The land fell off in a steep, jagged, ankle-breaking incline. It heaved up in nasty hillocks or rippled tables of rock. Acres of it, she thought. Acres of misery and shadows with only the undulating moan of a cold wind through the wild grass.

"Lots of places to hide," she commented. "We can use that as well as they can. Most of the fighting's going to have to be done on foot. Only the best riders could handle a mount on that ground."

She narrowed her eyes. "We'd better go down, take a look at what we're dealing with."

"How do you feel about riding a goat?"

"Unenthusiastic." But she gave his hand a squeeze. "Besides, if we can't negotiate it now, daylight, no pressure, we're not going to do very well at night, in the heat of battle."

Plenty of footholds, she discovered as they started down. And the ground was too mean and stubborn to crumble away under her boots. Maybe she'd have preferred a nice flat field for the mother of all battles, but there were ways to use what they had to their advantage.

"Some of these crevices, shallow caves could be useful. Hiding men and weapons."

"They would." Larkin crouched down, peered into a small opening. "They'd think

426

of that as well, as you said back in Ireland."

"So we get here first, block off some strategic points. Magically maybe — we can talk to Hoyt and Glenna about that. Or with crosses."

He nodded, straightened. "We'd want the high ground there, and perhaps there." He gestured as he studied the lay. "Flood down on them, that's what we'd do. Flood down on the bloody bastards, keeping archers on the high ground."

Blair climbed up on a shelf of rock. "We'll need light, that's essential."

"We can't count on the moon."

"Glenna conjured some sort of light the night we went head-to-head with Lora in that skirmish back at Cian's place. They'll slaughter us like flies if we fight in the dark. That's their turf. We can't lay traps here," she added with a thoughtful frown. "Can't risk our own men stumbling over or falling into one."

Larkin held up a hand for her as she prepared to jump down. "She'll come here as well, at night, to study, to work out her strategy. She may have been here before, before we were born. Before those who birthed us were born. Spinning out her web and dreaming of that single night to come."

"Yeah, she'll have been here. But . . ."

"What?"

"So have I. I've seen this place in my head as long as I can remember. From up there, from down here. In sunlight and silence, in the dark with the screams of battle. I know this place," she whispered. "I've been afraid of it all my life."

"Yet you come to it. You stand on it."

"Feels like I've been pushed here, closer and closer, every day. I don't want to die here, Larkin."

"Blair —"

"No, I'm not afraid to die. Or not obsessed with the idea of it. But, oh God, I don't want to end here, in this hard, lonely place. Drowning in my own blood."

"Stop." He took her shoulders. "Stop this."

Her eyes were huge now, and deep, deep blue. "You see, I don't know if I've seen it, or just imagined it because of the fear. I don't know if I've watched myself die here. Damn gods, anyway, for their mixed messages and unreasonable demands."

She patted her hands on his chest to ease him back, give herself a little space. "It's okay, I'm okay. Just a little panic attack."

"It's this place, this evil place. Slides under the skin and freezes the blood."

"So, advantage them. But you know what? You know something that tips onto our side? The people who'll come here, who'll take this ground and fight on this place, they'll have something inside them. Whatever it is, it'll already have given evil the finger."

"What finger?"

She hadn't thought it possible, not in this awful silence, not in this nightmare place, but she laughed until her sides ached.

She explained as they walked the broken ground. And it seemed easier then, to cross it, study it, to think clearly. When they climbed back up she felt more steady, more sure.

She brushed off her hands, started to speak. Then simply froze.

The goddess stood in a stream of light. It seemed to pulse from her white robe, and still it was dim compared to her luminous beauty.

I'm awake, Blair thought, so this is new. Wide awake, and there she is.

"Larkin, do you see —"

But he was going down on one knee, bowing his head. "My lady."

"My son, you would kneel before what you have never truly believed?"

"I have come to believe in many things."

"Then believe this," Morrigan said. "You

are precious to me. Each of you. All of you. I've watched you travel here, through the light and the dark. And you, daughter of my daughters, will you not kneel?"

"Is that what you need?"

"No." And she smiled. "I only wondered. Rise up, Larkin. You have my gratitude, and my pride."

"Would either of those come with an army of gods?" Blair asked her, and earned a shocked hushing sound from Larkin.

"You are my army, you and what you both carry inside you for tomorrow and tomorrow. Would I ask this thing of you if it were not possible?"

"I don't know," Blair answered. "I don't know if gods only ask the possible."

"And yet you come, you prepare, you battle. So you have my gratitude, my pride, and my admiration. This, the second month, the time of learning is nearly done. So will come the time of knowing. You must know if you are to win this thing."

"What, my lady, must we know?"

"You will know when you know."

"See." Blair spread her hands. "Cryptic. Why does it always have to be cryptic?"

"It frustrates you, I know." There might have been a laugh in Morrigan's eyes as she stepped closer. But there was no doubt of the affection in the brush of her fingers — warm and real — over Blair's cheek. "Mortals may see the path the gods have carved, but it's up to them to chose a direction and follow it. I will tell you that you are my hope, you and the four with you who forged the circle. You are my hope, the hope of mankind. You are my joy, and the future."

She touched Larkin's cheek now. "And you are blessed."

She stepped back, the laughter gone. In its place was a sorrow and a kind of steely strength. "What is coming must come. There will be pain, and blood and loss. There is no life without its price. The shadows will fall, dark upon dark, and demons rise from it. A sword flames through it, and a crown shines. Magic beats like a heart, and what was lost can be regained if that heart is willing. Give these words to all the circle, and remember them. For it is not the will of gods that will win the day, but the will of humankind."

She vanished with the light so Blair stood with Larkin on the edge of the cursed ground.

"Remember it?" Blair lifted her hands, let them fall. "How are we supposed to remember all that? Did you get it?"

"I'll remember it. It's my first conversation

with a goddess, so I can promise you I won't be forgetting the details of it."

They flew again, away from the valley to the first of the three points Blair had devised for traps. They set down in a green glade with a pretty river winding through it.

Standing beside the river, she took out the map the six of them had worked on. "Okay, if we go by the fact that our portal stands in nearly the same spot here as it does in Ireland, then we make the big leap of faith that the same would hold true for Lilith's way in, the cliffs are roughly twenty miles west."

"They are, as you see here." He traced his finger on the map, along the coastline. "And caves as well, which she could use for her base."

"Could," Blair agreed. "And she might put some troops there. But it makes more sense to base closer to the battleground. Even if she doesn't, at some point she'll have to move west to east, and if she's taking the most direct route, she'd have to cross this way. And this river." She nodded toward the water. "Smarter to cross it near this point, where it narrows. Moira said she took care of the mojo."

"She had the holy man brought here, as you wanted. The water was blessed."

"Not to question your holy man, but I'd feel better if I checked it out."

She dug in her pocket for a vial of blood. "Courtesy of the vampire you skewered into the ground the other night. Let's try a little chemistry."

Larkin took the water bag to the river to fill it. While he was there he cupped his hand, sampled straight from the river itself. "Fresh and cool in any case. Pity its not deep enough for a swim just here, or I'd talk you out of your clothes again."

"On the clock here, pretty boy." She crouched down beside him and opened the vial. "Just a couple of drops. It's either going to work or it's not."

He tapped a few drops into the vial. And the blood bubbled and steamed with the water mixed with it.

"All right! You've got yourself a happening holy man. Look at that boil." She straightened to do a quick happy dance. "Picture this. Along marches the evil vampire army. Gotta cross the river, if not at this point, at some point. Crap, going to get our feet wet, but we're the evil vampire army, we're not afraid of a little stinking water. Then they start across. Man, I can just *hear* it. 'Yipe, yipe, shit, fuck!' Splashing across, splashing back, just making it worse. Wet feet, hell.

Searing, burning feet — worse if some of them panic and knock each other down, slip. Oh joy, oh rapture."

Larkin stayed in his crouch, grinning at her pleasure. "It was damn clever of you."

"It was freaking brilliant. High five!" She grabbed his hand, slapped her palm to his. "It's a thing."

He got up, yanked her to him and kissed her long and deep. "It's a thing I like better."

"Who could argue? Wouldn't it be great, oh, wouldn't it be sweet, if Lilith was leading the way, starts her strut across the stream. The ultimate hot foot. I'm just loving this."

She took a huge breath. "Okay, that's enough fun and frivolity. Let's go check out the others."

A good day, Blair thought as they headed toward the second location. Rainbows, dragons, goddesses. She'd faced one of her personal nightmares by walking in the valley, and she'd come out of it again. Now she was seeing her guerilla warfare tactics take shape.

Lilith's army was going to take a few hard kicks in the ass long before Samhain. Since vamps weren't known for tending their wounded without a strong connection between them, she was likely going to lose a nice chunk of troops on the march toward destiny.

When Larkin started his descent she prepared herself for another pat on the back. Then he changed directions. Puzzled, she looked down and saw the overturned wagon.

There was a man lying beside it, and a woman standing with a toddler in her arms, and another at her skirts.

The youngest let out a squeal that might have been delight, might have been terror as a gold dragon with a woman on its back soared down to the road.

The young mother went pale as a sheet and stumbled back when the dragon shifted shape into a man.

"Oh, blessed mother!"

"Don't be frightened." Larkin spoke gently, added what Blair thought of as his thousand-watt smile. "Just a bit of magic, is all. I'm Larkin, son of Riddock."

"My lord." Her cheeks remained colorless, but she managed a curtsey.

"You've some trouble here. Your man is hurt?"

"It's me leg." The man struggled to sit up, but could only moan. "I fear it's broke."

"Let me have a look." Blair knelt down. His face was gray, she noted, with a good-sized bruise along his jawline.

"The axle, it broke. Thank the gods my family wasn't hurt, but I took a bad fall. Then the bloody horse runs off."

"Might have a small fracture here." Blair gave him a bolstering smile. "It's not as bad as your axle, but you're not going to be walking for a while. He's going to need help, Larkin."

Larkin studied the wheel. "There's no fixing that without some new wood. Where are you bound?" he asked the woman.

"My lord, we were going to stop at the wayfarers on the road to Geall City, then travel on from there on the morrow. My husband has relations in Geall City. His brother, Niall, is with the castle guards."

"I know Niall well. If you'd get what you feel you can't do without for the evening, we'll see you to the wayfarer."

The older child, a girl of about four, tugged on Larkin's tunic. "Where did your wings go?"

"I've just tucked them away for now, but I'll show them to you again. Help your mother now." He gestured to Blair.

"Can he ride?" he asked her.

"You'd have to go at a walk. We can put a temporary splint on that leg, but I don't think it should be jostled around. He's in a lot of pain."

"All right then, it'll have to be flying. It's only a few miles to the inn."

"You take them. Two adults — one of them hurt — a couple of kids. That's about all you can manage."

"I don't like leaving you alone."

"Broad daylight," she reminded him, "and I'm armed. I can head over, check out the next trap. It's what, about a quarter mile that way, right?"

"It is, but you could wait here. I wouldn't be much above a half hour."

"Kick my heels by a broken wagon? I can check it out and be back here by the time you make the round trip. Then we can swing by the last of them, and maybe do a sweep of the area, see if there are any stragglers that need a hand. We'll be back home before sunset, with time to spare."

"All right then, for you'll go anyway the minute I've gone."

"Nice to be so well understood."

It took time, not just to load the family on, but to first convince the woman that it could be done. That it had to be done.

"Now don't worry a bit, Breda." Larkin gave her full-power charm. "I'll be staying as low to the ground as I'm able. We'll have you and your family at the inn quick as a wink, and send off for help for your man here. I'll see that someone comes and fixes your wagon in the morning, and delivers it straight to you. Can't ask better than that."

"No, my lord, no. You're so kind." Still she stood, all but wringing her hands. "I've heard, of course, of your gift. All of Geall knows of it, but to see . . . And the idea of riding a dragon —"

"Won't your daughter have stories to tell? Come now, your husband needs help."

"Aye. Well, of course, of course."

He changed before she could balk, and left it to Blair to deal with the rest. She helped the injured man up, taking his weight as Larkin bellied to the ground. Using rope from the wagon, she tied him on.

"I'm grateful to you," he said to Blair. "I don't know how we'd have managed."

"If you're anything like your brother, you'd have figured something. He's a good man. You get on behind him," Blair instructed his wife. "Keep the kids between you. I'm going to tie you on his back. You'll be secure, I promise you."

"I like his wings." The girl clambered on before her mother could make a peep. "They shine."

When it was done, Larkin picked up the pack of possessions in his jeweled legs. Then turned his head to give Blair a nuzzle on the arm.

And he was rising up. Blair heard the little girl shouting with absolute delight as they skimmed down the road and away.

"Know just how you feel," Blair said with a laugh. With the map in hand, she crossed the road and started across the first field.

It felt good to walk, and to have a little alone time. Not that she wasn't nuts about the guy, Blair thought as she brushed her finger over the flower in her buttonhole. But she was so used to being on her own. This whole business had all but eliminated her solo time.

Since it started, she'd been part of a team — a circle, she corrected. People she respected and believed in, no question, but people who needed to be consulted.

All in all, she was better at teamwork than she'd imagined she would be. Maybe, she decided, it was all a matter of who was making up the team.

And somehow, through that team, she'd ended up being half of a couple. She hadn't believed that was in the cards for her, not again. Certainly not with a man who knew everything there was to know about her, and not only got it, but valued it.

She already knew it was going to rip her to

pieces when they went their separate ways. No choice there that she could see, so there wasn't much point in brooding about it, less point in wasting the time they had feeling sorry for herself.

In any case, they both had to live first before they could be miserable and alone.

It was better, all around better, to enjoy, and to cherish the time they had. When that time was done she could look back at it and know she'd loved, and had been loved.

She glanced up at the sky, wondering how the farmer and his family were faring with their first — and if she was any judge of the mother of the brood, their last — dragon flight.

Larkin would take care of them. It was one of the things he was good at. Taking care. When you added the fairy-tale-prince looks, the kick-ass attitude in battle, that quick grin and the excellent stamina in bed, he was just about perfect.

She checked her map again, hopped over a low stone fence to the next field.

Beyond it were a few trees, and the most direct route from the coast to the valley.

They'd move through here, Blair thought, two, maybe three hours before they reached the stream with the blessed water. And at night, go quickly through this open area toward the shelter of woods another few miles inland.

This route was logical, and it was efficient. Add in the scatter of farms, cottages sprinkled through, there was the possibility of fresh food.

Oh yeah, Blair mused, this is the way she'll come. Has to. In stages, maybe, leaving some at the caves, at various safe points along the way. For hunting, for ambushes, quick raids.

"It's what I'd do," Blair murmured, and with a last check of the map, headed southeast into a small, thin grove of trees.

She saw it almost immediately, and her first thought was some kid or passer-by had stumbled over the trap. And into it.

Her heart bounced straight into her throat. She sprinted toward the wide hole, terrified she'd see bodies impaled on the wooded spikes below.

What she saw was a scatter of weapons, and one very dead horse.

"Moved up the schedule," she said softly, and despite the sunlight, reached behind her to draw her sword.

Moved things up, Blair decided, when the reports came in that they'd gone to the Dance with supplies and weapons. And vanished.

She'd have known where they'd vanished,

Blair thought. So Lilith's army was already in Geall, already on the march. And had already passed this point. The trap had worked. From the weapon count, it looked to have taken out at least a dozen — and the very unlucky horse.

She crouched down, wishing she had some of the rope she'd used earlier. They needed to retrieve those weapons — waste not, want not — and get that poor horse out of there.

She was puzzling over how she and Larkin might do that when she realized the light had changed. Looking up, she saw the sky overhead was black with clouds.

As twilight fell in a fingersnap, she got to her feet. "Oh shit."

She backed up, backed away from the hole, and thought it wasn't just a dozen vamps who'd walked into a trap. She'd just walked into one herself.

And they came up, out of the ground.

CHAPTER 19

She took two out fast, an instinctive and wide sweep of her sword, before they were fully disinterred. But there were alarms shrilling in the back of her mind that said she was in big, bad trouble.

Eight, she counted, after the two she'd dusted. They had her surrounded, cutting off any chance of retreat. And she'd walked right into it, all but whistling a tune. If she managed to live — and the odds were against it — she'd curse herself for it later. Right now since flight wasn't an option, fight was all that was left.

The one thing she had, Blair reminded herself, was a lot of fight in her. She pulled her stake, blocked the first blade with her sword even as she pumped out a back kick. She spun, swinging out with the sword, scoring flesh, buying time. Spotting an opening, she rammed the stake.

One more down.

But these weren't green recruits who'd make many sloppy and fatal mistakes. What she was facing were trained and seasoned soldiers, and it was still seven against one.

She envisioned the fire, sending it rippling down the sword Glenna had charmed. "Yeah, come on. Come *on!*" Hacking out, she sent one falling back, his arm ablaze.

Then went flying as one caught her foot on the next kick and hurled her into the air. She slammed hard into the trunk of a tree, saw stars floating on a gray field edged with sickly red. But the one that charged her met fire and steel, and fell screaming into the trap.

She rolled, and with pain bursting through her, struck out with the flaming sword. Her left arm was numb from the shoulder down, and she'd lost the stake. She hacked, thrust, sliced, took a hard punch to the face that nearly sent her into the trap. She managed to spring over it, fight for footing. And with vicious, screaming blows, beat back the next attack.

One went for her throat, so she cracked the hilt of the sword on the bridge of his nose. She felt the chain that held her crosses snap as he fell back.

No stake, no cross. And five of them left.

She wasn't going to make it, no longer hoped she could hold them back until Larkin got to her to even the odds.

So she wouldn't die in the valley, but here and now. But by God, she'd take as many as she could with her first so that when Larkin came for her, he could finish the rest.

Her left arm was nearly useless, but she still had her feet, and kicked up, kicked out as she sliced out fire. They'd weakened her, breaking her form, her rhythm. She blocked an oncoming sword, but the tip of it scored a line down her thigh on the down swing. Her slight stumble left her open enough so that when another kicked, the blow plowed into her belly, stealing her breath as her body flew back.

She went down hard, felt something tear inside her. With what she had left, she thrust up blindly, had the grim satisfaction of seeing one burst into flame.

Then the sword was knocked out of her hand, and she had nothing left.

How many left? she wondered. Three? Maybe three. Larkin could take three. He'd be all right. Head swimming, she struggled back to her feet. She didn't want to die on her back. She fisted her hands, fought to get her balance.

Maybe, maybe she could take one more,

just one more, bare-handed, before they killed her.

But they'd stepped back, she saw. Three? Four? Her vision was doubling on her. But she willed it to focus, and saw Lora glide over the ground.

Weren't going to kill me, Blair thought dimly. Just working me over, wearing me down. Saving me for her. Worse than death, she realized as her blood went cold. She wondered if she could find a weapon and a way to end her own life before Lora made her a monster.

If she could manage it, she might be able to throw herself into the trap. Better staked than changed.

"I'm so impressed." Clapping her hands together lightly, Lora smiled. "You defeated seven of our seasoned warriors. I've lost a bet with Lilith. I wagered you'd take out no more than four."

"Happy to help you lose."

"Well, you did have a slight advantage. They were ordered not to kill you. That pleasure will be mine."

"You think?"

"Know. And that coat? I've admired that coat since I first saw you on the side of the road in Ireland. It's going to look marvelous on me."

"So that was you? Sorry, all of you smell the same to me."

"I can say the same about you mortals." Lora beamed out a gay smile. "Speaking of mortals, I have to say your Jeremy was absolutely delicious." Still smiling, she touched her fingertips to her lips, flicked them out as if reliving the moment.

Don't think about Jeremy, Blair ordered herself. Don't give her the satisfaction. So she said nothing, meeting Lora's laugh with stony silence.

"But where are my manners? We've met, of course, but haven't been formally introduced. I'm Lora, and I'll be your sire."

"Blair Murphy, and I'll be the one dusting you. And the coat looks better on me than it would on you."

"You're going to be the most delightful playmate! I can hardly wait. Because I have admiration and respect for you, we'll fight this out. Just you and I." Lora pointed a finger toward the trio of soldiers, wagged it. "Back, back, back now. This is between us girls."

"So, you want to fight?" Think, think, think, Blair ordered herself. Think over the pain. "Swords, knives, hand-to-hand?"

"I do love bare hands." Lora lifted hers, wiggled her fingers. "It's so intimate."

"Works for me." Blair spread her coat open to show she had no weapons. "Can I ask you a question?"

"Bien sur."

"Is that accent real, or do you just put it on?" She unhooked the water bottle from her belt.

"I was born in Paris, in the year fifteen-eighty-five."

Blair let out a snort. "Come on."

"All right," Lora said with a laugh, "fifteen-eighty-three. But what woman doesn't fudge a little about her age?"

"You were younger than me when you died."

"Younger when I was given true life."

"It's all a matter of perspective." Blair lifted the water sack, twisted it open. "Mind? Your boys gave me quite a workout. Feeling a little dehydrated."

"Be my guest."

Blair tipped the bag back, drank. The water felt like a miracle on her dry throat. "If I take you, are your boys going to finish me off?"

"You won't take me."

Blair angled her head, said a quick prayer. "Bet?"

And swung the bag so the blessed water splashed over Lora's face and throat.

The screams were like rusty razors slicing through Blair's brain. There was smoke, the nasty stench of burning flesh. She stumbled away from it as Lora ran shrieking.

A weapon, Blair thought, fighting to see, just to stay on her feet. Everything, anything was a weapon.

She grabbed a low branch of the tree as much for support as a last-ditch effort. Calling on whatever she had left she pulled at it, felt it crack. With something between a sob and a scream, she swung it at the three vampires who charged toward her.

The dragon dived out of the sky, tail lashing. Blair saw one of them fly headfirst into the trap as the man stood, drawing the sword from the harness that spilled around his feet.

The last thing she saw before she fell was the bright flame of it cleaving through the dark.

He fought like a madman, without a thought for his own safety. If they landed blows, he never felt them. His rage and his fear were beyond pain. There had been three, but if there'd been thirty he still would have cut through them like an avenging god.

His dragon had swept one into the stakes, and now he hacked through the shoulder of another. The arm that fell went to dust, and the creature that was left ran screaming across the field. The third rushed to retreat. Larkin swept up a stake on the run, flung it. And sent it to hell.

With his sword hand ready for however many more might spring out of the dark, he crouched to Blair. The words poured out of him, and were all her name. Her face had no color but the blood that streaked it, and the bruises already going black.

When her eyes fluttered open, he saw they were glassy with pain.

"My hero." Her voice was barely more than a thick whisper. "Gotta move, gotta go, could be more. Oh God, oh God, I'm hurt. You gotta help me up."

"Just be still a moment. I need to see how bad it is."

"It's bad. Just . . . is the light coming back or am I heading into that stupid white tunnel people talk about?"

"The sun's coming back. It's all right now."

"Ten, there were ten, and the French whore makes eleven. My head — damn it. Concussion. Vision keeps doubling on me. But —" She couldn't bite back the scream when he moved her shoulder.

"I'm sorry. *A stór, a stór,* I'm sorry."

"Dislocated. Don't think broken, just out of joint. Oh God. You have to fix it. I can't . . . I can't. You have to take care of it, okay? Then . . . Jesus, Jesus. Go get a wagon. I can't ride."

"You'll trust me now, won't you, my darling? Trust me to take care of you now."

"I do. I will. But I need you to —"

He did it quickly, bracing her back against the tree, pressing his body hard to her as he yanked her shoulder back into place.

She didn't scream this time. But he was watching her face, and saw her eyes roll up white before she slumped against him.

Ripping the sleeve of his tunic, he used the material to field dress the gash on her thigh before checking along her torso for broken ribs. When he'd done the best he could for her, Larkin laid her down gently before springing up to gather the weapons. After securing them in the harness, he draped it over himself and hoped it would hold.

Shimmered from man to dragon.

He picked her up, cradling her in his claws as if she were made of glass.

"Something's wrong." Glenna gripped Moira's arm as they stood on the practice field working with a handful of the more promising students. "Something bad, big. Wake Cian. Wake him now."

They both saw the black boil of the sky to

451

the southeast, and the rippling curtain of darkness that fell from it.

"Larkin. Blair."

"Get Cian," Glenna repeated, and began to run.

She didn't have to shout for Hoyt; he was already sprinting toward her. "Lilith," was all she said.

"Midir, her wizard." He took hold of her arm, pulling her toward the castle. "This would be his work."

"She's already here. Larkin and Blair are out there, out there in the dark. We need to do something, quickly. Counteract the spell. There must be a way."

"Riddock should send riders out."

"They'd never get there in time. It's miles off, Hoyt."

"They'll go in any case."

When they rushed inside, Cian was already coming down, Moira hard on his heels.

"He was already coming," Moira said.

"I felt the change. False night. I can get there quicker than you, or any mortal."

"And what good will it do if the sun comes back?" Moira demanded.

"Time I gave that bloody cloak a try."

"We don't separate. We can't risk it. And sending riders, Hoyt." Glenna shook her head. "They won't help now. We need a circle, and a counter spell." Maybe a miracle, she thought. "We need it fast."

"It has to be outside, under the sky." Hoyt looked into his brother's eyes. "Will you risk it? We can try it without you," he said before Cian could speak. "The three of us."

"But the odds are better with me. Let's get it done."

They gathered what they needed. Hoyt and Glenna were already outside making hurried preparations when Cian came down again with the cloak.

Moira stepped forward when he got to the base of the stairs. "I think faith in your brother will strengthen the spell."

"Do you?"

"I think," she said in the same measured tones, "your willingness to risk so much for friends has already given you protection."

"We're about to find out." He swirled the cloak on, pulled the hood up. "Nothing ventured," he added. And for the first time in nearly a thousand years stepped into the sun.

There was heat. He felt it weigh down on him — lead heated almost to burning. It pressed on his chest, shortened his breath, but he crossed the courtyard.

"I haven't turned into a human torch yet," he said, "but I wouldn't object if this didn't take long."

"Fast as we can," Glenna told him. "Bright blessings on you, Cian."

"Let's keep the bright off it, if it's all the same."

"Carnelian for speed." She began placing crystals in a pentagram pattern on the stones. "Sunstone for light. Agates — dendritic for protection, plume for binding."

Now she took up herbs, dropping them into a bowl. "Garlic for protection. Sorry," she said to Cian.

"That's a myth."

"Okay, good. Holly, restoration of balance. Rose and willow. Power and love. Join hands. Keep yours inside the cloak, Cian, we'll come to you."

"Focus," Hoyt ordered, with his eyes on the black sky, the bubble of night to the south and east. "Draw out what you have. Both of you have power inside you. Draw it out and forge the circle."

"Guardians of the Watchtowers," Glenna called out. "We summon you."

"Of the east, of the south, of the west, of the north, we call your fire to cast here this circle."

At Hoyt's words the yellow candles

Glenna had chosen to represent the sun sprang to light.

"Morrigan the mighty, join with us now," he continued. "We are your servants, we are your soldiers."

Casting her eyes to the sky, Glenna pulled everything she had inside her, and pushed. "Blessed are you and blessed are we who seek to fight this infamy. Magic against magic, white and pure against the black, here springs our power against this attack. Might and right push back the night. With our power joined we raise our cry, break this dark spell in the eastern sky. Hear our love and loyalty. As we will, so mote it be."

Her hand trembled in Hoyt's as the power spun round the circle. With her eyes still cast up, she saw the battle rage. Flashing lights, gushing black clashing together like swords to raise a thunder that sent the ground to quiver.

"We refute the dark magicks!" Hoyt shouted. "We cast them back, we cast them out. We call the sun to flame through the false night."

Overhead the war between the black and the white raged on.

Blair swam dizzily toward consciousness, and into the pain. She felt the wind rush by her, and thought she saw the blur of land below.

Flying? She was flying? Is this what happened after you were dead? But if she was dead, why the hell did she hurt so much?

She tried to move, but she was tied down, strapped in. Or maybe her body simply refused to work any longer. Then she managed to turn her head, and she was looking up at a golden throat.

She thought: Larkin. Then floated away once more.

He felt her stir, gently tightened his grip in hopes it would reassure her, make her feel more secure. He angled his head to look down at her, but her eyes were already closing again.

She looked so pale. She felt so fragile.

He'd left her alone.

He would live, all of his life, he would live with the image of her bleeding, left with nothing more than a tree branch for defense while monsters circled her like vultures.

If he'd been even seconds later, she would be dead. Because he hadn't been with her. He'd seen to the safety of others, and he'd tarried just a little longer so a young girl could pet his wings.

When the darkness had come, he hadn't been with her.

The fear ate through him that no matter how fast he'd flown to reach her, no matter if he'd stopped the three demons who'd stalked her from feeding, he'd still been too late to save her life.

Even when he saw the castle, the fear gnawed. He saw Moira rush out, and Hoyt, Glenna, his father and others. But still he knew nothing but that fear.

He'd barely touched the ground when he changed, and held Blair in his arms. "She's hurt. She's hurt."

"Bring her in, quickly." Sprinting alongside him, Glenna reached over to check the pulse in Blair's throat. "Up to her room. I'll get what I need. Moira, go with him, do what you can for her. I'll be quick."

"How bad?" Cian swung around to rush up the stairs beside Glenna.

"I don't know. Pulse is weak, thready. Her face . . . she took a beating."

"Bites?"

"I didn't see any." She grabbed her healing kit from her room, dashed out again.

Larkin had laid Blair on the bed, and stood as Moira laid hands on Blair's face, her shoulders, her heart.

"How long has she been unconscious?" Glenna snapped as she swept in.

"I . . . I don't know. She fainted," Larkin

managed. "I had to . . . her shoulder, it was out of the joint. I had to . . . she fainted when I snapped it back. I think she came around once on the way back, but I can't be sure. The dark, it came. I wasn't with her, and they set on her, and she was alone."

"You brought her back. Moira, help me get her coat off, her clothes. I have to see where she's hurt."

Cian stepped up himself to take off her boots.

"The men should go," Moira began.

"She isn't the first I've seen naked, and I don't think she'd be worried about it. How many were there?" Cian asked Larkin.

"She said ten. Ten and the French one as well. There were only three when I got to her."

"She made them pay." Cian gently tugged down her pants.

Glenna bit back a sound of distress as she saw the bruising, the cuts. "Ribs." She made her voice brisk. "Probably kidney. Bruised. Shoulder's bad, too. The gash on her leg is fairly shallow. But God, her knee. Not broken, at least. Nothing broken."

"She . . ." Larkin reached down, took one of Blair's limp hands. "She said her vision was going double. Concussion, she said."

Now Glenna spoke gently. "Why don't

you step out? Let Moira and me take care of her."

"No, I won't leave her again. She had pain. A lot of pain. You need to give her something that will take away the pain."

"I will, I promise I'll give her what I can for it. Why don't you build up the fire then? I want it warm for her."

Blair could hear them, the voices. She couldn't quite separate one from the other or pick out words, but the sounds were enough to assure her she was alive.

The pain spoke to her as well and that told her she'd gotten her ass thoroughly kicked.

She caught scents as well now. Peat smoke, Glenna, and something strong and floral. But when she tried to open her eyes, they wouldn't cooperate. That had panic trickling into her chest like nasty little drops of acid.

Coma? She didn't want to be in a coma. People fell into comas and sometimes they never climbed out. She'd rather be dead than trapped inside the dark, hearing, feeling, but not being able to see or speak.

Then she felt something slide over her, like silk. Just a flutter over her skin, under it, then deeper, deeper still to where the pain was clenched in fists.

Then the silk heated, then it burned. Oh

God. And the fire of it forced those fists open until the pain spread and broke into a thousand jagged pieces.

Her eyes flew open in blinding light that had her flailing out.

"Son of a *bitch!*" In her mind she screamed it, but it came out as a hoarse croak.

She sucked in breath to curse again, but the worst of it ebbed and became a slow, steady throbbing.

"It hurts, I know, it hurts to heal. Can you look at me? Blair? No, stay up here now, and look at me."

Blair forced her eyes open again. Glenna swam into view, her face close. Her hand cupped the back of Blair's neck, lifted it gently up. "Drink a little of this. Just a little now. I can't give you too much because of the head trauma. But this will help."

Blair swallowed, winced. "Tastes like liquid tree bark."

"Not that far off. Do you know where you are?"

"I'm back."

"What's your name?"

"Blair Murphy. Do you want rank and serial number?"

Glenna's lips curved. "How many fingers?"

"Two and a half. Vision's a little blurry." But she struggled to use it, to see. The room was full of people, she realized — the whole team. "Hey. Dorothy, Scarecrow, the Tin Man." She realized then her hand was gripping Larkin's, probably hard enough to grind bone to bone. She relaxed her fingers, managed a smile. "Thanks for saving my life back there."

"It was no trouble. You'd taken care of most of it yourself."

"I was done." She closed her eyes again. "Tapped out."

"I shouldn't have left you alone."

"Cut that out." Blair would have given him a light punch to go with the words if she'd had the strength. "It's wrong and it's useless."

"Why did you?" Cian asked him. "Why did you separate?"

As Larkin told them about the injured man, Blair closed her eyes again. She could hear Glenna and Moira murmuring to each other. Floating a little, she thought Glenna had a voice like silk — sort of sexy and sleek. Moira's was more like velvet, soft and warm.

And that was a really strange thought, she decided. But at least she was having thoughts.

As they worked on her, the pain bloomed,

then backed off, bloomed and died. She began to anticipate the rhythm of it before she made another realization.

"Am I naked?" She would have pushed up to her elbows, at least tried to, if Glenna hadn't eased her back. "I'm naked. Oh man."

"You're covered well enough with a sheet. We had to see your injuries," Glenna told her. "You're pretty well covered with gashes and bruises, too, so I wouldn't worry about modesty right now."

"My face." Blair lifted a hand to feel for herself. "How bad is my face?"

"Modesty and vanity," Glenna said. "Good signs. You wouldn't make the finals of the Miss Demon Hunter contest at the moment, but you look damn good to me."

"You're beautiful." Larkin took her hand, kissed it. "You couldn't be more beautiful."

"That bad, huh? Well, I heal fast. Not as fast as you guys," she said to Cian, "but fast enough."

"Can you tell us what happened when you and Larkin were apart?" Hoyt touched her ankle. "He said there were ten."

"Yeah, ten, and Lora, so that's eleven. Trap worked. Dead horse down there, and weapons. We should get those weapons. They were in the ground."

"The weapons?" Hoyt prompted.

"No, the vamps. Dug into the ground. Trap in a trap. It got dark — bam. Like a solar eclipse, but faster. And they came up out of the ground. I got the first two before they got all the way out. Realized after, later, they weren't trying to kill me — which to be honest, is why I'm not dead. They were just softening me up for her. Cowardly bitch."

"But you killed her."

She shook her head at Larkin, and immediately regretted the movement. "No. Don't think so. Couldn't have taken her in a fight, could barely keep my feet. She knew it. Comes strutting out, talking trash. Thinks she'll make me her lesbian vamp lover. As if. She's hurting now, too, oh yeah. And she doesn't look so good either. Water bag."

"Holy water," Larkin murmured. "Aren't you the clever one?"

"Everything's a weapon. I tossed as much as I could into her face. Hit her, too. Face, down the throat. I heard her screaming when she ran off. But that was it for me, pretty much all I had left. Good thing you came."

"You had a branch."

"A branch of what?"

"A tree branch," he told her, kissing her fingers again. "You were swinging a tree branch."

"Yeah. Huh, good for me. It's sort of blurry here and there."

"That's enough for now." Glenna held the cup back to Blair's lips. "A little more of this."

"Rather have a frozen margarita."

"Who wouldn't?" Glenna passed a hand over Blair's face. "Now sleep."

CHAPTER 20

She swam in and out, and the pain was waiting each time she surfaced. Weakness would drag her under again, but not before she heard whispers and murmurs. Not before she heard herself answering questions that seemed to be peppered over her every time she came back to the world.

Why wouldn't they just let her sleep?

Then someone would pour more tree bark down her throat, and she'd float away again.

Sometimes when she floated she went back to that field and relived every blow, every block, every movement of what she'd believed were the last moments of her life.

Sometimes she simply floated into nothing.

Larkin sat beside her, watching as Moira and Glenna took turns tending her. Watching as one of them came in to light candles, or add turf to the fire. Or just lay a hand over

Blair's brow to check for fever.

Every two hours by the clock, one of them would wake her, ask questions of her. Because of the concussion, Glenna had said. It was a precaution because she'd suffered such hard blows to her head.

Then he would think what might have happened if one of those blows had knocked her unconscious, what they would have done to her while she was alone.

Every time he thought of it, imagined it, he'd take her hand to feel her pulse beat under the scar on her wrist.

He passed the time talking nonsense to her, and for a time playing the pipe that Moira had brought to him. He thought — he hoped — she rested easier with the music.

"You should go, rest now for an hour or two." Moira stroked a hand down her hair as she spoke. "I'll sit with her."

"I can't."

"No. Nor could I in your place. She's so strong, Larkin, and Glenna so skilled. I wish you wouldn't worry so."

"I didn't know it was inside me. That I could feel so much for one person. That I could know, without question, without a single doubt, that this woman is . . . well, everything there is for me."

"I knew it. Not that it would be her, but

that there would be someone. And that when you found her, she'd change everything." Moira bent to press her lips to the top of his head. "I'm a little jealous. Do you mind?"

"No." He turned her head, pressed his face to her side. "I'll love you all my life. I think I could be a thousand miles from you, and still reach out my hand and touch yours."

Tears stung Moira's eyes. "I couldn't have chosen better for you if I'd chosen her myself. Still, she's the luckiest of women."

"She's waking."

"All right, talk to her now. We'll keep her with us a few moments, then I'll give her more medicine."

"There you are." Larkin spoke quietly, standing to take her hand. "*Mo chroi*. Open your eyes."

"What?" They fluttered open. "What is it?"

"Give me your name now."

"Scarlett O'Hara. Can't you remember it for five minutes?" she said testily. "Blair Murphy. I don't have brain damage. I'm just tired and annoyed."

"She's lucid enough," Moira decided, and poured more of Glenna's potion into a cup.

"I don't want any more of that." Hearing the petulance in her own voice, Blair closed

467

her eyes a moment. "Look, I don't mean to be pissy. Or, okay, maybe I do. So what? But that gunk makes me feel foggy and out of it. Which wouldn't be so bad if someone wasn't waking me up every freaking ten minutes to ask me my name."

Not at all displeased with the rant, Moira set the cup aside. "Glenna said I should wake her if Blair refused."

"Oh jeez, don't go get Nurse Rachett."

"I'll be a moment."

Larkin eased down on the side of the bed as Moira slipped out of the room. "Your color's come back, you know. It's a relief to me."

"I bet I'm all kinds of colors right now. Blue, black, purple, that sick-looking yellow. Good thing it's dark in here. Look, you don't have to hang around."

"I'm not going anywhere."

"I appreciate it. But . . . listen, can we talk about something other than me and my severely kicked ass? Tell me something. Tell me . . . when's the first time you knew you could shape-shift?"

"Oh, I'd have been about three. I wanted a puppy, you see. My father had his wolfhounds, but they were too dignified to play with the likes of me, to chase balls around and fetch sticks."

"A puppy." She relaxed with the sound of his voice. "What kind of puppy."

"Oh, any sort would do, but my mother said she wasn't after having another dog in the house, and that she already had me and the baby to deal with. That would be my brother, who would have been barely more than a year old. And I was unaware at the time she was already carrying my sister as well."

"Small wonder she wasn't up for house-breaking a dog."

"She's been in to see you, my mother. Twice tonight. My sister, my father as well."

"Oh." Blair patted her face, imagined how she looked. "Terrific."

"So, to continue the tale, I begged for the pup relentlessly, and to no avail. She would not be moved. I had a good sulk about it up in the nursery, imagining running off with the gypsies where I could have as many pups as I pleased, and so on. And I kept thinking about the pup, and then there was this . . . moving inside me. And this light was spinning around. I was frightened, and called out for my mother. And barked."

"You turned into a puppy."

Her eyes were clearer now; he could see it, see the fun in them as he told the story. "Oh, what terror — and what a thrill with it. I couldn't have a puppy, so I'd made myself one, and wasn't that an amazing thing."

"I'd make some crack about being able to play with yourself, but it's a cheap shot. Keep going."

"Well now, I went running out, and down the stairs where my mother caught sight of me. And thinking I'd gone and snuck a pup in the house despite her, she set off chasing me. I thought she'd hide me good when she realized what I'd done, and tried to run outside. But she cornered me. She's always been quick. Hauled me up, she did, by the scruff of the neck. I must have whimpered and looked plain pitiful, for she sighed, deep, and scratched my ears."

"Softie."

"Aye, she's a good, warm heart my mother. I heard her speak, plain as day. That boy, she said, what am I to do with that boy. And with you, she said to me — not knowing I *was* that boy. She sat down with me in her lap. When she began to pet me, I turned back."

"And when she regained consciousness?"

"Oh, she's made of sterner stuff than that, my mam. I remember her eyes popped wide — but mine must've been as big. I threw my arms around her neck, so glad to be a boy again. She laughed and laughed. Her granny, it seemed, had the same skill."

"Excellent. So it's a family trait."

"Here and there, it seems. By the end of the week, her granny, who I swear was older than the moon itself, came to stay with us and teach me what I needed to know. And she brought with her a little spotted puppy I named Conn, for the warrior of a thousand battles."

"That's a nice story." Her eyelids began to droop. "What happened to Conn?"

"He lived twelve good years, then went over the Bridge of Rainbows where he could be a puppy again, and play all day in the sun. Sleep now, *a ghrá*. I'll be with you when you wake."

He glanced over as Glenna came quietly in, and even managed a smile. "She's gone off to sleep again. Natural sleep. That would be good, wouldn't it?"

"Yes. No fever," Glenna said after laying her palm on Blair's forehead. "If she refused the medicine, I'd guess the pain's lessened. And her color's good. Moira says you won't leave her."

"How can I?"

"If it were Hoyt, I'd say the same. But why don't you lie down with her, get a little rest yourself?"

"I might jostle her in sleep. I don't want to hurt her."

"You won't hurt her." Glenna moved to the windows, drawing the drapes. "I don't want the sun to wake either of you. If you need me, come for me, or send for me. But I think she'll rest easy enough for a few hours now."

She put a hand on Larkin's shoulder, then leaned down to kiss his cheek. "Lie down beside her for a while, and do the same."

When he did, Blair stirred and turned, just a little, just enough so that her body curled toward his. As gently as he could, he took her hand. "She'll pay for what she did to you. I swear to you, she'll pay."

Listening to her low, steady breathing, he closed his eyes. And finally slept.

In another room a fire blazed, and the drapes were drawn tight against the glass. Against the dawn.

Lora's wild wails echoed through the room. She thrashed as Lilith, once again, slathered a pale green balm over the burns and the boils that covered Lora's face, her neck, even her breasts.

"There, there, don't. Don't, my darling, my sweet, sweet girl. Don't fight me. This will help."

"It burns! It burns!"

"I know." Tears gathered in Lilith's throat,

in her eyes, as she coated the vicious burns on Lora's neck. "Oh, my poor baby, I know. Here now, there now. Drink a little of this."

"I don't want it!" Lora turned her head away, clamping her eyes and mouth tightly shut.

"But you must." Though it scored her heart to cause Lora more pain, Lilith took a firm grip on the back of Lora's neck to force some of the liquid down. "Just a bit more, just a bit. Good, that's good, my own darling."

"She hurt me. Lilith, she hurt me."

"Hush, hush now. We'll fix it."

"She scarred me." Fresh tears spilled over the balm as Lora once again turned her face away. "I'm ugly and scarred. How can you even look at me after what she did to my face?"

"You're only more beautiful to me now. More precious to me." She laid her lips, gently, gently, on Lora's. Lilith had allowed no one else to tend Lora but herself. No one, she vowed, would touch that burned skin but herself. "You're my sweetest girl. My bravest."

"I had to hide in the dirt!"

"Ssh. It means nothing. You came back to me." Lilith took Lora's hand, turning it palm up to press kisses there. "I have you back."

The door opened, and Davey came in. He carried a crystal goblet on a silver tray, his lips pressed hard in concentration. "I didn't spill any. Not one drop."

"Such a big boy." Lilith took the goblet, ran her other hand down his hair.

Once again, Lora turned her face away. "He shouldn't see me like this."

"No. He should know what they're capable of, these *mortals*. Come, Davey, come sit with our Lora. Gently now, don't jostle her."

He climbed carefully onto the bed. "Does it hurt very bad?"

Lora nodded. "Very bad."

"I wish it didn't. I can bring you a toy."

In spite of the pain, Lora smiled. "Perhaps later."

"I brought you blood. It's still warm. I didn't sneak any," he added, stroking her hand as he'd seen Lilith do. "Mama said you need it all, so you can be strong and well again."

"That's right. Here now." Lilith held the goblet to Lora's lips. "Drink it, but slowly."

The blood calmed her, and the drug Lilith had given her earlier helped fog the worst of the pain. "It helps." She laid back, shut her eyes. "But I feel so weak. I thought, oh, Lilith, I thought at first I'd been blinded. It burned my eyes so. She tricked me. How could I have been so *stupid?*"

"You mustn't blame yourself. No, I won't have it."

"You should be furious with me."

"How could I be, at such a time? We've centuries together, my love, the good and the bad. Can I say you were foolish? Of course, but I might have done the same. What good is the kill without the flourish?" She lowered the bodice of her robes to reveal the pentagram scar between her breast. "Don't I carry this because I toyed too long with a mortal once?"

"Hoyt." Lora spat out the name. "You battled a sorcerer. There was no magic in that bitch who scarred me."

"When Mama kills the sorcerer, I can lap up his blood like a puppy does milk."

Lilith laughed, ruffled Davey's hair. "That's my boy. And don't be sure that demon hunter is without magic." She reached for Davey, setting him on her lap. "I don't believe she could have hurt you so without it."

"She was hurt, at least. Perhaps mortally."

"There, you see, always a bright side." Lilith kissed Davey. "It's Midir who must do better. Didn't night slip through his fingers? Didn't the white magic defeat his?"

Lilith had to take a moment to calm herself over the outrage of her wizard's incompetence. "I'd be rid of him if we had another nearly as powerful. But I promise you this, I swear this to you. They will pay. You'll bathe in her blood come Samhain, my darling girl. We'll all drink, long and deep. And when I rule, you'll be by my side."

Comforted, Lora reached out. "Will you stay awhile longer? Will you stay while I sleep?"

"Of course. We're family, after all."

Blair woke in stages. Her mind stirred first, circling slowly around where she was, what had happened. Her head began to ache in a low, steady drumming, then her eyes throbbed with it. She became aware of other pain — shoulder, ribs, belly, legs. As she lay quiet, taking stock, she realized there wasn't a spot on her that didn't hurt.

But it was manageable rather than the breath stealing pain that had flattened her. The aftertaste of the potion Glenna had poured down her coated her throat. Not horribly unpleasant, she decided. Just sort of smoky and thick, so that she wished for a gallon or two of water to clear it away.

Cautiously, she let her eyes open. Candlelight, firelight. So it was still shy of dawn, she decided. Good. She felt reasonably good, all in all.

In fact, she felt good enough to be hungry, which had to be a positive sign. She worked at sitting up just as she spotted Larkin crossing back toward the bed from the far window.

"Hey, go get some sleep."

He stopped, just stared for a moment. "You're awake."

"Yeah, and before you ask, my name's Blair Murphy, I'm in Geall, and I got my ass whooped by a bunch of vampires. Do you think I could get something to eat?"

"You're hungry." He all but sang the words as he rushed to the bed.

"Yeah. Maybe just a little midnight snack — or whatever time it is."

"You're having pain."

"The grandmother of all headaches," she admitted. "And some other twinges. Mostly, I feel sort of groggy and dopey. Also," she added with a quick wince, "I have an amazing need to pee. So, you know, shoo for a minute."

Instead, he picked her up, carried her to the chamber pot behind the painted screen.

"I can't do this with you in here. I just can't. Go outside the room and count to thirty." She squirmed as her bladder strained. "Make that forty. Come on, give a girl a private moment."

He rolled his eyes, but did as she asked. In exactly forty seconds he was back in the room where she was taking a few hesitant steps. He was at her side, taking her arm in an instant.

"Glenna said you might be dizzy."

"Little bit. Little dizzy, little wobbly, and it hurts pretty much everywhere. But it could be a whole lot worse, in that I could be dead or craving a nice slug of blood at this moment. I want to take a look."

With his help, she limped to the mirror. Her left cheek was scraped from nose to temple, and she was sporting two black eyes. Glenna had fashioned a kind of butterfly bandage to close the gash on her forehead. She turned, noted that while her shoulder was a mass of bruises, they were already going the sickly yellow-green of healing.

"Yeah, could've been worse." She ran a hand down her own ribs. "Pretty tender yet, but nothing got busted. There's a plus."

"I've never been so frightened in all my life."

"Me, either." She met his eyes in the glass. "I don't know if I thanked you or dreamed I did on one of my trips to La-La Land, but you saved me. I'll never forget watching you whip through those three vamps like they were nothing."

"If I'd been sooner —"

"Isn't this a lot about destiny, this whole business? If you were meant to be there sooner, you would've been. You were there in time, and that's what counts."

"Blair." He lowered his head to her good shoulder. He spoke in a quiet murmur, and in Gaelic.

"What was all that?"

"For later." He straightened. "But for now, I'll get you some food."

"I could use it. Feel like I haven't eaten in days. I'm not getting back in bed. I'll sit."

He helped her to the chair by the fire, then brought over a blanket for her legs. "Do you want the drapes open?"

"Yeah, sure. Listen, after you get someone to throw some food together, you should go, catch some sleep for the rest of the night — oh!"

She blinked, threw up a hand to block the glare of the sun through the glass.

"I slept a bit," he told her with a quick grin.

"Yeah, well, apparently so did I. What time is it?"

"I'd say well past midday."

"Mid —" She blew out a breath. "Guess my advanced healing powers have been getting a hell of a workout."

"I'll go see about some food if you promise to stay where I've put you."

Gingerly, she rubbed her aching knee. "I'm not going anywhere."

Obviously, he didn't take her at her word as Glenna came in moments later.

"You look better."

"Then I must've looked like the wrath of God."

"You did." Glenna set her case on a table, opened it.

And Blair gave it a long, meaningful frown. "I really don't need any more of that magic tree bark."

"We'll switch to something else. Double vision?"

"Down to the regular kind. Head aches like a mother."

"I can help with that." Glenna came over, laid her fingers on Blair's temples. "How's the shoulder?"

"Achy, worse than the ribs, but they're not too bad. Must've cracked my knee pretty good, too. It's a little wobbly."

"Considering it was about twice its normal size when Larkin got you here, a little wobbly's good. You know, this is the first time he's left this room since he brought you back."

"But he said he slept some."

"I convinced him to lie down next to you for a while."

"He blames himself. It's stupid."

"It's stupid, I agree. But that's only part of it. He's watched over you all night because he's desperately in love with you. How's the head now?"

"The what? Oh . . . Better," she realized. "A lot better. Thanks. Oh God, what am I going to do?"

"You'll figure it out. They'll be sending up some tea — one of my infusions. We'll add a little of this and that to it. You'll drink it all. Let's see what I can do about that shoulder."

"If I stayed here in Geall, I'd be turning my back on what I was born for. On what brought me to him in the first place. Glenna, I can't. Whatever I feel, whatever I want, I can't not be what I am."

"Duty and love. They can make their own nasty little wars, can't they? Relax now. Try some yoga breathing. You're a strong woman, Blair. Mind, body, heart. A lot of people don't understand how difficult it can be to be a strong woman. If I were taking bets, I'd say Larkin's a man who does."

Later, when she'd eaten and felt steadier, she convinced Larkin she needed to walk. She sensed he was waiting to scoop her up at the first sign of weakness. She did feel weak, but in heart rather than body. She had to tell him, he deserved to be told, that she couldn't make promises to him. When what they'd been charged to do had been done, she would have to leave him.

She knew what it was to be rejected, and wished with everything inside her things could be different. That she could be.

They walked to the courtyard with the fountain she could see from her window, where the sun was strong and the air cool with the first brush of autumn.

"Only a month left," he said, and sat with her on a bench of deep blue marble.

"We'll be ready."

"Aye, we will. In a few days, Moira will take her sword."

"What if it's not her? What if it's you?"

"It isn't." He lifted his shoulder. "I've searched myself on that, and I'd know if it was. I'd have always known, as in some part of her, Moira knows. And thank God."

"But your family. This place. You're tied to it, by birth. By blood."

"True enough." He took her hand, idly toying with her fingers. "It's the place of my birth, and I'll always miss it."

"You'll . . . what? Miss it? Why? We're going to win. Just because I got slapped around doesn't mean they're going to beat us."

"No, it doesn't, and they won't." He looked up from her fingers, into her eyes. And his were like gold steel. "Because we'll fight to the last man. To the last drop."

"So why —"

"Let me ask you a question, one none of us have voiced as yet. Have all the vampires from your world come here to follow Lilith?"

"No, of course not."

"Then when this battle's won, the fight goes on. You'll have to hunt, as you've always hunted. Here, if some survive, they'll be an army always to fight them. The people of Geall know what they are, as the people of your world don't."

"Yes." So he did understand. "I wish — I'm sorry. Going back, it's not a choice for me. If it were . . . But it's not."

"No, it can't be a choice for you. But it can be for me. So I'll be going back with you, to fight beside you."

"Excuse me?"

"*A stór.* Did you think I'd let you get away from me?"

"You can't leave here."

"Why? It's Moira who will rule, and my father will advise her as need be. There's my brother and my sister's husband to work the

483

land, and tend the horses."

She thought of his mother, his sister, brother. Of his father, and the look on Riddock's face when he'd embraced Larkin after his return. "You can't leave your family."

"It's hard, yes, to leave loved ones. It should be hard, I think, and should only be done when it needs to be done. It isn't, could never be, the way it was when your father left you, Blair."

"The result's the same."

"It's not, no. Not when the leaving is with love, all around. And it's true enough that a man often moves away from his parents. It's the way of things, a natural order."

"They move to the next town, or across the country. Not to another world."

"Trying to talk me out of it's a waste of breath. My mind's been made up to it for a while now. Moira knows it, though we haven't spoken of it right out. As does my mother."

He looked straight into her eyes. "Do you think I would fight, risk everything, then step aside from the one that matters most in this world, in any world to me? I'd give my life for this if that's what's needed. But if I live, you'll belong to me. And that's the end of it."

"The end of it?"

"I'm thinking, as you have no close family

at home, we could be married here. We can do the whole business again in your Chicago if you like."

"Married? I didn't say I would marry you. Anybody."

"Of course you'll marry me, don't be foolish." He gave her a friendly pat on her good knee. "You love me. And I love you," he said before she could speak. "I nearly told you that first night we were together. But a man shouldn't say such words when he's inside a woman, I think. How would she know, for certain, he was speaking with his heart and not, well, not with his . . ."

"Oh boy."

"I thought to tell you at other times, but told myself it should wait. I realize I nearly waited too long. You asked what I said to you, inside after you woke. I'll tell you now. So look at me when I do."

He laid his fingers on her cheeks. "I said you're my breath, and my pulse, my heart, my voice. I said, I'll love you even when all of them stop. I'll love you, and only you, until all the worlds are ended. So you'll marry me, Blair. And I'll go where you go, and fight beside you. We'll live together, and love together, and make a family."

"I have to . . . I have to stand up a minute." She got to her feet, shaky now, and walked to the fountain. Just to breathe, she thought, to let the cool spray of water wash her face.

"No one's ever loved me like this. I don't know, not for certain, that anyone's ever loved me at all until you. No one's ever offered me what you're offering me." She turned back to him. "I'd be a fool to push it away. I'm not a fool. I thought I loved someone once, but that was so pale compared to what I feel for you. I thought I'd have to be strong enough to leave you behind. I didn't know you could be strong enough to come with me. I should have."

She came back to him, offering her hand when he rose. "I'd marry you anywhere. I'd be so proud to marry you."

He kissed her hands, then drew her gently into his arms to meet her lips.

"Get a good grip, will you?" she murmured. "I'm a demon hunter. I'm not fragile."

He laughed, and swung her right off her feet.

"Have a care with her! Have you lost your mind?"

As Moira sprinted toward them, Larkin only grinned, and spun Blair again. "A bit. We're betrothed."

"Oh." Moira stopped, her hands fluttering

up to her heart. "Oh, well, that's wonderful. Blessings on you both. I'm so pleased for you."

She stepped up, kissed Blair's cheek, then Larkin's. "We need a celebration. I'll go back, tell the others. Cian had a notion . . . but it can wait."

"What notion?" Blair demanded.

"A way . . . how did he put it? To thumb our noses at Lilith. But —"

"I'm for that." Blair patted Larkin's arm. "Why don't you go in. I'll be right behind you. I just want a second with Moira."

"All right. But don't stay on your feet too long."

"Listen to him, after he's tossing you around in the air. I do wish you happy, Blair."

"I want you to know I'm going to try, every day of my life, to make him happy. I want you to know that."

"You do make him happy." Moira angled her head. "We're friends, aren't we, you and I?"

"You, Glenna, Hoyt, Cian. Best friends I ever had in my life."

"I feel the same, so I'm going to be honest with you. It will hurt when he goes. It will hurt my heart, and when he's out of sight I'll weep until my heart's dry of tears. Then I'll be light, and I'll be happy. Because I know he'll have what he needs, what he wants, what he deserves."

"If there's a way we can come back, to spend some time, to visit, you, his family, we'll find it."

"That's a nice thought to hold on to. And I will. Come now. He's right, you should be off your feet."

"I think I feel better than I ever have in my life."

"That's love for you, but still, you'll need your strength for what Cian has in mind."

It was nose-thumbing, Blair thought. And chest-beating. And it was perfect.

"Are you sure you're up for this?" Glenna asked her.

"I am so up for this. It's so in-your-face." Blair grinned at Cian. "Good thinking."

He looked up at the sky, watched the stars wink to life. "Good clear night for it. It's not what you'd call battle strategy, but —"

"Damn straight it is. Demoralizing the enemy is always good strategy." Blair turned the swords she held. "So I'm set?" she asked Glenna.

"You're set."

"Okay, handsome. Make like a dragon."

"In a moment. First, I have something for

you, and I want to give it to you here, in front of our circle. One of the symbols of Geall is the dragon. One of our symbols as well, you and I. So I want you to wear this, for our betrothal."

He drew out a ring of bright gold shaped like a dragon.

"Glenna drew a picture of it when I told her what I'd like. And the goldsmith used it to make the ring."

"It's perfect," she murmured when he slipped it on her finger.

"And to seal it." He framed her face, kissed her warmly. And shot her a grin when he eased back. "Now let's go thumb our noses at this bitch."

He flashed into the dragon. Leaping onto his back, Blair lifted both swords high.

"They rose into the sky," the old man said. "Across the moon and stars and the dark behind them. And over the world of Geall, those swords flashed flame for all to see. With them, the demon hunter carved these words into that sky.

"Bright blessings on Geall and all humankind. We," she wrote in fire, "are the future."

The old man lifted the wine that sat beside him. "It was said that the queen of the vampires stood below, cursing, shaking her fists as those words shone bright as the sun."

He sipped the wine, held up a hand when the children spread around him protested that couldn't be the end of the tale.

"Oh, there's more to tell. More indeed. But not tonight. Go on now, for I was told there'd be gingercakes in the kitchen for a treat before bedtime. I've a fondness for gingercake."

When he was alone, and the room quiet again, he sipped his wine. He nodded off with the fire warming his bones, and his mind drifting to the last of the story.

To the time of knowing.

GLOSSARY OF IRISH WORDS, CHARACTERS AND PLACES

a chroi (ah-REE), Gaelic term of endearment meaning "my heart," "my heart's beloved," "my darling"

a ghrá (ah-GHRA), Gaelic term of endearment meaning "my love," "dear"

a stór (ah-STOR), Gaelic term of endearment meaning "my darling"

Aideen (Ae-DEEN), Moira's young cousin

Alice McKenna, descendant of Cian and Hoyt Mac Cionaoith

An Clar (Ahn-CLAR), modern-day County Clare

Ballycloon (ba-LU-klun)

Beal (Bale), name Blair uses when acting as bait

bi istigh (vee-ISHtee), Gaelic term meaning "come in"

Blair Nola Bridgitt Murphy, one of the circle of six, the "warrior"; a demon hunter, a descendant of Nola Mac Cionaoith

491

(Cian and Hoyt's younger sister)

braes (BRO-sh), underdrawers or trousers, worn by the people of Geall

Breda (BREE-da), mother of family with overturned wagon

Bridget's Well, cemetery in County Clare, named after St. Bridget

Burren, the, a karst limestone region in County Clare, which features caves and underground streams

cailleach dearg (CAH-lic JAR-eg), witch with red hair, epithet for Glenna

cara (karu), Gaelic for "friend, relative"

Ceara, one of the village women

Cian (KEY-an) **Mac Cionaoith/McKenna**, Hoyt's twin brother, a vampire, Lord of Oiche, one of the circle of six, "the one who is lost"

Cillard, place in County Clare

Cirio, Lilith's human lover

ciunas (CYOON-as), Gaelic for "silence"; the battle takes place in the Valley of Ciunas — the Valley of Silence

claddaugh, the Celtic symbol of love, friendship, loyalty

Cliffs of Mohr (also Moher), the name given to the ruin of forts in the South of Ireland, on a cliff near Hag's Head, "Moher O'Ruan"

Conn, Larkin's childhood puppy

Dance of the Gods, the Dance, the place in which the circle of six passes through from the real world to the fantasy world of Geall

Dara (DARE-a), in modern day County Kildare

Davey, Lilith, the Vampire Queen's "son," a child vampire

Deirdre (DAIR-dhra) **Riddock**, Larkin's mother

Dervil (DAR-vel), one of the village women

Dunglas, place in Geall

Eire (AIR-reh), Gaelic for "Ireland"

Eogan (O-en), Ceara's husband

Eoin (OAN), Hoyt's brother-in-law

Eternity, the name of Cian's nightclub, located in New York City

Faerie Falls, imaginary place in Geall

fàilte à Geall (FALL-che ah GY-al), Gaelic for "Welcome to Geall"

Fearghus (FARE-gus), Hoyt's brother-in-law

Gaillimh (GALL-yuv), modern-day Galway, the capital of the west of Ireland

gaiscioch dorcha (GA-shuk DOR-ka), dark warrior or dark hero, epithet for Blair

Geall (GY-al), in Gaelic means "promise"; the city from which Moira and Larkin come; the city which Moira will someday rule

Glenna Ward, one of the circle of six, the "witch"; lives in modern-day New York City

Hoyt Mac Cionaoith/McKenna (mac KHEE-nee), one of the circle of six, the "sorcerer"

Isleen (Is-LEEN), a servant at Castle Geall

Jarl (Yarl), Lilith's sire, the vampire who turned her into a vampire

Jeremy Hilton, Blair Murphy's ex-fiance

King, the name of Cian's best friend, whom Cian befriended when King was a child; the manager of Eternity

Knockarague (KNOCKA-rig), town in Geall; home of Larlin's mother

Larkin Riddock, one of the circle of six, the "shifter of shapes," a cousin of Moira, Queen of Geall

Lilith, the Vampire Queen, aka Queen of the Demons; leader of the war against humankind; Cian's sire, the vampire who turned Cian from human to vampire

Lora, a vampire; Lilith's lover

Lucius, Lora's male vampire lover

Mac Dara, surname; part of one of Larkin's titles

Malvin, villager, soldier in Geallian army

Mam, term for mother

Manhattan, city in New York; where both Cian McKenna and Glenna Ward live

mathair (maahir), Gaelic word for "mother"

Michael Thomas McKenna, descendant of Cian and Hoyt Mac Cionaoith

Mick Murphy, Blair Murphy's younger brother

Midir (mee-DEER), vampire wizard to Lilith, Queen of the Vampires

miurnin (also sp. miurneach [mornukh]), Gaelic for "sweetheart," term of endearment

Mo chroi (mo-kree), Gaelic term meaning "my heart," "my sweetheart," "my darling" (see *a chroi*)

Moira (MWA-ra), one of the circle of six, the "scholar"; a princess, future queen of Geall

Morrigan (Mo-ree-ghan), Goddess of the Battle

Niall (Nile), a warrior in the Geallian army

Nola Mac Cionaoith, Hoyt and Cian's youngest sister

o Dubhuir (o DOVE-er), surname Blair uses when acting as bait

ogham (ä-gem) (also spelled ogam), fifth/sixth century Irish alphabet

oiche (EE-heh), Gaelic for "night"

Oran (O-ren), Riddock's youngest son, Larkin's younger brother

Phelan (FA-len), Larkin's brother-in-law

Prince Riddock, Larkin's father, acting king of Geall, Moira's maternal uncle

Region of Chiarrai (kee-U-ree), modern-day Kerry, situated in the extreme southwest of Ireland, sometimes referred to as "the Kingdom"

Samhain (SAM-en), summer's end (Celtic festival); the battle takes place on the Feast of Samhain, the feast celebrating the end of summer

Sean (Shawn) **Murphy**, Blair Murphy's father, a vampire hunter

Shop Street, cultural center of Galway

Sinann (shih-NAWN), Larkin's sister

sláinte (slawn-che), Gaelic term for "cheers!"

slán agat (shlahn u-gut), Gaelic for "goodbye," which is said to person staying

slán leat (shlahn ly-aht), Gaelic for "goodbye," which is said to the person leaving

Tuatha de Danaan (TOO-aha dai DON-nan), Welsh gods

Tynan (Ti-nin), guard at Castle Geall

Vlad, Cian's stallion

We hope you have enjoyed this Large Print book. Other Thorndike, Wheeler, and Chivers Press Large Print books are available at your library or directly from the publishers.

For information about current and upcoming titles, please call or write, without obligation, to:

Publisher
Thorndike Press
295 Kennedy Memorial Drive
Waterville, ME 04901
Tel. (800) 223-1244

or visit our Web site at:

www.gale.com/thorndike
www.gale.com/wheeler

OR

Chivers Large Print
published by BBC Audiobooks Ltd
St. James House, The Square
Lower Bristol Road
Bath BA2 3SB
England
Tel. +44(0) 800 136919
email: bbcaudiobooksbbc.co.uk
www.bbcaudiobooks.co.uk

All our Large Print titles are designed for easy reading, and all our books are made to last.

$L\,EO$

OCT 1 8 2006